I0593950

CONALL III
THE SISTERS
NA DEIRFIÚRACHA

DAVID H. MILLAR

TITLES BY DAVID H. MILLAR

Conall III: The Sisters—Na Deirfiúracha

DAVID H. MILLAR

Conall III: The Sisters—Na Deirfiúracha is a work of historical fiction. Apart from obviously historical figures and places, all names, characters, and incidents are either the product of the author's imagination or are used fictitiously. Any resemblance to actual persons, living or dead, establishments, events or locales is entirely coincidental.

Copyright © 2017 by David H. Millar
Revised 2023

All rights reserved. No part of this book may be reproduced or transmitted in any form or by any means, electronic or mechanical, including photocopy, recording, or any information and storage retrieval system now known or to be invented, without permission in writing from the publisher, except by a reviewer who wishes to quote brief passages in connection with a review written for inclusion in a magazine, newspaper, blog or broadcast.

A Wee Publishing Company
Houston, TX, USA
http://www.aweepublishingco.com/
Paperback ISBN 978-0-9916640-4-7
eBook ISBN 978-0-9916640-5-4
Library of Congress Control Number: 2018901994
A Wee Publishing Company, LLC, Houston, TX

The Princesses — Lucy, Chloe, and Sasha

ACKNOWLEDGEMENTS

'Team Conall' continues to grow. First and foremost, thanks to Lauren, my long-suffering editor who has to put up with my grumping at the red ink on my precious manuscript. Next is Pam, my long-time friend, who fills a multitude of vital roles — first chapters feedback, beta-reader and my encourager who is always asking, "Have you written the next one?" A big thank-you goes to my supportive team of beta-readers who valiantly read the draft manuscript and made extremely perceptive comments.

Thanks to Ida Jansson at Amygdala Book Design for the fantastic cover artwork and interior formatting. Finally, thanks to a great artist and friend, Michael McEvoy, from my hometown of Belfast, for the map illustrations.

CONTENTS

GAELIC PRONUNCIATIONS

Conall III: The Sisters—Na Deirfiúracha is a yarn set in ancient times. It revolves around the Celts and primarily Irish and Scottish Celts. As far as possible, I have attempted to use old Irish and Scots Gaelic words and phrases for personal and place names and the odd curse or two.

Gaelic in all its forms (Irish, Scottish, Welsh, Manx, Breton, and Cornish) is a difficult, if not impossible, language to comprehend. It is made more challenging by the regional dialects. I have often considered the language to result from a warped Celtic sense of humour. Rather than give a complete listing of the Gaelic words and phrases used in the story, I have opted for a compromise.

The following page lists the personal names of the main characters. Also, I recommend *A Beginner's Guide to Irish Gaelic Pronunciation*, which can be found at http://www.standingstones.com/gaelpron.html.

However, when all is said and done, it is the tale that counts. Feel free to pronounce the Gaelic in the way that gives you the most enjoyment.

IRISH GAELIC

Áine (**AW-nya**)

Aodán (**AY-awn**)

Bláithín (**BLAW-heen**)

Bréanainn (**BREH-neen**)

Brighid (**BREED**)

Brion (**BREE-un**)

Brocc (**BRUK**)

Cassán (**KAS-awn**)

Cathán (**KA-hawn**)

Conall (**KON-ul**)

Craiftine (**KRAFT-in**)

Cuán (**KOO-awn**)

Cúscraid (**KOO-skri**)

Danu (**DAH-noo**)

Deaglán (**DEG-lawn**)

Deda (**DAY-da**)

Eirnín (**ER-neen**)

Eochaidh (**OHY**)

Fearghal (**FER-ul**)

Fionnbharr (**FYUN-var**)

Íar (**EER**)

Labhraidh (**LA-ra**)

Lonán (**LUH-nawn**)

Macha (**MAHA**)

Manannán (**MAN-na-nawn**)

Medb (**MAY-ve**)

Mongfhionn (**MUNN-yung**)

Mórrígan (**Moe-Rig-gAHn**)

Sárán (**SAWR-awn**)

Tadhg (**TYG**)

Téide (**TYAY-d'yeh**)

Toirneach (**TOR-nah**)
Torcán (**TURK-awn**)
Tuathal (**TOO-al**)
Urard (**UR-urd**)

SCOTS GAELIC
Ailde (**AL-ja**)
Brandubh (**BRAN-doow**)
Camran (**KAM-uh-run**)
Carmag (**KAR-ah-mak**)
Ceana (**KEMA**)
Coireall (**KO-rull**)
Crum (**CROM**)
Diadhaidh (**JE-ah-ee**)
Drostan (**DROST-an**)
Eachdonn (**ISH-down**)
Failbhe (**FAL-uh-vuh**)
Finnean (**FIN-yan**)
Friseal (**FREE-shul**)
Gormal (**GAU-rum-ul**)
Gràinne (**GRAN-yuh**)
Iasg (**EE-ask**)
Mòrag (**MOR-ak**)
Ròidh (**ROY**)
Ualraig (**OO-ul-Rík**)

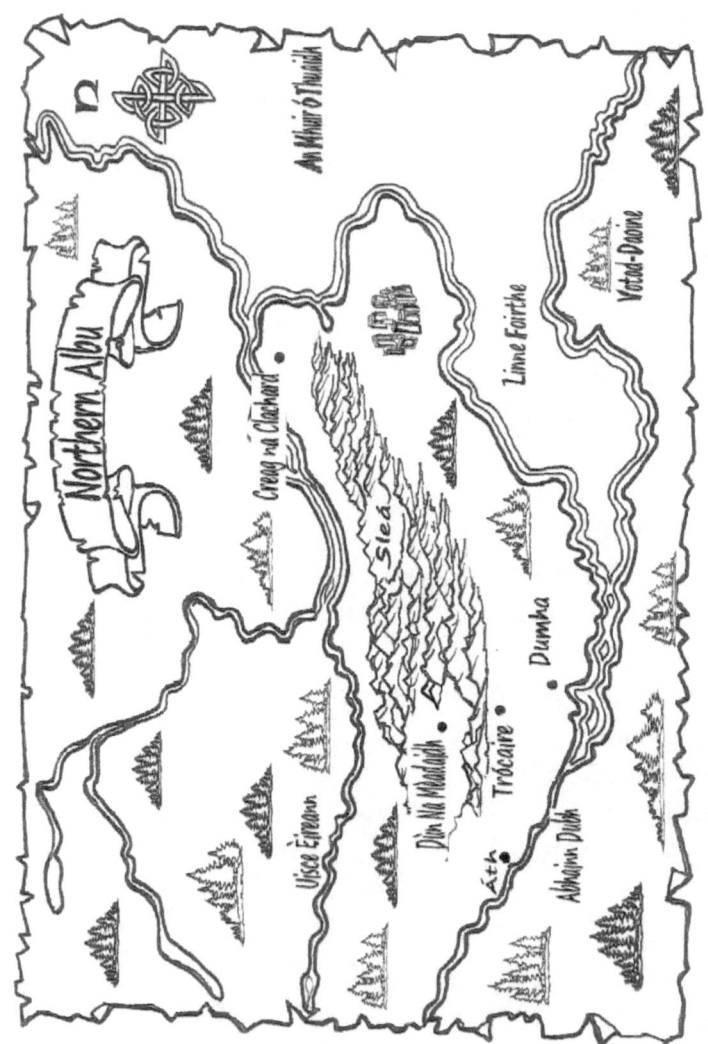

CHAPTER 1

406 B.C.—North-eastern Albu—Spring

Mórrígan withdrew blood-stained blades from the corpse's chest. The act was never easy. Flesh was fragile yet stubbornly reluctant to give up the cause of its demise. She dragged a hand scarred by battle and fire across her forehead. The crimson smear of blood, dirt, and sweat momentarily obscured the curling, indigo and white sigils that covered her face. She knelt on the cold earth, fighting to control her breathing. The skirmish had been brief but brutal.

Her *caomhnóirí*, a guard of two hundred mounted warriors, awaited their leader's orders. The men and women followed her without question and with a fervour that caused the king's commanders' concern. All were skilled with blades and bows. They rode their horses with what Íar Mac Dedad, the best horseman in the tribe, described as unnatural ease.

Rarely taking prisoners, the band left only death in its trail. Yet *An Fiagaí Dorcha's*—the Dark Huntress'—warband protected the army's eastern flank. Even their most vocal decriers acknowledged they carried out their commission with grisly efficiency.

The Dark Huntress glanced up. A sky filled with clouds threatened a heavy snowfall. It was the perfect setting for the gloomy silhouette of *Dùn Na Mèadaidh*. To Mórrígan, it seemed a short time since she had ended Finnean Mac Sèitheach's reign with an arrow that pierced his purple-violet eye. She shook her head. The fort had been her and Conall's home for several summers before they exchanged it for the broch in *Áth*.

Imagining the laughter of her daughters, Brighid and Danu, Mórrígan smiled. The twins were eight summers old, full of innocent mischief and already a handful for their tutors and guards. A new son, Aodán, filled the gap left by his ill-fated brother, Tuathal, and now vied for attention with his sisters.

With a mix of happiness and sorrow, Mórrígan passed a hand across her belly. Aodán's birth had been difficult. She sensed that she would give Conall no more sons or daughters. Jealousy's sharp blade stabbed her heart. She and Conall were finally joined by handfasting following the fight for Dùn Na Mèadaidh. Still, others, without hesitation, would seek to give Conall what she no longer could. They would spread their thighs for their king and delight as their bellies became swollen.

She had little recourse in the *Fénechas*, the Law of the Gaels. It allowed a man to have more than one partner. Many, especially nobles and kings, embraced this with enthusiasm. The stubborn blacksmith's apprentice with the piercing blue-grey eyes with whom she had grown up and loved was now *rí*—king. Famed for his prowess in battle, Conall was also burdened with the rule of the tribe. Only his deep sense of loyalty and an appealing naivety about women had delayed him from straying. Whether this would hold true in the future was known only by the Goddess.

The Dark Huntress thought wistfully of Urard, for so long her protector. The giant was now reassigned to Conall's inner guard. He had accepted this honour only after an appropriate level of protest. Mórrígan suspected the change came with some relief. Urard was not a complicated man, and she knew of his unease with her chosen path. *Also, he was not a horseman.*

"Mount up," ordered Mórrígan. Seizing her horse's mane, she swung up onto the *diallait*. It was less of an effort since she had trimmed her mail armour. Its previous mid-thigh length and weight had restricted her agility. The mail now barely touched her arse and thus was a good deal lighter. A crimson cloak, lined with curly fleece and trimmed with a silver-grey wolf pelt, lay across her pale shoulders. It was fastened with a fist-sized silver and gold brooch—a gift from Conall.

She adjusted the recurve bow across her back and slipped loops of leather over the twin, bone-handled daggers that hung in sheaths on a broad, leather belt. With the weapons secured, she placed an ornate, gold and silver helmet over long, red tresses. Black plumes trailed from the small golden raven at the helmet's crest and fluttered in the light breeze. Between the clasp, her helmet, and the gold and silver armbands that encircled taut muscles, Mórrígan was a pillager's dream.

Her brothers cantered over, taking up positions on either side. Beacán Ó Cathasaigh, now nineteen summers old, asked, "Where to?" Their presence was a bone of contention between Mórrígan, Conall, and her older brother, Brion. She knew their true purpose was to watch her, to keep her tied to her family. Yet both would die for her, if necessary. Mórrígan's emerald eyes clouded over. That was a real possibility.

"Back to Áth. The conflict we have been waiting for may not be far off."

***

A watery, early-spring sun held court in the mauve sky. Wet, clinging snow blanketed the marshlands, forests, and fields surrounding Dùn Na Mèadaidh. To many, it was a welcome relief from the interminable rain of northern *Albu*. The bogs were still ice-covered, and the land remained frozen under many layers of frost and ice. Yet it was solid enough for an army to fight and march on. The dirt would become impassably wet as the spring progressed before drying winds scoured the land and forests.

Mongfhionn, a member of the Aes Sídhe, an ancient race that inspired both awe and terror, faced into the blustering south-westerly wind. Her long, blonde hair flared. Highlights of burnished red shamed the sun. The statuesque sídhe projected great power and commanded reverence from all.

Peals of laughter drew her attention back to the landscape where purple heather, orange and yellow gorse and tufts of grass forced their heads through the snow. Soon the hill would be covered with a profusion of fragrant and brightly coloured wildflowers. Mongfhionn smiled at the screams of delight from Aodán and his sisters, playing tag with "uncle" Fearghal.

Fearghal Ruad, a king of the *Ulaid* and general of the *Cróeb Ruad,* a famed warrior clan, was Mongfhionn's lover. He was also the battle commander of Conall's army. Fearghal had a body sculpted in granite. At thirty-eight summers, he sported a few silver highlights within an unruly shock of red hair. A more able, loyal, or nobler man would be hard to find. Mongfhionn's eyes misted. She was ageless; Fearghal was not.

The Sídhe's pleasure in Conall and Mórrígan's twins was forever fused with reminiscences of her sisters, also named Brighid and Danu. Mongfhionn's fervent hope was that the memory and pain of her sisters' savage execution would diminish as Conall's daughters, so full of life, thrived. It was not to be. Each day she felt the sharp talons of guilt tighten around her heart. She was the one who had risen from the ashes of her sisters' funeral pyres.

Mongfhionn knew her thoughts were selfish. Her sisters did not hold her accountable. Their spirits, when the Ancient Ones permitted a visit to her dreams, told her as much. Yet, on one thing, all three sisters agreed. Their deaths should be avenged. That, however, was firmly tied to Conall's quest for justice for his slaughtered parents and sisters and the geis the Sídhe had laid upon him.

Mongfhionn looked down the broad river valley south of Dùn Na Mèadaidh. Soon, the armies of the *Aos na h-Àirde*—the High People— would march along it bringing war, death, and chaos. It was a testament to Conall's strength that they had been contained for several years.

The raids led by Ualraig were skirmishes aimed at testing Conall and his allies' defences and gathering information. Each time, the enemies learned a little bit more about each other. Each time, both sides adjusted their tactics. The simmering storm was not far off and was coming to the boil.

The Sídhe gripped her oak staff for strength. Her thoughts were troubled. As her spirit travelled forth, she sensed another darker force pushing back. Its presence clouded her vision with distractions and shadows. The Ancients were unhelpful when she inquired in her meditations as to the existence of other powers in the area. Forever strong and omniscient, their unease at her inquiries was something she had not hitherto experienced.

One had finally whispered a single word, *"Kartimandu."*

***

Ceana Nic Sèitheach, the tall, slender queen of the *Aos an Eich*—the Horse People—sat on her brother, Finnean Mac Sèitheach's carved, wooden throne. Finnean had been the king of the *Na Mèadaidh* and Dùn Na Mèadaidh his centre of power. His death at the hand of Mórrígan caused Ceana no unhappiness. He had murdered her father. There was no doubt that she would have suffered a similar fate if she had not, as a young girl, been carried off by Eachdonn Breac, king of the Aos an Eich.

She was, however, unhappy she had to steal such moments. Authority over the Na Mèadaidh tribe was firmly in Conall Mac Gabhann's hands. Her designs and plotting to have her, or her son, Ròidh, sit on the throne were thwarted by circumstance and her underestimation of the Ériu king.

Ceana knew her partner had an agreement with Conall to hand over the *dùn* when the Ériu army eventually decided to move on. Better still, the covenant was endorsed by Drostan Ruadh, the king of the *Aos na Coille*—the Forest People—both neighbours and the largest tribe in northern *Albu*.

Few disputed that the throne was hers by right of birth, but Ceana was an impatient woman. In her mind, she had already waited too long. Conall and his people might get too comfortable in the rich and fertile lands of the Na Mèadaidh. He needed to be persuaded to leave and leave quickly.

***

It was evident to all that, at eighteen summers, Gràinne had filled out nicely. As was the culture of most of the tribes of northeastern Albu, the *Cinn Péinteáilte*—the Painted Ones—Gràinne wore as few clothes as possible. Constant exercise and weapons training kept her slim body firmly muscled yet softly curved in all the right places.

According to comments made by many men and quite a few women, she had a fine arse. Her breasts were firm and not small by any measure. Unlike her friend Mòrag Nic Artair of the *Aos an Fhithich*—the Ravens—Gràinne needed no leather straps to restrain them, particularly in battle.

Gràinne's experience at the hands of her tribe of birth, the *Na Daoine Tùrsach*, had been appalling. Vicious whippings ordered by Diadhaidh, the tribe's Priest-queen and Gràinne's grandmother, gifted her with a spider's web of scars. They overlaid her body and the swirling tribal tattoos that covered it.

Her faith in the spiritual armour provided by the designs that covered her body was strong. Yet Gràinne was pragmatic and swore never again to be taken prisoner. Thus, at the very least, she wanted the capacity to inflict maximum pain on her enemies. With Conall's blessing, she approached the army's *ceannairí na míle*—leaders of one thousand—to determine her choice of weapon.

Initial efforts were discouraging. Gràinne was hopeless with bow and sling. She could not hit the largest of brochs at ten paces. Áine Ni Dedad, who had taken over from her sister-in-law, Mórrígan, as captain of the archers, quickly gave up on her.

Likewise, Brandubh, Prince of the Ravens and Mòrag's brother dismissed her attempts to master the spear. To Gràinne's embarrassment, Íar Mac Dedad and Nikandros of Sparta collapsed in laughter at her clumsy attempts to mount and ride even the most docile of horses.

However, to everyone's surprise, Gràinne took to swordplay like a *dobhran* to water. Even more impressively, her choice of weapon was the longsword. Thus, it was inevitable that she came under the tutelage of

Fearghal. The Ulaid king's love for and skill with his longsword was renowned and unmatched in Ériu and Albu.

Fearghal commissioned a sword for Gràinne. Five hands in length with a double edge for slashing, it was perfectly balanced and felt like a feather in her hands. Unlike most longswords, this weapon had an extended grip before the cross-piece. Thus it allowed Gràinne to wield the blade two-handed, compensating for her slight build. As an additional flourish, the last hand of steel was fashioned into a sharp tip, giving her the option of stabbing as well as slashing. Finally, a large cats-eye to match Gràinne's gold-flecked eyes capped the weapon's pommel.

That would have been enough for Conall, his generals, and his captains, the *ceannairí céad*—leaders of one hundred. Still, Gràinne the warrior added another dimension to her fighting style—the chariot. After badgering Brion endlessly for a chance to try out for a place on his chariot squad, he finally yielded and was thankful he did.

Gràinne may have been inept on a horse, but she was a figure of awe in the wicker *cret* of a chariot. Her natural balance and comfort with the longsword quickly established her reputation. Much to the annoyance of her current rutting partner, Tadhg Ó Cuileannáin, she did not lack volunteers for the position of her driver.

Hence, Gràinne developed into a very dangerous young woman.

***

Dawn broke as Mòrag rolled across Íar's belly, causing the tall, red-haired horseman to expel an explosive grunt. She smiled, stood up and stretched before grabbing a pair of black and forest-green plaid pants and her moss-green, fleece-lined cloak.

Were it not for the time of the year and her brother's pleading for modesty, the *Aos an Fhithich*—the Ravens—princess would have happily walked around Dùn Na Mèadaidh as naked as the day she was born. That said, the pants had been soaked in the river so often that they now resembled a tight skin and were strategically torn to leave little to the imagination.

A voluptuous, somewhat narcissistic beauty and an inveterate flirt, Mòrag was also a fierce warrior who could flatten most of the men in the army. She knew that her deep passions and thirst for adventure gave Brandubh nightmares. Most times, she ignored her brother's concerns and enjoyed tormenting him.

Mòrag was already riding two stallions in Íar and the dark-skinned Spartan, Nikandros. Even for lusty Celts, the arrangement was unconventional; for Mòrag, it was temporary. The princess had set her eyes on another. She observed him, stalked him like prey, and became well-acquainted with his habits.

At dawn, he would take his hounds and horse for morning exercise. He would ride the tall, black stallion, Toirneach, down to a nearby spring and waterfall, where they would drink and bathe in the cold waters. Mòrag licked full, red lips. Her cheeks flushed with anticipation, and her breathing increased. Dark, button-shaped nipples hardened. It was time for her to bathe.

CHAPTER 2

406 B.C.—Dun Na Mèadaidh

"We fight the bastards and drive them back to their precious mountains. Then we return to doing what we've always done—cattle raids, fighting and killing each other."

Conall laughed, took a gulp of beer, and wiped the foam from his mouth with the back of his hand. "That's your plan? You left out pillaging and deflowering virgins!"

Drostan stared at Conall with his one good eye. "Has the king of the Ériu—nae, *Clann Ui Flaithimh*, got a better idea?" He grinned at Conall's discomfort. The combined armies and people of the Ériu exiles and the Ravens numbered over ten thousand. While they would never disavow their heritage, the communities had voiced their desire for an identity that would enfold their disparate parts. They were a *clann*—a tribe, in all but name. Now, they wanted a suitable epithet.

It also seemed to the people that since the Goddess had blessed Conall with the title *Hand of the Goddess*, it would be churlish not to reflect this in the naming of the tribe. Thus, Clann Ui Flaithimh—the People of the Hand—was conceived and universally acclaimed. A meeting of civic Elders and Conall's *Chomhairle*—Council—gave their blessing to the name and then deliberated the status of the clann.

With more than a touch of swagger, they pronounced Clann Ui Flaithimh's standing equal to tribes such as the Ulaid or the *Connachta*. Thus, to his chagrin, Conall was immodestly designated *Rí Ruirech*—a king over kings. He shuddered to think how Ailill Mac Mata and Medb of the Connachta or Macha Mong Ruad of the Ulaid would react to his elevation. He was thankful for the sea that separated them.

The people of Clann Ui Flaithimh were comfortable within a defined structure. They had already begun re-organising themselves into clann, *sept*, and *fine*. The fine was an extended family group, and each sept comprised four or five *finte*. Each designation had its *flaith*—noble or leader—whose authority depended on the standing of the sept or fine.

Around the kinship groups circulated the *céile*—or free clansmen—who formed most of the army, and the *fuidhir*—the non-free and slaves. In their homeland of Ériu, rank was primarily based on wealth as determined by land and cattle. For the Clann Ui Flaithimh, it was a mix of gold, trade, and army rank.

Drostan interrupted Conall's musings with an "Or ye?" directed at Eachdonn Breac. "Ye hae a special stake in what happens, Eachdonn." The Forest People's king paused for effect. "Or is it just Ceana that has the interest?"

Eachdonn shifted uneasily in his chair. His normally sensible queen had become a different woman lately. Secure within the walls of Dùn Athad for over twenty summers, to a large extent, her brother, Finnean and Dùn Na Mèadaidh had become distant, ephemeral memories. With Finnean dead, Ceana constantly plagued Eachdonn with plots and schemes to reclaim the throne of the Na Mèadaidh.

It troubled Eachdonn that traces of Finnean's disturbed personality had surfaced in Ceana. At best, her machinations were a waste of time. At worst, it could make enemies of Conall and Drostan. Eachdonn had an agreement. When Conall resumed his quest, the dùn, with its lands and mines, would fall under Eachdonn's rule.

He would pay Conall a lump sum in gold on leaving and an annual tribute in gold and resources to Drostan. It was a deal that all could live with and was good enough for the king of the Aos an Eich. Apparently, it was unacceptable to his queen—or his increasingly petulant son, Ròidh.

He sighed.

"Well?" Drostan was annoyingly persistent.

Eachdonn smiled and nodded in Conall's direction. "*He* tricked me into giving him men and horses. His veterans and chariots held off the might of your Forest People while his cavalry rode to kidnap your heirs. He built up *A' Chrìon Làraich* as a trading centre and fortress for you. And he recruited a legion of Cinn Péinteáilte to his army.

"He has a better brain than the two of us put together, good commanders, disciplined men, and that dammed sídhe. Oh, and apparently, he has a leader of the druids in his camp—*your* brother. I'd listen to what he has to say."

Drostan's single, amber eye twinkled, "Of course, I'll listen to him, but why should I make it easy on him?"

The newly elected king of Clann Ui Flaithimh looked quizzically at the grizzled, red-haired king before him. He reflected that the scar that ran from Drostan's forehead to his chin did not lend itself to humour.

At twenty-seven summers, Conall considered himself a seasoned warrior, although not as accomplished as Fearghal, Íar, Cúscraid Mac Conchobar, and Nikandros, his top echelon of commanders. He swept shoulder-blade lengths of braided dark brown hair back from a winter-pale face. The fluttering flames of rushlights picked up the auburn highlights, an inheritance from his mother.

Conall's braids were tipped with rings of gold and silver and gemstones. According to Mórrígan, this was the current fashion. Often, he hankered after the time when his head was shaven. Yet that carried sad memories of his dead infant son, Tuathal.

"Good grief. Bring me more beer. I'm going to get drunk. Is everyone in a world of their own today?" An exasperated Drostan slammed his mug on the oak table, forgetting it had recently been filled. Beer splashed over Conall and galvanised him into action.

"The plan doesn't overly worry me. The High People have little choice. There is only one pass to the highlands and the forests of the north, and Dùn Na Mèadaidh guard it. The terrain is known to our enemy. Ualraig, their commander, is well-acquainted with the lie of the land from his time as the leader of Finnean's southern mercenaries. His raids and the spies we haven't caught have added to that knowledge.

"Once the bastards leave their strongholds of *Dùn Caen* and *An Balla Leac*, they have little choice but to march through our southern forests and along the river, which flows south of the *Sleá*. My guess is that Ualraig intends to cross the river you call the *Abhainn Dubh* southeast of us at the village of Áth and lay siege to Dùn Na Mèadaidh.

"I don't intend to let him cross. Even with Cúscraid's improvements to its defences, Dùn Na Mèadaidh is a piss-poor battleground. However, the landscape south of the river is ideal for fighting."

"Yes, the bastard farmers have cleared the land," growled Drostan.

Conall raised an eyebrow, making the dark-blue tattoo on his right temple crease. "We can avoid the twists and turns of the Abhainn Dubh. There's more than enough ground for manoeuvring men, cavalry, and chariots." He held Drostan's gaze. "Brandubh informs me there is more than enough forest for his and your men to the north, east, west, and south. Thick copses of birch, oak, and alder are scattered across the river plains." Drostan grunted and signalled Conall to proceed.

With a smile and a shrug, Conall continued. "According to Cúscraid, there is a crag a half-day's march southwest of here. That is where we should centre our fight. It's protected on three sides by cliffs. We can place and defend archers and slings on the hilltop.

"I'm amazed no one's thought of building an *ráth* on the crag. It's a much better location than Dùn Na Mèadaidh. A short distance south of the hill is another possible defensible area. There's an abandoned hillfort close to a small community. Its defences could quickly be upgraded."

"If the battle doesn't worry you, then what does?" asked Eachdonn.

"We know shite-all about Ualraig's king or queen. We know they can field more fighters than us, and their commander is no fool. Ualraig's spell as a mercenary with Finnean didn't work out so well, and, in the end, he and his men walked away from the battlefield."

Conall took a long drink of beer. It had the faint taste and fragrance of heather. Liquid dribbled down his chin onto the light woollen tunic covering his chainmail. Even with friends, Conall rarely removed his armour. Although weighty, the mail was a second skin.

"Mongfhionn is abnormally troubled. She can't push her spirit much further than the borders of High People's territory without something pushing back. Mórrígan's nightmares have increased in number and severity." Conall addressed Drostan directly. "Your brother, Crum, has not been lacking in effort, either. He met with other druids at several stone circles and travelled to the small settlements closest to the High People's northern borders.

"Your brother gained little information, but we gained more families seeking refuge. They are mostly farmers and appear frightened beyond comprehension at the mere mention of the High People's leader."

"Sheep frightened by old women's tales," said Drostan. "The High People is led by flesh and blood. Their warriors are no different to me or ye. An axe, sword or spear will send them to Mag Mell."

"I hope you're right," said Conall. "But the evil that Diadhaidh tried to resurrect is still fresh in my memory."

Drostan snorted. "Ye'r taking the Hand of the Goddess title too seriously. Ye see spirits and gods where there's only blood, bone, and flesh."

Conall grimaced at the mention of the title. "I hope you're right, Drostan. I hope you're right. With luck, Tadhg will bring us better news."

CHAPTER 3

406 B.C.—Dùn Caen

The midday sun rose in a rare powder blue sky. "Are they ready?" The voice was condescending and made clear there was but one acceptable response.

"Yes." Ualraig dipped his head stiffly, his disapproval barely disguised. The leader of the High People laughed. The objection of the tribe's highest-ranking commander was duly noted and summarily dismissed with a curl of the lip and a flash of teeth.

Ualraig's distaste for the upcoming display was considered a weakness and an ill-advised gesture. Only the loyalty of his men and his value as a sound tactician saved him from becoming part of the spectacle. As his ruler strode past him, the verdant green cloak that flowed from her slim shoulders created a soft wind tainted by the corruption of death.

Ròidh watched with mounting anxiety. At this moment, the prince of the Aos an Eich wished he was anywhere but the slush-covered sandstone ramparts of Dùn Caen. Sweat trickled down the bloodless face of Eachdonn Breac's son. Rivulets of moisture traced the curvature of his spine. His garments were uncomfortably damp and cold. Fear restrained him from any attempt to adjust his clothing. The last thing he wanted was to draw attention.

He cursed his mother. Ceana's plottings had sent him far south, delivering him into the hands of the High People. He shivered; if his father became aware of the mission, Ròidh's reward would be a slow and agonising traitor's death. A deal was struck with the High People, and gold changed hands. Intelligence, plans, and numbers were traded, and an unholy rendezvous was arranged. Now, the understanding was to be sealed in blood.

The ten that constituted Ròidh's guard were seized immediately upon arrival at Dùn Caen. Stripped and imprisoned, they were now arranged in a line along the fort's high, inner rampart. Each stood naked between two tall stakes, arms and legs held apart and secured with leather ties. Ròidh dropped his head, ashamed to meet their angry eyes. He wished he could close his ears and not listen to their abuse and shouts of condemnation.

Head held high, Kartimandu, Queen of the High People, ignored the cold. She walked gracefully barefoot, leaving only the faintest imprints in the wet, muddy snow. Once she stood before the condemned, the cloak slipped from her shoulders and was quickly taken away by a slave. The slave would be executed later. No one was allowed to touch the garments of the queen. Very few survived the touch of her body either. To become Kartimandu's lover was to invite death. No child had ever sucked on her nipples. The Goddess had decreed none ever would.

Kartimandu was tall, slender, and perfectly proportioned. Long, unbraided tresses of copper-red hair flowed smoothly over her shoulders, ending just above the cleft of a softly rounded arse. Her body gave the appearance of being sheathed in a fern-green garment that clung like a second skin. The queen, in fact, was unclothed. Paint was carefully applied daily to a body devoid of imperfection or hair—apart from her head. The solid colour was interrupted only at her neck and ankles, where it transformed into curling symbols and designs.

She faced the congregation who stood many rows deep before the ditch that paralleled Dùn Caen's rampart. As she lifted her hands, the army and citizenry cheered. To her subjects, Kartimandu was a goddess. Their queen had raised them up from nothing. She had brought them victories and immense wealth, subjugating neighbouring tribes until they were one. Unsated and unbounded, her ambitions lay towards the north beyond the range of mountains, moors, and valleys known as *Penn-inus*. Her people would follow without question.

The queen breathed deeply and savoured her people's worship. She pirouetted to face Ròidh's guard. They were not as appreciative of the queen. Neither was the gust of wind that danced along the rampart a respecter of royalty. It carried the men's voices and, lifting up the mist of spit and saliva from their mouths, threw it against the perfect canvas of Kartimandu's body. In an instant, the poise vanished. She snarled, angered at the lack of respect and devotion. Her eyes, black as a beetle's wings, looked with cruel relish upon her prey.

The warrior at the centre was chosen first. A hand reached out, seizing his flaccid manhood. The queen's lips formed a mocking smile as the man fought his erection. His uninvited stimulation was brief when his genitals were taken and crushed by a sadistic hand. A curved blade glinted as it sliced through the tender flesh of his balls and cock. Kartimandu held her bloody trophy before his face before tossing them to the hounds, who played tug-of-war with the lump of meat.

Crimson blood soaked the man's thighs, trickling down his legs to merge with puddles of slush and mud. His body shuddered, and he bit down on his tongue to stop screaming. His vow to show no fear remained unbroken. A trickle of blood flowed from lips blue with cold.

In place of his voice, his belly sighed as it was opened with swift horizontal and vertical slashes. A long trail of glistening guts slithered to the ground. They smelled of shite and lay in a steaming, reddish mass at his feet. He would have pissed himself had he the means.

The curved point of Kartimandu's blade pierced and then plucked his eyes from their sockets. Finally, the serrated outer edge of the knife was drawn across his throat. The dagger bit deeply through cartilage and muscle. Gouts of blood splattered the adjacent victims.

A rapidly beating heart strained to maintain life as its temple was desecrated. Finally, with a strength that belied her frame, Kartimandu cracked ribs to rip the organ from the victim's chest. A long, pointed tongue licked the heart, savouring its taste and smell before placing it on the platter held by a slave. The broken body slumped as the *bean sídhe* finally brought relief from the torment.

The queen of the High People made her next choice and sashayed to her prey. She was in no hurry and intended to savour the men's suffering fully. All met a similar fate. The screams of the sacrificed coursed across the ramparts of Dùn Caen. They were met by the ghoulish cheers of Kartimandu's subjects. Still, there were no pleas for mercy and, with their last breath, each cursed Ròidh and his mother.

***

Like his rí, Tadhg Ó Cuileannáin was slightly above average height. There the resemblance ended. Tadhg was slim and muscular, and his head was crowned with a mop of copper-straw hair. He was a talented poet, a *seanchaí*, and an able fighter. While not as experienced in warfare as Conall's ceannairí na míle, Tadhg was by far the cleverest of Conall's leaders, and his mind was as sharp as the keenest blade. Nikandros often referred to him as a "Young Odysseus," alluding to the famed Greek hero's cunning and resourcefulness.

Unfortunately, Tadhg's skills meant he was assigned tasks that, though vital, were unpleasant. This was not merely due to his flair for getting to the bottom of mysteries. Tadhg, like a dog with a bone, refused to give up. He was relentless in pursuit of his given quests.

The recent behaviour of Ceana and her ruddy-faced son raised Conall's suspicions, and he called for Tadhg. As a result, Tadhg was urged to take a particular interest in Ròidh.

Tadhg's band was small. Eight were from Clann Ui Flaithimh— Tadhg, the bullish Torcán Ó Dubhghaill, Mòrag, and five others from the Ravens. Conall had also insisted that Tadhg take at least one representative each from the Forest People and the Aos an Eich. If Conall's suspicions proved correct, they would be invaluable witnesses.

They travelled south on horseback for speed and because it was the only way to keep up with Ròidh. The Forest People warrior with them, one of Drostan's extended family, was bemused when he discovered that they were tracking Ròidh. Yet he was content to observe. However, Gormal Mac Eachdonn, the Aos an Eich representative, was outraged. He did not believe Tadhg's explanation that they were shadowing his brother as an extra security measure.

That implausible story fell apart at the border of the High People's lands. North of the hillfort of An Balla Leac, Ròidh was met by a large and apparently friendly warband and escorted towards the newly con-structed fort. The following dawn, Ròidh's party and escort departed and travelled south towards Dùn Caen. At this, Gormal grudgingly accepted that Ròidh's actions were peculiar, if not downright suspicious. Tadhg's band dismounted when they were within a half-day's ride of Dùn Caen. One of Mòrag's men was left to take care of the horses. The remainder continued on foot.

Dusk approached. From their vantage point of a small copse of alder and beech on the mountainside overlooking Dùn Caen, the band waited and observed. The thicket provided shelter from the driving south-westerly winds and the sleety rain. On the same level as the fort's ramparts, it offered an excellent view of the dùn while being far enough away to escape detection by occasional patrols.

It was bad enough that Ròidh apparently was a traitor. Still, now Tadhg fought to restrain himself as, helpless to intervene, he watched the sacrifices. Thankfully, distance hid the detail, if not the sound of the agonising deaths. The screams rose above the roar and cheers of Kartimandu's subjects. A scuffle from behind made Tadhg look around. Mòrag physically restrained Gormal.

"I'll kill the bastard!" cried Gormal, much too loudly for his com-rades. "The Hag bear witness. I'll kill him."

"*Dùn do bheal!*—shut your mouth," said Tadhg through clenched teeth. "I'll gag you if I have to." Gormal shook his head and slumped. Released by Mòrag, he crawled on hands and knees deeper into the copse. Soon the sour smell of vomit and the sound of muted sobs drifted back to the group. Tadhg glanced at a grim-faced Torcán. It was clear that Gormal would not have been alone had he chosen to charge Dùn Caen's defences.

Tadhg signalled to withdraw. A pale and solemn group reclaimed their horses and set out on the trail back to Dùn Na Mèadaidh.

As the sun slipped below the horizon, the High People celebrated, working themselves into a frenzy of bloodlust for Kartimandu. Spiked on stockade posts, ten Aos an Eich heads glared with black, empty eye sockets on the uninhibited carousing before them.

***

At the northeastern gateway of Dùn Caen, Kartimandu gripped the rail of her ornately decorated chariot tightly as it rumbled over a track deeply rutted by winter storms and iron-clad wheels. It was the fourth dawn after the executions.

Behind the queen, Ualraig led his detachment out of Dùn Caen. Ualraig's five thousand were the elite of Kartimandu's army. To her annoyance, the disciplined troops held their loyalty to Ualraig above their oaths to her. Bribes of wealth, elevated status, the offer of her body, and threats of terrible deaths failed to break the bonds between Ualraig and his warriors. Those tempted were soon revealed and found Ualraig's justice was quick and terminal. Thus, an uneasy stalemate had settled between the queen and her commander.

Kartimandu glanced over her shoulder towards the ramparts. To her disquiet, under the high winds that buffeted the Penn-inus, the victims' heads had rotated to face north. Bloody lips silently cursed her army as it staggered drunkenly towards the broad moorland and flat-topped hills.

Disconcertingly, no fowl feasted on the skull flesh. On each head perched a solitary raven, each both guardian and judge. A harsh, accusing *kraa kraa* sounded above the dull tramp of thousands of feet. For the first time, an icy finger of fear tracked along Kartimandu's spine. Ancient dreams, long smothered with the blood of countless sacrifices, rose up to threaten her steely composure.

The army marched along deep mountain valleys, across fast-flowing rivers and moorland trails still clothed in wet snow. In a cycle of the moon, they reached the borderlands of the High People. Their numbers had swollen to almost thirty thousand. If the weather improved, it would take the army another cycle of the moon before Kartimandu and Ualraig would look upon Dùn Na Mèadaidh.

That said, attaining their destination was not inevitable. There was another mountain range to cross. The warlike *Votod-Daoine* inhabited the lands around the southern shores of the *Linne Foirthe*. They would fight if they saw a clear opportunity for profit. Other tribes stood between them and Conall's armies, although all paid tribute to Kartimandu. Most would cower in their hillforts rather than confront the might of the High People.

Ualraig offered sacrifices of gold, silver, and armour for a quick victory at Dùn Na Mèadaidh. Ròidh had provided numbers and plans. Surprise should be on their side, and Conall Mac Gabhann's tactics countered. Ualraig snorted. *Some hope.* Underestimating the Ériu king was a sure path to defeat.

CHAPTER 4

406 B.C.—*Áth*

Swirls of late snow danced along the settlement's pathways and settled in stark, white drifts against the buildings. An undulating blue-grey veil of peat and wood smoke shimmered above the dark, thatched roofs.

Áth was situated a few hundred paces east of the Abhainn Dubh river. It had mushroomed from its humble beginnings as a few wooden shelters for hunters and fishers to the hum and bustle of Clann Ui Flaithimh's main settlement. Its population had grown from a few score to several hundred. Dry-stone walls edged the meandering paths connecting Áth's array of buildings. Hordes of red-cheeked, snot-nosed children shrieked with laughter as they played chase in and out of the maze.

At Áth's heart stood a sturdy, grey-stone broch topped with a steep, conical roof of brown thatch. Fifteen paces in diameter and twice that in height, the windowless sentinel towered over the nearby river ford. It cast a long shadow over Áth's thriving community of tradespeople and artisans. The broch had two floors, both made with planked wood.

Access to the upper level was via a curved stairway set into the building's double stone walls. The building could comfortably house thirty to forty people. This was the home of three couples: Conall and Mórrígan, Fearghal and Mongfhionn, Brion and Áine, their children and wolfhounds. Mórrígan had drawn the line at Conall's request for his horse, Toirneach, to be housed in the broch.

Adjacent to the home stood the *Halla Mór*—the Great Hall—where

Conall and his Chomhairle met with their allies to discuss battle strategies. It was also where an aged Seanán, the tribe's civic leader, met with the *flatha* to discuss trade and property; and where the druids sat to hear the pleadings of the people and interpret the Law.

The building was thirty-five paces long and ten paces broad and predominantly built of oak. Indeed, about thirty ancient oak trees had been sacrificed in its construction. The steep roof was made of thatch underpinned with long poles. A line of timber posts three paces apart with cross-braces formed the walls.

The Great Hall could comfortably hold a hundred. At feast times, this would swell to over three hundred. Its heavy oak doors swung on iron hinges. Once opened, they released an atmosphere redolent of peat and wood, sweat, beer and roasted food. The building's red-brown wood interior was austere. Nikandros described it as Spartan. Even the light from hundreds of wall-mounted rushlights and the glow from the smouldering fire-pits arrayed down the Hall's centre could not dispel the building's gloom. The room only came alive on feast nights when the fires roared high.

The Hall was divided into three aisles by two rows of de-barked oak poles. The rows were four paces apart and held the roof in place. Opposite the entrance and along the length of the building were two broad tiers of benches for eating, drinking, and sleeping. Scattered hides and pelts left behind by revellers broke the monotony of the décor. The *Ard-Bord*—High Table—was placed on the upper tier and against the wall opposite the entrance. Two carved seats for Conall and Mórrígan were placed at its centre.

Close to the Hall, skilled blacksmiths and apprentices, sweaty and covered in burns, stood half-naked by the roaring flames of forges. Here, metal was pounded into tools, horse tack, armour, and weapons. Their artisan neighbours inscribed and tapped gold, silver, and copper into exquisite torcs, armbands, brooches, bridles, and halters. Fletchers and bow-makers crafted for both hunter and warrior and vied with the harp-makers for the best quality strings.

The tanners and leather workers were exiled to the southern outskirts of Áth but close to the river. The smell of urine, animal shite, and decaying flesh hung like summer heat over their work. It clung to clothes and permeated deep into their pores. While their goods were appreciated and many were wealthy, few fathers wanted their daughters to marry into such a malodorous society. Thus, they lived in isolation, an essential yet separate part of the community.

In the scattering of stone, mud, and wood roundhouses, women with taut arm muscles ground barley and wheat on large, basalt quern stones. Bread baked on iron griddles, filling the air with mouth-watering aromas. Wheat cakes with honey were a rare treat appreciated by all. Great iron cauldrons, blackened with age and smoke, held simmering soups and stews.

Delicious smells rose up from the peat and wood-fired cooking pits. Cattle and pigs roasted over fires on spits hissed at passers-by as globs of fat splattered burning embers. Chickens clucked and scratched in the dirt for food or squawked as they were chased by children tasked with wringing their necks for the evening meal.

Homes, workshops, and most other buildings shared a lack of windows. The driving wind, rain and winter snowstorms dictated style. Most entrances faced east to face the morning sun. Inside dimly lit homes, men and women laboured over upright weaving looms to produce a diversity of brightly patterned cloth for *léinte* and *brait*. As the sun faded, work continued with eyes strained in the fluttering yellow flames of rushlights.

A man-high stockade enclosed Áth. The fence was of similar construction to the walls of the Great Hall, save for one aspect. In addition to cross-braces, stakes were sunk into the earth between the timber posts to form an intimidating palisade. A running platform was erected on the inside of the fence, giving defenders a height advantage over attackers and the ability to wield weapons more efficiently.

On its outside ran a ditch populated with blackthorn bushes and sharpened stakes. The trench was wide enough to prevent anyone from leaping across it. It was also deep enough that anyone fortunate to avoid the stakes would find it almost impossible to climb its muddy sides without aid. On the outer edge of the ditch, the excavated dirt was used to construct a man-high berm.

In contrast to the pleasant aromas of foods and fires, the pungent smells of shite, piss, rotting food, and the occasional carcass emanated from the ditch. In a warm summer, it was hard to tell which was riper: the smell from the trench or the tanners.

***

"That's not a happy group," remarked a passer-by as Tadhg, followed by Mòrag, Gormal, and Torcán, strode towards the Great Hall. It was not meant to be heard, but Tadhg fully agreed with the opinion.

Inside, the leaders and counsellors gathered around a solid oak table stained by grease and beer. The table ran the length of the shorter wall and could comfortably seat twenty. Faces were animated by the rush-lights and flushed with the heat from blazing log fires. A haze of peat and wood smoke stung eyes and settled a soft layer of grime on weather-beaten faces.

Beer flowed. According to the men, the copious volume consumed was needed to keep throats lubricated. Platters of bread, meat, and cheese were laid on the table. For the more abstemious, jugs of milk and water were available.

Much to Conall's delight, Carmag Mac an t-Sionnaich, the new general of the Forest People's army, sat at Drostan's shoulder. The former governor of *Cùil Daothail* had been unable to resist the challenge of Drostan's offer of command. On Drostan's right sat his father, Failbhe and the leader of Drostan's *Comhairle-Chatha*—the High Council of the Forest People. While aged and suffering from chronic back pain, Failbhe's mind remained alert, and his eyes undimmed. Drostan's brother, a tall, gaunt druid, chose to stand with the Clann Ui Flaithimh. It was a clear signal of his loyalty.

Eachdonn sat on Conall's left. The king, who usually loved an audience, was strangely subdued. His face gave the impression of a deep internal struggle. His eyes were distant, and his thoughts elsewhere. Periodically he would run restless fingers through a tangle of auburn hair and sigh. Gormal stood behind his father, stern-faced and plainly in anguish following his recent sortie.

Ceana did not attend the meeting. Conall suspected this was linked to Ròidh's return. As much as the queen's curiosity was piqued at the meeting, her priority would be to question her son and ensure her plans were followed. In this, Ceana was fatally naïve. Her accomplice, Kartimandu, cared for no one's plans save her own.

Around the table, the remainder of the seats were occupied by Conall's Chomhairle. Tadhg stood to the side. If the young man looked unhappy, he felt much worse. "We're glad to see you safely back, Tadhg," said Conall with genuine affection for the warrior. "Perhaps you would summarise what you observed in the land of the High People."

"If his face is anything to go by, I doubt he has any good news for us," Drostan said, "and neither would it appear do his companions."

With hands on the oak table as if to draw strength from its ancient timbers, Tadhg looked at the expectant faces while gathering his thoughts. "The High People's army left Dùn Caen a cycle of the moon past."

"So they're finally on the march. How many? How soon?" asked Fearghal.

"I make their size at least twenty thousand. They'll attract other clans and warbands on the way. So, their final numbers may be closer to thirty thousand. Maybe more. Likely, they near the northern borders of their territory today and will celebrate the feast of *Bealtaine* at the stronghold of An Balla-Leac."

"The confirmation is good, but we had already anticipated this, Tadhg. Is there anything else we should know?" asked Brion, tracing the long scar on his face with a dirt-ingrained fingernail. Tadhg paused, perhaps hoping that the Goddess would intervene. An almost imperceptible nod from Conall dashed that hope.

He breathed deeply and spoke bluntly. "My given mission was to observe the movements of Ròidh Mac Eachdonn." The room fell silent and then exploded in a wave of anger and astonishment. Thankfully, weapons had been surrendered before the meeting. They rested, out of reach, in wooden racks along the rear wall. Blood could still be spilt as each retained their daggers.

"This is how you treat a friend and ally?" Eachdonn glared at Conall. "My men and I will leave. Be thankful that we do not join the High People."

Yet as Eachdonn made to stand, a hand rested firmly on his shoulder. Gormal spoke quietly but with authority in the king's ear, "Be careful, father. Our friends have good cause to believe that the Aos an Eich are already in bed with the High People." Shocked, Eachdonn slumped back into his chair.

"Perhaps, we should allow Tadhg to continue his report," said Drostan, removing his booted feet from the table and sitting upright.

Tadhg acknowledged Drostan. "Ròidh and a guard of ten rode south towards Dùn Caen. I and nine others, chosen from each tribe present, followed."

"Now, wasn't that a fortunate mix?" said Failbhe looking at Conall. Conall just raised an eyebrow and smiled fleetingly.

"I apologise for my father. Once more, please continue, Tadhg," said Drostan.

"Ròidh met with the High People at the hillfort of An Balla-Leac. His party was escorted to Dùn Caen. When they reached the ráth, the guard was set upon, stripped, and dragged away. Ròidh was taken to meet with the High People's leaders. He did not appear to be under any restrictions." Tadhg paused, gathering strength for his subsequent revelations.

"Several sunsets later, Ròidh's guard were tied to stakes on the ramparts of Dùn Caen and sacrificed by the High People's queen."

"Queen?" snapped Mongfhionn rising from her seat.

"Yes. From the people's chants, Kartimandu is her name," said Tadhg. "She appeared to be sheathed in green."

"The Ancients preserve us all," murmured Mongfhionn and sat down as abruptly as she had stood.

Tadhg quickly ended his tale, sat down, and took a long gulp of beer. Mòrag stepped forward, glanced at Brandubh, and said, "I, Mòrag, Princess of the Ravens, bear witness to what Tadhg has spoken." She threw a hard look at Gormal.

As if aware of her gaze, Gormal looked up with deep sadness and said, "As did I."

"And ye?" queried Drostan of his kinsman. A sharp dip of the head elicited Drostan's response. "Shite! How far does this rot go in yer camp, Eachdonn?"

Eachdonn's demeanour changed from outraged and insulted to searching for a plausible explanation for his son's behaviour. His usually ruddy face was infused with anger at his betrayal and humiliation before Conall and Drostan. He rose stiffly from the table.

"Gormal and I will take our leave. At this time, there is little I can say to make amends. I believe I may know who is at the centre of this outrage. My son will seek evidence of the traitorous enclave. Once known, they will die very slowly and very publicly... no matter their status."

"We need an alternate battle plan," said Nikandros as Eachdonn exited the Hall. "We must assume Ròidh has told Kartimandu the current one... and our strength." The Spartan's dark eyes smouldered at the treachery. In the half-light of the broch, the remaining participants looked none too happy.

***

"Well?" snapped Ceana. A miserable Ròidh stood before her.

"You have your agreement with Kartimandu." Ceana smiled and reached to embrace her son until, in a flash of bravado, he added, "If you can trust that vicious bitseach. She gutted my men."

The warm embrace became a stinging slap in the face. "They are *my* men. Not yours. Some minor sacrifices are for the greater good." Ròidh's defiance melted like wax before a flame. With a sullen glance at his mother, he retreated to find solace in beer. He intended to drink as much as he could in as short a time as possible.

Left alone with her thoughts, Ceana congratulated herself. Unfortunately, her plan to gain the throne of Dùn Na Mèadaidh also depended on a minor coastal tribe, the *Aos nan Con-Seilge*—The People of the Hounds—honouring another of her arrangements. And why wouldn't they? It gave them a path to exact revenge on Mórrígan.

Soon she would take her rightful place as queen of the Na Mèadaidh. Conall and Drostan would be too preoccupied with Kartimandu's armies to pose a threat to her. Eachdonn, if he survived the war, would eventually come to see she had been right. The queen permitted herself a satisfied smile.

CHAPTER 5

406 B.C.— Creag na Clachard

The People of the Hounds were hunters. Like the hounds they reared, they were a hardy breed, and, as with many of the northern tribes, they favoured ginger-red hair and green eyes. Unlike the other tribes, they were a squat people, broad-shouldered, hard-muscled, and hirsute. The axe was their preferred weapon, and they had developed considerable skill in using a smaller version for throwing. Most carried several in their belts. Small round shields gave protection to their heavily tattooed and rarely covered torsos.

Creag na Clachard was the civil and military centre of the tribe. The hillfort commanded long sightlines due to its location on an escarpment overlooking the coastal plain to the north. Its name, translated as "the Crag of the High Stone", was derived from the enormous standing stone at its centre. The rock was forty paces high, ten paces wide, and towered over the landscape.

Many generations had carved swirling symbols into the rock's faces. It served as a religious focal point for the druids who provided spiritual oversight and guidance to the tribe. The monument also served as the assembly point for the tribe's warbands to receive blessings from the priests before setting out on raids.

Camran Mac Madadh, king of the People of the Hounds, scratched his scalp, scattering snow-white flakes of dry skin abroad. The king was a striking figure, noted for his hair or, rather, his hairstyle. A youthful thatch of thick, amber-red hair was streaked blonde after years of washing in limestone water. What remained stood in stiff spikes. Camran was a small, angry man, frustrated by the attacks on his territory by the *An Fiagaí Dorcha*—the Dark Huntress. That it was he who had initiated the raids on Clann Uí Flaithimh's communities and brought his tribe to the Huntress' attention was immaterial to Camran.

As he stood before his men, Camran smiled at the prospect of vengeance. Being somewhat of a brute and not overly endowed with wit or common sense, the king gave no thought to the disastrous consequences the raid might trigger. Camran's brain hung limply between short, sturdy legs. He was a fool.

Charmed by the willowy queen of the Aos an Eich, he thought only of her waist-long tresses of fair hair, her milk-pale skin, and the promise of her cleavage. Ceana's assurances of future wealth, cooperation, and hints of more intimate delights bound Camran as tightly as a wet leather thong.

In the shadow of the colossal stone and with the blessings of the druids, he watched fifty of his best marauders set out. They would travel north and then west along the foothills of the long ridge of mountains they knew as the Sleá. At the tip of the range sat Dùn Na Mèadaidh.

***

Kartimandu woke with a start. Cold sweat trickled down the queen's spine. She grabbed the highly polished bronze platter that was never far from her and held it close to her face. She expected that her flawless face would bear the red imprint of a hand. To her surprise, it did not. Yet she could feel the sting of that slap and see the monstrous face of the Hag who delivered it. In her head echoed a warning, *Turn back*.

Breathing heavily, Mongfhionn smiled as she rested on one arm. A droplet of perspiration flowed down her scarred throat and over a teardrop-shaped breast that curved delightfully upwards. The bead rested briefly on a prominent nipple before falling onto the bed of rushes and meadowsweet.

The Sídhe had expended considerable strength and concentration to accomplish her task. To deliver a warning at so great a distance and to such a loathsome creature drained her. Tadhg's description of the queen of the High People had opened Mongfhionn's eyes. Now she knew what manner of being she and Conall faced. *"Fuath,"* she whispered. The knowledge was both reassuring and alarming.

"Small, oddly coloured, furry creatures that live in lochs, rivers, and seas. They're a pain in the arse," mumbled a drowsy Fearghal as he turned on his side and raised his head.

"You're awake?"

"That obvious, is it?" A half-hearted slap on his stubbled cheek told Fearghal that further sarcasm would likely not be appreciated.

"Yes, most fuath are simply malevolent little bastards. Rarely seen, especially in daylight, and easily killed with an iron blade. But…"

The prolonged pause gained Fearghal's instant attention. "Spit it out, woman. What do a fuath and you sweating like a pig in the middle of the night have to do with us?"

"Every few generations, a special type of fuath emerges. A vicious creature with an insatiable hunger for blood and destruction. Like the Aes Sídhe, the creature is ageless and has… powers." Mongfhionn grimaced, for Fearghal's hand gripped like a vice.

"Again, what has this to do with us?"

The Sídhe took a deep breath and looked into Fearghal's hazel eyes with her obsidian pair. "I believe Kartimandu, the leader of the High People, is a fuath. She is close enough for me to visit in her dreams. Defeating the High People has become a hundred times more difficult and a thousand times more necessary."

"Shite! This and Ceana's plottings. What evil will crawl out from under the next rock?"

***

Dùn Na Mèadaidh lay at the far western end of the Sleá. The range was different from the high mountains of the north. Its crest could be readily gained by man and horse. The foothills on the northern side gently sloped down to a broad, tree-covered valley through which the *Uisce Èireann* flowed to the coast.

In the spring, a profusion of mosses, heathers, and gorse bushes covered the hills. Apart from scattered clusters of spindly trees on the slopes, any wood had long since been removed. The soil had been planted for grain, but the dirt had little depth, and the harvest was scant. Scattered flocks of scrawny sheep, chased by imaginary predators, scurried over the hills.

The fort had a commanding view of the surrounding land. It extended about one hundred and fifty paces in length and seventy across. Built parallel to each other, two thick outer walls of stone encircled the ráth. The fortifications were linked by spanning walls at the single western entrance. Within the enclosure, a second smaller but thicker defensive wall protected a tall wood and grey-stone building that contained the throne room and royal accommodation.

West of the gateway, a deep gorge ran north to south, almost splitting the Sleá in two. Along this defile, the People of the Hounds warband scrambled as the sun began its fiery descent.

With his back to the gully, Urard smiled as he watched Brighid and Danu go through their training exercises. Both girls had pleaded with Nikandros to let them start weapons training. The request met with little resistance from their father or mother. Aodán sat on Urard's tree trunk of a thigh and swung his play sword in the air as if directing his sisters' movements. In the stillness of the afternoon, the sound of wooden training swords clacked and echoed across the valley.

The girls had real swords. They were sheathed in beautifully designed scabbards and bound to their backs by equally ornate leather straps. The swords were a present from Nikandros and fashioned on a design the Spartan had seen on his travels. The blades were slimmer than, but just as deadly as, the xiphos the Spartan carried. They also could be held double-handed.

Absorbed with and enjoying the spectacle, Urard did not pick up the rustle of bushes or the shuffling feet in the gully behind him. He did not hear the *whish* of the axe as it tumbled through the air. The axe head struck the back of Urard's skull. Blackness overcame him as he pitched forward with Aodán trapped in his strong right arm.

Yelling, the raiders ran towards the twins. The shouts of panic and cries for help from Brighid and Danu reached the ears of those patrolling the walls of Dùn Na Mèadaidh. They responded with sneers, taunts, and laughter before they turned their backs. Although frightened beyond their wits, the girls remembered Nikandros' training. They dropped their training swords. There was a soft whisper as the twins drew swords from scabbards. Back-to-back and with hearts thumping in their young chests, the girls faced their attackers.

Jeers at the size of the swords were the response from the unwashed mob that encircled the girls. Tears stained the twin's cheeks as they slowly rotated, maintaining their balance and footing. Eventually, the leader of the warband lost patience and barked out commands in a strong brogue. Two thickset brutes strode forward, thinking to intimidate and grab the girls. Foolishly they had not seen fit to arm themselves, and their axes remained in their belts.

As the thugs came within striking distance, Brighid and Danu screamed and struck. Simultaneously, their swords slashed downwards. The move was followed by a step forward and a short thrust parallel to the ground. The difference in heights meant that the girls' diagonal slash, from right to left, opened up gashes from nipple to gut. Narrowly missing the men's cocks, the follow-up thrust punched through naked skin and muscle to pierce the men's bladders. As the swords were withdrawn, jets of blood and piss splashed the girls. The men slumped to the ground. Their fate was sealed.

Stunned, the mob was momentarily silenced. Then with a loud shriek, they rushed forward. The girls' blades fed greedily on soft flesh. A frenetic flurry of sword slashes left many with wounds that would inevitably become infected. A few would not survive.

The twins put up a brave fight, but while their skill did not let them down, age and the weight of their enemies did. Exhausted and bruised by the thumping of wooden shields against their young bodies, the girls eventually fell. They were tied, gagged, and thrown across the shoulders of two warriors. Like a withdrawing tentacle, the warband scrambled down the gully to the valley and began its journey back to Creag na Clachard with their prize.

CHAPTER 6

406 B.C.—Áth—Summer

Bealtaine passed, and summer arrived. The three kings, Conall, Drostan, and Eachdonn, met once again. Taking advantage of one of the few days without rain or sleet and accompanied by their advisors and commanders, they sat outside around a slumbering fire. Conall kicked the grey-black crust and tossed a few bricks of peat onto its smouldering ash-red heart. An earthy aroma permeated the air. Amid the uncertainty, it was a comforting, satisfying smell.

Unusually, Eachdonn had asked for the meeting. It was the first he had attended since the news of Ròidh's treachery. Ordinarily quite loquacious, Eachdonn became bitter and withdrawn. The visible change in the king's demeanour worried friends and alerted Ceana that all was not well. Immersed in her plottings, the queen failed to connect her handfast partner's demeanour to her activities. Instead, she believed Eachdonn had become disenchanted with his allies. It was an interpretation, which though gravely far from reality, greatly pleased Ceana.

"Ceana is the root and cause of the treachery. It goes no further than Ròidh and Ceana's guard and some malcontents— about two or three hundred men." The venom in Eachdonn's voice took Conall by surprise. Ceana had been his partner and queen for many years. It would have been kinder if Ceana had thrust a dagger into Eachdonn's heart. Her betrayal blighted his spirit, and its scabs festered within the king's mind.

"How do you intend to deal with the problem... and when?" asked

Conall. The Clann Ui Flaithimh king was reluctant to get involved in an internal matter of the Aos an Eich.

"There, we have a bit of good fortune. The bastards are all in Dùn Na Mèadaidh. Most of us have had important tasks to accomplish. The fort was low on our list of priorities. Conall resides in Áth. Thus, Ceana claimed it as her fiefdom under our noses and without resistance. I plan to surround it and starve the bitseach and her followers. When she surrenders, we'll march in, hang, and gut them all."

There was a silence as those present mulled over what Eachdonn had proposed. Drostan looked at Conall. "Yer son and daughters play on the slopes near Dùn Na Mèadaidh. Better get them away from the place quick."

"Urard is their guard. I can't imagine many getting past him." Glancing at Nikandros, Conall added, "And their weapons tutor has taught them some very unsavoury tactics. May the Goddess have mercy on any who stand in their way." Laughter rippled around the leaders.

"What about the new battle plans?" Eachdonn asked. It did not go unobserved to Eachdonn that there was a moment of hesitancy from Conall and Drostan. It was as if they were appraising his worth and trustworthiness. *Can I blame them?*

"The previous plan was based on taking the fight to the High People. The new one will concentrate on drawing them to us. It'll require a more defensive mind. We'll fight on the northern bank side of the Abhainn Dubh, using the river as the first line of defence. Cúscraid is in charge of developing a strategy. He'll inform you as to what and when resources are needed. It'll be mostly labour, I suspect."

"Are ye sure ye hae enough men?" asked Drostan. "If it's true that they have thirty thousand warriors, we'll be outnumbered. I can send for another ten thousand. Eachdonn can likely come up with another few thousand." Eachdonn grunted in agreement.

Íar laughed. "Where would be the glory in that fight?"

"The Hag can have the glory," snorted Drostan. "I want to be alive after the battle."

"We already have the best of our armies assembled. They'll not let us down," said Conall.

***

The sun burned orange and red in the evening sky as it slowly sank below the horizon. A groan escaped from the body sprawled in the dirt within sight of the gates of Dùn Na Mèadaidh. Slowly the massive frame of Urard stood. This startled Aodán. Frightened by Urard's sudden crash to the ground, the child had calmed himself by nestling in the crook of Urard's arm, close to the giant's chest.

He was about to scream in delight when Urard put a finger to his lips and said, "Shhhh, Aodán. We need to be very quiet." Happy that his friend was awake, Aodán smiled, hugged Urard with all his strength and nodded vigorously.

A sudden, sharp pain spiked through Urard's head, bringing him to his knees. Aodán flung his arms around his protector's neck and laid his head on his barrel chest. Concern marked the young boy's face, and a tear escaped his deep blue eyes. "I'll be fine, Aodán," reassured Urard. His arm cradled the child as he attempted to rise again.

"Climb on my back. We'll be quicker if I carry you." As he moved off, Urard's foot struck a hard object. The giant looked down at the throwing axe that had laid him out. In a twist of fate, the hatchet hit Urard with the flat side of its iron head. Thus, he fell to the dirt, unconscious but not lifeless.

Urard thanked the Goddess and promised a sacrifice. As his head cleared, he recalled the screams of Brighid and Danu and remembered the guards at Dùn Na Mèadaidh. They were laughing. Promising revenge on his charge's abductors and those within the fort, Urard scrambled down the gully and hillside and took up a brisk pace west towards Áth.

***

As the sun set, the leaders moved into Áth's Great Hall. The atmosphere was sombre. Rumours and tales of treachery and betrayal multiplied, feeding off each other and echoing off the wooden walls. Few of those present feared battles. It was how they lived. Dishonour was a blemish that could not be washed away except by blood.

Thus, there was a palatable unease at the presence of the Aos an Eich and the tribe's queen, Ceana. A veil of mistrust hung between the tribes. To quell the unhealthy chatter and confirm their ease with each other, Conall commanded the leaders of the armies to spend the evening circulating in small groups among their men and women.

Mid-evening, a breathless Deaglán Ó Néill rushed into the hall. His face flushed red, matching the colour of his long, braided hair. He caught Fearghal's eye and beckoned to him. The veteran rose from his place between Mongfhionn and Conall and sauntered towards Deaglán. There was a quick conversation before Fearghal walked back to the high table.

"What has got Deaglán so animated?" asked Conall.

"We have visitors," said Fearghal. He wore a troubled look. "A delegation from the High People waits at the ford and asks permission to join us."

"How many?"

"Fifty on foot. Two leaders on chariots." Fearghal paused briefly. "Ualraig and the High People's queen."

"Interesting," said Conall and called Deaglán over. "Inform the queen that she may join us." Deaglán nodded. Catching the eye of Cúscraid, Conall signalled his master of defence to his side. "We'll shortly have guests. Take who you need, check the defences and double the guard." Then he gestured to Íar, who reluctantly tore his gaze away from his study of Mòrag's breasts. "Send riders to the camps. Alert the men."

"This could be an entertaining evening," cackled Drostan as he called Carmag to his side. "Weapons would be a good idea." Carmag nodded and was about to move away when Drostan touched his forearm and added, "Not just our people, Carmag. To *all* in the Hall." Carmag smiled. The leaders of the other tribes dipped their heads to Drostan.

It seemed only a short time later when sword hilts pounded on the

Hall's oak doors. At a nod from Conall, the wooden bar securing the doors was withdrawn, and they swung inward. Iron hinges twisted and screamed as the massive doors slammed against the frame. Those nearby swore as they were showered with dust and spiders.

Soon, fifty pairs of feet muffled by leather boots thudded on the straw-covered, wooden floor. The intruders divided into two ranks and marched down the left and right aisles. As they came to a stop, the High People turned to face their hosts.

The sight did not fill them with confidence. Unusually for Kartimandu's men, they were heavily outnumbered. Two hundred fifty fully armed men and women stood on the lower tier. Many wore the famed armour and helmets of Clann Ui Flaithimh. Others sported the branch and sword tattoos of the Cróeb Ruad. The swirling designs of the Cinn Péinteáilte were noticeable.

All wore the scars of numerous engagements. These were the elite caomhnóirí of Clann Ui Flaithimh, the Forest People, the Aos an Eich, and the Ravens. Behind the warriors, archers waited on the second tier, each with an arrow nocked. At the high table, Conall sat on an ornately carved oak throne. On his left and right were Mongfhionn and Mórrígan. The others, leaders, chieftains, and Council members sat or stood nearby.

The confident footfall of Ualraig broke the tense atmosphere. The High People's commander walked at a measured pace down the centre aisle. His face was composed and neutral as he came to stand before Conall. He bowed and said, "As fated, we meet again, Conall Mac Gabhann, Rí Ruirech of Clann Ui Flaithimh and Dùn Na Mèadaidh."

Conall waved a hand to acknowledge Ualraig's presence. With cold blue eyes, he met and held his enemy's gaze. It was Ualraig who broke the glance. The High People's commander took an opportunity to appraise the leadership of the tribes.

The auras surrounding the Sídhe and Mórrígan made his mind uneasy. The scars on the exposed faces and limbs of the rest and the hard stares in their eyes informed him that these people would not be conquered without a high cost. His brief observation confirmed his knowledge and suspicions but told him little that he did not know before.

"I once told you to walk away, Ualraig. I'm disappointed, if unsurprised, you chose to return. I will make the same offer. Walk away. Leave these lands."

Ualraig paused as if considering the offer and said, "That would not be acceptable to my queen."

"Then you'll die, and with you, many thousands of your tribe," Conall spoke with an air of certainty that did nothing to lessen Ualraig's growing sense of unease.

The less-than-pleasant conversation shifted as Ualraig recalled his role this evening. Resuming his job as ambassador, he coughed, clearing his throat in the smoky atmosphere. In a voice that carried to the room's entrance, he proclaimed, "I am here to present Kartimandu, Queen of the High People, a follower of the Goddess Brighid…"

"I very much doubt the Goddess would concur," snapped Mongfhionn.

About to respond, Ualraig was arrested by a slender hand on his shoulder. He shivered at its touch, bowed deeply, and stepped to the side and a pace backwards. The iridescent figure of Kartimandu stood before the High Table.

"That is not very welcoming, my Lady Mongfhionn… and my sister."

"You are most certainly *not* my sister. Return to the stone from which you crawled, *fuath*." Mongfhionn stood, and as she did, her cloak slipped from her shoulders. The Sídhe stood statuesque, glowing with the symbols of power inscribed on her milk-white body. The red highlights in her white hair appeared to rise as vipers waiting to strike.

Kartimandu's attention was diverted by the scratching of a seat pushed back. To Conall's right stood an equally naked Dark Huntress. The curling sigils on her body radiated waves of dread and darkness, which startled Kartimandu and made her warriors gasp.

Calling on her considerable powers to regain composure and quell the unease that caused the vein in her neck to pulsate, Kartimandu looked imperiously around her. Her eyes met Ceana's with the briefest glimmer of recognition. It was a glance that would have drawn no comment had Conall not been forewarned of their conspiracy. Kartimandu bowed stiffly, acknowledging the kings and princes arrayed before her.

Involuntarily, the queen's eyes were drawn to the tall, granite-faced man who stood beside the Sídhe. It was not the sight of the drawn longsword upon which Fearghal's hands rested that unnerved her. Instead, it was the tattoo of a red branch entwined around a longsword on his right upper arm. Her hand reflexively rose to her throat before she snarled at the show of weakness.

"Ancient memories and old prophesies, *sister*," said Mongfhionn, for she had caught the glance.

Anger smouldered in Kartimandu's dark eyes. "A less than enthusiastic welcome for a visiting queen. Where is the vaunted hospitality of the Ériu? Can we not eat together?" she said, her eyes sweeping the table. The queen's painted body glistened as a sheen of perspiration was raised in the heat of the Great Hall's fires.

"You have an army of thirty thousand not far from my land. You brutally sacrificed Eachdonn's men for no reason apart from bloodlust. And yet you expect to share a meal. Why have you requested this meeting?"

The queen and Ceana were plainly startled at Conall's information and manner. Ceana glanced at Eachdonn, only to be greeted by a hard stare. The queen of the Aos an Eich feigned a dizzy spell, murmured that she was feeling unwell and excused herself. Her immediate thought was to flee to the safety of Dùn Na Mèadaidh, her son, and her men.

Tendrils of doubt slithered into Kartimandu's mind. *How much of her plans did this upstart king and his allies know?* Once more in control of her thoughts, she answered, "Why, to talk. I have no wish to see your people slaughtered. The tribes that follow me have gained incomparable wealth. We are feared across Albu. Join me." She looked at Drostan and Eachdonn.

"My offer is, of course, to all the kings present. Join me. "Join me or die. You cannot possibly win."

"Go back and rule your lands as you wish. No matter how detestable we find you, we'll not interfere. Remain here, and your people will feed the land with their blood. Their flesh will be torn and bones broken. The Hand of the Goddess has spoken." That Conall spoke with the full consent of Drostan and Eachdonn did not go unnoticed.

Kartimandu winced at Conall's use of his title, then smiled and licked her full lips. With a rumbling purr, she said, "Perhaps you and I could discuss this in a more private location. I am sure I could convince you of the benefits of my offer." The queen's aura changed subtly. Its tone was one of seduction, and she breathed in deeply, emphasising her full, round breasts. A long finger traced a route from her lips to a very prominent nipple.

"She's a wee bit obvious," said one wit loud enough to be heard across the hall. A thread of laughter rippled through the ranks of those present. Their leaders cupped chins in their hands to hide adolescent smirks. Humour destroyed the impact of Kartimandu's offer.

Angrily Kartimandu rounded on Conall. Any response to the growing wave of laughter and mockery was halted by angry voices and scuffling at the entrance. Hands went to swords and axes but relaxed as the hulking shape of Urard staggered towards the high table. The back of his head was matted with dried blood. Aodán rested his head on his shoulder.

"What is the meaning of this?" cried Mórrígan as Urard lowered a drowsy Aodán into his nurse's arms. "Where are my daughters?"

Urard looked to Conall and dropped to one knee. "Treachery, my king."

"I hear that word a lot recently," Conall said. "Stand. Speak."

Urard related the kidnapping of Brighid and Danu to the sound of mounting anger and calls for vengeance across the Great Hall. A patently distraught Urard, having told his story, knelt again, this time baring his neck. His meaning was manifest, and the response from Conall was equally clear. "You took a bloody axe to the head, yet brought Aodán safely home. Have Fionnbharr's healers dress your wound. Get a good meal and some rest. Then report back to me. This will be a long night."

It was Eachdonn Breac who spoke first as Fionnbharr led Urard away. He spied Ceana, threading her way to the doors. "Seize that woman! Bind her until we have time to hang her." This elicited a startled scream from Ceana at the realisation her plans had unravelled. She stared at Eachdonn in disbelief and mounting horror at his following words.

"Gormal, assemble the men. We attack Dùn Na Mèadaidh immediately. Kill everyone in the dùn. Keep Ròidh alive if possible." At his last words, Ceana grasped at the expectation of mercy. Her hope was dashed as Eachdonn finished. "The queen will watch her son die before she meets her executioner." Dragged from the Great Hall, Ceana cursed her partner.

"No!"

The voice of Mórrígan rang out over the clamour. "Dùn Na Mèadaidh is well stocked. It will take many sunsets to besiege and take the ráth by starvation. My caomhnóirí will take the fort before the sun rises." An uncomfortable silence pervaded the room. While most acknowledged the truth in Mórrígan's words, they had little empathy with her methods or that of her warriors.

"The task is Mórrígan's," conceded Conall to groans of protest from Eachdonn's people. The blemish of dishonour was a stain on their tribe. "When the sun rises, we will seek out and destroy the kidnappers of my daughters."

Shite, they know everything. Ualraig scanned the room for possible escape routes.

"We have divided their forces," Kartimandu murmured. Ualraig did not share her claim of victory.

"That's all well and good. How do you propose we get out of this building alive?"

As if he had heard Ualraig's words, Conall turned to Kartimandu and her commander. There was a terrible chill in his speech. "This wicked deed is on your heads. Now, hear my oath to the Goddess.

"Until I recover my daughters, I will burn every ráth, settlement, and home of High People. I will slaughter your people until they are a faint memory among the tribes of Albu."

Conall raised his hand as he spoke and drew a blade across the palm. "With my blood, this, I swear." The soft whisper of blades withdrawn from sheaths followed as each of the warriors present in like manner swore assent to Conall's oath.

"We shall leave," said Kartimandu, turning to face the Great Hall's doors.

"You and Ualraig may leave. Your men will not."

"We came here in peace," the Queen hissed. "My men will return with me."

"I see *your* hand behind my daughters' peril. Choose, Kartimandu, Queen of the High People. Your life or your warriors."

There was little doubt which the queen would choose. With a swirl of her lustrous, red hair Kartimandu looked to the door. She glided towards the Great Hall's exit, followed by Ualraig. As she crossed the oak sill, a shout from Conall brought her to a halt.

"*Imeacht gan teacht ort*—may you leave without returning."

The ancient curse rang in the queen's ears as she and Ualraig mounted their chariots. As did the shouts and curses of her men as their blood was spilt on the wooden floors.

On the hillside, the *mná sídhe* howled. Souls awaited the harvest.

CHAPTER 7

406 B.C.—Dùn Na Mèadaidh

Ròidh paced the Throne Room of Dùn Na Mèadaidh in a state of nervous agitation. His footfalls echoed off the cold, grey stone walls. Periodically, he glanced at the carved throne and stepped closer, steeling himself to claim it. Each time he was halted by visions of his grandfather, Finnean Mac Sèitheach.

In death, the spirit of the king of the Na Mèadaidh differed little from his human appearance: sharply featured, pale-skinned, and white-haired. Only his eyes had changed from a vibrant purple to silver-grey. Finnean's ghost was mocking and contemptuous of Ròidh.

On the sole occasion, Ròidh's courage had not failed him, and his arse touched the throne; he had been discovered by his mother. Ceana had been furious. The throne was hers and hers alone. The memory of her slap still made his ruddy face flame with embarrassment. In his mind, he swore to get even, but the bravery that accompanies petulance is fleeting. Thus, in the dead of night, Ròidh paced the oak floor, alone save for the spectre of Finnean. The throne remained empty.

Whispered rumours and dropped glances troubled Ròidh. His brother, Gormal, had been overheard asking questions about those encamped at Dùn Na Mèadaidh. The inquiries concerned their loyalties and the recent movements of Ròidh and the queen. A cold chill ran up his spine. Surely, his Da did not know of his mother's conspiracies. He smiled. Of course not. His father was ruthless, and action would have been taken before now.

At the western gatepost, those on guard duty watched with mounting curiosity as splashes of yellow and red light floated haphazardly in the inky blackness. They flickered in the breeze and thus seemed to come and go. "Faerie fire," one opined. He looked at his companion and nodded in the direction of the lights.

His comrade spat into the night. The first man was not clear whether his partner had insulted him, but as a precaution slacked off the guard on his dagger. There was no trust or comradeship between those who garrisoned Dùn Na Mèadaidh. The kidnapping of the girls became a canker infecting all within the fort's walls.

On the hilltop west of the fort, Mongfhionn raised her arms. Slategrey clouds gathered, blotting out an already waning moon. A heart-stopping shriek from the Sídhe was echoed by a second from Mórrígan. Red, orange, and yellow balls with long, burning tails arched high over the dùn. The acrid smell of oil and smoke broke the night's spell. The Dark Huntress stood before the gates of Dùn Na Mèadaidh, flaming arrow in hand. She sought retribution. On the bridge between life and death, the mná sídhe gathered and began to wail. They would soon harvest the souls of the newly dead.

Arrows from two hundred archers swooped upwards. At the apex of the arc, they seemed to pause before dropping on the ráth. The steady *thunk* of arrowheads sinking into wood filled the air. Soon anything that would burn was ablaze. Thickening smoke choked shrieks of terror from those caught in the firestorm. Burning carcasses replaced the torchlights on the ramparts as oil-soaked fire arrows bit into flesh. Wounds cauterised by the arrows' flames left the men to die slowly, their flesh consumed by fire.

The western entrance, guarded by solid oak gates, burned furiously. Mórrígan listened. The Dark Huntress had learned to temper fury with patience. Contrary to the common talk among the people of Clann Ui Flaithimh, she never threw her band recklessly into conflict. While not averse to taking risks, her decisions were measured and undertaken with reliable intelligence.

In the stillness of the night, Mórrígan paid attention to the sounds from within the ráth. The roar of the flames, the crack of roofing timbers weakened by the talons of fire, the crash of stone walls no longer supported by thick, oak beams. The funeral pyre of Dùn Na Mèadaidh was visible far across the valley.

***

His sleep was already tormented by nightmares. Friseal, the leader of the People of the Hounds warband, awoke to see the vermilion glow in the west. He knew it could only be one thing. He shivered, not at the early morning chill, but at the wrath Dùn Na Mèadaidh had drawn upon itself.

Friseal looked across the slumbering campfire. Its light momentarily resurged, and he saw the faces of the kidnapped girls. As one, they mouthed, "Our Da is coming." It was enough to spur Friseal to rouse his men and, in the half-light, urge them back on the trail to Creag na Clachard.

***

The dùn smouldered in the pre-dawn, a charred ruin silhouetted against an indigo sky. With a kick, the gates crashed inward, throwing splinters and glowing ash into the air. Flanked by her brothers, Bricriu and Beacán, Mórrígan led her warriors into the maw of the Otherworld.

Bows were slung across backs, shields raised, and weapons unsheathed as boots crunched over cinders. They passed the charred, misshapen remains of men. Infrequently, there was a hoarse cry as a smoke-blackened survivor tried to escape. Weakened by fire and smoke, they were no match for the blades of Mórrígan's band.

In one sense, Ròidh's prayers to the Goddess had been answered. She had indeed preserved his life. As to the wisdom of the prayer, that was doubtful. Held between her brothers, Ròidh looked into the cold, dark eyes of Mórrígan. Her stare showed no mercy, only the promise of a slow and agonising death.

***

Ceana stumbled as she was half-marched, half-dragged to the ruins of Dùn Na Mèadaidh. Thorns tore her white dress. Arms and legs became a patchwork of cuts and bruises, and bare feet bled, pierced by sharp stones. The queen's treatment was symbolic of her fall from power and payback for the loss of face the tribe suffered.

When Ceana looked upon the devastation visited upon her former home, it was possible that some recognition of her folly permeated her mind. However, when Eachdonn grabbed the tresses of her long hair and forced her to look to the ramparts, Ceana's sanity broke. The body of Ròidh swung from one of the few remaining crossbeams that jutted out above the tower's entrance.

The prince of the Aos an Eich was barely recognisable. The twist of his neck suggested it was broken. His hair and eyebrows were singed, and his face was blistered and swollen. Only a remnant of his eyelids remained, providing no protection for his eyes from the fires. Permanently open, his eyes stared without seeing. Guts streamed from his belly to settle on the stone rampart. A thousand cuts mutilated his body.

Despite his torment, the bean sídhe had not come for Ròidh. He lived. He moaned. He would have wept had the flames not deprived him of that comfort. His body shuddered. The tension in the rope made him rotate in a slow semi-circle presenting his torment to all present. From burnt lips, he called "Ma" like a child over and over. He could not see that she kneeled before him.

Ceana shrieked. It was the heart-breaking cry of a mother's anguish. Ròidh's body twitched at the sound. Ceana pounded the dirt until her hands bled. Mother and son shared their torment. A sob of despair welled up from within Ceana.

Drawing herself up, she stood before Eachdonn and snarled a curse of revenge and death. Of the two, the queen was the more fortunate. Her suffering ended as Eachdonn brought an axe down on her skull. A javelin from Conall brought Ròidh's agonies to an end.

The king looked at a disappointed Mórrígan. "His loyalty to his mother was true but misplaced. He has paid enough for both of them." Conall expected a sharp retort. When there was none, he turned to Gormal. "Bury the queen and her son in the ruins of Dùn Na Mèadaidh."

The ghost of Finnean Mac Sèitheach hovered above the ramparts of Dùn Na Mèadaidh. His arms stretched out, and he was soon joined by two others. Behind the trio stood the spirits of the warriors consumed in the inferno. Forever tied to the ráth's stone walls, the souls of Finnean, Ceana, and Ròidh smiled. The family was united, and they had a kingdom to rule.

***

Brion looked at the bodies lying on the dirt. "People of the Hounds," he spat. In a moment of anger, he looked at Mórrígan with a hardness she had not witnessed before. "It seems your raids have reaped their harvest." She turned away, unable to hold his gaze or respond to his words. "They were taken from this spot. My nieces put up a fight."

Nikandros found Danu and Brighid's swords. He lifted them with a gentle reverence before sheathing them in his belt. The Spartan growled, "The blood on the blades tells they fought well. I'll bury these in the bastards who took them."

"Not if I get to them first."

A shaven-headed Urard stood beside Nikandros. Previously, the bear of a man had sported a burly beauty. Now he was downright frightening. From the top of his head, almost to the base of his skull, ran a blood-encrusted gash. The ragged sides of the cut were held together by a series of ugly black stitches. Urard's choice to have his head shaved did little to improve his demeanour.

Conall gazed eastward along the ridge of rolling hills. "They'll make for Creag na Clachard. In this weather, it should take them two, maybe three sunsets. We're a sunset behind." He turned as Tadhg and Deaglán jogged up to the circle of leaders.

"A small warband of about fifty raiders on foot. They're taking the wagon trail along the foothills," reported Tadhg.

"Horses might intercept them before they reach their ráth," said Íar.

"My men will be on their way immediately," responded Mórrígan.

Her declaration was met with a stern look from Conall. "No. Your riders will provide a mounted strike force for Drostan. You will take your orders from him." Still smarting from her brother's remark, Mórrígan dipped her head in sullen acquiescence. "Brion, Eachdonn's men only use their horses for getting from place to place. You will remain and guard his flanks with your chariots."

Conall turned to Íar and Nikandros. Before he could speak, Íar nodded in the direction of the corrals. Good fortune had placed the pens between the Uisce Èireann and the northern side of the Sleá. From the crest, Conall observed a hive of activity as riders readied mounts and strapped weapons onto their broad flanks. "Toirneach is ready to ride," he said. Conall flashed a quick look of thanks to both men.

It was then that Urard spoke. "Which horse is mine?"

There was a stunned silence as those nearby pondered how to respond diplomatically while not hurting Urard's feelings and avoiding bloodshed. "You hate riding. You're uncomfortable around horses," said Íar, "and you're still recovering from a bloody great wound on your head. A lesser man would be dead. Rest at Áth. No one will think ill of you."

Urard left no one in any doubt of his intentions. "Which horse?"

CHAPTER 8

406 B.C.—Creag na Clachard

Danu's face was streaked with strings of rotting vegetation, the debris kicked up by her mule as he splashed through stagnant pools of bog water. Her teeth rattled as she was dumped on the dirt with no more consideration than a sack of parsnips.

Anxiously, Danu looked around and was relieved to see Brighid's transport drop her to the ground. Bound with thin strips of leather, their wrists and ankles were blood-raw from constant chafing and fumbled escape attempts. Purple-black bruises highlighted the twins' cheeks, punishment for obstinacy.

Their eyes held wells of tears, which threatened to overflow. Yet both refused to give their captors that pleasure. Crying and laughter would come later when they were rescued. Neither doubted that their Da or Ma would save them. At each stop, they contrived some scene to signpost their path. Petulant screaming and fits of temper with exaggerated foot stamping. While the spoilt behaviour resulted in hard slaps to their heads and arses, it also left small footprints in the dirt.

It was evening. The clouds retreated. Silvery-blue moonlight bathed Danu and Brighid as they slept in each other's embrace. They slumbered, reassured by the warmth of each other's bodies, the steady beat of their hearts, and the presence of the Sídhe in their dreams. Her voice gave comfort and strength. It soothed anxious moments, encouraged them to be brave, and promised rescue. Within her message, there was an emotion they did not fully understand… retribution.

***

In the cobalt darkness of the morning's early hours, Mongfhionn slept fitfully, and in her slumbers, she wept. In her dreams, the Sídhe fought a lonely struggle for Brighid and Danu. She sensed the strong arms of Fearghal that held her close and took comfort from the warm dampness on her cheeks as her head rested on the hair of his tear-soaked chest. She felt his sorrow at not being able to help. He could do little more. Mongfhionn sighed. He should not worry; his arms were all she needed.

Still, the brave hero of Clann Uí Flaithimh was troubled. He feared what would happen if Mongfhionn lost the twins as she had her sisters. The Hag would dominate, and her wrath would know no boundaries. Moreover, Fearghal dreaded the cold fury of Conall and the dark vengeance of Mórrígan.

Untempered, this triumvirate would lay waste to all before it. No distinction would be made between the guilty and the innocent. Yet Fearghal feared one more thing. The transformation of his heart to stone. He would not permit his lover or friends to travel this dark path alone. Of his own choice, he would stand with them in the blood and gore.

***

As the sun rose above the horizon, Friseal listened to the familiar crackle of twigs catching alight. He was reluctant to waste time but had pushed his men hard and sensed that a hot meal to break their fast was preferable to rebellion. A smile crossed his face as he gazed upon the twins. It was not a smile of victory or conquest but the smile of a father. Friseal had children of a similar age.

At heart, the chieftain was an honourable man and disliked his task. Subterfuge and kidnapping of children did not sit well with his sense of honour. Yet he would do his duty and deliver the girls to his king. Friseal had little choice, for Camran would make his family suffer if he failed. A sigh of misery escaped his lips as he stood up, walked over to the girls, and gently nudged them.

"Time to go."

***

It was not difficult to track the People of the Hounds' warband. Their destination was obvious. Only the land resisted the horses that galloped through marshes, scattered copses of fully leafed hardwoods, and flatlands covered in swathes of brightly coloured wildflowers. The riders paralleled the path of the Uisce Èireann as the fast-flowing river burbled and splashed towards the coast. Conall grimaced at the charred remains of small settlements and farms that heretofore had thrived on the river's banks. This legacy of the raiders did little to improve the king's humour.

The cavalry, one thousand horses strong, rounded a broad loop of the Uisce Èireann, slowing to a halt as Conall raised a hand. The coastal plain stretched before them. It was a flat, fertile land which, apart from a few hillocks, did not offer much concealment. In the distance, less than a morning's ride away, was the escarpment upon which Creag na Clachard sat. Surrounded by terraced slopes on three sides, the ráth's primary defences were a series of concentric, timber-laced stone earthworks. A precipitous cliff guarded its eastern side.

Nikandros pointed eastward. Through the early morning mist that swirled over the land, it was possible to make out Friseal's warband as it approached the ráth. Curses rippled through the ranks as the riders realised how close they had been to intercepting the raiders. Conall, aware that their task had become more complicated, ordered the men to rest and conferred with Íar and Nikandros.

***

Friseal heaved a sigh of relief as he strode through the entrance of Creag na Clachard. The chieftain was glad to be within the safety of its ramparts. Well aware of the riders that tracked him, he could imagine their anger at losing their prey in sight of the dùn.

As Friseal made his way to the substantial stone building that was

Camran's sanctuary, he heard the sobbing of Brighid and Danu. Both put on a bold face but were understandably disappointed their father was unable to close on them. That their hoped-for rescue had become tougher did not escape them.

Roused by the commotion, Camran emerged from his broch. A swaggering cock with a spiked comb, he puffed out his chest and glowered at the twins. "Shut those children up. Gag them if ye have to."

The girls stared at the comical figure of Camran. In the midst of their anxiety, they could not resist giggling at the king's deportment. Unfortunately, this did not help their cause. Camran's face turned red as the *blaeberry* shrubs that flourished on the eastern face of the crag. With an unpleasant curl of his lip, he said, "Take them to the boat. It waits in the harbour."

Rid of the girls, he turned to Friseal. "My informant tells me that yer capture of the girls was clumsy. Ye have provoked the bastards from Dùn Na Mèadaidh. That could be regrettable for ye... and yer kin." To Camran's delight, Friseal blanched. The strawberry birthmark covering his left cheek and neck blushed deep purple, and he glanced nervously around him.

"I suppose that we'll have to put up with more raids by that witch who styles herself the Dark Huntress," said Camran, his face set in its usual scowl. Friseal, his moment of anxiety past, simply nodded and vowed to find the turncoat within his band.

"I think it would be prudent for ye to go to the watchtower," said Friseal.

The look in his chieftain's eyes convinced Camran to take Friseal's advice. He stomped to the nearest tower. Not in prime condition, it took physical effort accompanied by much grumbling for Camran to haul himself up a wooden ladder that threatened to split with each heavy step. At the top, he paused briefly, caught his breath, and brusquely shoved aside the guard's proffered hand.

Friseal stood behind and to the side of his king. "Look to the west," he said. His reward was watching the blood drain slowly from the king's face. Curling charcoal trails of smoke continued to rise from the fort's ruins. Camran's dismay deepened as Friseal added, "Dùn Na Mèadaidh is no more. It sits a burned and blackened shell. *My* informants tell me that all in the dùn were slaughtered. Ceana, Queen of the Aos an Eich and her son were executed. The wrath of the Rí Ruirech of Clann Ui Flaithimh and the Dark Huntress spared no one."

"Close the gates. Assemble the warriors on the inner walls. Make the dogs ready," shouted an unnerved Camran. As he spoke, a drop of sweat rolled down his forehead, paused on the tip of his fleshy bent nose and splashed onto the back of a hand that gripped the wooden rail before him. Had he made a terrible misjudgement?

***

Mongfhionn paused a thousand paces southwest of Creag na Clachard and dismounted on a grassy knoll. The land around the fort was fertile. Neat fields of yellow-gold wheat and barley bent their heads in the wind. Small farm holdings with two or three wood and stone roundhouses tended clusters of cropland. Wooden pens held cattle and pigs. Chickens, free to roam, scratched in the dirt.

Closer to Creag na Clachard, larger dwellings housed the artisans, the smiths, and other trades. Wisps of blue-grey smoke curled upwards from hundreds of untended cooking fires. A haze of heat shimmered above the thatch and sod roofs. On this day, the buildings were deserted. The population had fled to safety within the dùn's fortifications.

To Mongfhionn's left and at the bottom of the mound stood the cavalry of Clann Ui Flaithimh. The metal fittings of reins, bridles and girths chinked in the quiet of the morning. Horses dipped their heads to graze on summer grass. Impatient for battle, riders exchanged words and glances while checking their weapons—javelins, axes, and swords.

Each had his or her routine that they instinctively repeated. Each had their heavy gold torcs and armlets of gold, silver, and copper arranged how they believed the Goddess had blessed. Each had dropped sacrifices into the waters of Uisce Èireann. Now they wanted to fight.

Even had they not been paces ahead of the cavalry, the Sídhe would have recognised the three leaders. The gold and silver helmet of Conall, a gift from the artisans of Ráth Na Conall, was topped by a gold raven complete with trailing blue-black plumes.

Íar stood out due to his physical presence. A helmet of bronze and iron with a red and black foxtail hanging from its apex strained to contain his wild mane of ginger-red hair. His riders also sported similar foxtails on their helmets. All wore boiled brownish-red leather breastplates reinforced with iron scales. Even the horses bore similarly fashioned armour on their broad chests.

The Sídhe smiled at the sight of Nikandros, her adopted brother. The veteran had fought alongside his fellow Spartans in many actions in faraway lands. Yet there, he would not have stood apart among his comrades. In Ériu and Albu, sheathed head-to-toe in bronze, the Spartan glittered in the weak morning sun.

His helmet's red horsehair flared in the breeze. Mongfhionn watched as he adjusted his round, bronze shield and the black ash doru, a spear whose reputation almost overshadowed that of its wielder. His black horse sensed his master's mood and pawed impatiently at the dirt with bony hoofs. Now and then, the Spartan glanced backwards and exchanged friendly nods, insults, and *craic* with the other riders.

A thin smile lifted the edge of the Sídhe's lips as she looked beyond the three leaders to where Urard stood. Taking advantage of the rest, he dismounted from a large dapple grey and rubbed his arse with vigour. The horse also appeared to appreciate the respite.

Conall looked at Mongfhionn and nodded. The Sídhe lifted her hands, and the sky began to darken. Charcoal-grey clouds scudded across the expanse, pausing to gather over Creag na Clachard. A flock of ravens swooped upwards from a nearby copse, circled the cavalry and flew towards the dùn. No one dared look at the Sídhe. She had transformed into a stooped and aged crone drawing strength from an ancient oak staff.

The screech of the Hag was borne on the rising wind and assaulted the ears of the fort's residents.

In response, the druids of Creag na Clachard circled the obelisk at its centre, chanting and hurling dark curses at the Hag and the attackers. A cruel smile twisted the crone's face. She mocked their feeble efforts, lifted her staff, and pointed. Lightning struck the obelisk. Sharp chips of smouldering, red hot rock flayed the unprotected faces of the druids gathered in the stone's shadow. Their eyes and mouths were sealed with blood and fire. Their incantations would never be heard again.

The riders had covered half the distance to the fort when the lightning struck. Conall, Íar, and Nikandros rode at the apex of the wedge formation. Grim-faced riders struggled to control their mounts in the growing wind and storm but steadily closed on the ráth.

The dùn's main entrance was a channel carved into the south-eastern earthworks. On the higher terraces, the ramparts had two parallel, non-aligned gaps. They were close, opening onto a gentle, broad slope and the cattle pens of the dùn. Camran's tower stood at the northern end of the final defences.

From the watchtower on the ramparts, Camran watched. His gut twisted with growing fear. Creag na Clachard was not designed to withstand a siege. He did not have the vast number of fighters that Drostan or Eachdonn could call on. The time was long past when he could call upon his neighbours for aid.

***

With a sharp cuff to the back of their heads, Danu and Brighid were shoved into the boat. Foul water sloshed in the bow, splashing them and soaking their soft boots and pants. The bottom of the craft was awash with salt water and, from the smell, piss.

Compared to the sweet-scented, cedar-built galleys that sailed the Great Sea and beyond, this was a crudely constructed vessel. The hull was flat, built from four large oak planks attached to a frame of slender timbers by chains and leather ropes. At its widest point, it was not much more than a tall man in breadth.

It was an old vessel. The ship's faded grey-black timbers smelt of smoke, urine, and rotting vegetation. Water seeped through cracks caused by numerous collisions with submerged rocks and unyielding jetties. Tufts of grass sprouted from the clods of plant fibres rammed into the fissures to stem an increasing number of leaks. Aged and heavy, the boat had toiled on the sea for many years but always within clear sight of the shore. While the ship's high bow and stern offered some protection in heavy seas, even fully manned, it had never been a ship to venture into deeper waters.

The crew of eight, less than half of its usual compliment, were plainly nervous. Given a choice, they would have remained safely sheltered in the cove north of Creag na Clachard. Already superstitious, the wailing of the bean sídhe and the sudden rise of the storm were ill omens. However, they had been paid generously. On the jetty, the squad of pock-faced thugs who delivered the girls showed no sign of leaving until the boat was well underway.

With a sigh, the captain ordered the ship's square sail, itself a tired and mildewed patchwork of canvas and leather, unfurled. The vessel bumped against the dock's timbers and entered the estuary. Brighid and Danu looked at each other with mounting fear. How would their Da find them?

***

The alarm spread quickly from community to community. Soon labourers, villagers, artisans, and farmers with bellowing cows and squealing pigs sought refuge within Creag na Clachard's inner ramparts. In the tight confines of the hillfort, the unwashed jostled each other to stake out their space.

Assaulted by the smell of the crowd and their animals, Camran's nose twitched. The fort lacked basic sanitation for so many. Human excrement quickly filled and overflowed the shallow waste pits near the ramparts. Men stood, and women squatted to piss. Only the livestock appeared to have any sense of propriety.

Ambition far outweighed Camran's resources. Just five hundred men garrisoned Creag na Clachard. His was not a powerful tribe. Its strength was scattered throughout its territory. There were barely enough men to man the inner defences, let alone the two earthworks further down the terraces.

Camran hoped to remain within the fort, or even better, within his stone sanctuary. His motive was purely self-preservation, and as such, it was a good plan. Nonetheless, the increasing rage of the population and calls for action made it an impossible strategy.

In Camran's favour, the people's anger was directed at the riders who were methodically laying waste to their homes and crops. Without the season's growth, the settlement would starve. No reserves would be available to barter or trade during the fall and winter. Farmers wailed as they watched ivory-coloured hoofs trample crops into the dirt. Across the landscape, roundhouses burned. Thatches and timbers robbed of their strength fell, and stone walls collapsed.

The king furiously rubbed and scratched the back of his neck. The many rewards promised by Ceana were chaff scattered to the wind. Like rocks, hard stares and glances were thrown at him. The rumble of discontent rose.

A low murmur soon built into a loud demand for action. Camran groaned. *What can I do?* His men were outnumbered and ill-equipped for a battle against horsemen. In an act of bravado that brought half-hearted cheers from the crowd, he snarled and shouted, "Let the dogs loose!"

Alerted by barking and howling, Íar put his bronze horn to his lips. Several crisp blasts rose above the wind. Conall brought his mighty horse, Toirneach, to a slow canter. The horse, its jet-black coat flecked with sweat, tossed its head in defiance at the oncoming pack of hounds. Beside him, the rest of the horses had spread out left and right. The dogs would not find an easy target.

A shadow of sadness darkened Conall's face. These were not

half-starved dogs kept in cages of rough wood. The deerhounds, with their short, wiry coats of blue-grey, brindle, and red fawn, were the hunting companions of the tribe. They lived and slept with their master and his family; they played with his children. Now, tasked with protecting their masters, the multi-hued pack charged forward, taking no thought for safety.

A past encounter with the wolves at A' Chrìon Làraich had prompted Íar to ponder the problem of future four-legged attacks. He blasted out a second signal on his horn. The riders divided into two ranks, leaving a gap of a hundred paces between each row. Íar's strategy was to break the pack's charge and trap the beasts in the space between.

The front rank threw a hopeful and hurried volley of javelins before bearing the brunt of the snarling canine assault. Men shouted and swung long-handled axes or slashed down with swords. Horses screamed, lashing out with yellowed teeth and hoofs. Bloodied but not stopped, momentum drove the hounds forward and past the first row of horses.

At another series of horn blasts, the front row turned. The ends of the two ranks moved together, forming a rough circle that steadily shrank as the formation closed up. The hounds threw themselves in a frantic rage at horses and riders. Still, even the bravest and strongest succumbed to tiredness, a myriad of cuts or a blade that opened their skulls to the elements.

The hounds left the riders bloodied and bearing gashes and bites before they were finally put down. Now, Conall's riders tended to each other's wounds before turning their faces to Creag na Clachard.

CHAPTER 9

406 B.C.—Abhainn Dubh

Damp, black soil clung to the iron-rimmed wheels of Gràinne's chariot as it bumped along the trail bordering the Abhainn Dubh. Cleared of trees, the river plain stretched for five hundred paces on each bank. On the eastern side, rich farmland merged with gently rolling hills swathed in dense forests and a flourishing undergrowth of ferns, thistles, and mosses. It was a land that was pleasing to the eye.

Hundreds of small family crofts spotted the landscape. Each housed three or four generations, thirty to forty people, in squat roundhouses. The fields were ribbed with uniform drills of wheat and barley. Some farms had dry, stone walls separating their land from their neighbours. This was mainly for show as each farmer knew his cropland and handiwork. Each planting and ploughing was unique.

A handful of larger settlements supported the farms. They lay further from the river or nestled in the foothills below Dùn Na Mèadaidh. Typically resounding with the grunt of labour, the grinding of flour, hammers striking iron and children laughing, the communities were deserted and silent.

The fires were cold, and the embers black. War had arrived. Crofts on the western side of the river burned, sending ribbons of smoke curling upwards. The population had long moved to shelter in the shadow of the Sleá.

Gràinne did not fully comprehend what thirty thousand meant. Still, as she looked across the muddy Abhainn Dubh, she saw an endless, disorderly array of tents. Coarse shouts, promising how she would be raped, by how many, and how often, resounded across the river. Usually, they were accompanied by what Gràinne considered unimpressive shows of cocks and pale, scabby arses that rarely saw the sun.

An occasional spear was hurled in her direction. The effort was futile and brought snorts of derision from Gràinne. The river at its narrowest was at least eighty paces wide. Only an arrow or a slingshot could reach her. It was unlikely that the High People had archers, and so far, they showed no inclination to waste slingshots.

The chariot driver, a sturdy rust-haired man with bulging upper arm muscles, put a foot on the long wooden shaft, pulled on the reins, and brought the chariot to a halt on the crest of a small hillock. He looked at Gràinne and winked.

Unsurprisingly, Gràinne was naked, apart from a leather belt and a narrow ribbon of cloth that barely covered the regrown auburn triangle between her thighs. She climbed onto the rail of the cret and found her balance. It was a deft feat of poise. The chariot "box" was open-ended at the front and rear, leaving two parallel sides. Long toes gripped the rail; legs a pace apart, Gràinne stood defiant.

A sword was drawn from the ornately designed leather and wood scabbard strapped to her back. Loops of leather were typically used to hold weapons on warriors' backs. Gràinne's longsword had cut through so many she persuaded the armourer to design a sheath for her.

Although young, Gràinne's voice rang out loud with a clear and loud burr, taunting and cursing the enemy. She offered her painted body to any who could take it. She mocked their impotent fury with peals of derision. Then, having tired of the sport, she dropped down onto the floor of the wicker cret. Her driver flicked the reins of the pair of white horses, and they wheeled about.

The chariot bounced northwest along a rutted wagon trail until it came to a small mound. Gràinne waved to the tall, broad-shouldered warrior who stood at its summit, leapt from her vehicle, and charged up the hill.

There was a heated discussion in progress between Fearghal, Cúscraid, Drostan, and Eachdonn. Brion stood nearby with a whimsical look on his face. As she neared the group, the argument appeared to be about who would take first blood and how much glory they would get. It was apparent that Drostan thought he was being short-changed.

An exasperated Cúscraid scratched short, sandy hair, looked at a grinning Fearghal, and finally overrode the two kings. He pointed west to an almost square-shaped loop in the river. "*That* is where the High People will cross. The ford at Áth is the only one upstream. It's wide, and its length will allow a rank of a thousand attackers to cross.

The river gets increasingly wider below this, and its waters deeper. It makes no sense for them to cross anywhere else." Conall's master of defence stared at Drostan and Eachdonn with hazel-green eyes, challenging them to disagree. None did, for they were neither blind nor stupid.

Cúscraid faced Eachdonn and said, "*You* will conceal your spears in the forests north of the ford, but not as far as the boglands. When Kartimandu's army reaches the main defences, your men will mount up, ride to, and attack their rear. Brion will provide support with his chariots."

Eachdonn looked at Drostan. "Seems fair." Drostan shrugged and grunted more in acquiescence than agreement.

"There will be more than enough blood for you, Drostan." Cúscraid pointed to Áth's defences. It was here the Ravens, under Brandubh and Mòrag, would make their stand. A long, shallow channel had been excavated at the crossing, and the dirt used to build a man-high berm.

Crossed stakes, sharpened, and hardened by fire, provided a hedgehog of barbs along the ditch. The slope of the defence was engineered to encourage the attacker's momentum, resulting in impalement. Brandubh's men would stand on the berm and flay the enemy with spears and slings.

South-east of Áth, between the mountains and the river, was a choke point. Using the natural advantages of the land, the ramparts raised up were broken only by the hill upon which they now stood and a small lake to the north. Ditches dug midway up steep inclines to the broad, flat crest of the earthworks had been populated with sharpened stakes and thorns and sewn liberally with iron thistles.

On the Dùn Na Mèadaidh side, the slopes were gentler and longer, and the ditches bridged by narrow dirt causeways. Beyond the primary defences, small, shallow channels seeded with sharpened sticks and covered with grass and dirt on a frame of branches added an extra challenge.

"The warriors of Clann Ui Flaithimh will make their stand here. *But* we'll not be able to withstand thirty thousand. We'll break, but we'll break only on Fearghal's command and make an orderly withdrawal north and south."

Drostan dipped his head to Cúscraid. "And the Forest People?"

Cúscraid smiled, "I expect Ualraig and his army to flood through the gap. You get to fight tens of thousands of unwashed, angry assholes. Mórrígan's mounted caomhnóirí will support you. The main force will probably break up once past the defences. Mórrígan will give you a small but nimble force to chase down breakaway groups."

"I'm more disturbed about having Mórrígan close to me than the High People," growled Drostan. "Don't you have any ordinary women?"

"Like that one?" said Cúscraid.

All turned to look at Gràinne. Bored with the talk of strategies and plans, she went through a series of practice exercises with her longsword. Her body glowed with a film of sweat. The sheen accentuated the swirling tattoos that covered her. Her plaid loincloth had given up long ago. Modesty lay in the dirt.

Fearghal grinned and looked at Gràinne with the pride of a well-pleased mentor. "Give her a few summers, and I'll have trouble besting her."

***

It was sunrise. A stiff breeze caused wavelets to form on the water's surface, sweeping the morning smoke aside. It was a wet morning. The constant rain soaked into woollen clothes. It made men miserable, warped wooden shields and made slings and bows virtually useless.

At least it's not snowing. At the river's edge, Ualraig shielded his eyes from the sun and squinted at the defences that dominated the far side of the ford at Áth. The High People's commander swore, not at the physical presence of the rampart and not at the cruel line of stakes.

He cursed at the fifty spears, the fifty heads that dressed them, and the fifty black ravens that perched silently on the skulls. They were his men, and he knew each of them by name. He had shared bread with their families. It was an unmistakable message from Conall.

Ualraig shivered in the morning air as he quizzed his scouts. They belonged to an exclusive and shrinking band. These were brave men who were able to swim the cold waters of the Abhainn Dubh and return alive. Conall's commanders had proven to be efficient at tracking and killing his spies. Ualraig was aware of the defences thrown across the valley.

He knew they were manned by Clann Ui Flaithimh and their allies. There was little information on the locations of the Aos an Eich or the Forest People, but his instinct told him to look to the forest. He huffed. His men were mountain and valley fighters, unused to low rolling hills swathed in thick forests where each tree was a potential ambush.

His strategy was simple. Get as many of the army across the river as quickly as possible. A night crossing was considered but discarded in light of Clann Ui Flaithimh's prowess with bows and their fondness for fire. Ualraig was convinced that, ultimately, his superior numbers would triumph.

Dùn Na Mèadaidh, the symbol of regional power, lay in ruins, apparently raised to the ground by Conall and Mórrígan. *Who defied him?* The settlements and farms were deserted. Any stores were carted away, and the livestock were driven to safer pastures. The fields were not near the time for harvesting. The battle would have to be fast and decisive. With such lean pickings, Ualraig could not risk a prolonged campaign. His men would starve or, more likely, desert.

The kidnapping of Conall Mac Gabhann's daughters had complicated matters. In Ualraig's opinion, it was an act that added an unpredictable dynamic to what he believed to be a relatively inevitable outcome. Superior numbers always prevail. Yet, the look on the king of the Clann Ui Flaithimh's face and the promise of revenge without mercy could not be lightly dismissed.

The gleaming skulls on the berm at Áth left Ualraig in no doubt. Unless Conall was slain and his forces destroyed, the journey back to Dùn Caen would be perilous. The moorlands and valleys of his beloved Penn-inus would be stained with the blood of many.

It also seemed to Ualraig that Kartimandu was quieter and more contemplative since sparring with the Sídhe. Truthfully, the queen's previous conquests had been relatively straightforward. A demonstration of her undoubted powers backed up by overwhelming numbers was usually sufficient to make enemies cower.

Faced with the Ancient Sídhe, an unpredictable Dark Huntress, and the Druid, Kartimandu's advantage, if not nullified, was diminished. Far from her strongholds at Dùn Caen and An Bella Leac, the queen was more vulnerable than ever.

***

Fearghal raised a fist. The young girls and boys waving the army's crimson-red and gold banners cheered. Others thumped out a thunderous rhythm on hundreds of *bodhráin*. A few older ones spat, moistened their lips, and tested their horns. They would transmit crucial commands during the clash. Fearghal took a long, steadying breath and inspected his battle line. Two thousand heavily armoured warriors waited in two rows behind the ramparts. Five hundred stood behind the earthworks in reserve.

Led by their ceannairí céad, the front rank was the most experienced. Tall, oblong shields painted red and embellished with a black raven rested against the fence, their iron edges embedded in the soft dirt. Each defender had four javelins, three for throwing and one for stabbing. All were pushed, iron spike first into the soil.

Helmet straps were continuously adjusted, and weapons were checked for ease of release. Neighbours examined each other's armour. Each warrior ensured the calf-wrappings over his or her brightly coloured pants were tied tight with leather thongs. Boots and *bróga* were secured.

To his southwest, in Áth, Fearghal watched Brandubh and Mòrag position their forces along the embankment. It would be their honour to meet the enemy first. The Ravens were almost naked to a man or woman. It was, after all, officially summer. They were much faster than Fearghal's shield-wall since they wore no armour save their curling tattoos and blue paint.

All carried a spear, a small round shield, and an array of daggers attached to limbs or held between flesh and their leather belts. Each also brought three or four slings and leather pouches heavy with stones and iron slugs. Fearghal prayed to the Goddess that Brandubh would keep to the agreed plan. He did not want the doubtful privilege of supervising the construction of hundreds of Raven funeral pyres.

He wished that Íar and his cavalry were at hand. The red-haired titan and his horde of unruly riders could change the course of a battle with a single charge. Fearghal allowed himself another sigh. It was shortened by a cacophony of war horns and shouting from across the river.

***

The chariot of Kartimandu did not so much wend its way through the rank and file as plough a furrow. Long scythes attached to the vehicle's axle hubs grazed some and lopped the limbs of others too slow to get out of its path. Reaching the riverside, the queen halted and turned to face her army.

She sensed Mongfhionn was not with the enemy this day, and the Dark Huntress was too distant to be little more than an annoyance. And, since she considered herself more than a match for any druid, Kartimandu was about to take full advantage of the more favourable circumstances.

"Witness the power of your queen and goddess," shouted Kartimandu to a mostly drunk congregation occupied with thoughts of rape and looting.

"*Kartimandu!*" came the roared response.

Thousands stamped feet and slammed weapons against shields. The queen turned to face the river. Hands raised, she called to the waters. At first, the Abhainn Dubh roiled as if determined to resist Kartimandu's commands. Still, its struggle was useless, and the waters ebbed. Thousands of fish gasped for air, flapping futilely in the muddy silt of the river bottom.

Basking in her miracle, Kartimandu turned to Ualraig. "*Now* would be a good time to attack." Ualraig spat into the waterless channel and nodded to the barrel-chested horn-blower beside him. A great bronze instrument was raised, and hundreds of others soon took up its mournful refrain. The High People's army rushed forward. Those with rafts tossed them onto the mud. Given the river's width, the pallets provided only the slimmest opportunities to avoid the squelching sludge.

***

"Shite!" Cúscraid swore at the developing chaos. His prediction that the enemy would storm across the river-ford was incorrect. Instead, the horde advanced along the river's length between the ford and his defensive position. His one consolation was instead of the enemy wading through waist-high water, it floundered in the thick river mud. Despite his well-known agnosticism, he thanked the Goddess that the fuath did not control the skies. A drying wind was the last thing he needed.

Cúscraid and Fearghal watched the first to cross escape the mire and slip and slide up the riverbank. Fearghal swore at being unable to take advantage of his enemy's vulnerability. A cavalry charge along the riverbank might have halted the invasion before it could gather momentum. Yet his army was out of position and had no mounted troops. They could do little more than watch and wait.

At a tap on his shoulder, Fearghal turned and looked to where

Cúscraid pointed. Standing back from the far riverbank, about five thousand held to a disciplined formation. They waited for a signal from their commander, Ualraig. "The Hag's arse. Ualraig's no fool. He'll let us waste our strength on the assholes and then attack with the veterans," said Fearghal. A sigh was Cúscraid's response.

***

Mòrag looked at her brother and shook her head. Few of the enemy chose to attack the river-ford. Any fools who did fell to the slings of the Ravens or stumbled into the ditch, impaling themselves on roughly hewed stakes. They moaned in agony as their blood washed the wood.

Brandubh signalled to abandon the position and withdraw to Áth. Inside its sturdy stockade and dry-stone walls, they waited. "They don't seem interested in us," said Mòrag, pointing to the mass of mud and slime-covered warriors who milled around looking for direction. Brandubh tugged at the raven's feather that hung on a thin, neatly twisted braid in his thinning red hair. His forehead wrinkled as he frowned.

"We're one thousand against more than thirty. It would be foolish of us to draw attention to ourselves. We'd be easily overwhelmed."

"We can't just hold here and do nothing, brother," the voluptuous princess declared, tugging at the leather cross-straps that secured her bosom. The straps chaffed her nipples, and she hoped that the rigour of the promised onslaught would break the bindings. "That wouldn't be honourable."

"I think it won't be long before we have company. They'll soon see that Áth would make a good headquarters. It's unlikely they'll breach Cúscraid's defences this day, so we'll inevitably become the target." Mòrag nodded. There was no disputing her brother's analysis. "Have our warriors line up to face the enemy. Position them in two rows around the stockade. Front row with spears ready, second with slings."

Mòrag pointed to the fence, "Pity, it's there. Our slings will have to rely on volume rather than accuracy. Brandubh smiled; his sister was right. The slings could only be swung overhand. Their stones and slugs would fly high and fall on the enemy causing significant pain and injury. Underhand, however, they could have picked off the High People's chieftains.

"Put small groups on the roofs. They can target the chieftains." Brandubh looked again at the growing horde as it crossed the river and then at the sky. "They'll be across by *meadhan-latha*. Let the men rest. They'll get little respite later."

***

A chariot drew up before Eachdonn Breac. The scarred face of Brion Ó Cathasaigh twisted around to look at the Aos an Eich king. "So much for plans," said Brion. "They'll turn on Brandubh's force soon. He'll be stranded and cut to pieces. I'm taking my chariots to harass the High People. Hopefully, we can relieve the pressure on the Ravens and allow time for some to escape." The king noted that this was a statement rather than a request.

Eachdonn tugged at an unkempt beard, which matched his knotted thatch of shoulder-length red hair. The king had not been himself since the executions of Ceana and Ròidh. Always at Eachdonn's side, Gormal knew that the king suffered severe headaches.

Dark shadows below Eachdonn's eyes signalled rest was a stranger during the night. What sleep he snatched was a mélange of nightmares. The curses of Ceana rang loudly in his mind. The king knew Brion, and other leaders and chieftains blamed him for their current predicament. It was, after all, from the Aos an Eich that Kartimandu learned their plans.

The king gathered himself, holding Brion's stare with deep green eyes that had not wholly lost their fire. "The Aos an Eich will lead." Ignoring the slight curl of dissension at the edges of Brion's lips, Eachdonn pointed to the terrain. "The land is a mix of sodden bogs, flat land, and low grassy hills. My horses are sturdy and will carry my spearmen to the battleground faster than your chariots. We can engage quicker than you." A snort from the second chariot that accompanied Brion suggested that Gràinne intended to prove the king wrong.

"Then the Goddess go with you," said Brion as he ordered his driver to join the remainder of his chariots. Eachdonn smiled. Brion's prayer was the friendliest the king had heard in a while.

CHAPTER 10

406. B.C.—Creag na Clachard

Camran faced a crescendo of demands for him to do something. The hitherto docile people of Creag na Clachard had witnessed their farms and homes set alight and crops and livelihoods destroyed. From the ramparts, they watched in despair as their hunting dogs died. Fear and anger passed simmering and rose to boiling with curses, threats, and demands for action.

The king considered whether he had enough men to slaughter the dissenters and repopulate Creag na Clachard with a fresh and more compliant stock. As he looked at Friseal, standing with his family, Camran reluctantly discarded that option. Too many of his men had family in the fort, a mistake he would not repeat. Worse, their kin was among those calling for Camran to do something. In this, Camran was incredulous. Did the women not realise their mates, whose arms kept them warm and for whom they lifted their skirts, would likely not return?

That his only negotiating pieces were bound hand-and-foot in an old boat off the eastern coast was not lost on Camran. Given the decrepit state of the vessel, its crew and the girls had probably drowned. It was another in a list of unwise choices to haunt him.

An able fighter in his youth, Camran sat on the tribe's throne because he killed anyone in his way. In a small clann, this was not difficult since rivals were readily identified, easily challenged, and quickly disposed of. Opponents not overcome in combat would be silenced with a knife in the back.

Camran's brutal myopia did not require him to think much beyond his next murder. Hence, his experience and skills left him unprepared to face the mounted horde advancing on his gates. Exasperated, Camran shouted to Friseal, "Select a hundred of the best. They'll remain under yer command in the dùn."

Then he turned to face his other chieftains. "As for the rest of ye. It's the time to earn yer gold. Arm yer men. If ye keep your head, spears and throwing axes should be good enough against horses." Grimly the four chieftains accepted their king's orders. To Camran, it was all too easy to see that each chieftain was feverishly considering how they might survive the coming skirmish. "Break open the beer barrels. Let the men drink their fill."

***

Like the lochs of Northern Albu, Conall's love for his daughters was bottomless. He would go to the gates of the Otherworld or fight legions of enemies to get them back. The king grimaced at the pitiful mob of warriors, lurching towards his position.

Conall sorely regretted his rashness in bringing all his riders on the raid. He had made a poor choice for a king. A quick prayer was offered to the Goddess that his cavalry's absence from the strife at Áth would not foretell disaster.

Turning to face Íar and Nikandros, he said tersely, "Give them a swift death."

From the safety of the walls of Creag na Clachard, the horses seemed small and inconsequential. At eye level, they were monstrous beasts. Horns blared as the mounted Clann Ui Flaithimh formed a wedge with their leaders at its apex. Seemingly as one, the cavalry took off at a brisk canter, which quickly became a gallop. The ground trembled, and hoof-sized clods of earth were tossed into the air as the riders closed on the Camran's rabble.

The confrontation was little more than a brief and pitiless execution.

It would never earn the title of a battle or be remembered in sagas told over roaring fires. Most of Camran's warriors were battered to the ground by broad, heavily muscled equine bodies and trampled by hard hoofs. Skulls crushed and bones shattered, the People of the Hounds lay bloodied and misshapen on a green sward. Few had the honour of greeting death with the swift cut of a sharp blade.

Íar removed his helmet, shook free hair damp with sweat, and wiped blood and mud from his face. He watched as his men dismounted and moved through the bodies. The corpses were stripped of anything of value. Those who still had a few breaths of life were silenced when their throats were cut and their heads hacked off.

"Brave men," Íar commented.

"Drunken fools," Conall responded.

"Drunk or not, they never turned their backs on us."

Íar guided his horse to where Nikandros surveyed the field on his black stallion. "And it's best not to tell the families of our dead that they were killed by drunks throwing axes," said Íar, pointing to a dozen riderless horses. Conall blushed, acknowledging his words were ill-chosen.

From the ramparts of Creag na Clachard, a terrible wailing rose as families mourned fathers, lovers, mothers, sons, and daughters. Friseal stood with his partner. Ignoring her protests and the tears of his children, he ordered her to flee. Left unsaid was that they would never comfort each other again.

Soon comprehension of their precarious plight dawned on the more nimble-minded residents of Creag na Clachard. The able quickly grabbed their belongings and, shepherding tearful children and livestock before them, scrambled to escape from the dùn. Once beyond the fort's outer perimeter, the people scattered, fleeing east and south.

Several riders leapt onto their mounts, intending to cut off the escape. Much to the relief of Íar and Nikandros, a sharp "No!" from Conall stopped them.

"Íar, take half the riders and return to Áth. Battles rarely go the way they are planned. Hopefully, you can make a difference," ordered Conall. Íar dipped his head in agreement and relief. A few blasts of his hunting horn divided the company into two. As Íar turned to join his men, Conall placed a hand on his arm. "Prevail on the Lady Mongfhionn to go with you."

***

Before Íar led his riders away, he brought his chestnut bay alongside Nikandros' horse. Nikandros looked at his friend curiously. "Is there something on your mind?"

"About Mòrag," said Íar, his face reddening in discomfort.

"No," said Nikandros with a long, almost mournful sigh. "Tell me you're not getting serious." Íar's horse shuffled as if embarrassed for his master.

"Would you step aside if I asked?"

"Of course I would, you big eejit," said Nikandros. "She's not the only woman with friendly thighs and a pronounced appetite for rutting in the camp." The Spartan gazed with sadness at the improvement in his friend's bearing. "Are *you* sure you know what you are doing?"

"What do you mean?"

"The girl has her eyes set on a more esteemed target than you or me," said Nikandros with a knowing glance in Conall's direction.

Íar nodded, disappointment clouding his usually cheerful face. "I was hoping I was mistaken."

As Íar's men and horses rode west, Conall trotted alongside Nikandros. "Anything I should know about?" he said, indicating the departing Íar.

"You're more perceptive than most, Conall. But sometimes you're stubbornly blind to what's in front of your nose." Nikandros shook his head.

Conall responded curtly. "Let's go find my daughters."

***

Brighid and Danu hugged each other and shrieked with each lurch and dip of the boat. Their throats were raw from screaming and dry from the saltwater spray they swallowed. Their kidnappers paid them no heed. No one could hear their cries over the storm.

The twins' grit had taken a severe pounding. At just eight summers old, their reserves were almost exhausted. Each gust of wind or splash of the sea on their faces seemed to further erode their hopes for rescue. Inexperienced as they were, Brighid and Danu recognised the skills of the rough, foul-mouthed men that guided the boat through the churning coastal waters. More than once, they heard the crack and scrape of wood on a rock. Only Coireall's quick thinking and skilful manoeuvring saved them.

The boat dipped once more, and water cascaded over its sides. Two wooden jugs were tossed to the girls. "Make yerselves useful if ye want to see tomorrow. Scoop the water and toss it over the side." The girls shivered and then set to work at a feverish rate. It was not long before their arm muscles ached, but the work served to take their mind off their predicament.

***

Mongfhionn watched as Iar's band drew closer. The Hag had withdrawn, and the Sídhe leant heavily on her oak staff. She was weak, having drained much of her reserves to encourage and hold the storm. Iar's horse separated from the riders, galloped up the hill and stopped at her side. "It goes well, Iar?" she asked. Although more to start the conversation than to elicit information she already knew.

Iar nodded, "We're to return to add our numbers to the fight with the High People."

"*We?*" asked the Sídhe. She was not fond of receiving commands from others and at second-hand.

The warrior smiled, bowed, took a deep breath, and rephrased his directive. "Conall has suggested that your help would be of more use at Áth and asks that you accompany me."

"You're not quite as accomplished a diplomat as your father, Deda

Mac Sin," said Mongfhionn, "but you are improving. I will return when…" The scream from the Sídhe was beyond anything that Íar had ever heard. It started as a cry of loss and pain but quickly became coloured with dark shades of wrath and vengeance.

Its pitch was such that ears bled as far as the rock at Creag na Clachard. The storm suddenly abated, the wind became a mere whisper, and the sky cleared to a blue-grey colour. On her knees, the Sídhe beat the ground in helpless rage.

"By the Goddess, Mongfhionn, what brings such a reaction?" asked Íar, fearful of the answer.

Mongfhionn rose and regarded Íar with a look that chilled his bones, "Brighid and Danu are not in Creag na Clachard."

"They're not…"

"No, the Goddess protects them. They are not dead. Their cries to me finally rose above the storm. Camran sold them to Kartimandu. Their destination is Dùn Caen by sea."

"Horse piss and shite! I'll ride and tell Conall."

"Conall approaches the gates of Creag na Clachard. He will know soon enough. You will ride as Conall instructed, but I will remain. I have a task to complete," said the Sídhe.

***

"Apollo's plague. What disturbs Mongfhionn so much that her cries rise beyond the skies?" Nikandros wiped a smear of blood from his helmet and used a strip of his tunic to clear his ears. Conall shivered with a sense of foreboding. He shook his head to dispel the ringing in his ears that threatened to bring on one of his headaches.

"I dread to think. Let's finish this and return home." At Conall's signal, the cavalry rode towards the entrance of Creag na Clachard. The dùn's defences were in three tiers. Each had an entranceway placed at a different location on each level. As with most forts, the outer defensive rings were mostly to slow an enemy's attack and lay them open to traps, slings, and other thrown weapons. Only the inner ramparts were manned. In the case of Creag na Clachard, too few remained to man, even the inner wall.

Eventually, the riders curled into an open area filled with livestock pens. The cattle were silent, and many lay on the ground, stunned by the Sídhe's ululations. Large brown eyes tracked Conall's riders as they threaded a path to the open area before Camran's stone broch.

Five hundred riders formed a semi-circle around the remnant of Creag na Clachard's defenders. Opponents glared at each other. The People of the Hounds looked upon their enemy with fear, the Clann Ui Flaithimh with resignation. To the side, a group of sightless druids rocked from foot to foot as, in muted silence, they exhorted their gods for protection.

"Send out my daughters," barked Conall. "Send them out if you want to live."

A solitary figure took several steps forward and stood between his men and Conall. "They're not here. They only stopped for a short time." Blood drained from Conall's face as the shock of the chieftain's words sank in.

"*Where* are my daughters?" Conall asked through clenched jaws.

A tremble of fear and acceptance of his likely fate shaded Friseal's voice as he spoke, "There was an agreement with Kartimandu. A boat was waiting."

A dark silence hung in the air. Friseal's death was swift. He did not have time to consider his family or ask his gods for journey's mercies to Mag Mell. His head tumbled as the keen edge of Urard's great axe cleaved it from Friseal's neck.

The headless body pitched forward, gushing blood over the dirt. Taking Urard's lead, a volley of axes and javelins felled the remainder of Camran's fighters and the druids where they stood. The grey stone building at their back was soon drenched in blood.

"Why?" asked Conall with a pained look at Urard as he sheathed his axe.

"I've told you before, my lord. You're a king. Not an executioner," said Urard. "It would have been unseemly to split the head of a helpless man as your subjects looked on."

Conall's thanks to Urard were heartfelt, although he was bitterly disappointed at not having rescued his daughters. He also felt shame at Urard's quiet chastisement. He looked with a king's resignation at Nikandros. "We'll return with all speed to Áth. We have a battle to win and a queen to slay."

Barely able to contain his anger, the Spartan bent his head and signalled the riders to mount up. Conall touched the Spartan's forearm and added, "Make no mistake. If needed, I will track them to the gates of Dùn Caen and the Maw of the Otherworld. I *will* have my daughters back."

As he prepared to mount Toirneach, Conall paused and thought for a moment. He knew little of the lie of the land on the east coast of Albu, save for what his merchant friend, Pytheas, had said of its many inlets, some small, some vast. He prayed to the Goddess that it would take many sunsets before the boat with Brighid and Danu arrived at Dùn Caen. Their captors would likely need to replenish fresh food and water, further extending the journey.

Calling a plainly distressed Urard to him, Conall said, "Take twenty men. Ride to the coast and follow it until you find an inhabited fishing settlement." Conall reached into a leather bag strapped to Toirneach, withdrew a smaller pouch, and tossed it to Urard. "Use your judgement as to whether gold or blade will loosen tongues. I want information on the vessel that holds my daughters captive. Get the information… at any cost."

With renewed purpose, Urard turned to walk to his horse. Conall's hand on his shoulder caused him to pause. With ice in his voice, Conall said, "You will kill *anyone* who tries to delay or prevent you from completing this task."

Urard saluted Conall with steely determination. "I'll not fail you, my king."

***

Camran waited for what seemed like an eternity before venturing from his grey, stone sanctuary. Immediately, he slipped on a pile of shite and guts. Uttering a mouthful of curses, he threw his hands out and was barely able to prevent himself from falling into the blood and gore. He wiped blood-stained hands on the nearest corpse and took in the slaughter before him. It was only a short time before he smiled broadly and laughed aloud.

The stupid son of a *striopach*, king of the Clann Ui Flaithimh, had assumed Friseal was the leader of the tribe. In his gloating, it did not cross Camran's mind to give a word of thanks or even offer a blessing for Friseal. He gazed across the inner perimeter yard to the pens. All were in good order. He had a healthy herd of cattle and some pigs that he could legitimately claim as his own. He had enough gold buried to recruit another army. To Camran's limited way of thinking, the day's events were little more than a temporary setback.

Had he been observant or even curious, the flock of ravens that interrupted their feeding and swooped upwards with a loud *kraa kraa* should have been a warning. Similarly, he did not see that the livestock was quiet and huddled together as far from his sanctuary as they could manage. Above Creag na Clachard, the skies became iron-grey. The air crackled with unnatural energy. A sharp and pungent odour filled the ether.

Upon completing a quick survey of his domain, Camran's stomach grumbled, and so did the king. Since his slaves were gone, he would have to prepare and cook a meal. With a disgruntled sigh, he stepped across the entrance of the stone building.

Camran's trailing foot had barely traversed the sill when lightning struck with an unearthly ferocity. Fingers of white fire hit wood and stone ramparts, setting them ablaze. A jagged bolt turned Camran's tower into an inferno that collapsed inward and then exploded, throwing rocks and flaming cinders far and wide.

The bean sídhe wailed, and Camran uttered a long and terrifying scream.

On a hillock west of Creag na Clachard, the Sídhe swung a leg over her horse's back. Her full red lips spread, and she smiled with perfectly formed white teeth. High cheeks flushed pink, aided by no unnatural colouring, and eyes gleamed with a dark, sinister beauty. Mongfhionn's face had all the elements of perfection and elegance.

To Conall, as he approached, it was the face of a nightmare. The primaeval snarl from her throat did nothing to change his first impression.

Of Camran Mac Madadh, king of the People of the Hounds, nothing was ever heard, and no trace was ever found.

CHAPTER 11

406 B.C—Áth

The morning mizzle increased to a dense, opaque rain. At each crack in the striated-grey clouds, the sun paused to hurl shafts of gold earthwards. These brief glimpses of sunshine made an otherwise miserable day tolerable. Kartimandu crossed the river with her thousand-strong personal guard and immediately went to a stubby knoll between Áth and the Clann Ui Flaithimh defences. It was a position that gave her a commanding view of the battlefield.

In her army's mind, lowering the river waters reinforced the belief that the queen was an all-powerful goddess. Yet it also created total disorder. With prior warning, Ualraig could have used the "miracle" to a much better advantage. Oblivious to criticism, Kartimandu blamed Ualraig and the clan chieftains for the chaos she now witnessed. She watched with imperious disinterest from her chariot as Ualraig tried to restore order.

Ualraig's five thousand were an island of discipline in a sea of confusion. They stood at ease, waiting for the signal to advance. His chieftains, without much effort, maintained a higher level of order than the mob that flowed around them. Kartimandu grudgingly admitted that Ualraig was progressing in bringing the army under control.

She watched chariots race through the horde, carrying messengers to the chieftains. Kartimandu smiled. Knowing Ualraig, the messengers threatened painful deaths unless their men were reined in. Horns blasted another signal for the unruly mob to halt, take stock, and wait for orders.

Yet, it was meadhan-latha before Ualraig regained any semblance of control over the army. A third of the force, still enthralled, stormed towards the defences of Clann Ui Flaithimh in a mindless frenzy.

Kartimandu sniffed the air. Her nose was small, sloping upward and added to her arrogant aura. The taint of iron filled her nostrils. Soon it would be joined with the distinctive metallic smell of blood. Being a fuath, iron was a grave concern to the queen. The slightest touch was exceedingly unpleasant. Her chariot fittings were made of bronze, silver, copper, and gold. The metal buckles and links in the horse's tack were made from hardened gold. The scythes protruding from the wooden wheels were bronze.

The queen preferred to remain apart from the battle. In her favour and to her frustration, Kartimandu accepted that she was no general. While she enjoyed the carnage, for the most part, the queen left warfare in the hands of men and the gods that accepted their sacrifices. That said, she was not averse to causing mischief.

It had taken most of Kartimandu's strength to abate the river waters. That said, her siren chants still controlled the minds of the weak and easily inflamed. Her will drove the foolish towards a miserable death on the ramparts of Clann Ui Flaithimh.

In normal circumstances, the same warriors would have exhausted their passion and given up. Kartimandu scowled as she sensed the druidic power on Clann Ui Flaithimh's ramparts. Not as powerful as the Sídhe, their connection with the earth was a shield for Conall's warriors' minds.

In a futile hope and with more than a touch of irony, the queen offered up a prayer to the tribe's titular Goddess, Brighid. The deafening silence from the Goddess left her unruffled. Brighid had yet to answer any of Kartimandu's previous supplications.

***

Like a loose ball of rags in a stiff wind, the enemy rolled towards the earthworks of Clann Ui Flaithimh. War had no respect for age or sex. Children of twelve summers fought alongside veterans of forty. While

Kartimandu's horde was dominated by men, there were many females. Indeed, many asserted they were better warriors.

The screams, taunts, and curses of the High People clashed with the thunder of bodhráin thumped out by the Ériu. Called to action by a long, deep blast from an Ériu horn, large conspiracies of ravens left their forest sanctuaries and took to the sky. They added their harsh *kraa kraa* to the assembled orchestra and choir.

A roar of defiance from Clann Ui Flaithimh's fighters accompanied the horn. On the ramparts, javelins were slammed rhythmically against hide-covered wooden shields. The challenge reverberated across the battlefield.

On the summit of the Sleá, the banners of the tribe and king flapped in the wind. Conall's flag, black ravens on a sky of crimson red, were interspersed with the new clann banner, a blood-red fist on a field of gold. Behind the chest-high stockade, Fearghal's men stood in two ranks, each warrior a pace apart. Each man or woman held their red and black shields high and plucked a javelin from the soft dirt.

Áine's archers stood a pace in front of the stockade, bows ready and quivers full. She signalled with a nod. Arrows were put to bowstrings and drawn back to cheeks. Upper arm muscles held taut until Áine released her barb. The single black shaft, with its red and white fletching, rose high, paused as if choosing its target and plunged earthward.

A man of no significance chose that moment to glance upwards. The arrow took his eye first and then his life. The first blood was Áine's. Her shaft was closely followed by a hundred, then hundreds and thousands more. Keenly aware that the threatening rain would weaken the bowstrings, she cajoled and encouraged her bowmen to greater effort. Muscles burned as arrows flew.

Showers of iron-tipped missiles fell on Kartimandu's army as it ran towards the rampart ditch. Unused to the long-range attack, the crowd shuddered. Their steps faltered. Men and women shrieked. Without armour, their only protection was the small, round shields some carried. It was inadequate.

Many died from their wounds, others from being trampled underfoot by their comrades. They paused. An ululating, wolf-like wail came from Kartimandu, and the momentum of her army recovered. Spurred on by their nightmarish queen, they closed on the perimeter ditches.

***

Fearghal paced along the central rampart watching as the archers whittled away at the enemy. A thousand Clann Ui Flaithimh shuffled feet in the dirt and gravel to gain a firmer purchase. Cúscraid, Tadhg, and Brocc stood ready before the front row.

Behind the wall of shields, there stood twenty druids. Another ten were divided equally between each of the smaller flanking ramparts. Each wore a black cloak with its hood raised. Each carried a sword sheathed in a plain scabbard that hung from an equally nondescript leather belt. The Druid had assembled his band from the neighbouring lands. They were not hard to convince. Kartimandu brooked no spiritual influences on her tribe save her own. All knew that life under the queen would be painful and of very short duration.

"Do you know how to use that sword, Druid?" asked Fearghal. The Druid smiled. In answer, there was a soft whisper as the sword was drawn from its sheath. It was no surprise to Fearghal that the sword was as unremarkable as its wielder. Yet to his trained eye, it was well-oiled and keenly edged.

"Our work is to administer the Law and care for the minds and spirits of the tribe with our prayers and chants. We will, however, not shrink from the battle. Death holds no fear for us." The Druid's dark eyes, framed with swirls of blue-painted tattoos, held Fearghal's.

"If we're to fight alongside each other, I should know your name, Druid."

The Druid smiled and bowed almost imperceptibly. "Crum, my name is Crum Dubh."

Fearghal dipped his head and turned to Cúscraid, "The archers must have killed or wounded at least a thousand of the *tuilithe*."

"That's wonderful. We'll be finished in time for the evening meal," replied Cúscraid.

"You know what they say about sarcasm."

A gust of wind lifted the stink of the enemy horde and flung it at the fortifications. "Do we smell as bad as that?" asked Cúscraid. The tall warrior's nose scrunched, and hazel-green eyes twinkled as he pointed to the horde. On the ramparts, those within range of his voice roared with laughter.

One wag shouted, "Aye, we do!" Fearghal chuckled and turned to Cúscraid.

"They're almost within javelin range. Our height gives us a much better length of throw. Ularaig's men won't see the ditch beyond the berm. Fewer will tumble into it if we can hit them before they reach the ditch. That'll leave more stakes to impale their comrades."

"You can be a cold-blooded bastard, Cúscraid," snorted Fearghal. Then he called to Brocc, "Get Áine and her archers to safety behind the stockade."

Brocc smiled impishly and, with mock concern, shouted, "Time for us men to take over, Áine." He pushed out his chest while attempting to keep a straight face. "You'd better get your lot on this side of the fence so we can protect your delicate arses."

A flash of anger lit up Áine's deep blue eyes. It was well-known that the sister of Íar, and princess of Curraghatoor, had a prickly temperament. Catching the glint in Brocc's eyes, she paused and took the last black shaft from her quiver. Her lips flickered between a scowl and a smirk as she said, "This arrow up your manly arse will take that grin off your face, Brocc Ó Cathasaigh."

Then Áine signalled to her archers. They turned as one. A fringe of hundreds of arms stretched across the wooden stockade to help them surmount the fence and thread their way through the two rows of Brocc's men.

Moments later, Fearghal called upon the hornblower. A triple-pitch note sounded out above the noise of the enemy cacophony. There was a soft, damp *plop* as each man pulled a javelin from the wet earth. It was followed by the sharp report of iron against the fence as points were tapped to dislodge clumps of dirt.

A creak of leather and a communal grunt accompanied the raft of javelins tossed into the midst of the attackers. Two more volleys followed. In less time than it would take to gulp down a horn or two of beer, over four thousand missiles were launched at the enemy. The dead numbered over one thousand, the injured twice that number.

Ualraig's attack floundered, slipping and sliding on the guts, shite, and gore that dressed the outer incline. Many chieftains, choosing to lead from the front, were crippled by the arms-length spikes of iron that erupted from gaping, bloody holes in their backs. After a moment of excruciating pain, they crossed the bridge to Mag Mell.

The injured were not as fortunate. Maimed, they were kicked aside and trampled by friends. If fate favoured them, their life would be ended with a quick spear thrust or blade across their throats. If they survived, a lingering death from fevers and infections would be their reward. Useless to their families, many would choose to end their own lives.

***

Unable to retreat because of the crush from behind, the wings of Kartimandu's army split left and right. Screaming with anger and fear, they surged to the right and left flanks of the daunting defences.

At the sight, Torcán Ó Dubhghaill's features resolved into a savage grin. He signalled to the tall, sandy-haired warrior further along the rank. "Time for a quick tune, Craiftine?" Craiftine Ó Cuileannáin stood near the end of the front row and laughed. An excellent harpist rarely without his instrument, on this day, he had left it with Sárán Mac Craobhach, the army's eccentric but dependable quartermaster.

"Maybe later. We'll down a few beers and sing a song or two. As usual, you'll exaggerate your deeds and prowess with that sword between your legs."

Torcán smiled broadly and then howled at the oncoming horde. The reddish-purple mark on his neck, a "gift" from Mongfhionn, was even more striking than usual. It and the livid scar across his forehead were clear signs that he was looking forward with unabashed fervour to the battle. Craiftine chuckled. He knew that while Torcán lacked common sense, he was ferocious and unrelenting in a fight.

The musician looked at the pack charging towards the ditch. Unlike the main force that challenged Fearghal's defences, this leaderless and ragged mob was too spread out for a volley of javelins to have maximum impact. Craiftine thought for a moment and then roared, "Hold your spears! Wait until they reach the ditch. They'll hesitate at the edge. Throw the first volley as one, then choose your targets." The loudest cheer of assent came from Torcán's men. Brave and fierce to the point of rashness, they were as crazy as their leader.

***

On the right flank, Deaglán secured his helmet comfortably over braided red hair and checked his weapons. He stood before his men and watched the enemy. This section of the defences, wedged between a small loch and the forested foothills, would be the last to join the fray. Deaglán could hear the enemy's war cries and the steady thump of weapons on shields as they skirted the shoreline and sprinted towards his position.

At thirty-two summers, Deaglán was no novice. As the tattoo on his right shoulder proclaimed, he was a member of the famed Ulaid elite—the Cróeb Ruad. Yet Deaglán was tense, for behind him stood Conall's caomhnóirí, the best-of-the-best. The two hundred veterans had fought beside Conall in the worst circumstances and prevailed. They were exceedingly unhappy at being left behind by Conall and sought someone to vent their spleen.

As if reading his thoughts, a voice behind Deaglán spoke, "Don't worry, son. If you're alive tomorrow, you'll be one of us."

To his right, Fionnbharr Ó Cuileannáin, the eldest of the Ó

Cuileannáin brothers, chuckled. Fionnbharr was twenty-four summers old and the army's chief healer. Tall and fair-haired, he, too, was a veteran of many battles. Deaglán smiled at his friend and then hefted his javelin. The shuffle of feet, the sound of shields being settled against armour and the soft *sloop* of spears tugged from the soggy ground told him the men had followed his lead.

CHAPTER 12

Dusk approached. The old vessel hugged the shoreline. Eventually, the estuary would merge with the cold waters of *An Mhuir Ó Thuaidh*. The captain, Coireall, a squat man well past fifty summers, tugged at a short, grizzled beard. It was the only hair on his weather-beaten and salt-scarred head. Thankful for the calmer wind conditions, he looked back with mounting apprehension at the assault of the gods on Creag na Clachard. *Shite! What have I got us into?*

His crew were fishermen accustomed to trading their white-fleshed catch along the eastern coast. Oft times they transported trade goods, sometimes people. Their hands were calloused from pulling on oars and burned by the rough cables that sped through fingers whose grasp had weakened over the years. They had bodies bruised from being slammed against the boat's wooden hull in angry seas and brawls. Slashes from filleting knives left thin scars and shortened fingers.

The wind and sun gave the seamen's skin its reddish-brown hue. It looked, felt, and sometimes smelled like boiled leather. Apart from his second, the crew were in their mid-years, and none were too bright. They were foul-mouthed and foul-smelling, but they followed his orders without question. He cared for them and fed and clothed them and their families.

"Stuck upstream in a river of shite without an oar. That's us." It was one of the longest sentences the ordinarily laconic mate had spoken since joining the crew.

Coireall nodded, "If we stick to the plan, and the weather holds fair, it'll take us one or two sunsets to navigate the Linne Foirthe and another eight to reach the head of the *Abus*. From there, Dùn Caen is a further four or five sunsets overland."

The second nodded in the direction of Brighid and Danu. Exhausted, the girls succumbed to sleep. "My opinion. Drop them over the side."

The older man shook his head, "We've had enough trouble with gods and goddesses without adding Manannán Mac Lir to the mix." Coireall looked at the twins. "I'm nae child murderer." He gripped the wooden rudder. "This'll be our last voyage. The boat is old and leaks like a sieve. It's beyond repair and won't last another sail. I took a job that would see us all with enough money to do whatever we wanted. It was a bad decision."

"If not us, someone else would've done it."

The captain grunted, savouring the cool salt spray on his face as they cut through the waters, "Camran saw the desperation in me, and the bastard was right. I don't even know who the girls are."

At that moment, Danu awakened from her slumbers. She was slightly older than Brighid. Both were born on the cusp of dawn. Danu's life began under the moon and stars, Brighid's as the morning sun rose above the horizon. The sisters were the same physically: their height, emerald-green eyes, auburn hair, and pale skin. Only one aspect set them apart—the highlights in their hair. Danu's hair was laced with threads of silver-blue and Brighid's with gossamers of gold.

Sound travelled clearly in the calm evening. The older twin, wakened by the last of the conversation, stood up. She paused a few moments to get her balance. With shoulders straight, head held high and chin firmly set, she said, "I am Danu Ni Conall, Princess of the Ériu and Clann Ui Flaithimh."

She gripped the hand of Brighid, who had joined her. "This is my sister, Brighid Ni Conall. She is also a Princess of the Ériu and Clann Ui

Flaithimh. "Our Da is Conall Mac Gabhann, Rí of Ráth Na Conall, Rí Ruirech of Clann Ui Flaithimh, conqueror of Rí Eochaidh Ruad, the scourge of Medb of the Connachta, humiliator of Macha Mong Ruad, High Queen of the Ériu, and destroyer of Diadhaidh of the Na Daoine Tùrsach. He is also known as the Hand of the Goddess.

"Our Ma is Mórrígan Ni Cathasaigh, Queen of Clann Ui Flaithimh and known as An Fiagaí Dorcha—The Dark Huntress." Sensing the fear mounting in the captain, she thrust her final words forward like a dagger, "Our protector is the Lady Mongfhionn of the Aes Sídhe."

The mate looked at his ashen-faced captain and said, "Two choices. Cut their throats and toss them overboard. It'll be quick and relatively painless or..." He paused to lick cracked lips. "Give them a knife. They can do us a mercy and slit our throats."

The elderly captain scowled, "There'll only be fileting of fish on this boat." Then he stared at the girls, "As for ye two, go back to sleep. I'm short for a crew. Ye'll be worked hard this voyage."

As he slumped over a navigation platform smoothed with age, Coireall gripped the rail of the boat as if hoping to draw strength from its ancient timbers. Caught between gods and kings, his future appeared bleak. A flicker of hope stilled his fears. A memory of a meeting long forgotten revived. The captain allowed himself a small smile of comfort, dropped a band of silver into the sea and offered a prayer to Manannán Mac Lir.

Then to the crew, he said, "Steer for the shore. We'll beach the ship, make camp for the night, and set sail on the morning high tide."

CHAPTER 13

406 B.C.—Áth

The warrior's long hair had seen neither comb nor water for many seasons. It hung limp and thick with grease from a pock-marked scalp. Ragged tails clung to scabby shoulders. There was no telling its actual colour.

A shield slammed against his mud-bespattered face, dislodging the few remaining teeth. It was neither difficult nor painful. The teeth's roots had rotted a long time ago. Carried on a pungently sweet and sour breath, he sprayed bloody saliva from a yawning mouth.

He felt good. His battle cry was loud and defiant. He was lucky, having first bridged the perimeter ditch and then breached the fence encircling Áth. It was here the Goddess withdrew her favour.

First, Mòrag's shield stunned him. Next, her spear thrust ground past his breastbone and broke several ribs before piercing his heart. She had little time to dwell on his death. A blood and gore-streaked body testified this was not her first kill of the day. It would not be her last.

The slingers, their supplies of stones and slugs exhausted, took up spears and joined their comrades at Áth's stockade. Evidence of their work was evident. Beyond the heaving mass of the enemy, packed into the narrow band of dirt between ditch and fence, lay the bodies of the broken. Cracked skulls oozed greyish-pink brain matter.

Others seemed, at a glance, in a peaceful repose, apparently for no reason. Closer examination revealed ragged-edged bruises marking the location of missiles buried deep in soft flesh. Beneath the surface, cracked and splintered bones pierced vital organs or ruptured blood vessels. The injured flailed around in shock. The trauma of sudden, blunt injury subdued their senses. They were bumped roughly aside by their brothers. Their presence was a hindrance to the assault.

Dùn Na Mèadaidh's ruins, smoke-blackened and inhabited by spirits, ceased to have any use for Kartimandu. Thus, Ualraig turned his attention to Áth. The settlement became a strategic goal. A quick victory over the forces within its fence would raise the army's spirits. More than this, it would give him a defensible location at the river's main crossing and a potential launching platform for forays into the north. Thus, Ualraig despatched five thousand against the settlement's defenders.

Much to their annoyance, Ualraig kept his restless elite from the mêlée. They would be needed later when the real battle was enjoined. In the remaining hours of light, Ualraig was under little illusion about the fate of the thousands of eejits who rushed the formidable ramparts that stretched from the Abhainn Dubh to the foothills of the Sleá. He had no pity for them. Hopefully, a few thousand of the best and those with wiser heads would survive the shield-wall of Clann Ui Flaithimh.

***

Mòrag's task was to command a reserve force to plug breaches in Áth's defences. The maze of dry-stone walls within the settlement was an effective barrier and provided cover for her band. Thus far, she had efficiently dealt with any intrusion.

However, Mòrag knew it would not be long before someone got the bright idea of cutting down trees from nearby copses and using them as rams against the east-facing gate. The Ravens' princess looked upwards. *Could they hold out until the sun slid below the horizon and make their escape to the forests in the gloom?*

Brandubh gazed along the fence. So far, the stockade held firm despite the crazed, phlegm-spitting besiegers pressing against it. The attackers' position remained perilous and unstable. The perimeter ditch, long since filled with the dead and debris of war, was a precarious platform for fighting.

The dirt lip between the ditch and stockade was just three paces wide, enough to ensure the wooden stakes were well-grounded in the earth. Thankfully, fewer than three men deep could stand and fight on the crumbling and now blood-soaked ledge. It evened the odds, which was good. Brandubh's force was massively outnumbered.

The prince of the Ravens' attention was diverted when the man to his front fell to an axe blow. The blade sliced through a muscled shoulder, exposing the gleaming white bone. Hooked by the axe's curvature, the defender was jerked against the fence and finished off by a spear thrust to his head.

His death was caused by a heavy-set battler whose torso rippled with cords of muscle and myriad scars. The man roared in delight, hawked up a glob of saliva and phlegm, and spat on his victim as he wrenched the blade from the flesh. Those around him cheered his victory, jeered at their enemy, and attacked the fence with renewed vigour.

Angry, Brandubh raised his spear and made to step forward. He was blocked by two Ravens, one male and one female, who stood on either side of the fallen man. The younger female fighter acknowledged his intent with a quick smile before she turned her attention to the stockade.

The bull-necked belligerent would have claimed another victim without her fast, almost involuntary movement. His swinging axe should have taken most of her face and shoulder. Instead, it shaved a curling splinter of wood from her shield as it continued its downward arc.

For a fleeting moment, the veteran attacker was off-balance. It was enough to seal his fate. The female's companion thrust from the side. His leaf-shaped spearhead punched through the bluish-purple, rope-like vein on the man's neck and exited, having cut sinew and bone. Hot arterial blood gushed in rhythmical, diminishing pulses, spraying those nearby.

Transfixed and unable to move, the man's eyes stared forward. He watched the female raise her spear. The tip of the blade entered his nose.

His throat was already ruined, and thus he could not howl at the intense pain. It seemed to take an eternity for the point to finally exit his skull in an explosion of blood, brain, and shards of bone. The venom behind the thrust was such that the spear also skewered the one behind.

A shout of anger burst from the female Raven. Her weapon was wrenched from her blood-slicked hands by the falling corpse. Brandubh grabbed her by the shoulders and pulled her back from the stockade. Anger and frustration smouldered in blue-green eyes. Before her leader and prince of the tribe, she fought to control her breathing.

Brandubh examined her closely and saw a naked body shrouded in a veneer of blood, dirt, and sweat. There was little of her tribal paint visible. Nevertheless, the gore did little to disguise her beauty. Her chest heaved, and Brandubh became aware that her breasts had a pleasing fullness. The furious passion of the clash caused her nipples to stand proud at the centre of a corona of blood.

For all that was to take place before sunset, it was this image that Brandubh would bring to his dreams. He held out his spear. "You'll need this," he said.

She smiled broadly. "The Raven, go with you and protect you, My Lord."

***

Eachdonn Breac urged his shaggy-haired pony to a final burst of effort as Áth came into sight. At his side, Gormal kept pace with the king. Behind, the Aos an Eich rode as a long, squat wedge with Eachdonn at its point. On their left flank and, much to the tribe's delight, several hundred paces behind were Brion's chariots. Gormal wondered what the plan was, for Eachdonn had given little direction apart from "Mount up and ride."

Gormal was not alone. Eachdonn had given little consideration to a plan beyond washing the stain of treachery from his tribe's memory and restoring his reputation with Conall and Drostan. A hundred paces from the battle that raged around Áth, the king drew up, inhaled deeply, and leapt from his horse. He grabbed his spear and shield and, in a rare flash of clarity of purpose, roared, "For the Goddess! Relieve our friends. Give no quarter."

The king's call was echoed by his men as they dismounted and formed behind their leaders. The ponies surprisingly did not scatter but trotted to a nearby grassy knoll. Their duty completed in an exemplary fashion, and unconcerned about the blood-fest, they proceeded to chomp on lush, early summer grass.

Turning to his hornblower, Eachdonn said, "Let them know we're here." Then, with a bellow, he raised his spear and charged the enemy's ranks.

"Rut the Hag!" cried Gormal. In the few moments before the Aos an Eich charged in their king's wake, the long stride of Eachdonn had already put him twenty paces ahead.

**

Doubled over and with hands on her knees, Mòrag heaved. Irritated, she swept a thin braid of copper-red hair from her face. Wet with sweat and slick with gore, Mòrag's tresses clung tenaciously to her face.

Mòrag's harsh and deep breathing put an intolerable strain on the harness that "protected" her chest. Mere threads held the blood-soaked straps in place. It would not be long before her magnificent bosom would find release. She had no qualms about this. Her breasts had caused many to pause for a few fateful moments.

It took Mòrag a few deep breaths to calm her heartbeat and martial her senses. In Cúscraid's design, the stockade at the gate curved first outwards and then back towards the fence. The effect was to corral besiegers into a triangular killing field with the gateway at its narrowest point.

Yet the portal had been breached. As Mòrag anticipated, the enemy had finally listened to someone with common sense. Gates designed to protect from the odd wild beast and smash-and-grab warbands were shattered by a few crude battering rams.

Before Mòrag, a mix of attackers and defenders lay prone on the blood-soaked dirt. Their twisted bodies were a ghoulish microcosm of the encounter. The moaning of the injured rose up but elicited no succour. Left unattended, enemies lying side-by-side were united in their need for relief from their agony. Aid never came.

A roar from outside the gateway signalled that more High People were pushing forward. Only the narrowness of the entrance, which was no more than fifteen paces wide, gave Mòrag hope of staunching the attackers' momentum. Once more, she yelled, "Hold!"

The princess' parched throat screamed for water. Still, her band knew what she wanted. The front rank knelt with spearheads at waist height and butts braced in the dirt. The rear row raised spears and readied to stab and thrust over the heads of their comrades.

At first, Mòrag thought it the clamour of battle. Plugs of blood and more than a few blows to the head had diminished her hearing. Hence, she ignored the solitary blare of a horn. After several blasts and a noticeable ripple of uncertainty within the enemy's ranks, she ordered one of her men to climb a nearby roundhouse. His news prompted Mòrag to offer a prayer of thanks to the Goddess.

"Eachdonn Breac has arrived. His men appear to be pushing the enemy back and south from us. If they continue, it should allow us to escape." Mòrag's shouted news raised a smile of hope on her brother's face and a wild cheer from the defenders. "Pity we don't have a hundred of Conall's men. Their shields would be useful in forcing a path out of the gateway," said Mòrag. Hindsight, as ever, was a useless companion.

Brandubh nodded in agreement, "If we survive this assault, we'll have those men in the future. In the meantime, your band will hold its position, but be prepared to abandon Áth on my command."

***

Eachdonn Breac was thirty-eight summers old and in his prime. He was above average height. Long, auburn hair hung like a horse's mane over broad shoulders. His physique was muscular, and his stamina was as durable as the ponies his tribe bred.

This day, wrath overcame good sense and took command of his body. Thus, Eachdonn fought with reckless abandon without mercy or fear of death. Berserk, he slaughtered a path through his enemy. His shield was abandoned, shattered by the impact of many spears, clubs, and axes. He fought with his spear and an axe torn from the hands of one of his victims.

Many drew back from his presence, recoiling at his frightening appearance. Others charged forward to challenge him. Spear thrusts, axe swings, head butts and bites left a trail of the dead and the dismembered. Enrobed in a mist of blood, a maddened Eachdonn battled his foes. Yet he fought too far—and alone. Severed from his army, Eachdonn brawled in an ever-shrinking circle. Perhaps it was for the best. His unhinged mind was unable to differentiate friend from enemy.

An axe, thrown in frustration, halted Eachdonn's epic fight. The spinning weapon hit him with a glancing blow on his spear arm. It did not do a great deal of damage, but his arm was numbed, and his spear slipped from his grasp. Worse, the knock brought the king momentarily out of his madness. It was with a sad smile, but in complete control of his mind, that Eachdonn Breac assailed his adversaries one final time.

Howling, the enemy horde enclosed the king. Blades slashed and pierced his body until it was a lump of meat. Eachdonn's assault would be regaled forever in the odes sung by friends and enemies. Cut down like a rabid dog, his death would be remembered with a kindness that bore little relation to reality.

***

Standing in his chariot, Brion raised his hands to the sky in helpless frustration and shouted, "The Hag save me, Gràinne. What possessed Eachdonn?"

"It was a hero's death. He killed many enemies," said Gràinne with a shrug of her shoulders.

"You've spent too much time with Tadhg, listening to ballads of mythical heroes and glorious contests," retorted Brion. "Eachdonn's pride leaves Brandubh and Mòrag stranded in Áth. Mark my words. Gormal will fight to recover the king's body and leave the field."

Under the stomp and twisting of thousands of boots and bróga and the incessant rain, lush meadowland became a morass of mud and blood. The battle for Áth was a vicious, torturous fight. Dulled blades ripped flesh. Within the crush, men and women, old and young, fought thousands of grim duels. Gràinne could see that both sides had taken substantial losses from her vantage point.

Trapped in the settlement, the Ravens increasingly became spectators, unable to influence their fate. Mòrag and her brother could do little save defend against increasingly frenzied assaults on the stockade.

Brion was proved right. The Aos an Eich, under Gormal's leadership, fought to retrieve Eachdonn's corpse. They surged forward with fanatical zeal, pushing against a belligerent foe. Rain streamed over blood and sweat as they screamed themselves hoarse and hacked through the High People's lines.

***

Ualraig watched the fight for Áth ebb and flow as pride and stubbornness struggled to overcome tiredness. There was little art or honour in the contest. Men and women fought, their faces no more apart than the smell of a stinking breath. The rain gradually ceased, but feet still slipped in the slop of mud, blood, and guts. Blades hacked at exposed flesh. Clubs bludgeoned skulls. Warriors cursed in frustration at the lack of a clear killing opportunity. In the crushing maw of the front line, men died unintentionally shouldered into the path of a blade.

On a rocky outcrop beyond Áth, Ualraig was in excellent humour. The Aos an Eich finally recovered their heroic king and were making a bloody withdrawal. He was tempted to sound a halt to the fighting, yet the voice of Kartimandu rang insistently in his head.

While he was strong enough to resist the urge to run into the battle, the same was not true for those attacking Áth. So he watched as the tide of the skirmish once more turned to the settlement's walls.

✳✳✳

Each Clann Ui Flaithimh chariot was as unique as the men and women who drove and fought from it. Ever individuals, each team chose a colour for the box. The leather harness and metallic fittings were made for function and service and were ornately decorated. Garishly coloured clann and tribal banners hung from long poles lashed to the cret. They flapped in concert with the wheels as the chariots trundled forward.

Brion stopped a respectful distance from where Gormal dressed Eachdonn's body for his final journey to Dùn Athad. With a shrug at Gràinne at his anticipated reception, Brion jumped from his chariot and strode to Gormal.

"The fight is not over. Our friends... *your* friends need your help," said Brion.

"I've lost over half my men. I won't lose more. The Aos an Eich will return to Dùn Athad and our lands."

"Eachdonn had an agreement with Conall and Drostan," growled Brion, annoyed at the young man's petulance. "I expect *you* to keep to it."

"I'm the king, and I made no such agreement." Gormal scowled as he signalled his men to mount up.

A firm hand clamped down on Gormal's naked shoulder, making him wince. "You're not king *yet*." Hard eyes, the match of Mórrígan's colouring, were made more sinister by Brion's scarred face. They held Gormal's gaze less than a hand's length away.

"You are honour bound to keep Eachdonn's oath," Brion spoke softly but firmly. "And *you will*, or the Aos an Eich will lose a prionnsa." Gormal's spear lay on the ground beside the king's body. His hand went to the dagger in his belt; the soft whisper of steel on wool forestalled his movement. Gràinne smiled as the tip of her sword pricked Gormal's neck.

"We outnumber you." Gormal spat for emphasis, careful not to cut himself further by moving. The crunch of iron-rimmed wheels on the stony ground drew Gormal's eyes to the rest of Brion's chariots.

Grim-faced men held javelins ready. The long scythes jutting out from iron hubs added credence to the threat.

"*You* will certainly die. Many of your warriors will die," said Brion. "The Aos an Eich are not mounted fighters. Our chariots will outrun your men and your spears. Fight with honour or die here... now." Gormal spat and wiped the back of his hand across his mouth.

"If he spits again, I'm going to kill him anyway," murmured Gràinne. Brion choked down the urge to laugh, instead signalling Gràinne to sheath her weapon.

With a final glare at Brion, Gormal turned to his men, lifted his spear in the air and roared, "For Eachdonn Breac!" As one, once more, the Aos an Eich charged towards the blood-soaked fields of Áth.

"Perhaps we should have discussed tactics," said Gràinne as their allies streamed past.

"Like father, like son," Brion replied. Then to the waiting chariots, he said, "We'll attack the eastern side of Áth. Focus on breaking up the attack so that our friends can escape."

***

There were times when Brandubh wished he was a simple warrior and only had to think about obeying orders. Battles would be fought. He would either die and go to Mag Mell or survive and spread the legs of a willing maiden. He sighed and recalled the young woman from earlier. Maybe if they both lived...

The thought lasted little more than a heartbeat, and he turned to Mòrag. "I'll not die caged within stone and wood. We attack now. You lead from the front. I'll take the rear." His sister smiled in agreement.

"Abandon the walls!" shouted Brandubh. "Form in rows of eight behind Mòrag. Spears of the outer ranks defend the column."

***

Madness shackled the Kartimandu's army and hurled them at the Clann Ui Flaithimh defences. They suffered cruel spikes and barbs but still surged forward and upward. The ground, a quagmire of blood and dirt, gave no advantage. Ditches dug into the slopes and packed with stakes and thorns, quickly filled with corpses. At the crest of the ramparts, the flat plateau presented another challenge—the stockade.

Behind the fence, overlapping scarlet-coloured shields gave little hope to the attackers. Severe-faced men and women raised javelins to kill and maim. Short swords were unfastened from leather belts and slapped against plaid-covered thighs. Behind the shield-wall, the druids chanted. On the adjacent Sleá's hills, bodhráin continued to beat out a wall of sound. Attackers and defenders hurled curses and taunts at each other in an unintelligible cry of rage.

From her vantage point, Kartimandu defended her army against the spiritual onslaught of the druids. The High People had a single advantage—numbers. The queen threw her army at the ramparts, overwhelming their natural instincts and impressing her will on the minds of her followers. However, like Ualraig, she kept her guard from the slaughter.

On the left flank, Torcán laughed at the labouring enemy who crested the summit, only to face the stockade. A few scrambled over. Their reward was to have their bodies slammed against the wood and backs broken by the iron bosses of Clann Ui Flaithimh's shields. Soft flesh and hard bone yielded to iron spikes and blades.

More scrambled over the chest-high fence. A hesitant trickle became a surge. The attackers sank to their ankles and slipped in the gore of their comrades. They could not get a good purchase for the fight, yet numbers eventually prevailed. Those at the front fell, but the attackers steadily gained ground.

"*Hold!*" bellowed Torcán.

The rear row shouted, stamped, and crouched. One foot forward, one trailing, shoulders braced shields against the front row. The front row roared, "*Tuilithe!*" Whether the target of the insult was the enemy or their friends who had pinned them in place was debatable.

***

Gormal's men pressed the attack on the besiegers of Áth to pry them from the ramparts of the settlement. However, he was well outnumbered. Minds, shackled by Kartimandu, resisted any retreat. Within Áth, more of the enemy scrambled over the stockade and made their way deeper into the settlement.

Only Brandubh's spears and the maze of stone walls slowed their progress. At the gateway, Mòrag fought against the press in a bloody and increasingly hopeless task. Their opponents formed a solid plug of flesh and bone. Brandubh cried out in frustration as the Ravens' escape was thwarted.

Brion's chariots swept around Gormal and charged the enemy from the east. Forewarned by war cries and the screams and squeals of ten teams of horses, the besiegers of Áth scrambled to get out of the way. Iron-rimmed wheels churned the ground into a worse mess.

Only an eejit voluntarily stands in the path of a chariot and its spinning scythes. Those who had fought chariots before knew there was only one plan. Get out of the way and hit the vehicles from behind. Hence, with surprising alacrity and efficiency, the ranks of the High People parted.

Gràinne howled in anger and ordered her driver to swerve towards the receding line of the enemy. The cret shuddered as spinning knives snagged those too slow to get out of her way. Gripped in both hands, her longsword swung at shaggy-haired heads, delivering death to anyone within her reach. She hissed like an angry *lince* torn from its prey when her driver directed his team back to join the other chariots.

At last, they broke through to the curved stockade and gateway of Áth. Faced with chariots on one side and Ravens on the other, the rump of the enemy besieging the gateway broke. Most were killed by Mòrag's men from behind or by the chariots as they tried to dodge and weave a path to safety. Gràinne gave Mòrag a bloody smile.

"We need to move before our wheels sink in this muck. Are you ready?" In reply, Mòrag screamed and charged forward.

From his vantage point, Ualraig swore. He watched the enemy's war chariots swing around to face his men. Once more, instinct made them give way. In the wake of Clann Ui Flaithimh's two-horse war chariots, the Ravens flowed east from Áth. Ualraig's men, now thinly spread, came under renewed pressure from Gormal, the Ravens, and Clann Ui Flaithimh chariots.

With a sigh of resignation, Ualraig signalled his hornblower to sound disengage. He would suffer no more needless casualties but, doubtless, would face an angry queen. The battle for Áth ended in a bloody stalemate. He had lost several thousand men, injured or dead, but he had won Áth and the strategic river ford. The Ravens and their allies escaped and would fight him on another day.

***

Dusk fell as another wave of attackers was repulsed. The stockade from the Abhainn Dubh to the slopes of the Sleá was stained dark with the blood of thousands. Fearghal rubbed at the grime that filled the crevices and pores of his face and surveyed the battlefield. "Do you think they'll ever stop?"

"I hope so. I need a piss," said an equally dirty Cúscraid. He grinned and scratched his groin.

"Since when have you been so modest?" Fearghal wrinkled his nose. "Use the fence like everyone else.

"It's getting dark. I'm hoping they'll retreat to their camp soon." Cúscraid groaned in sympathy with his weary muscles as he thrust his sword into another attacker.

"It's Kartimandu. She's controlling them," said the druid, Crum Dubh. "She only has to control a small group. The rest will follow. Like cattle in a stampede."

Even as they spoke, Kartimandu's wailing ceased, and horns blared across the battlefield. Exhausted, the High People disengaged and trudged away with heavy legs. They were met and herded towards Áth and the river crossing by the queen's and Ualraig's guards. Neither queen nor her commander would risk some chieftains taking their warbands and fleeing. Before long, Kartimandu's army was no more than shadows in the deepening dusk.

Fearghal spun around. "Brocc, take your men onto the field and behead a few hundred. Put their heads on spearheads along the stockade, and organize a watch along the fence. Make sure there are plenty of torches along the ramparts. I want Ualraig to think we're still here." He half-turned to Cúscraid.

"You know what to do."

Cúscraid dipped his head and paused. "Did you see their eyes? Sends shivers up my spine."

***

Brion cursed the rapidly dimming light. Brandubh and Mòrag's men trotted parallel but several hundred paces away from his chariots. They parted with a sour-faced Gormal shortly after Kartimandu's army removed themselves from the field. Now, they were making their way towards the forested foothills of the Sleá. It would have been impossible for Brion's chariots to cross the dense tangle of undergrowth carpeting the wildwood. But Cúscraid had the foresight to cut several paths into the woods—if only Brion could find them.

The Ravens had no such challenge. As soon as they reached the edge of the forest, Brandubh called out a quick goodbye, and he and his sister disappeared into the gloom and cover of the dense forest. "Our paths should be close by," said Brion to Gràinne. "We'll travel along the edge one more time. If we've no luck, we'll camp here and wait for the dawn. We're too far from Áth to have any serious trouble from Ualraig."

Gràinne nodded. "I'll go in the direction of the ramparts. I'll circle back if I find the trail."

It was no one's fault, yet several bore the blame like heavy yokes on their shoulders. Gràinne found an opening and wheeled her chariot around to find Brion. Yet Brion had also found a gap and was driving towards Gràinne. In their enthusiasm, both travelled with less caution and at too high a speed in the half-light of dusk.

It would have been hard for Brion to see the rock in the daytime. It was impossible in the gloom. The chariot's wheel crunched against the stone. With the vehicle's momentum, the wheel attempted to climb the moss-covered rock. The cret flipped, flinging Brion and his driver to the ground. Horses screamed as the pole between them twisted, pulling their reins.

Brion hit the ground with little more than a surprised "Oomph!" as the wind was knocked from him. Hearing the rumble of wheels and hoof beats, he tried to raise himself from the dirt as Gràinne's chariot rushed out of the darkness.

CHAPTER 14

It was the third cluster of shacks along the shoreline. Urard's nose crinkled, and his stomach churned at the strong smell of rotting fish and seaweed. Fish was not his favourite food. He entered the settlement warily, axe at the ready and with his men in a loose semi-circle behind him. They passed several hovels where silver-brown pieces of carefully chosen driftwood had been interlinked to form a second layer on the thatched roofs. Benches, drying racks, and cages were similarly constructed from the sea's wooden harvest.

As far as Urard could make out, there were about thirty people in the community. All kin, no doubt, and aged from one to one hundred. Raggedly dressed children with dirty faces wiped snotty noses on mothers' skirts or peered from behind barrels of water and salted fish. The adolescents adopted an air of casual disinterest. Young men and women looked with silent curiosity as Urard walked his dapple-grey mare towards the centre. The older residents looked on with helpless resignation, accepting there was little they could do to influence their fate.

An ancient iron cauldron blackened with years of smoke hung on an iron lifting bar over a roaring fire. Bread cooked on flat iron griddles and the hot stones surrounding the fire. The aroma, carried on the light easterly breeze, was welcoming. A rumbling from his stomach reminded Urard that it had been a long time since he had eaten. Now was not the time to be choosy about hot food.

Beside the fire stood a man. Urard judged him to be about fifty summers. In the dimming light, the older man smiled and extended his hands in welcome as Urard slowly dismounted. It was a friendly greeting, and the smile was genuine. At the edges of the elder's eyes, lines of anxiety bore witness to how past visitors had behaved. Urard grimaced, although not at the man's unease. A sore arse and raw inner thighs were reminders that a horse was not his favourite means of travel.

"Will ye join us for some food? I'm sure we can make what we have stretch. Hope ye like fish."

Urard groaned. "Just fish?"

His host chuckled. "Oh, I'm sure a few rabbits are in the stew. Maybe a viper or two. The snakes like to lie beside the warm fire during the night. They end up in the pot if they're not away by morning." He paused briefly and added, "Come to think of it, the goat's missing. Tough old bastard. Ye'll have to chew that meat well."

"You don't seem afraid of us," Urard said.

The old man shrugged. "What could we do against ye? Our only protection is the will of the gods. So we may as well be happy and hope for the best."

"You'll likely know who we are."

"Ye'r part of the raiders who burned Camran's dùn to the ground. Likely him with it, which is no big loss to anyone. He was a bastard. I hear that most of the village folk and farmers got away. Sad about the warriors, but then fighting is what they're paid fer." The man held Urard's gaze. "Should I be worried?"

"I hope not. I'm looking for information." Urard patted the pouch that hung from his belt. The chink of gold was unmistakable. "I'd prefer to pay rather than use this." He lowered his massive axe to the ground.

The elder nodded. "Let's eat and talk." The food was simple but filling. There was no beer, so the food was washed down with spring water or milk that had an edge of sourness. Urard described how he was looking for two girls, believed to be on board a boat heading for Dùn Caen.

The elder scratched the stubble on his swarthy, weather-beaten face. He shook his head and sighed unhappily.

"I was offered that contract but turned it down. I have no love for that strange woman who leads the High People. As for kidnapping children, I don't think Mac Lir would approve. Still, don't think too badly of Coireall. At heart, he's a good man, and I doubt he'll harm the girls. He was desperate. His boat is old. His crew and their families needed feeding."

"Can I catch him? What's the best way to Dùn Caen?"

"Your first problem is the Linne Foirthe. It's a huge bay, about a day's ride south. It's wide… about…" The elder halted as if searching for words before asking, "What way did ye come to Albu? Did ye land at *Maol Chinn Tìre*?" Urard nodded. "Well, the Linne Foirthe is about same distance at its widest point. It's deep too. There's nae way a horse will swim that distance."

"Boats?"

"There are larger ships, but they're all on the other side of the estuary. They belong to the Votod-Daoine and are protected by their hillforts along the coastline." Urard let out a long sigh of disappointment. "Yet ye have one thing in yer favour. Yer horses will travel twice as fast as Coireall's boat. And ye'll likely ride for longer. Coireall's vessel is undermanned; he's probably only got a half-crew. He'll need to rest up a lot and get new provisions."

"You're leaving something out," said Urard.

The man breathed in, not wanting to be the bearer of bad news. "The best crossing is south of Dùn Na Mèadaidh on the Abhainn Dubh. As to where? Ye'll have to judge how far your horses can swim." The look on Urard's face troubled the fisherman. "Rumours are that war is imminent further up the Abhainn Dubh. Yer face tells me the rumours have substance."

Urard dipped his head. "It's true." His hand reached for his belt, brushing against the hilt of a dagger the size of a small sword. The elder flinched and looked nervously around him. The Clann Ui Flaithimh warrior smiled and shook his head as he untied the pouch from his belt. "Your information was good. Maybe not welcome, but that's hardly your fault. I keep my word." He tossed the pouch to the fisherman.

"I can do one more service for ye," the elder said. Urard looked at him, one eyebrow raised. "Take my... grandson, Iasg, with you. He's a good lad. Knows the rivers and coastline well. He'll save ye time."

"How will he get back to you?"

"If he wants to, he'll find his way back. Personally, I'd be happy if he stayed with yer folk. Better prospects than this life." Urard nodded and stretched out his hand. Both men clasped each other's forearms to seal the agreement.

***

In Mórrígan's camp, the air was filled with snoring, farting, and the occasional unintelligible grunt as the sleek rat wended through the encampment. To the intruder, the horses were better behaved with their soft nickering. Chilled by night, camp guards stamped feet, rubbed hands, and pulled damp brats closer. They looked at the moon, hoping that their shift was soon over.

The creature paused to warm its tight, mud-brown fur at one of the campfires. Its nose twitched, and its whiskers flickered as it balanced the desire for food with staying alive. Men were not friendly. The rat remembered leaving part of its foot in a trap when it was younger. With an uneven gait, it wandered on.

It paused to stand on its hind legs and looked condescendingly at the dozens of mice scurrying across the camp. His was a path of deliberation, not frenzy. The rat's long, furless tail swept the dirt behind him. He could not understand man's aversion to his race.

Apart from the odd bite prompted by curiosity, he had never sought to harm the two-legs. His tail touched the warm skin of a foot. The rat froze, feeling the foot instinctively flinch from the brief caress. He waited until reassured the man had relaxed back to sleep and continued his journey.

The pain was excruciating, and the rat squealed a short prayer for relief. His entreaty was answered, and death took him. "Snack for breakfast?" queried an adjacent comrade, looking at the carcass pinned to the earth by his neighbour's dagger.

"A *francach* bit me in the crib. It still gives me nightmares. I hate them," said the rat killer, retrieving his blood-stained dagger. He smiled and pointed at the impaled rodent. "I'm not hungry for rats yet. But you can have it if your belly's that needy." His comrade laughed and turned over to resume his sleep. The rat was flicked into the fire. With a shiver of remembrance at the touch of the tail, the rodent killer continued a sleep disturbed by dreams of a cradle.

Mórrígan woke from a fitful sleep disturbed by nightmares of Brighid and Danu. No matter how hard she tried, they were impossible to control. She was helpless. Knowing she could do little to change the circumstances increased her anxiety. It was impossible to set aside the dark images in her mind.

A momentary flash of jealousy of Mongfhionn reared up. The Sídhe was powerful and could speak to the girls in their dreams. Mórrígan had no such connection. In frustration, she stabbed the ground over and over. Not far away, Bricriu and Beacán watched with growing concern and prayed to the Goddess for mercies for both sister and nieces.

***

Conall awoke with a start and a stabbing pain in the back of his head. The anguish of Mórrígan's despair had pierced his dreams. In the inky darkness before sunrise, the ruler of Clann Ui Flaithimh felt her despondency. It added to the already deep well of his sorrow. His children were sorely missed, and his heart felt as if crushed by a heavy yoke. He scratched at the dark stubble on his chin and fingered braided hair with weapon-calloused fingers.

Instinctively, Conall's hand reached out and grasped his axe. He smiled. He had discarded his twin axes and now carried just one. The hulking Urard, the most proficient fighter with a *tuagh* or battle-axe, had, in a moment of rare criticism of his king, suggested having two axes was a young man's vanity.

He strongly hinted that Conall would be better served by being excellent with one weapon than modestly skilled with two. And so, Conall now fought with axe and shield. The arm's length weapon had a double blade at one end and an iron-butt piece at the other. Above the butt, a strip of leather was wound around the oak haft to make a grip large enough for two hands if needed. At the insistence of the Sídhe, the shaft and blade had been inscribed with swirling designs.

The fire smouldering at his feet suddenly flared as several logs were tossed onto it, breaking the crust. Startled, Conall looked up. Íar towered over him. "It's still chilly at this hour, and clothes never dry in this bloody rain, but at least you can be warm." Conall dipped his head in appreciation as his friend turned and strode across the camp.

"Are you sure *she* has her eye on Conall?"

In the still of the morning, whispered voices carried far. As he stood near the cooking fires, the lilting, southern brogue of Íar was readily distinguished. He had never quite mastered the art of speaking softly.

"Keep it down, you eejit. As sure as I can be," whispered Nikandros. "I've watched her, and not just when she's left my bed. A fine arse she has."

"Did you have to add that bit?" Íar sighed and picked at a lump of congealed fat in his beard.

Nikandros laughed. "She tracks him like a hunter. Knows his habits. Where he bathes. Where he goes for solitude." He paused briefly. "Fortunately, she's not a threat to his life, or we'd have to deal with that. She wants to impale herself on *his* spear."

"Again, did you have to add that final bit?"

Conall's cheeks flushed red, and he was thankful that twilight masked his discomfort and embarrassment at overhearing his friends' conversation. It was as if a blindfold had been removed. *The Hag's tits. That's all I need.* It was, however, accompanied by no small measure of pleasure that such a beautiful young woman desired him. The stirring between his legs betrayed his thoughts, if not his intentions.

"The odd thing is that Conall hasn't a clue about what is going on," Nikandros' voice continued. "That's good in some ways, but there'll be others who'll offer their bodies and whose motives won't be as obvious or harmless."

"In that case, we'll need to keep our eyes open and blades sharp." The two spotted Conall's approach and turned to face him.

A head lifted up in the shadows beyond the light of the campfires. Mongfhionn shook her head at the stupidity of men and the complicity of women. Men were weak when presented with a shapely body and friendly thighs. For many, the only barrier to infidelity was the opportunity. Even her stalwart Fearghal could no more resist dalliances with Macha of the Ériu and Medb of the Connachta than a moth could resist candlelight.

Temptation stared Conall in the face. However, the timing was particularly bad. All their minds needed to concentrate on dealing with Kartimandu and retrieving Brighid and Danu from her captors. Sadly, Mongfhionn knew one other who could rival the voluptuous Mòrag for Conall's attention. The Sídhe sighed. If only the Law were on her side. She growled. The Fénechas practically encouraged men to have more than one partner.

A not insignificant question was how Mórrígan would react to sharing her bed with another woman? Mórrígan spent too much time away from Conall, which was not good. Mongfhionn sighed again in resignation and determined to have a stern talk with Mórrígan's rivals and Mórrígan.

***

Life went on, thought Brighid, as an orange-gold sun rose up through banks of grey clouds on the eastern horizon. She carved a small track in the wooden rail with her thumbnail. It was her way of knowing how many sunsets had passed. Under the prodding of Brighid's middle finger, Danu awoke, rubbing the last vestiges of sleep from her eyes.

Danu was not a morning person. Unlike Brighid, she did not appreciate the glory of the sunrise. She was very grumpy until she had warm food in her belly. On this dawn, there was no food, warm or cold. The night had been spent on the boat, drifting with the coastal currents, and Danu was more than a little irked.

She looked at Coireall and his crew. Young as they were, the sisters realised that while Coireall had a rough nature, he was neither evil nor cruel. He was an exceptional seaman and was never happier than when standing on the stern's boards, hands on the tiller, threading the boat through rocks and currents. Strangely, she and Brighid felt safe while at sea. Their concern was what would happen when they reached their destination, but that was many sunsets distant.

Still, both also knew Coireall was a man of poor judgment.

***

Brion's spirit was trapped. The bean sídhe had not claimed him, so he drifted on the periphery of life. The plains of Mag Mell remained a distant golden glow. Fevers racked his body, drenching him in sweat. Cold chills made him shiver uncontrollably even though he lay close to the fire. He felt little pain. That had passed with the onset of shock. In moments of clarity, he unsuccessfully tried to piece together what had happened. At intervals, he was aware of arguing voices.

"You'll have to do it," said Gràinne's broad-shouldered driver. "Look at him. He'll die if we do nothing, and we can't wait until we get back to the healers."

Gràinne glared at the man and spat. "Since when was I appointed leader?"

"It was our chariot that slammed into him and just about broke every bone on his left side. It was our wheel that crushed his arm to a pulp. I'm astonished he managed to avoid the scythe from taking his head." The driver looked around at the other chariot teams.

In a softer tone, he said, "*They* don't want to be leaders, Gràinne. They're good fighters, but they're followers. They simply want to be pointed in the right direction and told who to kill." He pointed to Brion. "The Goddess wants him alive."

The young woman paced back and forward. Her slender shoulders slumped. Neck muscles that were cramped and knotted pushed a throbbing ache deeper into her head. She fought the waterfall of tears that threatened to overwhelm her. Yet the decision was inevitable. "Are the hot knives ready?" Her driver nodded. "Gather him up... gently. Lay him with his arm over that thick branch."

Gràinne did not have the luxury of contemplating the situation. Unable to hold back the tears streaming from golden eyes, she stepped forward. Time seemed to pause. The whisper of a longsword drawn from its scabbard, a cry of bitterness at the inescapable, and the *thunk* as the blade severed Brion's left arm. The smell of seared flesh broke the moment as red-hot daggers cauterised the bloody stump.

Brion's body lifted in a slow spasm, and a groan escaped bloody lips. Emerald eyes opened briefly to hold Gràinne's. They carried no guilt, and yet she felt remorse. "Lay him on the chariot. Unless we can get him to the healers, he may still make the journey to Mag Mell." Sombre chariot teams rumbled through the wildwood and into the old forest.

CHAPTER 15

406 B.C.—Áth

Ualraig rubbed the nape of his neck and slowly rotated his head. In the silence, he detected the crunching sound of bones grating over each other. His ill temper grew in concert with the sun as it rose over the Sleá. Kartimandu had commandeered Áth for her personal use, forbidding all others from the comfort of its stone walls, thatched roofs, and the warmth of its firepits. The queen and her slaves rested within Áth's broch.

Her caomhnóirí stood around the settlement's stockade. Kartimandu's personal guard was a strange battalion. Comprising one thousand of the best warriors, they were uniformly tall and hard-muscled. They fought with unnatural automation and had eyes that matched the colour of the queen's painted skin. They gave Ualraig the willies.

The battle commander's lousy humour was well-founded. There were no tents for shelter. Thus, his warriors lay on the other side of the river with the slaves, smiths, supplies, and camp whores. The plan to transport the supply wagons across the river by the time the sun rose to its zenith was of little consolation. Ualraig had spent the night huddled against Áth's stockade seeking shelter from the wind and the cursed, never-ending mizzle. His bones ached, and his knuckles were painful and slow to function.

Now, Ualraig stood warily on the central rampart of the Clann Ui Flaithimh defences. The defenders had slipped away during the night, leaving a fence of skulls and scattered traps and snares. South of the fortifications, the clans of the High People filled their bellies.

Copious horns of alcohol were guzzled down. The men and women smelt of stale beer and unwashed bodies. Soon tongues would loosen; they would become fractious, and old grievances would surface. If Ualraig waited, they would start arguing with each other. Someone would inevitably kill someone, clanns would fight clanns, and he would lose half his army. It was their nature.

To forestall such a disaster, Ualraig issued his orders. His single-horse chariots, much lighter, but not as solidly built or as fast as the Clann Uí Flaithimh vehicles, scurried around the army, delivering commands to the chieftains. All were left in no doubt as to their fate should they disobey. As a further measure, squads, each containing a score of his trusted men, policed the camp, settling disputes with brutal efficiency.

He slowly turned a full circle to survey the deserted defences. Ignoring the more minor fortifications on the right and left flanks, Ualraig concentrated his deliberations on the central earthworks. The solid ramparts had been engineered with pride, efficiency, and strength.

Midway up their slopes, deep ditches paralleled the wall of rock, wood, and dirt. By themselves, they were formidable barriers. It had several dirt bridges on the southern side, but they were too narrow to allow more than two men to cross. His army would be at the mercy of the cursed Clann Uí Flaithimh's arrows and throwing spears.

Thus, rather than fight, the army of Kartimandu stripped and laboured. Teams cut down trees from the nearby forest and split them with iron spikes and hammers. Others began to fill in the ditches; more began excavating a broad path to breach the rampart. Apart from some skirmishes, there would be no more fighting before the next sunrise. It was doubtful whether Kartimandu would understand the need for the activity. She would not be pleased. Of that, Ualraig was never in doubt.

The sun was high in the sky, although the only clue to this was the presence of a bright aura behind thickening grey clouds. Raucous cheers drew Ualraig's eyes to the front line of the Clann Ui Flaithimh. He watched the Ravens jog from the forest, led by their striking princess and her brother. Several of the Clann Ui Flaithimh embraced the pair and then pointed.

The Cinn Péinteáilte took up a position before the shield wall. Ualraig watched as they stuck spears in the dirt and leaned their small round shields against them. Hands went to waists, and as Ualraig watched, he sighed… slings. Several stones rattled the wooden stockade as they tested the range and adjusted their position.

The archers of Clann Ui Flaithimh stood to the right of the Ravens. Each had several quivers of arrows slung from their belts. More were stabbed into the dirt before them. They selected their victims with care and precision. Cries' from the ramparts told of their skill. Occasionally a flight was launched high, dropping on the vulnerable workers.

To the left of the Ravens, two hundred horses and riders milled around. Occasionally, they charged forward to the edge of the ditch, dismounted, and loosed a hail of arrows. Shrieks of pain and furious curses were the High People's only response.

There was a shouted command. Ualraig watched as the leader of the horse archers walked a pale, golden horse to stand beside the tall, red-haired figure of Fearghal. Ualraig recognised Mórrígan from her ornate helmet with its raven crest and feathers. He shuddered. Tales of the Dark Huntress and her savage riders were well-known, even in Dùn Caen. As Mórrígan bent over the velvet shoulder of her mount, the warrior spoke and pointed to the west.

A perplexed Ualraig watched the riders gallop towards the Abhainn Dubh. The river had returned to its normal state, and its waters churned as the horses entered it. A long whistle pierced the air. From the wheat and barley fields, a grey mist rose up. Ualraig swore as Clann Ui Flaithimh's wolfhounds howled and followed Mórrígan's riders into the river. Ualraig now understood. He called for his hornblower, and several deep blasts sounded out.

A thousand men protected his army's encampment and its stocks of provisions and weapons. Ualraig doubted it would be enough. They were not the best warriors; many were malingerers or the sick. Ualraig had little concern about the hundreds of slaves and whores in the camp. They were expendable. Not even the lithe, young girl who usually warmed his bed entered his calculations of loss. His jaw stiffened, and his teeth ground.

As if sensing Ualraig's dilemma, Clann Ui Flaithimh's army took up their taunting battle chants. On the Sleá, bodhráin thumped out a steady beat. Flag bearers waved banners. In the shadow of the range, two thousand men and women stood in the familiar shield wall formation. Two rows, two paces from each other and each an arm's length from his neighbour. It was their configuration for hurling javelins. Once their supply was exhausted, the ranks would tighten up, and shields would lock to present an unbroken line of crimson and black. Behind them stood another five hundred, a reserve to protect their supply wagons.

Ualraig strained his eyes to little avail as he sought to find a hint of where Drostan's Forest People were concealed. The forests could hide Drostan's ten thousand with ease.

***

His people knew him as a man of extravagant excesses and appetites. This night he had been particularly brutal as he used the young woman to satisfy himself. She winced as she levered herself from his bed and padded unsteadily towards the doorway. In the moonlight, the bruising on her breasts showed black against her porcelain white skin. She could feel the other bruises, some new, many old.

It had been this way since she was fourteen, over ten summers ago. He took others during the night, but she was always the last. She was the only one who could lead him to sleep. She listened briefly to his snores, drew the heavy cloak around her, and returned home.

Votod awoke mid-morning. He gasped in pain, reached out, gripped his ash staff with both hands and hauled himself upwards from his bed of straw and pelts. It was always worse in the mornings. He straightened his back, stretched his arms high over his head, and flexed arm muscles in slow circles.

By any measure, Votod had the appearance of an impressive man. A head taller than his tribe and built like an oak tree, his legs were thick and sturdy, his torso solid and sculpted, and his long arms ended in hands whose vice-like grip could snap a neck with a quick twist.

Sadly, the king of the Votod-Daoine was also a dead man.

The pain doubled him over. It had been getting progressively worse. Blood stained his pee, although that, in itself, was not new to him. He was well-acquainted with fights and hard kicks to the gut. Lately, however, he had noticed the small, red clots when he moved his bowels. Even the act of taking a shite was painful. His da and grand-da had suffered the same curse. His sons would likely inherit it.

No longer able to cope with the pain, his father had slashed his wrists. Votod growled at what he perceived as weakness. In contrast, his grand-da had challenged the best warriors in the tribe to fight to the death. He killed eight before tiredness dulled his reflexes, allowing a spear blade to slip through his defences. Ironically, the blade punched through the growth that had taken over his belly. Thus, before he went to Mag Mell, and, as his guts lay a steaming pile in the dirt, he could appreciate what had killed him.

The Votod-Daoine inhabited the lands between Kartimandu's High People and the southern coastline of the Linne Foirthe. As illustrated by their appellations, the people and their kings lacked a certain amount of imagination. The kings were named Votod, and the tribe was the Votod-Daoine—the People of Votod.

The lowland kingdom was as vast as the Forest and High Peoples, although not as populous. It was defended by three massive hillforts and the kingdom's fleet of ships. Votod's people were skilled shipbuilders, mostly constructing the vessels needed to transport tin ingots, essential in producing bronze, from the mines in the far south of Albu. This made sense. The north of Albu was well forested, whereas the south had been mainly cleared for grain crops and cattle grazing.

Votod pulled on *triubhas*, laced up soft leather boots, grabbed his axe, and strode to the door of his broch and into the morning sunshine. He blinked a few times to adjust his eyes and then marched to the sheltered cove where ships were built and berthed.

Narrow, wooden jetties reached out into the estuary. It was high tide, and two thousand of Votod's best raiders were waiting in boats that rocked gently with the swell or knocked against their moorings.

A roar greeted him as he half-ran, half-walked down the steep, winding path to the harbour. His eyes glinted mischievously. An epic battle would soon be fought on the other side of the Linne Foirthe. To Votod, a raid on the lands of the Na Mèadaidh was the perfect way to immortalise his name in an epic ballad. This was his chance to have a glorious death like his grand-da.

***

"Eachdonn Breac is dead. His son, Gormal, has withdrawn from the alliance. They lost a lot of men at Áth, and the Aos an Eich are vulnerable. Ye should, at the least, consider 'acquiring' the territory. Ye could put our king in place." Failbhe looked at Drostan and Carmag Mac an t-Sionnaich.

Drostan grunted. "It's an opportunity, perhaps. Any news, Carmag?"

"The chariot teams tracking Conall tell me his force should rejoin us on the morrow by meadhan-latha." Carmag paused and continued, "Cúscraid's defences were exceptionally well built. My guess is that it'll take Ualraig the rest of this day to break a path through. The serious fighting will not begin before the next dawn."

"What about Conall's daughters?" Drostan and Carmag had children around the same age as Brighid and Danu.

Carmag's reply was filled with sorrow. "He didn't find them. Something about boats and Kartimandu. The Sídhe and Conall levelled Creag na Clachard in revenge. Slaughtered the garrison to a man."

"I'd have done the same, m'self," said Drostan. "What about

Mórrígan?"

"Fearghal sent her across the river with the hounds."

"Keeps her out of my hair." Then he asked, "Does *she* know about the girls?"

"She does now. One of her riders brought the news earlier."

"Those poor bastards across the river have no idea what is coming to them." Drostan thought for a moment. "The best thing for that woman and Conall would be if she met with an accident." The startled look on Carmag and Failbhe's faces told Drostan his spoken thoughts were perhaps too pointed.

He snorted. "Don't worry. That's one path I won't be going down. Mórrígan's protected and not by flesh and blood. We have enough to contend with without angering the Goddess." The tense moment passed, although the look on Failbhe's face suggested that he agreed with his son's conclusion that Mórrígan needed to die.

Drostan rose, signalling Carmag and Failbhe to go about their duties. He noted Carmag's hesitation. "There's something more?"

"Two things. Votod has crossed the Linne Foirthe. About two thousand of his tribe accompany him."

"A raid?" Carmag dipped his head.

Drostan laughed. "Ever the opportunist, but the family is cursed. If they could stay alive for more than thirty summers, they would be a force to be reckoned with." Drostan scratched his chin. "The timing is a wee bit inconvenient. I'll take five thousand to meet him. I'll suggest that he returns to Dùn Votod. If he disagrees, we'll drive him back into Linne Foirthe.

"What's the second thing?"

"There's a rumour Brion's been badly injured. Might have gone to Mag Mell by now." Drostan's eye misted over. The king of the Forest People had a soft spot for Brion.

"*Ar shlí na fírinne.* If he's gone on the path of truth, I'll deeply regret his passing."

***

Someone with a dark sense of humour named the village *Trócaire*—Mercy. It was smaller than Áth and nestled in a clearing at the foot of the Sleá, in the shadow of the charred ruins of Dùn Na Mèadaidh.

In normal times, Trócaire hummed with activity and the rise and fall of voices as merchants bartered everything from chickens to brightly coloured garments. Small hammers tapped on metal as artisans made and sold beautiful gold and silver jewellery. Warriors favoured thick torcs and armbands. Beautiful pins adorned the lush, red hair of the women. There were brooches strong enough to keep cloaks secure in the wind and rain but which did not forego the intricately beaten and engraved designs loved by the people.

Trócaire was the cultural centre for those who felt that Áth and its Great Hall were too formal a venue for the arts and carousing. It was a rare night if there was no *céilí*. Skilled musicians like Craiftine played to appreciative, if often drunk, audiences. At times *seanchaithe*—storytellers such as Tadhg would step forward and recite epic tales of combat and heroes of myth and legend. Of course, their king, Conall, the Hand of the Goddess, had ballads dedicated to his triumphs.

They were a proud and noble people. Many were tall and pale-skinned with copper-red hair and emerald-green eyes. This was a common misperception of the Gaels from Ériu and northern Albu. The tribes had more blonde or dark hair and blue, brown, or hazel-coloured eyes.

Those blessed with dark hair were able to appreciate the sun better. Their skin darkened by degree rather than flaring red like their blonde or red-haired brothers and sisters. It was a people who had profound paradoxes. While appreciating design, music, and the arts, they were warrior people with quick tempers and long, unforgiving memories. They fought expecting no mercy and gave none.

Trócaire had bowed to the demands of war. Its people retreated to the heights of the Sleá, and the settlement became the headquarters and logistical centre for the upcoming conflict. It was also where the wounded were treated or dispatched to Mag Mell. Healers and druids walked the narrow pathways and contemplated what was to come.

A sombre group gathered around the injured Brion in the circular, stone and wood building that squatted at the centre of Trócaire. The Clann Ui Flaithimh leader lay on a pallet of meadowsweet, straw, and pelts. He was not dead. Whether that was mercy was as yet unclear. Fionnbharr wished that Mongfhionn was with them, but his healers had done all they could in her absence.

Brion was alive only by the whim of the Goddess. Thus, the druids continued their entreaties for healing or a swift journey to Mag Mell. Áine screeched. This was expected. However, the wailing was not that of a distraught lover or partner. Cries of "*Bitseach!*" and "*Striapach!*" were hurled at Gràinne.

It was the third time the insults were flung at the young woman. The first time she burst into tears, for indeed, Gràinne was burdened with guilt for Brion's condition despite the consolation of others. The second time, her eyes lowered to the dirt floor, and her body trembled as she sobbed.

On the third occurrence, Gràinne's eyes lifted and held Áine's. This time her look was grim, if not frightening. Áine flinched and took a step back. She felt a hand on her shoulder as Brocc, her brother by hand-fasting, tried to give succour and restore some calmness. His good intentions were lost on Áine. Unhinged by events, Áine's hand reached for her dagger, and she moved towards Gràinne.

She was stopped in her tracks by the point of Gràinne's sword. Few had heard the longsword unsheathed, but all could see the trickle of blood that flowed down Áine's neck. They wondered how far the blade had penetrated. To their relief, Gràinne took a half-step back and raised the sword diagonally above her right shoulder. Áine had suffered only a slight nick. However, Gràinne's posture made no one doubt that she would take no more insults. All present knew one slash would end

Áine's life.

"Maybe I should kill ye now. Better that than an arrow or dagger in ma back," said Gràinne in her rich burr. Áine stared in helpless rage.

"Enough!" roared Crum Dubh. The druid brushed aside both sword and dagger to stand between the women. "It was an accident. No one is to blame. No one deserves or will be punished."

"Look at him," spat Áine. "He's a… *cripple*." At that moment, any sympathy for Áine dissipated as quickly as the morning mist in a warm sun. She did not notice the change in the atmosphere and continued her tirade. "How will he clothe himself? How will he ride a horse or chariot? He cannot stand in the shield wall. What example will he be to our son?

"What use will he be?"

Taken aback, the Druid started to retort. He was held back by Brocc, who spoke quietly and in a tone mixed with anger and regret. "You bring shame to our family, Áine. Obviously, you do not know my brother at all."

Brocc had lost his best friend, Labhraidh, similarly, and the memory still haunted him. He had no intention of giving up on his older brother. He walked towards the entranceway. Before exiting, he turned to Fionnbharr and said, "Please let me know when my brother awakes."

"You, too, should leave," said Crum to Gràinne. "There is a battle imminent. You have chariots to command." Gràinne glanced at Brion, and the druid smiled, "I will inform you of his progress." In a swift, smooth movement, Gràinne sheathed her longsword and followed in Brocc's footsteps. Áine made to follow but was brought up short when Crum asked, "Where do you think you're going? Brion is your partner by hand-fasting. Your place is by his side. Your vows to each other were not just for better times."

"I can do nothing for him, Druid. My prayer is that he makes the journey to Mag Mell. There, the Goddess will make him whole again."

Crum flinched at Áine's cold words. All knew Áine could be wilful and sharp-tongued but allowed that this was merely the result of her upbringing as a princess. Unlike her brother, Íar, she had not developed an affinity for people. Now her words revealed a shocking callousness.

"Your betrayal stinks. It seeps from your pores," replied Crum. "Brion's spirit is whole and strong. The Goddess has a purpose for him." "As for you…" He stopped and, choosing his words carefully, said, "Consider your path before it is too late."

***

Áine gasped, her face flushed a deep pink, and she rushed out into the daylight. *How did the druid know? It was just one night.* She had drunk more than usual after the skirmish. The young bowman had been persuasive, and she had not felt Brion inside her for many sunsets. The archer's hands swiftly disrobed her, and she moaned as he kissed and kneaded her breasts. She had willingly opened her legs for his manhood, and he had not refused her gift. Áine had not regretted offering her *pit…* until now.

Her escape took her past a campfire, and she spotted her erstwhile lover. He turned and waved, but she ignored him. With a shrug of asymmetrically muscled shoulders, which were common to most archers, he turned back to his friends. They laughed out loud. *The bastard. The bastard has told his friends. How else could the druid have known?* In the fertile soil of guilt, seeds of paranoia took root.

Meanwhile, Crum scratched a stubbled chin. He was deeply perturbed as he watched Áine rush away. His words, meant as a reminder of her hand-fasting vows, appeared to have struck a dissonant chord.

***

After sharing a meal at the fishing village, Urard regretfully declined the offer of a roof and bed for him and his men. Instead, they filled their water pouches, made their apologies, and rode through the night. It was mid-day when Urard trotted into Conall's camp. Eager to hear any news, Conall strode across the field and clasped Urard's arms.

Urard repeated what the elder at the fishing village had told him. He nodded in the direction of Iasg, who was rocking nervously from one foot to the other while deep green eyes watched and took in all around.

Conall summoned Íar. "Choose a hundred riders to accompany Urard. He'll be leaving to find and return Brighid and Danu to us. It will be a long and hazardous journey, so choose well."

When Conall had finished, there was a tap on Urard's shoulder. "These belong to the girls." In Nikandros' hands were the blades he had fashioned for Brighid and Danu. Urard nodded and took the swords, slipping them into his belt.

"They will receive them. You have my word."

Iasg grew more anxious as the leaders of the clann talked. Used to living in a small, closely-knit fishing community, there were few dealings with kings and nobles. Any contact often ended in rape for the women and a beating for the men. She watched Conall break from the group and walk towards her. He offered thanks for her help; Iasg's response was lowered eyes, mumbled words, and a clumsy attempt at a bow.

However, if Conall made Iasg nervous, the Sídhe's presence terrified her. As if knowing Iasg's thoughts, the Sídhe said, "I'm not so dreadful... to my friends."

Iasg jumped, startled by the sudden appearance of Mongfhionn. The Sídhe stood back a pace, and her eyes narrowed as she inspected Iasg from head to toe. A smile lifted the ends of full, ruby-red lips, "Your father is quite clever, but I think before you ride off with Urard and a hundred men, you should be honest with him."

"I don't know what ye mean," stammered Iasg, now aware of the curious looks from the others.

"Let me ask you one question first. Are you, in truth, a good guide?"

"I am. There's none better," said Iasg. This time with more confidence and a chin that spoke of defiance.

"Then, being a woman should not change that."

A stunned silence followed Mongfhionn's announcement. Conall, Íar, Nikandros, and Urard moved closer and looked at Iasg with a mix of concern and amusement. "Remove that ridiculous cap. I suspect there's a full head of hair under it. How you can breathe with the binding around your breasts is an astonishing feat," said Mongfhionn.

"Well?" It was Conall who spoke.

Iasg flushed deeply and removed the hat and pins. Dark, nut-brown hair with blond highlights, a gift from constant work in the sun, fell over Iasg's shoulders. The shoulders seemed narrower. Her face was subtly feminine with high cheeks and lips that could not make up their mind whether to pout or thin into a sharp retort.

A peal of laughter from Nikandros made Iasg redden, this time with anger. He slapped Urard on his broad shoulders. "Really observant, big man," Urard growled at the Spartan, who added, "Are we going to watch as 'he' removes the binding, so we're sure?"

At a glare from Mongfhionn and the sight of Urard's fists, the Spartan raised his hands, but not before a parting shot. "They can't be that big with all that binding."

This time the stare was from Iasg, who snapped, "Ma tits are big enough for any man, but ye'll never get yer hands on them."

"What age are you, girl?" asked Conall.

"Seventeen summers."

"More like fifteen, I think," said Conall. "The life of my daughters is in Urard's hands. His life may be in yours. Can I trust you?"

Iasg nodded. "The only one who knows the estuaries and coastline better is my da. I've sailed them since I could walk and steered our boats through their waters."

"Then I suggest you change into more appropriate and less restrictive clothing. Enough time has been wasted." Conall paused. "You should apologise to Urard." Iasg's eyes met Urard's with some discomfort, but she was rewarded with a glimmer of a smile. The bluff warrior was not one to hold a grudge. "Do you carry a weapon? Can you use a weapon?"

Conall's words brought a frown to Iasg's face. "I've not needed a sword, axe, or spear." She thought momentarily, adding, "I know how to filet a fish, and I'm good at throwing a knife. It was how we entertained ourselves."

"Find Iasg a baldric and throwing knives if their owners will give them up. Fetch two of the smaller axes for her belt. Fists will not be much use when you've thrown all your knives." Conall looked at Mongfhionn. "Perhaps you could help with the clothes? And she'll need riding armour... at least the breastplate."

Urard's warband rode from the camp a short time later. As they cantered by, Nikandros laughed and said, "I wish I'd got my hands on her tits." Mongfhionn shook her head in exasperation.

CHAPTER 16

406 B.C.—Abhainn Dubh

The Abhainn Dubh coiled and twisted from the tip of the Sleá to the Linne Foirthe and finally to the sea. It was a shallow, slow-moving tidal river, teeming with silver-scaled, pink-fleshed fish that thrived in the brackish waters. Muddy banks rose up steeply from the water. A tangled skein of roots sprouted from the brown-black dirt providing shelter for the river's fish and a snare for the unwary.

Shaggy bushes and brambles bearded the water's edge. Masses of creamy-white blossoms from thorn bushes relieved the monotony of green and brown. They were a pleasant sight, contrasting with the blackish bark of the blackthorn whose glorious flowering had just passed. A delight to look on, yet the bushes' stiff spines were more than capable of tearing flesh.

Adjacent to the crofts peppering the river plain, the profusion of flora had been hacked back to allow access to the river for farmers and cattle. Once vibrant and productive, the farms smouldered, victims of the enemy's malicious vandalism. The river paths, however, remained intact, and it was to these that the Huntress' riders guided their mounts.

The High People's camp stretched as far as the eye could see. It was a motley collection of shelters ranging from the relatively luxurious, tented enclosures of the nobles and chieftains to structures with little more than four sticks and a scrap of hide. Curls of smoke from hundreds of fires rose lazily into a summer sky that always held the threat of rain.

Soft-leather boots cross-laced to the top of her calves overlapped Mórrígan's plaid pants. Her horse nickered, not minding the imposition of the boots against its flanks but reminding Mórrígan that a few slices of winter-sweetened parsnips were the price of its tolerance.

No perimeter fence or ditch protected the camp. There was no sign of guards, although they were probably clustered around the pavilions of the leaders. Warning blasts from Ualraig's horns in the distance prompted little activity. Mórrígan suspected that the civilians did not understand the signal. As for the guards, they were likely rutting the camp whores or, for the more parsimonious, the slaves.

Mórrígan settled on the diallait covering her mount's back. The thick blanket was deep green with gold fringing. It was a present from Íar, yet the queen of Clann Uí Flaithimh would have gladly paid her weight in gold for it. No more was her arse a perpetual riot of colour after a long ride.

She stirred from her reverie and looked pointedly at the dog handler who accompanied her band. A series of piercing whistles roused the hounds, and they sped towards the camp. Their barking would alert the encampment, but it would be too late by that time.

Beyond the river but distant from the enemy camp, a cluster of farm buildings perched on a natural hillock. They held a good position overlooking neat grain fields and lush meadows where cattle would graze. The roundhouses and the dry stone wall surrounding them were well maintained.

The farmer obviously took immense pride in his labour. Yet vanity blinded him to the necessity to flee and condemned his family. As Mórrígan approached, three semi-naked men scrambled from the central roundhouse, pursued by wolfhounds who snapped at their pale, scabby arses. The men abruptly halted at the sight of the riders, and the javelins pointed at them.

At a nod from Mórrígan, several riders dismounted and entered the home. Moments later, they emerged. Their faces were grim with unconcealed anger, and their bróga stained red. Between them, they escorted a shell of a woman. The brat draped over her shoulder struggled to cover her nakedness.

Bald patches on her head bore witness to how, in her anguish, she had ripped tresses of apple-red hair from her skull. Her jaw hung slack, broken; bloody drool flowed from a toothless mouth. Arms, limp and useless, dangled by her side, the circlet of bruising and outline of bones pushing at her skin told the story.

Once proud breasts that fed her children and gave her mate pleasure sagged. Constant battering had left them mottled blue, green, and purple. Her misery had lasted for several sunsets. Blood and fluids from countless penetrations flowed down her thighs, pooling below her ankles.

Eyes filled with torment and pleading looked up at Mórrígan. The Huntress dismounted and embraced the woman, gasping as the wretch's pain touched her. "Family?" she asked, looking over the woman's shoulder. The older man nodded.

"Four: her mate, two young daughters and a baby boy." The man paused. "They were too far gone. They'd been used by more than these three *heroes*." He spat at Ualraig's men. "We sent them to Tír Tairngire." The memory of the look in one of the girls' eyes, opening for one final time as he slit her throat, troubled the younger of the two men. Unable to hold his bile, he walked away.

Tears flowed down Mórrígan's cheeks as she whispered to the mother, "Your grief will always be with me. The Goddess will take you to join your family." The long blade slipped between the woman's ribs, piercing a heart that was already dead. The escort took the corpse from Mórrígan arms.

A hundred images of how she would punish the captured men flooded Mórrígan's mind. Each was more cruel and painful than the last. Yet they gave her no satisfaction. She focused. She had little time. The camp had been alerted. Her eyes hardened as she glanced down at the bloody stain on her tunic. Mórrígan pointed to the wooden outbuilding.

Straw was scattered in the dirt at its entrance; cut logs and bricks of peat were stacked high against its walls. "Wrap the bodies and lay them in the hut."

Reluctantly she forced her attention back to the assailants and, in a voice made terrible by its calmness, said, "Cut off their cocks. Bind them and throw them into the building along with their victims. Barricade the entrance. Make sure there is enough kindling to burn everything inside to ash."

The violators screamed for mercy, but just as they had ignored the family's cries, their pleadings fell on deaf ears.

***

Ships' bows crunched reassuringly on stones smoothed by wind and sea. Men jumped into foaming waters as the vessels came to a halt, bobbing on the waves of an inflowing tide. They splashed and waded to the beach carrying thick, wooden stakes. The sound of hammering was loud and brief. Shouts followed it, and thick ropes were hurled from each ship. Caught with casual ease, they were quickly looped around the stakes and tied off. No one wanted the embarrassment of watching their ship float away.

It was high tide, meaning the shoreline was narrow and rocky. An almost vertical dirt bank constrained the beach, but beyond the bank lay gentle, grass-covered hills with thick forests in the distance. Fortunately, the embankment was just the height of a man, and the second group were able to use the backs of their comrades as a platform to clamber up. Once on the firm ground, they constructed a fence from more stakes.

The joints of Votod's hands and legs cracked, causing his shield-man to wince. The king paced along the perimeter fence, letting his legs adjust to being on land. Naturally impulsive, Votod's thinking had not gone much beyond fighting to a glorious death.

From a practical perspective, he needed to find opportunistic targets to satisfy his army's desire for plunder and mayhem. He did not care much whether the spoils were gold or slaves, who were as good as gold.

Votod was astute enough to lead his band in a north-eastern direction, away from the Abhainn Dubh.

The sound of chanting drew Votod to a clearing in the middle of the ancient forest. Before him was a shallow, nearly circular ditch. On its outer edge, an earthen bank rose up. Higher than an average-sized man, the rampart partially concealed the view of the inside. Thus it gave a measure of privacy to any activities within.

Two tall upright stones guarded the west-facing entrance of the circle. Curious and with axe in hand, Votod crossed the causeway, bridging the ditch. The hair on the back of his neck stood on end as he passed the sentinel stones. Both resonated with the essence of countless primaeval souls.

Inside were two concentric stone circles standing on a flat, grass-covered mound. Each ring comprised thirty-three stones. The diameter of the inner circle was thirty-three paces. Irregular in shape, the rocks were as tall as Votod but at least twice his girth.

At the centre, a rectangular mound of dirt had been uncovered. *Its size was enough to contain a body or perhaps a treasure chest.* That it was surrounded by thirty-three druids cloaked in black convinced Votod that something of real value was hidden in the earth.

The druids turned to face Votod and his men. "Leave this hallowed place," said one who stood apart. "It holds nothing good for you."

"I've heard that many times, druid," said Votod. "More times than enough, it proved false. Stand aside." The druids quietly formed two ranks behind their leader and continued their incantations. Votod turned to his men. "Tie them to their stones while we unearth the treasure they protect."

In the remaining time before sunset, Votod's men dug up the pit at the centre of the stone circle. They were disappointed. It contained the skeleton of a young man holding a flint knife. Infuriated, they turned their anger on the druids, stripping them of their garments and cutting them with blades. As the druids' blood stained the stones, others searched the site, finding only smaller pits containing memories of past people but nothing of value.

Furious, the younger among the raiding party fell on the druids. The lucky were disembowelled and left to bleed to death. Others had their genitals mutilated and eventually sliced off. Perhaps, in recognition that being visited by angry druidic spirits would not be a pleasant experience, the priests were beheaded, but only after they were abused.

Campfires threw showers of embers into the night sky. The young slaked their thirst for blood with the beer they carried. The veterans and the more religiously minded prayed for mercy to their gods while glancing nervously at the headless corpses. The druids were some god's followers. He or she would not be amused at the slaughter. A troubled army settled down to sleep by the fires.

Votod woke with a start, dagger in hand and sweating profusely in the chill of the night. The camp was quiet, and the fires had fallen to a black and ash-grey crust. Only the smell of wood smoke marked their presence. Votod stood. His senses told him that all was not as it should be, so his stance remained guarded.

It was not that his eyes had become used to the darkness or that the clouds fled the sky to reveal a pale three-quarter moon. It was more the simultaneous appearance of the spirits. Before each stone stood an opaque, silver-white apparition. Each was illuminated from within by a diffuse bluish light. Behind them, blood-drenched pillars glistened liquid-black in the moonlight. The wraiths made no sound. They merely watched and counted. Every warrior within the stone circle was noted. When the task was completed, the spectres receded into the stones.

Votod shuddered. He looked around and wondered why no one had witnessed the strange apparitions. Around the camp, bodies lay covered in brats, undisturbed in their sleep. He shook his head and turned to lie down. It took him several moments to realise that the body already asleep in his place was his.

Dawn broke. The sun crept upwards, suffusing the clouds with a pink and yellow glow. Early morning birds began their song, and animals stirred in dens and burrows. A rough tug at his shoulder roused Votod. "Are ye going to sleep all day?" It was his incorrigible friend, and shield-man, proffering a horn of hot, honeyed beer. "Get this in yer belly. It'll take the night's chill away."

Votod muttered a muted "Thanks" as he regarded the standing stones. The headless bodies of the druids still clung to the rocks. "Cut those bloody corpses down and bury them," he shouted. His friend gazed curiously at his king.

***

It was a chilling mimicry. Above, flocks of ravens soared, glided, and tumbled in a sweeping aerial ballet. Below, on the verdant green, the riders of the Dark Huntress swept through Kartimandu's camp with a merciless elegance. Had the camp guards been in one or two large groups, they would have taken longer to die. However, they were in a score of small groups and incapable of withstanding the concerted onslaught of hounds and horses.

Pushed effortlessly aside by broad shoulders, the High People were assailed by bony hoofs. Chests and skulls were crushed or cracked open. Faces were bitten to the bone by grass-stained teeth. Ivory hoofs were soon stained red and covered with the gore that burst from broken bodies.

The wolfhounds were not to be left out. Blood-covered snouts and strings of muscle and skin caught in razor-sharp teeth told their story as the pack roamed the camp, bringing down man, woman, child, and beast. The animals had the day.

Indeed, the blades of the riders were barely wet. A few brave guards challenged them, but the numbers were not in their favour, and Mórrígan's instructions had been unambiguous. Destroy the warriors quickly and efficiently. Thus, her band had little to do but strip the bodies of valuables and, where needed, deliver a final stab to end the suffering. Mórrígan watched as small groups of camp followers and slaves fled to the south and west. Those that survived the forests and mountains would spread tales of terror and savagery. It was the only reason they were allowed to live.

At Mórrígan's command, the hounds' master recalled the pack. Together with her riders, she surveyed the shattered camp. Gritty smoke, black with charred camp debris, smudged the sky. The air was infused with the smell of roasted flesh. Numerous fires discouraged scavengers from feasting on the dead or nearly dead, though this would not last long. The ravens would descend, and the echoes of their throaty *kraa kraa* would fill the river plain. When dusk fell, silver-grey shapes with yellow eyes would emerge from the forests.

Mórrígan removed her helmet and shook her hair free. Her long hair was dark with sweat, and she was grateful for the breeze that swept away the stale smell. She looked north towards the crossing at Áth and smiled at her brothers. Beacán and Bricriu mouthed a silent "No," but shortly after, they were cantering beside their sister.

From the rampart, Ualraig watched the destruction of the army's camp and supplies with conflicting emotions of anger and professional admiration. He grumped at having to spend another night under the sky while Kartimandu and her entourage shared the dry, warm environs of Áth. His interest perked up as he watched Mórrígan's wolfhounds use powerful legs to bound back to the river and safety. His curiosity continued when, rather than following the hounds, Mórrígan's troop galloped north.

Slightly south of the crossing at Áth, the lay of the land gave the riders a good perspective of the settlement. Mórrígan barked out instructions. Her cavalry dismounted and slid their bows from their backs. Each stabbed a quiver of arrows into the soft dirt. Several additional shafts were laid on the ground. Wisps of white smoke rose up behind the cavalry.

In Áth, Kartimandu's elite looked on with mounting interest. The main army laboured to tear down the Clann Ui Flaithimh defences.

Hence there was no one to guard Áth should her caomhnóirí choose to attack the riders. So they stood their ground. A few braver members walked to Áth's broch, bowed, and entered. Presently, they were followed out by a plainly irritated Kartimandu.

Mórrígan smiled as she dipped an arrow into the small fire. Below the arrowhead, the oil-soaked cloth flared up. She nocked the shaft, pulled the bowstring back and released the missile. Accompanied by two hundred others, the missiles left ghostly trails in the early evening sky. Two more flights followed them before the warband turned to its more traditional projectiles.

Smouldering fires in Áth burst into flames. The ongoing hail of arrows that followed prevented any but the foolish from attempting to douse the many blazes that erupted from timbers and thatched roofs. Men held shields up and cowered in the shadows of Áth's stone walls for protection. They could do little else.

Kartimandu quivered with rage at the audacity of the onslaught, yet she was helpless. The iron arrowheads that rained down threatened her immortality. She shivered and, with a thought, replaced another member of her human shield. They were disposable; she was not. In her mind, she heard the taunting laughter of the Huntress. For the first time, Kartimandu knew fear.

Ualraig allowed himself a smile of satisfaction. He would not be the only one to sleep on the damp ground or to wake up in clothes wet from the constant mizzle. In his head, he could hear Kartimandu scream.

***

"Good of them to pick a nice open space to fight." Drostan looked from the cover of the forest across to the stone circle. With professional disgust, he noted the lack of camp sentries and defences. For once, he wished his brother, Crum, was with him. You could never tell what mischief gods and druids might create at one of their holy shrines. This one was strange. A single entrance and the perimeter ditch were not substantial barriers to a half-determined attacker.

Votod had brought about two thousand with him. In normal circumstances, that was a good-sized raiding band. Nearly half were within the grounds of the stone circle. The rest, located on the western side, were stirring from their night's sleep. Drostan, needing a quick resolution, was in no mood to be generous. Behind him, at the edge of the forest, stood five thousand warriors. They were arrayed in a rough semi-circle facing Votod's army.

"Go back to yer lands and hillforts, Votod." Drostan's deep voice boomed as he stepped into the clearing and placed himself opposite the causeway. He was an impressive man, tall, red-haired, and well-muscled. His body bore the marks of many battles, and his face had a fierce look forged by the long scar from his forehead to his chin. That he had but one amber eye added to his menace.

A roar of laughter greeted Drostan as Votod strode across the causeway, stopping at its end. "My friend, it's a glorious day for fighting. Let's ye and I start."

"When I kill ye, will yer men go home?" asked Drostan.

"Probably not. They're an unruly lot. Ye could offer them gold or slaves. They might go home then."

Drostan sighed. "I have nae time for this. Go or die." He turned his back on Votod and started to walk back to the forest edge. It was a calculated insult. Not the most stable of kings and yearning for a hero's death, Votod cursed the departing king of the Forest People. The king's frustration flowed like water off Drostan's scarred back.

Finally, Votod shouted, "Gold and cattle for the man who brings me the head of Drostan Ruadh." There was a short pause, followed by loud cheering as the Votod-Daoine roused themselves and charged. Drostan allowed himself a crooked smile before diving to the ground.

With slings loaded, a thousand of his men stepped from the cover of the forest and loosed the first volley of stones. The thrum of displaced air was brief. The impact of rock and lead was traumatic. Many staggered, bleeding from head wounds. The second and third volleys scythed them down like summer hay.

Drostan stood, surveyed the theatre, and shouted, "Kill the bastards." War horns reverberated throughout the forest as the might of the Forest People charged. The purpose of the standing stone circle was spiritual and cultural. Its perimeter rampart and ditch were designed for privacy, not defence. The embankment was too low and had a gentle incline; the trench was shallow and not populated with stakes, iron thistles or even random thorn bushes.

With a tremendous roar, the Drostan's warriors swept through the marauders outside the ring, cleaving heads and hamstringing legs. Men and women were impaled on leaf-shaped spearheads. Soon, Drostan's force was within the stone circle.

Inside the confined space, the fighting slowed as individuals fought toe-to-toe. Blood splattered, body parts littered the dirt, and the scene took on a lurid red hue. The Votod-Daoine fought stubbornly but were outnumbered. The fighting lulled as a small remnant of the Votod's band fell back, forming a small circle around their king.

"Honour and glory, Drostan," shouted Votod from the centre of his men. "Where's your honour?" Drostan looked at the standing stones, taking in the dried splashes of blood and the desecrated corpses of the druids.

"Ye talk about honour after this," said Drostan, gesturing at the dead druids. "Ye'r a stupid bastard, Votod. Ye leave me no room for mercy." The Forest People's king turned to his shield-man, "Kill them all, save Votod. I want him alive."

***

Votod knelt, bound, and guarded. He watched as Drostan's men walked around the stone circle. Sharp cries rang out as an axe or spear finished off another of his men. His gaze looked along the line of the causeway to observe the fate of his men beyond the circle. They fared no better. The severely injured were given a mercy blade. The remaining who could walk unaided or with a comrade's help were bound and lined up. A life of slavery awaited.

"Fight me, Drostan," Votod pleaded one more time.

Drostan spat on the ground. "There will be no glory for ye. Nae glorious arrival in Mag Mell. For this…" Drostan's hand swept around the blood-stained stones, "Ye'll be lucky if the Otherworld takes ye." Drostan turned to his men. "Stake him. Let the spirits decide his fate."

Votod screamed as a stake was driven into his arse, leaving a forearm's length of wood jutting from the flesh. Then, he was lifted up and dropped into a hole that snuggly fitted the stake's butt. He shrieked at the sharp pain. The stake ripped through his insides but skirted his heart, so he lived. He breathed in short, laboured pants. Surrounded by his dead, Votod screamed as Drostan departed.

As dusk fell, the spectres of the druids appeared. He pleaded for mercy, but they, too, turned away. A short while later, he felt a sharp tug on his pants. He looked up and saw a pair of golden-yellow eyes that seemed to glow white in the moonlight. Hot breath that stank of raw meat wafted across his face. Long strings of drool dripped onto his face and chest. The rows of sharp teeth as the wolf slavered were mesmerising.

Votod was admiring the magnificent beast when another padded behind him and ripped a chunk of flesh from his shoulder. Others fed on his thickly muscled chest, arms, and legs. Votod screamed; his cries ended when one wolf tore out his throat. After that, he suffered in silence until his final breath.

Votod was a good meal, and the wolves savoured the meat. Yet they avoided his belly. Perhaps they sensed his disease and wanted none of it.

***

"Yer Goddess must favour ye," said Iasg, admiring the row of ships stranded on the sand and mud flats of the Linne Foirthe. The tide was out. Thus, even had the ships' captains wanted to flee, there was no opportunity. The Votod-Daoine sailors shared anxious looks as they gazed upon the line of riders that suddenly appeared on the crest of the bank bordering the beach. The pitiful and somewhat resentful small guard that Votod left to defend the seamen took to their heels as soon as they sighted the riders.

Urard studied the scene before him and looked across the estuary. He groaned. First, he had to get used to travelling by horse; now, his stomach turned over several times as he contemplated another sea journey. Iasg took Urard's silence as an opportunity for comment.

"I know where we could sell these ships. They'd fetch a good price in gold."

At that, the ears of the closest riders pricked up. Rumbles of "No harm in making a wee profit" flowed through the band.

A shake of Urard's head halted their embryonic dreams of wealth and whores. "We take what we need. Leave the rest." With a collective sigh, the riders guided their mounts over the grassy lip and to the ships. Once they were promised their freedom in exchange for steering the vessels to the other side of the Linne Foirthe, it was not difficult to recruit the sailors. Iasg knew of a sheltered cove that they could make before dark. Orders were issued, and the boats slid into the water.

***

Coireall was surprised by the ships that crossed the estuary. Shipping traffic was rarely this heavy. Instinct told him he should avoid contact, so he navigated a path away from the flotilla. He was unlikely to be seen or pursued in the dusk light.

The boat's motion on the gentle swell had lulled the already tired Brighid and Danu into sleep. They breathed a word as if dreaming. "Urard."

CHAPTER 17

406 B.C.—Trócaire

The ancient oak shook violently, scattering leaves and branches to the forest floor. Two magnificent birds more ancient than the tree launched dark-brown bodies into the morning sky. Mighty wings, each spanning six hands, pummelled the air as the eagles broke through the leafy canopy. Shafts of sunlight highlighted the raptors' golden-amber neck feathers as their flight took them high into the powder blue sky.

Far above the land, the eagles soared. They circled and glided effortlessly, watching with bright, amber eyes as the humans prepared for war. The Goddess breathed deeply, relishing the fresh air. This was her favourite physical form. Alongside her, Fate's eyes flickered rapidly, taking inventory of the tiny figures scurrying below. The Goddess smiled. It would be a fascinating contest in the skies as well as on the earth.

Trócaire hosted an early morning meeting of senior commanders. Fortified with warm, honeyed beer and bowls of steaming hot oatmeal infused with berries, pine, and hazelnuts, they considered what the day might hold.

Mórrígan, the only female present, was, at twenty-three summers, also the youngest. Brandubh, at twenty-six, was the closest to her age. The rest of the group—Fearghal, Cúscraid, Crum Dubh and Carmag ranged from thirty-three to thirty-eight summers. Regardless of age, all bore the scars and some the silver-grey hairs of experience.

Fearghal scratched his scalp in frustration. "So... Gormal has taken the Aos an Eich home. We've lost one of our ceannairí na míle to a stupid accident. Drostan has taken half of his men to fight a Votod-Daoine raiding party. And, excepting Mórrígan's two hundred, we have no cavalry.

"The Sídhe is the Hag knows where and a slip of a girl with little experience has assumed command of our chariots. Have I missed anything?" The grizzled warrior paused and, before anyone could speak, said, "Oh yes. As soon as dawn breaks, we'll have about thirty thousand bastards led by a crazed, green demi-goddess slavering at us. If their blades don't kill us, their body odour and bad breath will."

"Could be worse."

Everyone looked incredulously at Cúscraid. He smirked. "If Sárán had his way, we'd have to queue up and sign for our weapons in triplicate... and blood."

Fearghal growled, "Yes, he only requests a bloody thumbprint in times of war." Unable to hold back fits of laughter, the tension in the roundhouse eased. "You all know what you have to do. We'll meet later here—or in Mag Mell.

"*Ní ghéillfear, nó cúlú...* No retreat, no surrender."

As one, the group reached out fists to touch each other's knuckles, repeating Fearghal's final command, "*Ní ghéillfear, nó cúlú.*"

***

Ualraig's army was tired, covered in mud after clawing through the Clann Ui Flaithimh defences from sunrise to sunset, and very irritable. Given a choice, Ualraig would have opened the beer barrels, set the remaining cattle and pigs over the firepits, and rested the men for another sunset.

However, Kartimandu was practically foaming at the mouth after Mórrígan had set Áth alight, depriving her of dry and comfortable accommodation. The queen made it clear that if the army did not engage, she would be looking for a new general. The look of relish on her face as she made her pronouncement left Ualraig in little doubt that his resignation would be long and painful.

From his vantage point on the huge mound of dirt, Ualraig sent final orders to the nobles and chieftains. Before him, the battlefield was mainly open ground with a smattering of smaller hills. Ualraig's plan was straightforward. Send the inexperienced, the drunk, and the glory-hunters to bridge and cross the final ditches.

The ones who survived the slings and arrows of Clann Ui Flaithimh would likely be slaughtered on the shield-wall. However, they would provide time for the veterans and Ualraig's elite to cross largely unscathed. At that time, the real battle would begin. In Ualraig's mind, he could sacrifice half of his army and still win.

***

The citizens of Clann Ui Flaithimh and the Forest People massed on the summit of the Sleá. The air was filled with the thumping of hundreds of bodhráin. Thousands of sticks and utensils beat against giant cooking cauldrons, pots, and pans. Banners flapped in the stiff breeze.

Those too young to fight joined with the old in singing and shouting tribal chants. Ancient curses were hurled at the enemy. The sound rode on the morning breeze, entreating those still not present to urge their mounts or increase the length of their steps.

In the forests below the charred ruins of Dùn Na Mèadaidh, Carmag was kept fully informed by a constant flow of runners. He cut an impressive figure. Tall and with a girth that suggested he was fond of his food, Carmag had a presence that radiated "do not mess with me." The chieftain fought with a hammer. It was, in effect, a big lump of iron on a stick. He could not recall why or when this began. He just knew it felt comfortable. It had always felt comfortable.

Carmag rested one hand on the butt end of the hammer's shaft. With the other, he tugged at a shaggy, rust-red beard. It was braided into four tresses and rested on his upper chest. The ends of a full moustache were twisted and tied with leather thongs. In a mêlée, his hair was tied back into a messy but serviceable ponytail.

Beards were common among the Celts. It was principally the

nobles, chieftains, and *flaith-fine* or those who favoured tattoos and tribal designs, who persisted in shaving their faces. Many kept small blades with extremely sharp edges for the sole purpose of shaving. The sight of bleeding faces and the noise of loud curses in the mornings were commonplace.

Some tried to fashion face and head hair into patterns or only shave specific areas. Mostly this was a disaster. Others spiked their hair with lime wash, beeswax, and pine resin. If they had a friend or a woman, they would be called upon to trim the peacock's glory. As a young man, Carmag had let his beard grow. Now, the pain and inconvenience of shaving had removed any incentive to be clean-shaven.

***

Eirnín Mac Gabhann looked around the settlement of Trócaire, which was a hive of activity. Twenty-one summers old, Eirnín lived in the shadow of his older brother, Conall. He often felt aggrieved, believing he deserved more respect. It aggravated him that while he constantly demanded more responsibility, Conall appeared to give him tasks that kept him out of harm's way—until now. *What had changed his brother's mind?*

Unexpectedly charged with the defence of Trócaire, Eirnín shivered with apprehension and wished he had kept his mouth shut. His command comprised five hundred Clann Ui Flaithimh shield-warriors and a few handfuls of archers and slingers.

Kartimandu's army totalled thirty thousand. To Eirnín, it took no great stretch of the imagination to project that a good proportion would eventually direct their attention towards Trócaire. As he conducted a final inspection of the settlement, Eirnín took solace in the veteran ceannairí céad that supported him.

The fiery-haired Deaglán Ó Néill relished battles and spent his free time honing his skills and undoubted flair for swordplay. The slim, fair-haired Fionnbharr Ó Cuileannáin wanted to be a healer. Fionnbharr had amassed a wealth of knowledge from the Sídhe and found much more satisfaction in healing than in warfare. Yet he was a veteran warrior, too.

The chants of druids drew Eirnín's attention uneasily to his priestly cohort. Led by the sallow-complexioned Crum Dubh, the druids provided a spiritual barrier against the High People's queen. Crum made it plain he did not like mingling swordplay and sanctity. However, according to Fearghal and Cúscraid, the druids were well-skilled in using the swords that hung on their belts.

Finally, there was Sárán. The gangly quartermaster knew his limitations. He was good at organisation but, unlike many of his friends, was not overly enamoured with fighting. Sárán was a head taller than most of the army, with a shock of short, blond-red hair. That, and his love of bright orange clothing, meant he was instantly recognisable by the enemy.

"Shite, Sárán. You'll be the death of us. Stop growing and wear other colours," called out the men around him. He smiled, knowing that this was precisely why the men kept close to him. He was the guarantor of a good fight.

***

Fearghal stood with Cúscraid before the shield-wall. Both peered at the ruined ramparts and ditches. Cúscraid grunted in disgust. "That could have been Albu's Black Pig's Dyke." He referred to the colossal earthworks that separated the kingdom of the Ulaid from the rest of Ériu's tribes.

"I could have been famous." Fearghal snorted and looked at Cúscraid. Sometimes it was difficult to tell whether his friend was serious or jesting. Five hundred paces south of the mountain of dirt that had replaced Cúscraid's well-engineered defences stood the shield-wall of two thousand men.

The double row of warriors stood in a loose formation. Once their javelins were exhausted, the rows would tighten up. Either way, the human wall was broad enough to block the path of the Kartimandu's horde. The enemy had no choice but confrontation.

Áine's archers, one hundred skilled bowmen and women, stood before the wall. It had taken a long time for archers to be accepted into the

Clann Uí Flaithimh ranks. Now, Fearghal wished he had double or triple their numbers. He looked on approvingly as Áine walked up and down the line, ensuring all were prepared with extra bowstrings. Arrows were stabbed into the ground; full quivers hung from belt loops. Nevertheless, Fearghal considered Áine's prowess an inadequate compensation for her treatment of Brion.

On each of the wall's flanks, Fearghal positioned five hundred spearmen led by Brandubh and Mòrag. Naked, unless you counted the intricate paint and tattoos that covered their bodies, the Ravens took up a tribal chant, matching the beat of spears on shields with feet that stamped hard on the dirt.

Like the shield-wall, they formed up in two rows. Once the onslaught commenced, the Ravens' first line would kneel with spear butts rammed into the ground and the spear tips at waist level. The rear rank would ready slings. The land between them and the ramparts was clear of trees and shrubs and a perfect killing ground for the simple yet deadly weapon.

Five hundred paces south, on his left flank, Mórrígan's band stood beside their horses with bows ready. Not far from them, Gràinne and her chariots waited. Their job was to discourage the enemy from breaking away and outflanking the shield-wall.

Fearghal sighed. "We are too few."

"We're always too few," replied Cúscraid. "It's why our opponents always think they have a chance. Otherwise, they'd just run away and leave us be."

"*Bollocks!*"

The repartee ceased when a war horn blast reverberated behind Ualraig's lines. For a fraction of time, no longer than the snap of a finger against the thumb, there was total silence. Then, like water bursting from a crack in a dam, the High People gushed from the ruined earthworks.

They scrambled like ants over mounds of soft, damp dirt; charged through the considerable gap excavated in the embankment; and threw split logs across the ditches separating them from their foes. The noise level on each side quickly reached a crescendo.

The defence began with Fearghal's deep-throated shout, "Archers and slingers!" Arrows arched high in the air, falling indiscriminately on the attackers. Eyes were plucked from the curious, unable to resist the instinct to look upwards at the humming, black cloud. There was no escape, for few had shields. Even fewer wore armour. In the sky, Fate and the Goddess dipped and glided on warm updrafts, arguing with piercing shrieks which were the winners and losers of this lottery.

In contrast to the bowmen, the slingers kept a low trajectory as they hurled a hail of stones and iron at the rushing tidal wave. Comrades stumbled over comrades. They fell to their knees, grasping heads as slugs of metal and rock made a bloody mess of unfriendly faces. Bones in limbs cracked and shattered, leaving off-white shards exposed to the summer air. Hit by multiple slugs, some twisted and were flung aside. With no chest armour and little by way of clothing, the projectiles left angry red weals that masked inner traumas.

Ualraig watched as his front ranks were scourged with ruthless efficiency. Soon, the ground was littered with the broken and the dead. The attackers' horns continued to sound the attack. Chieftains kicked, shoved, and cajoled the reluctant forward. The assault advanced closer to the red and black shields of Clann Ui Flaithimh. "Numbers," repeated Ualraig like a litany. "I have the numbers to grind the bastards down."

At Ualraig's signal, a war horn blasted out a different pattern of notes. Five thousand on his right flank broke from the main body, bypassing Fearghal's forces. Their destination was Trócaire.

***

A weakness of Kartimandu was her inability to prioritise strategic tasks over personal feelings. Even though her army had engaged in the greatest conflict of her reign, Kartimandu's anger at Mórrígan consumed her thoughts. She wanted to teach Clann Ui Flaithimh's queen a painful lesson. After which, her head would be mounted on a spear outside Kartimandu's residence in Dùn Caen.

Thus, when she espied Mórrígan's warband holding its position, the temptation proved irresistible, and she ordered her guard to engage. Ualraig watched and shook his head. His queen was a force to be reckoned with when she stuck to what she did well. Using her dark powers to consolidate power, scheming and removing opponents by politics and assassination, and even wielding her armies as a hammer to crush stubborn resistance.

Unlike Mórrígan, however, Kartimandu was not a battle queen. With more than enough to keep him occupied, Ualraig did nothing to forestall his queen's intent. A fierce grin swept across Mórrígan's face as she watched Kartimandu's chariot lead her personal guard at a fast jog towards her.

The Dark Huntress looked to her right and held her bow above her head. In answer, Gràinne raised her longsword. The younger woman's chariots rocked back and forward on spoked wheels. Drivers flicked whips and juggled reins to control mounts whose nostrils flared at the scent of blood.

Both women were confident until pain suddenly surged through everyone's minds, disorienting men, women, and horses. Charioteers were thrown to the ground as horses reared. Fighters grasped heads or fell on all fours and threw up. Horses squealed with wide-eyed terror.

An Fiagaí Dorcha snarled like a highland *lincse* as she fought to regain control of her mind. She glanced skyward and felt the gaze of an eagle's eye on her. Grinding blood-stained teeth, Mórrígan nocked an arrow and drew the bowstring back. Her shoulder muscles tensed and then relaxed as she loosed the black shaft. It rose high into the air, held at the peak of the arc, and then dropped. It was a shot of defiance carried by prayer and anger. The distance was impossible.

Passion overruled prudence in Kartimandu's thirst for vengeance. Inspired by his queen's ululations, her charioteer whipped the horse, propelling the chariot forward. Unsurprisingly, the vehicle closed on Mórrígan's band much faster than Kartimandu's guards, who were on foot. In his enthusiasm for the fight, the chariot driver unwittingly put his queen within range of Mórrígan's arrow.

Epic ballads would later tell of the beat of an eagle's wing that shifted the arrow's flight. The arrowhead caused minor damage, barely grazing Kartimandu's perfectly round shoulder before dropping to the cret floor. A thin, uneven line of blood seeped from the shallow cut.

However, the barb was made of iron. Kartimandu felt as if she had been felled by an axe. Excruciating pain flowed through her veins, setting nerve endings on fire. Her body convulsed, and she flopped to the cret's wooden floor. Wide-eyed with fear, the driver pulled hard on the reins, wheeled the vehicle around, and sped to safety.

Freed from Kartimandu's mental snare, Mórrígan ordered her band to dismount and form two lines. It irked Mórrígan that even a well-trained horse was still unstable as a platform to send multiple flights into the enemy's ranks. The likelihood of diallait and belly-belt slipping as the rider attempted to control the horse with knees while drawing and loosing arrows was high. At least with javelins or swords, it was still possible to guide a horse with one hand while using the weapon with the other.

Before long, Kartimandu regained control of herself and her guard. Once more, she drove them towards Mórrígan. This time she directed her attack from well behind her warriors. They held spears grasped with strong hands and wedged firmly between the arm and solid side muscles. Small, round shields were strapped to their naked backs. Guttural cries and curses rang out as they gathered pace and closed on Mórrígan.

Three rapid volleys of arrows curbed the guard's enthusiasm, and their pace faltered. They had no response except to swerve to avoid being hit. In doing this, they knocked their comrades aside, creating additional gaps and disarray in their ranks.

Mórrígan shouted for the archers to mount up. With the precision of constant practice, they swung onto their horse's backs. Cantering a further two hundred paces distant from the approaching enemy, they waited. Kartimandu howled in anger, frustrated at the apparent cowardice of her prey.

On the right flank, partially concealed by a shallow dip in the land-scape, Gràinne admired the smooth manoeuvring of Mórrígan. She watched the riders dismount for the second time. More volleys of black-shafted arrows fell on Kartimandu's ranks.

As the missiles flew, Gràinne's chariots were already moving. Several more volleys of arrows scattered Kartimandu's formation. Gaps appeared as men swerved, anticipating the flight of the shafts. Others tripped over the fallen. The looser array was an invitation made for chariots, and one Gràinne did not refuse.

Gràinne's *carbad* shuddered as its spinning blades ground through muscle and bone, flinging shards and cords of bloody flesh. Her chariot swerved between gaps in the ragged ranks of the enemy. With a boldness that belied her age, Gràinne stood barefoot on the floor of the vehicle's blood-splattered cret and hurled her javelins. Once these were exhausted, she reached over her shoulder and tugged, releasing her longsword.

The blade swept up and down, doling out deep gashes to uncovered heads and unclothed torsos. As Gràinne reached the far end of the enemy's formation, she lifted her sword in a circular motion above her head, directing the chariots to turn for another pass. Kartimandu's warriors fled before the chariots. By the time Gràinne completed her bloody manoeuvre, Mórrígan's riders were already galloping towards the rapidly disintegrating unity of Kartimandu's elite guards.

A real pig's arse, this is. Ualraig's assault on Fearghal's men progressed but slowed to a crawl. The last thing he needed was to send part of his force to rescue Kartimandu. *Do I have a choice?*

Mórrígan spied new warbands peel off and sprint to aid their queen. She laughed, halted her attack, and retreated. With Kartimandu's guard reduced by half, it had been a successful mission.

***

From Áth to Trócaire, the trail skirted the foothills of the Sleá. Forest and dense undergrowth spilt onto the path. It was well-used and wide enough to take two wagons side-by-side with room to spare. Still, it was the line of least resistance for the thousands of sweating attackers who hurtled along the rutted track and skirted muddy pools in search of plunder.

Eirnín's choice was clear. Fight behind the chest-high stone wall that encircled the settlement, or fight outside. To a few raised eyebrows, Eirnín elected for compromise. Half his warriors were placed in front of the western-facing wall, javelins ready. The other half of his men were inside the perimeter under Sárán's command. They were supported by the druids and a small band of archers and slingers.

His rationale was reasonable. If those outside were slaughtered. *A more than likely outcome.* There should be enough remaining within Trócaire to defend the supplies and the injured. Eirnín was not optimistic about their chances. His actions were brave, and to the approval of his men, he took up a central position outside the wall.

Shielded by trees, a broad curve in the track opened without warning onto the open expanse before the settlement. Thus, the roar of the enemy preceded their sighting. Shouts and screams rose to a frenzied and derisory crescendo as they spotted Eirnín's small force. Insulted by the number of defenders before them, they hoped for rich plunder within the settlement. At the wall, Eirnín braced himself and hefted a javelin. "Engage when you have a target!" His shout was taken up by the other commanders.

The battle for Trócaire began.

***

The Clann Ui Flaithimh shield-wall closed ranks when the supply of javelins was exhausted. Now, they waited. The rear row braced themselves against their comrades, ignoring muttered growls and threats as protruding iron bosses scraped and bruised spines.

On the wings, Mòrag and Brandubh's force maintained a solid hail of stones and slugs into the flanks of the oncoming horde. Áine retreated with her archers, taking up position behind the wall. Once in place, the bowmen sent flight after flight upwards.

Meanwhile, the High People's army slipped and stumbled over bodies and doggedly churned through the blood-soaked mud and gore. It was approaching mid-morning when the first wave of Kartimandu's army smashed against the shield-wall. There was a communal grunt from both sides, followed by a pastel-pink mist of blood and spit released into the air. Partially toothless mouths gaped, howling for blood while drool trickled down unshaven chins. The stench of unwashed bodies, stale beer and piss assaulted the senses.

Bloody págánaigh. Fearghal briefly wondered if he smelled as bad. He hoped he did not. He shook his head and smiled. Mongfhionn, who bathed quite often, would have quickly and, in blunt language, informed him of her disapproval. Above the curses and taunts of the enemy, his voice roared with the strength of a great bear. "Hold the line. *Ní ghéillfear, nó cúlú!*" Along the wall, the commanders and warriors echoed his battle cry. The slaughter resumed.

***

Mass conflicts make very little sense unless you are a god or goddess who savours the bloody sacrifice made in his or her name. For men and women of ambition, the motives are sometimes an intoxicating brew of power, madness, and glory. Still, for many, it is a matter of being in the wrong place at the wrong time. The ones at the front of the assault were most definitely in the latter category.

They had little choice and no escape but death. Pushed by their comrades from behind, they launched themselves at the red wall. Beady, black eyes glittered at them from the ravens emblazoned on Clann Ui Flaithimh's shields. They fought with spears, axes, swords, and clubs, but the crush constrained their use. They pushed backwards and sideways to secure room to swing or raise their weapons. It was a hopeless task. Once enough space was gained, they were momentarily off-balance. The press behind pushed them onto the spears of the enemy.

As the sun rose higher, the injured and the dead formed a bloody berm before the shield-wall. Loosened bowels and eviscerated bellies intensified the stench along the front lines. Tadhg lunged forward and lamented at how differently and gloriously the battle would be portrayed in future epic tales and poems. The warrior in him screamed as he plunged his blade's tip into the face of another transient enemy. The poet captured the look of shock in deep, blue eyes before a half arm's length of iron continued its path between blood-stained lips.

Tadhg sighed, wrenched the blade from its fleshy scabbard and thrust forward again. His new enemy was a boy of no more than fourteen summers. The enemy's horns sounded. With surprising discipline, the attackers halted and pulled back twenty paces.

Fearghal roared, "Hold!" as the Clann Ui Flaithimh line wavered and some in the shield-wall made to charge the retreating enemy. Two bloodied sides snarled at each other. Red and yellow stained teeth were bared in the rictus of the strife. Men and women on both sides turned around and exposed bare, milk-white arses to their opponents. Others grabbed their crotches and, with thrusting pelvises, insulted the manhood of their enemy.

The horns sounded again. New fighters kicked and shoved their way to the front. They crowed at the opportunity to show how much better they were than the fallen. At the third horn, they stormed forward.

***

Clever tactics. Fearghal watched the tenth of Ualraig's waves slam against Clann Ui Flaithimh's shields. After the fifth, the rear row of the shield-wall exchanged places with the front. Brandubh and Mòrag did the same with their spears.

Mòrag walked along the Ravens' line, encouraging, cajoling, and cursing her band. Her lines were in constant flux, with the injured pulled out of the front ranks and replaced with her finite reserves. Broken spears were strewn about the ground, their points firmly embedded in corpses. The Cinn Péinteáilte princess uttered a quick prayer of thanks to Sárán. His uncanny knack for knowing how many additional spears would be needed gained him an admirer and her respect.

Bodies piled up before the shield-wall, forcing it to step several paces back. Fearghal listened to the laboured breathing of his men. Blood dripped from cuts and slashes. Those that survived would sport an impressive array of new scars. The greater numbers of Ualraig began to tell. Yet Fearghal sensed that the morning's assailants were not veterans. Their job was to exhaust his force, make them careless, and set them up as easy prey for his veterans. *That bastard, Ualraig, is a shrewd tactician.*

Unfortunately, Fearghal was correct. Ualraig was delighted. So far, his plan was working, a viewpoint unlikely to gain much support from the hundreds of broken or dead. Like waves crashing against a sea wall, his men threw themselves against Conall's shields. Instead of great, white gouts of salt spray ascending, there was blood, gore, and spit.

Clann Ui Flaithimh's warriors were pushed back five, ten, and twenty paces. Meanwhile, Kartimandu had returned to safety. There, she re-focused her powers on ensuring the weak-minded fools at the front of the attack sacrificed themselves for the benefit of her imminent victory.

The victory is ours. What could go wrong? Ualraig's hubris proved foolish and an irresistible challenge to the brace of eagles in the skies above. Fate connived with the Goddess. Nearby, Serendipity was always looking to create chaos. Soon after Ualraig indulged the thought, he sensed that something was different. Something had altered in the ambience of the theatre of conflict. Silence fell upon the crowds gathered on the Sleá.

They know their army is beaten. Ualraig said a short prayer to his Goddess, Brighid. However, this was not Brighid's domain, and, besides, the Ancient was no friend of Kartimandu. From the higher peak of the Sleá, an eardrum-shattering series of screams pierced the air.

The cloaked figure of the Sídhe sat on a remarkably calm black horse. With arms outstretched, Mongfhionn summoned her powers. Her cries were amplified by those on the summit and thrown like a hammer at Kartimandu's horde. In the clouds and on distant hills, the mná sídhe shrieked the names of the future dead.

In the shield-wall, the pain of tired, bruised, and bloody bodies dissipated, and spines stiffened. There would be no retreat… no surrender. Once more, the anthem *"Ní ghéillfear, nó cúlú!"* was hurled at the enemy.

***

Carmag watched the enemy emerge from the forest and onto the open ground before Trócaire. Guttural commands echoed along their ragged ranks. It was followed by loud cheering and the banging of weapons against shields. Shortly after, Kartimandu's warriors swarmed the neat, grey walls of Trócaire.

The composed expression on Carmag's face belied his true feelings. As his chieftains bombarded him with pleading looks to intervene, Carmag held firm. His timing had to be perfect. The defenders of Trócaire would have no immediate relief.

Eirnín cried out as a brute, more beast than man, surmounted Trócaire's perimeter ditch and swung an impossibly sized club at his shield. The force jarred his arm and knocked him back against a particularly sharp rock jutting from the wall. *No favours from the gods today.* To his surprise, the shield did not shatter. Perhaps the gods had not wholly deserted him.

As the club's shadow crossed his face and again was raised high in the air, Eirnín stretched forward with his javelin. It was to be the last time he held the spear. It disappeared into and was held firmly by multiple folds of fat. Still, the thrust did not halt the brute's attack. Perhaps, the message that a spear was in his belly had not penetrated his feeble brain.

The club descended. A glancing blow to his helmet stunned Eirnín. For a second time, his shield bore the full force of the strike. His arm hung numb and useless. As he scrambled to unsheathe his sword with his right hand, Eirnín was vaguely aware that the human-bear was limbering up for another attack. *A short command, this was.* Eirnín resigned himself to being pulped by the heavy club.

Instead, he was anointed from above with bright blood. With a high degree of distaste, he spat out the warm, viscous blood that trickled down his face, over his lips and into his mouth. His vision slowly cleared, and Eirnín watched his two adjacent comrades repeatedly stab his assailant in the neck. By the time they had finished, the man's head was barely connected to his body. He fell backwards into the stinking shite, piss, and communal debris at the bottom of the ditch.

"Next time, pick on someone smaller. You might last longer," said the veteran.

Eirnín blinked at the unfairness of the comment and was about to protest when the scarred face split into an enormous grin. Eirnín shook his head, muttered, "Thanks," and then, "Bastards," as he took up his place. Above his head, the swish of javelins thrown by those behind the wall brought shrieks from the attackers. To the assailants, the stream of missiles appeared endless. In this, they were rightly observant. Sárán kept both an ongoing supply and a tally of each weapon.

While the enemy's main force sought to crush Eirnín's shield-wall, a thousand besiegers broke to the right. Their chieftain's intent was to attack the lightly defended southern wall. The dry-stone defence was not high. Neither it nor the wooden gateway were much of a barrier to the fighters who brushed the handful of defenders aside. They smashed their way through the gate and clambered over the wall.

Only Trócaire's maze of narrow, walled avenues slowed their advance. The small band of Clann Ui Flaithimh archers and slingers positioned on the settlement's higher vantage points were the first to react, initially with cries and shouts to warn the defenders and then with arrows and stones. The attackers fell, although not in significant numbers. However, an irresistible urge to search for plunder and vandalise any building in their path conspired to slow the besiegers' advance.

The mob finally reached the roundhouse and healing centre at the heart of Trócaire and was confronted by the druids. The sight of the black-cloaked priests, their faces sinisterly veiled by cavernous hoods, unnerved the attackers. The druids' monophonic chanting served to heighten the throng's trepidation.

The horde's anxiety rose further as they observed that each druid's tattooed hands were crossed and rested on the smooth pommels of heavy, iron swords. The tips were placed in the dirt, midway between open bróga. A tall, sallow-faced druid with piercing eyes, the colour of the blue ink of his tattoos, stepped forward. In a commanding voice, Crum Dubh said, "Leave this place."

The avenue to the druids, although broader than the narrow streets that fed into it, was wide enough to allow the passage of about eight or nine men. The attackers slowed to an uneven halt and watched the druids warily. No one wanted to be the first to strike at another god's followers. A burly chieftain pushed his way forward, pointed his spear at Crum and shouted, "Kill the bastard!" The man obviously had issues with religion.

The stand-off was terminated. Relieved of responsibility, the crowd rushed forward. To the attackers' chagrin, the druids wielded their blades with an unholy. Although the priests would say blessed, skill and bloody efficiency. Ably, the wiry Crum swept the deeply pockmarked head of the unbelieving chieftain from his neck with an almost effortless, two-hand-ed cut.

Uninterrupted, the sword continued its arc, slashing an adjacent war-rior's cheek to the bone. Blood welled from the gash in the wind-scoured face. In shock, the man, through force of habit, raised his axe. The Druid's sword swept upwards and then swiftly downwards. The man's face fell apart. His arms continued to lift his axe, then paused as if waiting for instruction. He tumbled forward, the weapon still firmly in his hands.

Sárán's choice of weapon was a hawthorn staff. Cut when the tree was in bloom, the pole came with the blessing of the Aes Sídhe and the fae. It was the height of a tall man and tipped with iron at each end. Grasping the stave in both hands, the fair-haired quartermaster shouted instructions to his men and charged into the fray.

A long semi-circular swing of the staff had his opponents reflexively bend backwards to avoid being struck. His first thrust forward smacked the group's leader on the forehead. Perhaps he had a thin skull, or maybe

Sárán was stronger than he realised. The iron-capped staff punched an almost perfect circle in the man's forehead. Lifeless, he dropped to the dirt.

In the cramped inner precincts of Trócaire, the fight was less than elegant. Biting and head-butting, knees to the groin and fists wrapped in studded leather were much more effective than swords or axes. Fingers tipped with broken, bloody, and dirt-encrusted nails gouged eyes. Daggers slipped between ribs or raked along necks. Loose rocks crushed skulls.

Outside Trócaire, the shield-wall was battered on three sides. It shrank as the injured fell and stood close to being overwhelmed by the frenzied horde. An exhausted Deaglán clenched his teeth, slammed his shield against a ruddy-faced assailant, and slashed downwards.

His blade dulled by countless blows ripped rather than sliced through his opponent's arm. It fell, fingers twitching, to the dirt. Before the shock of injury overcame his rage, he roared and thrust his spear into Deaglán's shoulder. Deaglán slumped against the stone wall and added his blood to the drying gore.

***

Carmag paced along his front line as the battle around and within Trócaire ebbed and flowed. Observing the full force of the enemy committed, he raised his hammer above his head. However, his signal to attack was pre-empted by the loud screeching from the Sídhe. He smiled and, taking this as confirmation to proceed, called to his hornblower. "Now." The war horn of the Forest People sounded a mournful, deep *barrr-ewww*. Its refrain was taken up by many others.

To the enemy, wearied from battling most of the morning yet fighting with confidence in their belief of inevitable victory, it seemed as if the forest came alive. A hail of stones and iron slugs flayed the outer margins of the besiegers, instantly dropping hundreds to the dirt. Then, with a marvellous roar, Carmag's battalion of belligerents, naked and tattooed from head-to-toe, descended from the foothills of the Sleá.

The man was fleetingly aware of his fate before his head caved in under the impact of Carmag's hammer. Wielded with a two-handed grip, Carmag swung and bludgeoned his way towards the beleaguered defenders of Trócaire.

"You took your bloody time," snarled the ceannairí céad. His face was covered in blood and gore. His fair hair, trailing from a badly dented helmet, had a distinctive blood-red tint. Fionnbharr was the antithesis of a caring healer.

"Timing, son. It's all about timing." Carmag grinned. "And outnumbering the bastards." Fionnbharr did not appear placated. "Look on the positive side. Tadhg will immortalise ye in one of his epic tales. Then ye'll never have to pay for a striopach for the rest of yer life." This did not seem to relieve Fionnbharr's irritation. However, several around him with less-than-handsome features smirked at a potential path to friendlier thighs.

On surer ground, Carmag reverted to his role as a commander. "Get yer men behind the walls. Secure Trócaire and the supplies. I'll leave a few hundred men to replace your injured."

"Thanks," mumbled Fionnbharr and turned to organise his men.

"The young can be very touchy," remarked Carmag to the salt and pepper-haired veteran beside him. It drew a toothless smile of agreement.

***

The two, male and female, sat back-to-back in the centre of the blood-stained field. Chins resting on their chests, arms by their sides, they looked like lovers in quiet repose, enjoying the early summer sun. A shadow passed overhead. The air beat with the swish of feathers and filled with a strangled *kraa kraa* as a flock of ravens swooped and circled the field. The couple neither felt nor heard the birds. Nor did they move. The rigour of death had not taken hold, but the spear thrust through both chest and back ensured the pose was sustained.

A passing warrior lifted the woman's head. Her slashed throat gave him a gory smile. The long scab broke and wept with the watery blood pooling behind the wound. He looked down. An encrusted bib of purple covered her naked chest. He shook his head. *Pity, she had nice tits.*

A few swings with his axe removed both heads. He methodically stripped the gold and silver armbands and torcs from the bodies, pulled leather belts away and ripped the triubhas to ensure nothing of value was missed. He considered cutting off the man's cock but disregarded the thought. After all, he was not a barbarian.

***

Taken by surprise, the enemy had little choice but to turn and confront Carmag's force. The two sides stood evenly numbered. However, held at bay by the stubbornness of the Clann Uí Flaithimh defenders, Kartimandu's men were no longer fresh.

With hindsight, Ualraig's decision to send a force to attack the settlement was foolish. Dismayed and weary, the attackers were steadily driven back to the edge of the southern forest. Many turned to run but were skewered by spears or had their spines opened to the air by axe and sword blades.

Carmag's men were accustomed to fighting in the pine forests of the north. The High People fought in the vast expanses of the mountains, valleys, and moorlands of the Penn-inus. To the harried enemy, the forest appeared to signal safety and a chance to reunite with the main force. The retreating warbands gained several hundred paces into the trees without opposition. They breathed easier.

A fifth of Carmag's command remained unseen in the shadows of the woods. Camouflaged, the Forest People appeared silently from behind trees or dropped from overhead branches. Taken unawares, hundreds of the enemy died instantly. With clubs and spears, Carmag's warriors bludgeoned and cut a bloody swathe through the heart of the Ualraig's force.

The High People's retreat from Trócaire stalled and then disintegrated into chaos. Men and women searched for paths to avoid being caught between the ambushers in their midst and the foe advancing from behind. Many, confused by the forest, lost their sense of direction.

They ran around in circles before falling to the spears of their enemy. The orange-brown tones of the forest floor became infused with red as Carmag's men methodically tracked and slaughtered their foe.

No more than seventeen summers, the two dark-haired sisters had fought for Kartimandu on other campaigns. Used to victory, they had little fear of battle, and their knives had taken many lives. They believed totally, fanatically, in their queen. Their skin had been tinted green to emulate and honour Kartimandu. The style of clothes they wore was minimal. This was not to flaunt their bodies but to expose more green-painted skin areas.

On this day and in this fracas, they resembled their attackers more than their tribe. Unlike their comrades, it served them well in the forest, helping them avoid the enemy and even allowing them to strike back. Now, the pair ran for their lives. They scrambled through undergrowth that grasped and tore at their flesh, slipped on lichen-covered boulders and stumps of trees, and tripped over fallen branches.

Chased by a determined group of men, the younger sister hurdled a tree stump that lay across their escape route. The elder misjudged her step and yelped as she struck her head on the tree's rough bark. In her head, the younger sibling knew there was little she could do to help. She ran another twenty paces before turning around. Blood is blood.

She heard her sister's cry and watched a tall, muscled warrior throw her with a sickening thump across the stump. He was naked, and it was evident that the thrill of the fight had made a singular impact on his manhood. With one hand on her neck and the other holding his spear, he thrust inside the girl. She shrieked helplessly.

The battleground is no place for leisurely rutting. He climaxed quickly with a loud grunt, withdrew, stepped back a half-pace and released his hand from her neck. Any thought of relief or mercy vanished when her head, split from her neck by the leaf-shaped spearhead, rolled to the forest floor. With practised ease, the slayer of her sister proceeded to remove any valuables before continuing the hunt.

The remaining sister looked on, numbed with shock. Not at her sister being abused. That was an occupational hazard. Even among their own sweaty comrades, oft-times, one or both would be hauled to the side and rutted. It was the cold, emotionless way that her sister had been penetrated, beheaded, stripped of anything of value, and left for the forest beasts. It made her blood boil. She turned, not sure in her mind whether she would fight or flee.

The pain in her belly made her gasp. She looked down at the protruding spear shaft. Her toes barely touched the ground. The upward spear thrust lifted her and pinned her to the tree. She felt hot blood flow down her belly and thighs as she hung. The blade edge cut through her guts as her weight pressed down on it.

"Ye should have run," said the warrior in a broad brogue.

She smiled. "Sister."

"Would she have wanted ye dead?" She shook her head feebly.

"Then ye should have run."

Moments later, her head fell to the ground, and she joined her sister in Mag Mell.

***

It was a minor wound, barely more than a scratch, yet Kartimandu's shoulder burned. Her previously perfect body was spoiled by a thin, red scar the length of a middle finger. She knew it would never heal and cried out with frustrated rage as her nemesis' screams shredded the ties with which she controlled the minds of her army.

By the time the queen had replenished her power from the waters of the Abhainn Dubh and re-established her dominance, the army's push forward had stuttered. Confused for moments, it was enough to allow Clann Ui Flaithimh's red wall to press on.

Tramping over the blood and gore of the dead, the shield-wall remorselessly slashed and hacked. Ravens' spears impaled scores and channelled many others onto the shields and swords of their comrades. Ualraig watched, helpless, as his attack lost its shape and momentum.

The slaughter in the teeth of the Clann Ui Flaithimh advance grew.

Furious commands to hold the ground were relayed to shocked chieftains. As usual, they were accompanied by death threats to leaders and their families. Snarling warband chieftains kicked and cajoled their men. Ualraig's ranks stiffened, and with the strength of numbers, once more, they pushed forward.

"That advantage didn't last the time for a leisurely piss," muttered Fearghal as he fought to maintain traction in the slurry of gore and mud around him. His feet squelched in rapidly disintegrating boots. *The boot and bróga makers will greatly increase trade after this.* As he looked down the line, he saw that his struggle was no different than the rest in the ranks.

There was little chance his men could push their foe back. Yet that had never been an option. The ground was unfavourable, and the enemy's numbers were too numerous. Fearghal glanced to his rear and bellowed, "Fall back twenty paces to solid ground. Slowly and in order."

***

On the Sleá, Mongfhionn slipped from her mount after a hard ride, patted its black velvet shoulder, and said, "Thanks." The big horse nodded in acceptance and walked several paces to graze. The Sídhe was restrained in what she could do. The cloudless, blue skies gave her little room to use the weather. And so, for now, she focused on playing with Kartimandu's mind. This was made easier by the druids at Trócaire. Their endless incantations raised and maintained a barrier between the queen and the battlers of Clann Ui Flaithimh.

Retreat or die fuath. The persistent message from Mongfhionn drove Kartimandu to the point of insanity. Although many would maintain that the queen had crossed that bridge long ago. The waters of the Abhainn Dubh churned as the queen of the High People fought the intrusions. For a short time, it seemed the fighters in Ualraig's latest wave fought with reduced zealotry.

The Sídhe looked to the Clann Ui Flaithimh lines and smiled. Fearghal stood a head taller than most, and his gravelly voice roared commands and encouragement to his men. Her lover was a good-hearted man with a fiery temper and a hard body that appeared to be forged from *eibhear*. Mongfhionn sighed. Fearghal was in his prime. He was at an age when many heroes fell gloriously in battle and were remembered forever in the tribe's communal memory through the epic tales that birthed legends.

She knew that one day, the astuteness he had amassed would not save him from a fatal sword stroke or spear thrust, but Mongfhionn was selfish when it came to Fearghal. She would not let the bean sídhe take him to Mag Mell without a fight. Thus, the zephyr of wind that suddenly flurried around Fearghal refreshed him. It also caused the two-handed slash from his opponent to open up a gash on his shoulder, not sever his neck.

The numbers favoured Kartimandu. The Sídhe knew if this battle could not be ended soon, the sea of the enemy would overwhelm the valiant but tired sword arms of Clann Ui Flaithimh and the spears of the Ravens. She allowed herself a stamp of the foot in frustration at her impotence.

Movement in the forest caught the Sídhe's attention. Full, ruby-red lips parted in a smile. An ancient oak staff was raised and pointed to the woods. Carmag's forces effortlessly ghosted through the wild woods in pursuit of their quarry. Now they moved more swiftly.

***

Ualraig's face broke into a broad grin as the raiders of Trócaire broke from the nearby forest and sprinted, screaming to join the main force. Kartimandu's general hoped it would be enough to tip the balance in his favour. That was dashed when he saw how few they were. He estimated less than a third of his men remained.

He was puzzled that their cries appeared to be of panic, not triumph. Then Ualraig realised they were pursued by a horde of howling, painted warriors led by a red-haired giant swinging a massive war hammer. It was a shock, for it had never occurred to Ualraig that his men could have been defeated at Trócaire.

Carmag's cohort gathered momentum as they charged from the forest to the ragged northern edge of Ualraig's army. Focused on defeating Clann Uí Flaithimh's shield-wall, Ualraig's troops had little warning or time to turn and defend against the marauding Carmag. The High People's assault on Fearghal's defensive line wavered.

Amid loud shouts from Carmag's band and the resonating *barrr ewww* from horns, Fearghal gestured frantically at a blood-spattered Cúscraid. "Turn the formation. We'll catch them between our two forces."

Ualraig's most forward fighters were caught like a beast's snout in a trap. As the cruel iron jaws of the snare snapped shut, the latest wave of his raiders was sundered from the main body. A thousand spears of Mòrag and Brandubh quickly formed a barrier to prevent enemy reinforcements from rescuing their isolated comrades. The move was redundant. Taken aback by Carmag's intervention, Ualraig's main force turned tail and fled. The remnant was slaughtered.

Ualraig cursed and sounded the withdrawal. His opponents had proved more resourceful than he anticipated. As he left the field, he scowled and shook his head. Kartimandu would not be pleased.

CHAPTER 18

406 B.C.—Dumha

The settlement of *Dumha* sat on a grassy mound, midway between the Sleá and the Linne Foirthe estuary and halfway between the Abhainn Dubh and the eastern forest. Rumour had it that the hill was an ancient burial site. It was a credible story, given the number of bones uncovered by curious children and bored hounds. That the spirits of the dead freely roamed the area did not seem to overly concern the pragmatic families who farmed the surrounding land. Gifts to the Goddess and the spirits kept everyone on friendly terms.

It was to Dumha that the tired Clann Ui Flaithimh battalions led by Brandubh, Carmag, Cúscraid, and Fearghal retired. Sárán soon commandeered the settlement, a flattering description for the cluster of farm dwellings and animal pens. Thus, Dumha became the official centre of logistics, storage, and repair.

Teams of blacksmiths and their apprentices soon had Dumha's forges fired up. Ere long, the air was filled with the hammering of metal on metal as the armourers repaired and rebuilt weapons. Metal rasped on whetstones as men queued to have dulled blades sharpened by apprentices.

By dusk, the tents and campfires of Clann Ui Flaithimh and their allies encircled Dumha. There was a perceptible rise in morale among the army as Conall, Nikandros, and Íar rode into the camp. The Sidhe had arrived earlier. Conall took a long and deliberately circuitous route to the main tents. He paused many times to share the craic or congratulate the men and women for their steady defiance in the face of superior numbers. Fearghal and his weary commanders rose from the roaring fire, delighted to see their comrades return. It meant their cavalry was close.

The women stood a short distance from the campfire. There was a noticeable tension between Áine and the rest of the group. Mórrígan was devastated over Brion's injuries, and she and Mongfhionn were outraged at Áine's behaviour.

Gràinne stood with her head hung down. She had been taken severely to task by the Sídhe for being "Bloody stupid". Still, she was surprised when Mórrígan embraced her and told her any fault should be shared equally between her and Brion.

Mongfhionn snorted as Conall, Íar, and Nikandros dismounted. Yet they did not approach the campfire, choosing to brush, feed, and water their horses before handing the reins to several boys. "You can see where we are ranked in our men's affections," said Mongfhionn. "First their horses, second their hounds, and then us."

"Fearghal prefers the comfort of solid ground to a horse," countered Mórrígan, "so you only compete with his dogs." The Sídhe laughed.

"When will Drostan and his men arrive?" asked Conall. The senior commanders, the ceannairí na míle, sat on broad logs around the fire as they ate and drank. The ceannairí céad, except the injured Deaglán, stood in groups within earshot. Deaglán remained at Trócaire, recuperating from the spear thrust that cracked his collarbone.

"His messengers say later this evening. Definitely by sunrise," said Carmag.

"Do you think Ualraig will attack or rest his army? Or do we have to provide some bait?"

"He'll attack," answered Mongfhionn. "He may not consider it the wisest of strategies, but Kartimandu's impatience will not allow otherwise. That is assuming she has not already replaced Ualraig. The queen will not have been pleased with today's performance." She raised an eyebrow. "What were you thinking about regarding bait? And what is *your* strategy?"

Conall laughed, "I'm thinking of something I learned from the Romans." He paused and added ominously, "As for the plan. We drive them into the Abhainn Dubh and slaughter them in the water and mud. *Then*, the army will follow them to Dùn Caen, killing all in our path until my daughters are returned." All contemplated this silently.

Fearghal broke the tense atmosphere. "We're no longer a large warband, Conall. Such a venture will not happen until the nobles, flaith-fine, ceannairí na míle, and ceannairí céad have to assemble, discuss, and agree to the move. The army will not march without their clann and families' consent. It will be after the feast of Lugnasad before we have gathered the support to march… and then there is the winter to consider."

Conall spoke with deep resignation, "Of that, I'm aware. I am their king, not their tyrant." He then looked at Mongfhionn and said, "We will prevail upon the Goddess and the Aes Sídhe to keep Brighid and Danu safe." The Sídhe smiled and nodded. "And, of course, we'll pray that Urard and his hundred will find and protect them."

***

As Mongfhionn suspected, it was an unhappy evening in the camp of the High People. Kartimandu's command for Ualraig to present himself at her hastily constructed pavilion could not be refused. Even the sight of the flaunted nakedness of the queen and her retinue was little compensation.

A stinging rebuke from Kartimandu in front of his captains left Ualraig in no doubt about the tenuous nature of his future. Should he not redeem himself in the next attack, his life, and quite possibly his spirit, was forfeit.

Ualraig exited the tent and heaved a sigh of relief. *At least, the queen had not demanded he take part in satisfying her voracious hunger for rutting.* Frequently prompted by fierce passion and anger, the act of having her body stimulated to equally intense and multiple orgasms seemed to have a soothing effect on the queen's temper.

This was beneficial for the tribe but not so rewarding for those chosen as her partners, whether male or female. After they rutted the queen, they were executed, sometimes as part of the night's entertainment. As Ualraig passed the "chosen", the look in their eyes told him they were fully aware of their fate.

Cold rage at his humiliation at first simmered but quickly bubbled to the surface. That evening, groups of Ualraig's trusted elite were sent to the tents of those chieftains he deemed the more reluctant. Punishments ranged from a sharp blade to the throat to breaking legs, or a stake rammed up arses. The choice of death depended on the whims of those administering the sentence. Few had any compassion, so the cries of the suffering rang out long into the night. The lesson was not lost on the spared.

Ualraig retired to his paltry tent, taking comfort from the warmth of the fire that crackled at its entrance and the spitted rabbit roasting over it. He knew he had to win this battle. His army was not prepared or provisioned for a long campaign. Any supplies brought with them had been destroyed by Mórrígan. The land provided little beyond what they could hunt, trap or fish.

Viewed simply, this was no more than a raid. It was the biggest ever known in Albu, but it was still just a raid. Ualraig knew he had to win decisively and quickly to secure the settlements around the Sleá. Not unreasonably, he remained confident of victory. Even with their losses, the army numbered almost twenty-five thousand. If he failed, it would be a long and perilous walk back to Dùn Caen with a moribund army and a wrathful Conall snapping at his heels.

Dawn was cloaked in a miserable wet mist. With much cursing, kicking, and shoving, Ualraig's chieftains herded their clans and warbands back to the river plain. That he had accomplished this without harassment from his enemies made Ualraig uneasy.

He and Kartimandu stood in adjacent wagons. To their left and right, the army's fifty chariots rocked back and forth as their drivers pulled on reins and traces to keep the eager horses from dashing forward. At their rear, the army stamped feet, exchanged insults, and spat voluminous gobs of phlegm on the dirt.

Although the chariots had limb-slashing scythes on their wheel hubs, Ualraig considered them a pain in the arse. A charioteer's vision was narrow, and they rarely cared about those they manoeuvred through. He would likely lose men trying to avoid their whirling blades.

In Ualraig's opinion, the vehicles were helpful in communications but not on the battlefield. By contrast, the two-horse war chariots of Clann Uí Flaithimh were bigger, faster, and better equipped. That his chariots would cause disarray in the Clann Uí Flaithimh ranks before being overwhelmed was the best hope that Ualraig could entertain.

However, Ualraig's immediate concern was the dense fog. He could hardly see more than a hundred paces in front of him. He looked to Kartimandu, watching her shiver as a fresh morning breeze played with the ends of her long hair. "Can you not do something about this fog?"

The queen glared at Ualraig. The combined powers of the Sídhe, Mórrígan and the druids severely constrained her and impeded her control over her army. Her head thumped under the assault. Her belly roiled, and nausea welled up.

"Making excuses already? Just do your job. And do it well, Ualraig or your time as my commander will cease."

✳✳✳

"It's raining," said Brocc.

"This surprises you, how?" replied Torcán.

"Smart-arse," countered Brocc.

The two friends tramped across the field to take up their positions. The settlement and surrounding land were shrouded in a dense, damp mist. Only the occasional sighting of a dark-brown thatched roof gave any hint of Dumha's location. It was, as Brocc indicated, also raining.

"Do you think this will work?" asked Brocc.

"Probably not. We'll all get slaughtered. And you'll stop asking me dumb questions," said Torcán.

"*Póg mo thoin.*"

"Never going to happen, Brocc. You may have a fine arse, but I like women too much." Torcán grinned at his friend. "Look, if you wanted intelligent conversation, you've picked the wrong person. I don't think. I fight, I drink, and I spread girls' thighs. And I'm very good at all three." Torcán pointed to a small group standing around Conall. "They are the ones who think and they can have the job. I'm like a well-trained wolf-hound. Point me at the enemy and tell me who to kill."

Brocc slapped Torcán's back and laughed, "You're still an arsehole."

River smoke floated in undulating layers on the Abhainn Dubh. To the north and east of Dumha, ribbons of silver-white fog snaked through the forest's tall trees. As the mist enveloping the croft retreated, it revealed the red and black shields of Clann Ui Flaithimh.

Conall's phalanx bristled with spears. Each side had four hundred and fifty men in two ranks. One hundred archers and one hundred sling-ers readied bows and slings at its centre. Two hundred shields stood with them in reserve. On the left and right flanks were Clann Ui Flaithimh's chariots.

"Shite!" cursed Ualraig. It was a formation he had no experience with, and he needed time to think.

Conall gave Ualraig no reprieve. Rather than waiting to defend their position, the phalanx moved to confront the enemy. To stall the advance, Ualraig ordered his chariots to attack. Conall's shields halted and opened ranks until each man was a pace apart from his neighbour. Javelins were gripped in rough hands, and spear butts were rammed into the soft earth. As Ualraig's chariots moved within range, they were met with arrows, stones, and a volley of javelins. Men and horses screamed.

Over a third of Ualraig's chariots were destroyed or incapacitated in the first skirmish. After regrouping, the remaining vehicles trundled forward. Conall's phalanx closed ranks. At a shouted command, the front row bent to one knee, resting the bottom edge of their red and black shields on the ground and rammed the butts of their spears into the dirt. The rear rows kept a javelin ready to throw. Íar and Nikandros contended that horses would not cross the hedge of spears. Conall stood, lance in hand, hoping they were right.

Íar later remarked that horses showed a lot more common sense than men. For the horse teams had baulked at the bristling wall of iron. Frantically, their drivers tried to bring them under control and swerve away from the phalanx. The manoeuvre was met by another volley of javelins, arrows, and slingshots.

Their predicament worsened for Ualraig's chariots when they heard Gràinne's war cry and watched her *carbaid* rumble into action. Grainne led her group along the rear of the High People's chariots, cutting them off from the main body, which maintained its position a thousand paces away.

Horses screamed as tendons were slashed and the rotating scythes severed legs. Blades snapped and spun through the air with a savage disregard for who they maimed. Wheels smashed on half-hidden rocks. Wooden spokes splintered and wheels buckled, tossing chariot occupants into the path of iron-rimmed wheels and hard hoofs.

Gràinne's blood-stained longsword swung left and right, renting flesh and bone. Cries for mercy were met with brutal slashes. In battle, Gràinne found relief from the cruel abuse delivered by her grandmother, Diadhaidh, and the guilt she still felt for Brion. With a feral cry, she leapt from her chariot and waded through the gore, searching for more victims for her rage.

"The Hag's tits. Tadhg had better watch out if she ever takes a dislike to him," said Fearghal. His voice had a definite tenor of pride as he watched his apprentice cause mayhem among Kartimandu's warriors.

Conall nodded, "Maybe we should just send her, Mongfhionn, Mórrígan, and Mòrag into the middle of Kartimandu's army. They'd frighten them to death." He laughed momentarily and then called to the reserves, "Support Gràinne. Finish off the chariots and drag them out of our path." The double front row moved aside, allowing the reserves to jog through.

"The Goddess give me strength. What is she doing now?" As the wreckage of chariots and men were dragged aside, many grumbled that Gràinne left them with few opponents to fight. Conall pointed to her green-painted vehicle. Banners flapping in the wind, it hurtled towards the enemy lines.

"Maybe she heard you," answered Fearghal.

The chariot pulled up a hundred paces from Ualraig and Kartimandu. Legs apart, her body enrobed in blood, Gràinne perched on the rail of the cret. Longsword brandished in the air, she howled like a wolf, taunting the High People's leaders and their army. To the enemy, she was a terrifying sight. Along the ridge of the Sleá, the people of Clann Ui Flaithimh waved a multitude of banners and cheered raucously in support of Gràinne.

In the sky above, an eagle's cry showed the Goddess' approval.

***

"How long will you let our army be insulted by this barbarian bitseach?" Kartimandu was in a foul mood. Still, Ualraig was reluctant to commit his army until the fog fully cleared. The hairs on the back of his neck told him to be wary. Unfortunately, the queen's demeanour allowed him little latitude to delay engaging Conall. Thus, Ualraig compromised and ordered half of the army to battle. The war horns of the High People reverberated across the river plain as the army advanced.

"Kartimandu is offended by Gràinne," said Conall wryly. He watched the High People, weapons held high, gather momentum. As a final insult, Gràinne grabbed the chariot's rear handrails, bent over, and wiggled her arse at the enemy. Perhaps she thought Kartimandu's horde would not fight as well with erections. At that moment, Gràinne's driver, having more sense than his companion, swung the chariot around and sped back to safety.

Fearghal laughed and bellowed, "Forward!" The Clann Ui Flaithimh square marched moved to meet their enemy. Ualraig and Kartimandu took their chariots to a grassy *droimnín*, which provided a good view of the location. Around them, the remnant of the queen's guard stood alert.

Ualraig, to his disgust, discovered that his earlier unease was justified. The swirling mist rolled back with a discomfiting exactness and eventually dissipated over the waters of the Linne Foirthe. The settlement of Dumha was revealed, as was Carmag's five thousand and Brandubh's thousand. Ualraig cursed as Clann Ui Flaithimh and Cinn Péinteáilte horns sounded out.

The deafening roar of the enemy washed over Nikandros, along with the rank smells of unwashed bodies and piss. For the Spartan, being part of the phalanx brought back vivid memories of epic encounters in much warmer and distant lands. His long doru was ideal for Conall's chosen strategy. It was an arm's length longer than his comrades' spears, causing a ripple of good-humoured craic and comparisons with his manhood.

With a high level of professional admiration, Ualraig watched Conall's square stab, slash and grind its way slowly and inexorably forward. In its wake, the phalanx left a trail of bloody corpses. "Bastards," muttered Ualraig.

Although battered and bloodied, the integrity of the Clann Ui Flaithimh formation held steady. Shields were locked; the front row stabbed low and the rear row high. The archers and slingers continued a hail of missiles that decimated Ualraig's farther ranks, creating gaps and weaknesses that the square could exploit.

Kartimandu looked at Ualraig with spiteful green eyes. "Do we have a problem?"

"We will if that bloody formation can't be stopped."

"You had better see that it is."

Ualraig called his hornblower to him and snapped several orders. The warband chieftains were alerted to Carmag and Brandubh's forces. With a roar, the remaining half of Kartimandu's army, including Ualraig's elite battalions, jogged into the bloody arena.

In the forests east of Dumha, Íar grinned, tightened the chin strap on his helmet, and brought his hunting horn to lips almost hidden by his thick, ginger beard. To his right, Mórrígan stood up in the girth loops of her mount, gesticulating and shouting orders to her warband. Over a thousand horses thundered from the forest. Íar's cavalry attacked Ualraig's left flank; Mórrígan's force rode hard to flank the enemy on its northern side.

Kartimandu's eyes blinked rapidly as she watched Íar's riders enter the battle. *It's only a thousand warriors. Surely, they will not make a significant difference.* Typically, horses were used to transport warriors to the front. Thus, Kartimandu fully expected the riders to dismount and fight.

Instead, she watched her army's flank shatter under volleys of javelins thrown from horseback. Her people were trampled by hard hoofs or brushed aside by broad equine shoulders. The queen watched with rising anxiety as the horsemen unsheathed axes and swords and began to cleave flesh and bone.

She cried, "No!" when the great war horns of the Forest People reverberated from the northern forests. Then she watched in disbelief as Drostan, battle axe in hand, led five thousand out of the woods.

"At least there should be no more surprises," said Ualraig.

The tall, swarthy-skinned commander sighed and nodded to his driver. Like many of his men, Ualraig fought bare-chested and with dark brown hair in long plaits. He wore no armour, preferring to protect his torso with a large, round, wooden shield and his expertise with a sword, axe, and dagger. With a curt nod to Kartimandu, he directed his chariot towards the skirmish.

From the settlement of Dumha, the screams and shrieks of the Sídhe, accompanied by the druids' chanting, rose above the battle's cacophony.

In her head, Kartimandu heard one word repeated over and over. *Flee.*

***

The eagles soared high over the theatre. Fate cried, "You cannot interfere."

"Of course, I can. That's what gods do. The humans pray to us, and we meddle with godly capriciousness." The Goddess dived and swept low along the waters of the Abhainn Dubh. Sharp talons plucked a huge, silver fish from the river. She loved to hunt. The fish was a fighter and furiously slapped its head and tail against her plumage.

The Goddess appreciated the struggle but declined to release the fish into the water. Instead, she dropped it at the feet of a massive brown bear trolling for food along the riverbank. It stood on its hind legs and roared its appreciation.

As the eagle gained height, the river smoke appeared to take on the shape of a ghostly apparition. Long tendrils of gossamer white hair flared in the breeze. The face was a skull with sunken black eyes and a cavernous maw. One hand raised a spectral spear and pointed to the river. The waters roared, gathered in a turbulent froth, and rushed towards the sea. In their place was left an expanse of mud.

Cut off from the river and the wellspring of her power, Kartimandu swore. With a howl of anger, she ordered her chariot driver and guard towards Áth and the higher waters of the Abhainn Dubh. She urgently needed another source of water and power.

***

The Cinn Péinteáilte crashed into Ualraig's divisions, battering their front ranks. Mòrag screamed herself hoarse and laid about her with a spear slick with the blood of many. Her stance alternated between stabbing high to pierce soft upper body and head tissues and swinging low in long low arcs to slash leg muscles and tendons.

Blood spurted around Mòrag, painting her body with garish crimson swirls. She forced a path to the shield-wall, and a great cheer rose. The straps constraining her breasts had finally succumbed to the inevitable. She grinned through a mask of blood, accepted the rash of indelicate compliments, and turned to head-butt a new opponent.

Carmag's force split, targeting the enemy's left and right flanks. There was little room for heroic duels in the free-for-all. Indeed, Carmag's men gave him a wide berth. His hammer was held high, and he swung the weapon steadied by a foundation of thighs as broad as tree trunks and feet that took a cow's hide to cover.

He roared orders to push Ualraig's men onto the spears of Conall's square. Under the relentless onslaught, the enemy's attack fractured. Unable to maintain command of their men, the clann leaders shrugged bloodied shoulders. Those with hornblowers not lying in the mud and gore sounded the retreat and ran for the river and forest.

Mórrígan ignored the central conflict. Clods of dirt flew high into the air as she rode hard towards the warband that was making a desperate attempt to reach Áth. Horses snorted and sweated, and muzzles streamed froth. The Huntress had at first dismissed the small band as cowards leaving the fight. Still, the gaudiness of Kartimandu's chariot caught her attention. Now Mórrígan gritted her teeth and determined to close the distance. The abomination that was Kartimandu had stolen her babies, and the Huntress had every intention of administering a painful retribution.

Kartimandu watched Mórrígan's riders gaining on her party. *Our retreat is too slow, but my chariot will make the ford if an obstacle is placed in the path of that bitseach.* Weakened by the loss of the river waters, the queen still retained command over the five hundred elite guards that accompanied her. She brought her chariot to a halt and addressed the group.

"Twenty will run with me. The rest will engage the queen of Clann Ui Flaithimh. Serve your queen and Goddess well, and you will be rewarded. Do not disappoint me, for my vengeance is terrible." Without a backward glance, the chariot sped away. The guard spread out to form a barrier of flesh and bone.

Mórrígan's horses slammed into Kartimandu's guard, knocking many brutally aside. Stunned, they were open to a skull-cracking sword blade or axe. The Dark Huntress leapt from her horse, rolled forward and, pulling the twin daggers she favoured from her belt, disembowelled one man, and slit the throat of another. She walked through a curtain of spurting blood.

In vain, Mórrígan wiped her mouth with the back of an equally bloody hand and tasted the gore. Like a wolf, she howled rather than shouted orders to her men. The skirmish was fought on a green canvas splashed garishly with crimson. If horses were considered combatants, then both sides were evenly matched. The beasts bit with grass-stained teeth and reared up on hind legs to deliver crushing blows with lashing hoofs.

Men and women fought in a chaotic frenzy of blood, piss, and shite as they dodged and slid underneath the horses. Soon the ground was carpeted with bodies. Blood seeped into an already saturated earth. Bloated, the land groaned but was unwilling to reject the sacrifice. Severed heads looked astonished. Their eyes were unable to comprehend they were dead.

Kartimandu's hold over her guard meant they would never yield. Thus, the skirmish was fought to an inevitable conclusion. Most lay dead; others awaited a stab to the heart or the slash of a blade across their throats. None pleaded for mercy. Mórrígan looked into their eyes and shivered. Their bodies moved and breathed, but their spirits had been sucked from them.

High-pitched squeals of injured horses blended with the groans and sobs of men. The animals' broken legs and mortal slashes to chests and flanks brought tears to hard men and women. They gently stroked their friend's velvet head and whispered heartfelt farewells before ending the beast's suffering with a dagger or sword thrust.

Mórrígan was dismayed. Of her original two hundred, half were dead or injured. She would be fortunate if more than a score of the wounded recovered to ride with her again. Her loss was felt more as she watched Kartimandu's chariot cross the ford at Áth. The queen's guard had served her well.

***

Ualraig knew the day was lost. *Conall probably played a mean game of fidchell.* His remaining forces were pressed on all flanks by a combination of cavalry and Drostan's warriors. Conall's highly effective square, having survived what should have been a crushing onslaught, was reinforced.

Kartimandu's battle commander watched as his men fled east to the forest or west to the Abhainn Dubh. With commendable discipline, Conall's formation reorganised and approached Ualraig's flank as four distinct shield-walls. Beset by enemies on three sides, Ualraig's choice was simple, fight to a glorious defeat and certain death or retreat.

The High People's commander was no coward. However, he was in no mood to sacrifice any more men for a queen who had fled the field. He grabbed a hornblower by the shoulder and rasped, *"Sound the retreat!"* Standing on the small dirt ridge, Ualraig roared, *"Retreat to the river!"* That said, Ualraig failed to consider that the river was no more than an expanse of wet mud.

All retreats are bloody because an army falling back is always in two minds. They can stand and fight, hoping to clear a route or run and outpace their pursuers' blades. Conall was impressed. Ualraig's flight had much more order than the chaotic fragmentation of many of the battle commander's warbands.

When those under Ualraig's command reached the riverbank, a third of his force, over ten thousand men and women, lay dead or injured. A sickening realisation dawned on him. Without water in the river, his men faced a lethally slow trudge through cloying silt and slime.

The allies hurled spears, axes, rocks, and even logs, at the mass of High People struggling in the muck of the Abhainn Dubh. Many re-treating warbands used the bodies of their fallen comrades as stepping stones to cross the riverbed. Indeed, some precipitated the fall of fellow warriors with a spear or axe in the back. The death toll was substantially higher downstream, where the river widened to several hundred paces.

When the High People's army finally gathered together, a headcount found that less than half had survived. Many died quickly from mortal injuries; the wounded lingered, awaiting infection or a merciful blade. Those on the opposite bank faced a life in chains, likely far away from their homeland.

Ualraig listened to taunts and curses from the far side of the Abhainn Dubh and the mountaintop of the Sleá. His army faced a long tramp to Dùn Caen. The words of Conall were recalled, and Ualraig shivered. Yes, it would be a long and dangerous journey.

***

Like a flock of crows, the people of Clann Ui Flaithimh descended the foothills of the Sleá. Many joined the wailing of the mná sídhe as loved ones were carried to the funeral pyres. The rest worked alongside kin to strip bodies and send the mortally injured to Mag Mell. The latter mercy was a judgment call regarding the enemy's injuries.

Thousands of the enemy had been captured, prompting Drostan to propose the prisoners should be executed. The king of the Forest People's opinion was that while women and children made valuable slaves, men were troublemakers and a pain in the arse. Besides, he maintained that if they were true warriors, they should have chosen death over capture. In the end, economics prevailed, and the prisoners were sent to the coastal communities where slave galleys made regular stops.

As the day drew in around the many fires and piles of plunder, the battle frenzy evolved into impromptu feasting, drinking, and celebrating heroic contests. Relief at having survived inflamed the loins and passions of men and women. It was not long before carousing rapidly descended into unrestrained rutting.

The feast of Imbolg after the coming winter would welcome a fresh crop of Crobh-Daoine to the world.

CHAPTER 19

406 B.C.—Abus

Curiosity nibbled at Coireall's mind. The twins and he had come to an accommodation. For the duration of the journey, they would be treated as part of his crew, helping in whatever way they could. In the end, they would let the gods sort out the mess. However, in the past few sunsets, the girls' demeanour had shown a marked improvement that could not be adequately explained by the physically exhausting, if less stressful, atmosphere on the boat.

Brighid and Danu were young and had not developed the adult art of bare-faced deceit. The boat rocked gently on a shallow swell this evening as the sun settled below the horizon. Yellow flames from stern and bow lamps flickered in the pleasant sea breeze, flooding the vessel with the distinctive smell of burning fish oil. Coireall watched. In the half-light of the stuttering flames, his answer came quickly.

Danu nudged her sister and pointed towards the shore. The bald-headed captain followed her line of interest. On a rocky headland, a signal fire with a distinctive blue-green flame burst into life. *Lots of birch wood.*

The vision for both girls came from the Sídhe. It was no more than a suggestion to be watchful and a reminder that coincidences are rarely what they seem. The distance between them was almost impossible. Mongfhionn fought, draining much of her powers to bridge the physical gap and brush aside the veils that protected human minds from unearthly intrusions. Her goal was to plant one final thought... one name.

One of the twins whispered, "Urard."

It was the second time the name had been spoken. In his bones, Coireall knew this was not good news.

***

If the fair weather kept up, the ship was two sunsets from the mouth of the *Abus*. From there, navigating the estuary and the trek overland to Kartimandu's seat of power at Dùn Caen would take a quarter of the moon. As he was calculating distances, Coireall's thoughts were interrupted by a shout, "*Sail!*"

The captain screwed up his eyes, squinting to see better, and then gave up. Any more than a few hundred paces and all he could see was a shimmering mist of ghostly shapes and colours. The mate laughed. "It's too far for me to make out. Ye have no chance."

Coireall's ship hugged the coastline. Its ancient timbers groaned, protesting each of the many subtle alterations to its course. Occasionally, the vessel's bow rose and slapped the cold salt waters, dousing the ship's crew. Squeals from the girls brought a smile to Coireall's weather-beaten face.

The other boat paralleled the shore but maintained a course much farther out in the deeper waters. Coireall and the girls recognised the ship's outline, rigging, and square sail. "Pytheas!" they exclaimed.

A thick, ginger-grey eyebrow rose as Coireall peered at the girls. "Ye know Pytheas?"

Brighid sported a self-satisfied smile. "Pytheas is a good friend of our Da."

Coireall's mate looked at him and said, "Ye just cannae get a break, can ye?"

The older man sighed. He was past caring and tired of running, and it seemed appropriate to put his fate in the hands of a fellow sailor. He watched the sleek galley with some envy. It was a design that he knew well. The long, narrow cedarwood hull was braced with thick cables that sprouted like octopus' tentacles from a single mast top.

The ship abruptly changed direction. Its build allowed it to turn on a pinhead. Now it cut through the waves of *An Mhuir Ó Thuaidh* towards them. As the vessel closed on Coireall's boat, he heard the resounding thump of a beat drum. He visualised two banks of oars dipping synchronously into the waters. The hair on the back of Coireall's sunburnt neck stood up.

Coireall stood on his platform. His hand was steady on the tiller as he navigated a course through submerged nearshore rocks. This was a particularly treacherous strip of coastline, made more deceptive by the beautiful white sand beach that swept north and south as far as the eye could see. A perpetual sea breeze threaded through the skeletons of animals and ocean debris, creating a soft, female singing sound. Indeed, many ships and crews, attracted by the beach's music and the pristine sands, met their fate on the rocks.

Once again, Coireall squinted hard. This time his gut twisted.

The bireme climbed a larger-than-usual wave, exposing its signature flat hull. It also revealed a blunt-nosed, bronze-covered ram. The length of a spear, the ram would find little resistance from the old timbers of his ship. The vessel's sail was deep green, not black. To Coireall, it was more evidence the gods had deserted him. Deaf to his pleadings, they disdained his gifts. He looked at his mate, saw resignation in his eyes, and roared, "*Sea Peoples!*"

"They've eyes and ears along the coast," said Coireall. "Likely, we were betrayed for gold by one of the fishing settlements where we bought supplies. The girls are worth much gold, either as slaves or ransom."

"They'll catch us before we make the shore. Six score oars to our eight," said the mate.

Coireall called the twins to him. "Can ye swim?"

"In rivers, yes. Never in the sea," said Danu.

"Same principle. It can be rougher in the sea but more buoyant due to the salt. Keep yer heads up and yer mouths shut. Turn on yer back if you get tired. The tide is coming in and running fast. It will bring you ashore." The girls nodded.

"Once ashore, head west, away from the sea." The elderly captain handed the girls a pair of knives. "Take these. Dinnae trust anyone you don't know." He breathed deeply and exhaled, "I'm sorry for what has happened. Ye know yer Da is looking for ye. Stay together, stay strong, and never give up. Some of us might make it to the shore, but likely not."

Brighid whispered, "Thank you."

Calloused hands grabbed the twins and tossed them into the sea. They broke the surface with a splash and splutter of mouths filled with saltwater. "I said keep yer mouths shut," shouted the captain before returning to his predicament.

"Will they make it ashore?" asked the mate.

"Likely not, but better Manannán Mac Lir takes them than slavers. I doubt these pirates have anything pleasant in mind for them. Their age will not protect them." The captain thought for a moment. "Right. Get yerself and the men into the water. Swim for the shore. Some of ye might make it. Ye certainly won't if ye remain with the boat."

The mate asked, "And ye?" Coireall nodded towards the bireme. His friend clasped his arm, shook his head, and said, "Ye'r an eejit." Then he leapt into the waters.

***

Coireall intended to avoid striking the galley bow-to-bow. The ram would shatter the ancient timbers of his boat, leaving the pirate's course unchanged. He would have sacrificed everything for no gain. The elderly seaman manoeuvred his ship with all the knowledge he had amassed over a lifetime on the sea.

The tide was not running in his favour, but beneath the water's surface, a god finally listened. Manannán Mac Lir reached out. Coireall relished the unexpected gust of wind and the feel of an uncharted current taking hold of his boat. The old vessel struck the bireme's bow on the port side just beyond the ram with unnatural momentum and impact.

The old sailor heard the crack of timbers and knew they were not his. It was the last sound Coireall heard. The galley, thrown off-course by the unexpectedly fierce blow, twisted and mounted the ancient ship, crushing it into a thousand pieces of flotsam.

The bireme's cables, their tension released, lashed the pirates. Some lost limbs, others their fingers, and one lost his head. The angry sea roared at them. In reply, they cursed the sea gods and raised clenched fists. The sea current gripped the flat-bottomed galley. For a moment, all was calm. Then Manannán Mac Lir dashed the trespassers against the rocks.

***

Brighid and Danu lay on the wet sand, clothed in kelp and bladderwrack. They coughed, throwing up salt water and chunks of food until their bellies ached. They longed for a cold drink of spring water. Crabs scuttled away from them, seabirds ignored them, and rabbits took shelter in dune burrows.

A rough hand grabbed them by the shoulders, hauling them to their feet. "This is nae the time to rest." Through a mist of tears and encrusted sand, the girls fought to make sense of their situation. Before them stood the mate of the ship. Water dripped from his straggly hair. Behind him, three others waited. All looked more miserable than usual. The girls twisted free of the mate's grip, which was not difficult. He was exhausted, his fingers a waxy white with numbness, and they were still draped in seaweed. Instinctively, they stood back-to-back, knives raised.

He laughed. "Someone trained ye well." Then, in a more serious tone, he pointed to the sea. "Look." The Sea Peoples' galley was stranded on the rocks. The motion of the waves carried the ship back and forward across rows of stone teeth. From the cracking sounds, the ship's timbers were slowly and inevitably rent asunder.

Men jumped over the side. Some dashed their skulls on submerged rocks, turning the foam around the vessel a delicate shade of pink. Triangular fins began to appear. The sharks in the cold waters around Albu were curious creatures but tended to keep their distance. But every sailor knew it only took one thrash and snap from a hungry predator, and the waters would churn in a bloody feeding frenzy.

"The water is not deep between the shore and the ship. These men have lost much. They will be furious. They're well-armed and will delight in doing as much harm as possible to ye without harming yer value." The man pointed towards the high sand that rose like mountains between sea and forest. "Ye need to get over those dunes and into the forest beyond."

The girls nodded and began to move. It was easy at first. The sand was wet and packed solid. Soon it became drier, looser, and deeper. Tiny feet sank into the fine grit. They floundered, tripped, and fell flat on their faces. Sand crunched in their teeth and clogged their nostrils.

After this trial, they hit a belt of wave-smoothed rocks and pebbles that ran the length of the long beach. Toes were stubbed on stones. They cried as thorns, broken shells, and dried seaweed pierced their soft feet. Knees and elbows bled from cuts and grazes when they stumbled.

Breathing harshly, they finally reached the base of the dunes. Brighid and Danu loved playing in the sand dunes of the northeastern coast of Ériu. Now, they cried as the mountains of sand towered over them. Only tufts of spiky, yellow, and green grasses provided handholds to prevent them from slipping back down the steep, constantly moving slopes. To misstep was to court disaster. The pirates had gained the beach and were quickly closing the gap.

Rough hands came to their rescue as former shipmates hauled the girls over the lip of the first line of dunes. Out of breath, the mate could only point inland and rasp, "Run!" He shouted before turning to help the last seaman.

Brighid and Danu would later wonder where they got the strength to keep their legs pumping. They raced blindly through a maze of chest-high grasses, praying to the Goddess that they were travelling in the right direction.

The girls ran screaming, unaware that this pinpointed their position to enemies. Today the Goddess watched over them. They stumbled over the lip of a small sandbank and fell at the feet of a pair of red and black plaid-covered legs that ended in soft leather boots.

"Help us, please." Unseeing in the panic of terror, Danu uttered the plea and collapsed.

***

Urard gently lifted the girls with massively muscled arms, quickly checked to make sure they were not injured and then passed them to Iasg. "Take several men. Go to the camp. Feed them. Dry their clothes. Try and get them to rest. Guard them with your life." He turned to face the sea. Across sandy ridges, several men in ragged clothes staggered towards him. Several hundred paces behind, a pack of howling pirates chased them.

"We're in an alien land. We've no time to question who are friends or enemies. Kill them all." The warband's response was definitely on Urard's side. Helmets, studded fist wraps, and small round, leather and wood shields were quickly tightened into position. Axes and swords were loosened and checked for easy release. The single javelin that each carried was balanced, ready to throw. These were warriors used to fighting on horseback, but their fighting skills were well-honed. As one, led by Urard, they strode forward.

Coireall's remaining crew could scarcely believe their misfortune. To their rear, over a hundred brigands from the shipwreck steadily gained on them. To their front, they were faced with an equal number of red-haired, fierce-looking men who, from their manner, appeared to have little interest in talking. They dropped to their knees and prayed to any god who might listen.

Urard swept past the mate. Without breaking his stride, the battle-axe inscribed with the word *Breith*—judgment, swept in a low, rising arc. For a fleeting moment, the mate's head appeared to lead Urard's charge before it lost momentum and dropped with a dull thud to the sand. The other crew members were put down with the stab of a javelin.

It occurred to Urard the men charging towards him, screaming in an unintelligible language, were dressed, after a fashion, like Nikandros. Urard very much doubted that they were exchanging greetings. They carried large, circular bronze shields, spears, and swords and wore bronze breastplates and shin armour. A few had helmets with long, flaring black horsehair plumes. Most had black hair in long, tight plaits. Their skin varied in colour from ivory cream to almost black.

***

Chios was beautiful but, by no measurement, the largest of the Greek islands. Yet Chios was a great naval power with a long tradition of waging war at sea. Tired of fighting for no personal gain, Orestes of Chios had been an eager recruit to the Sea Peoples. He preferred that name to "pirate", which had such an unfortunate connotation.

He saw himself as a benign adventurer of the sea. However, no one could recall a single charitable act associated with his name. His speciality was kidnapping for ransom and slave trading. In these, he was both an expert and very successful.

Orestes had assembled a crew of like-minded villains. That, in itself, was a slur on the term "villain." His gang quickly gained a reputation for having no measure of compassion or mercy and no loyalty except, perhaps, to each other. To them, anyone man, woman, and child with a tradable value in gold was a fair target. Without conscience, they would kill any who stood between them and their profit.

Orestes and his men outstripped their peers in a profession unknown for its niceties or pleasant personalities. Hence, they stood a pinnacle of black-heartedness. Many had tried to defeat him. All had failed, and most were dead. Orestes paid well for intelligence, and a network of informers kept him well-supplied. Beyond this, his crew comprised the best fighters in the Great Sea.

To put it mildly, the predicament in which Orestes found himself was unfavourable. His ship was gone. His profit, the children, were temporarily beyond his grasp. His men were exhausted, having chased the remaining crew of the bastard who had sunk them across the beach and up steeply inclined sand dunes.

Since they had been at sea for a full moon, they were unsteady on their feet. As they crested the dune, they faced a band of tall, heavily armed barbarians whose demeanour did not look forgiving and who were much fresher. Their leader, a colossus made taller by an iron, horned helmet, wielded an oversized axe like a twig. Their similarity of dress concerned him. Did they have friends nearby?

There was little to be done or said. This was going to be a scrap. Orestes smiled confidently. His men were the dirtiest fighters in the known world. He would bet his life on them. *"Kill the Keltoi!"* he roared. He drew his sword and charged with the sure knowledge that the crew would follow.

Urard did not consider that he was a leader. Like most Clann Ui Flaithimh warriors, he was content to take his lead from the ceannairí céad or ceannairí na míle. As his men closed the final few hundred paces, he felt an uncomfortable urge to say something inspiring. Therefore, while maintaining his stride, Urard turned, faced his men, and shouted, "Heads, arms, and legs. We'll kill them later."

His words were met with a roar of approval, informing Urard he had said the right thing. The warband picked up the pace and charged. As Urard led his assault, his men strained to keep up the pace set by his huge leg muscles. Yet they maintained a tight formation of two rows of fifty men.

Orestes' pace noticeably slackened, and he fell behind such that five men were ahead of him. It was no accident. Orestes was a veteran. He wanted to see if the colossus thundering towards his men was also a good fighter.

Clann Ui Flaithimh's riders were accustomed to throwing javelins while moving, although usually from horseback. Therefore, as they closed within javelin range, their stride remained constant as they hurled a hundred missiles into the air.

Unlike their usual enemies, Orestes' men were better armoured and used their bronze shields to deflect most projectiles. That said, they lost a tenth of their band. More importantly, their momentum faltered. Not by much, but enough to make the impact of the Urard's band more effective as they swept spears aside with long swords and axes.

In the lands surrounding the Great Sea, the Keltoi's zeal for a fight was well known. Warbands of the red-haired fighters were highly prized as mercenaries. Hence, Orestes' men were unnerved. Tales they previously considered wild exaggerations sounded ominously accurate. The already ragged centre of the pirates shattered as the Urard's band punched through. Screams filled the air as Urard's men swiftly hamstrung dozens of men with vicious backslashes of axe and sword.

The five before Urard were brave, but their spears became firewood as his double-bladed weapon carved an arc to the right and left. Two lost their lives as they scrambled to unsheathe swords from leather baldrics. Urard's chest-high swing opened their throats and almost cleaved heads from necks.

Three remained and had the presence of mind to swing their shields around before unsheathing their weapons. Even then, they staggered backwards as Urard's curved blade carved deep gouges into their shields' bronze covering. The giant's drive carried him forward. His strength was unabated.

Orestes watched with mounting concern. His force was reduced by a third on the first assault. The skirmish quickly descended into a melee of duels. His men were over-confident in their bronze armour. They found underneath plain Keltoi clothing was boiled leather armour with iron fish scales stitched between its layers. A few had chainmail. Blade strokes that should have been deadly achieved little apart from putting them at the mercy of their opponents.

The formidable warrior who led the Keltoi appeared unstoppable. With men on three sides, Urard feinted left, crouched, and swung his axe low and parallel to the ground. Orestes winced as one assailant's leg was severed at the knee. The man fell, with blood pumping from the stump.

His screams were loud but ignored.

Another leapt at Urard's back. He was halted by the iron-ringed butt-end of the axe as it was driven backwards. The force took the breath from the pirate, bending him double. With a bellow, Urard turned. The axe cleaved the gasping man's skull in two, scattering pink-grey brains on the sand.

A pleading look from the fifth pirate gained no help from Orestes. The man spat his disgust in the sand, raised his shield, balanced his sword, and approached Urard. There was no avoiding the giant. That was perfectly clear from the man's aggressive stance. The pirate knew the reach of his sword was too short. He needed to survive the first blow and close quickly on his opponent. It was a good plan—for anyone other than Urard.

Breith was restless in Urard's large hands. It was as if man and axe were communicating the best tactics. Never one to think overlong, Urard lifted the axe high and stepped forward. His two-handed grip lent speed and strength to the swing. The axe head arched in a half-circle that ended at his opponent's shield, striking the top edge and cracking bronze and wood.

The force wrenched the pirate's arm, numbing it from shoulder to elbow. With another man and another axe, he might have survived. The long, curved edge of Urard's blade carved a path starting at the pirate's forehead, splitting his nose and sundering his mouth and jaw in two. The fact that his arm was numb was irrelevant. He was already dead.

The pirate leader sheathed his xiphos and picked up a spear. He needed an advantage. As he looked around, it was apparent no help would come from his remaining crew. Those closest had stepped back, clearing an arena in the sand. The only thing that suggested the warrior approaching had just killed five of his foes was the gore-splattered cloth-ing. Orestes admired his talent for killing and was puzzled by the anger on his blood-streaked face. *Why is he taking this so personally?*

It was true that Urard was angry. He was also annoyed, although not about the skirmish. With every step, his boots filled with more sand and gravel. One particular piece of grit insisted on lodging in the most sensitive areas of his sole. It resisted all efforts to remove it or move to a less painful location. Therefore, Urard wanted the confrontation over with all speed. Killing the leader of the pirates seemed an excellent way to achieve his goal.

"You and your men would make great pirates. May I offer you a new profession?" Orestes called out as he moved within spear range. The pirate was well-travelled and knew enough of the Keltoi language to make himself understood. Urard snorted, his hand swept in a circular motion indicating the battlefield. The sand was crimson-red and littered with bodies.

"You've lost. Surrender. I promise a swift death."

"What? No negotiation on who lives or dies?"

"You're pirates. You chose the life. You know the penalty." Urard watched as Orestes slowly, fluidly circled. Dark brown eyes never strayed from Urard as the pirate leader probed for weakness. He considered but ruled out throwing the spear. A miss would put him at the mercy of the axe's curved edge.

"You chased the girls. That sealed your fate."

"Ah, the girls. Then perhaps we could trade my freedom for information on that contract." Urard saw a glimmer of hope in Orestes' eyes.

"No pleading for mercy for your men?"

"Leaders are a scarce commodity. Crews are found in many places."

"I know who your contract is with." The Greek pirate looked startled. Urard tapped his head and smiled, "I'm big but not thick in the head. When we strip your bodies, we'll find Roman gold. You spoke of a contract and not a simple opportunity that came your way. That means it could be from only one source. However, I am thankful for the information. My king will be grateful. He thought this was a simple kidnapping by Kartimandu of the High People."

Orestes snarled and lunged.

The pirate chose his time well. The spearhead sliced through Urard's pants, causing a long gash on his left thigh. The slash smarted. It was deep enough that it would leave a scar but did not result in any loss of motion. Urard grasped Orestes' spear and pulled it forward abruptly. With a forehead that was just as hard as his iron helmet, Urard smashed the pirate's nose beyond fixing.

The pirate leader staggered backwards, blinking furiously to clear eyes blurred with tears. Blood and snot gushed from his mangled nose, but he was no amateur. Playing for time, he crouched and swung his spear in a long arc. The tip grazed across Urard's knees, making the enormous man grunt. It was one of those cuts that stung and would keep opening up because of its location but caused no real damage. A swift swing of the axe cut the spear in two.

Pirates rely on surprise and speed. On a galley with one hundred and twenty men, carrying heavy infantry shields would reduce the vessel's speed, losing a vital advantage. Hence, Orestes and his men had ones that were thinner, lighter, and designed to deflect rather than absorb sword blade strikes. For a flutter of time, Orestes was unarmed as he reached to draw his sword from the scabbard. Were it not for the shield protecting his trunk, the two-handed, backward blow from Urard's axe would have carved him in two.

As it was, Urard's blade struck a horizontal blow across the centre of the shield. The lighter shield buckled. Fortunately for Orestes, shield straps held his arm level. Instead of the axe-blade lopping off his arm, it merely opened up his flesh from elbow to wrist.

The pirate cried out as he lost the power of his arm. Arm and shield hung limply against his body. More worrying was the steady flow of blood that coursed down the inside of the broken shield and dripped on the sand. Orestes brushed aside the light-headedness that threatened to swamp his senses and moved forward.

"That's bright blood. You're a dead man. Kneel. I'll end your life swiftly."

Enraged, Orestes dropped his shield and rushed Urard. He found the colossal man was surprisingly nimble and sidestepped the oncoming charge. The axe swung, and Orestes' forearm fell to the sand, severed at the elbow. The follow-through pierced his side, opening up a deep gash in his abdomen, just below the ribs. He screamed, cursed, and called on his gods. Blood spurted rhythmically from the stump of his arm, its force diminishing as Orestes' heart faltered. He slumped to his knees and looked pleadingly at Urard.

The usually good-hearted warrior shook his head. "You shouldn't have come after the girls and should have taken my offer." Urard walked away. In the corner of his eye, he watched Orestes struggle to position his sword before falling forward. The pirate was unsuccessful. The blade did little more than add another slash along his ribcage before resting between his side and arm. Orestes bled to death. It was a painful and fitting end.

Stunned, the remaining pirates turned to flee. "Finish this rabble," bellowed Urard. The warband roared in response and fell on the pirates. None lived. All were beheaded. Their bodies were stripped of anything valuable and left to the scavengers. Urard had lost five men; another score had minor injuries.

***

Urard's camp was in a sheltered hollow between dunes. Close by, horses grazed in a makeshift corral, nipping at tufts of grass with large, yellowed teeth. Beyond the encampment, the dirt mixed with sand, and the grass became less patchy and finer-bladed. A green swathe sprinkled with late-spring wildflowers carpeted the land.

Eventually, the wildwood overwhelmed the grass with its thick undergrowth of ferns, bushes, and brambles. Further west, the tangle of the brush surrendered to the order of tall, majestic trees more ancient than man. The old forest spread over the vast slopes of the Penn-inus—the spine of mountains that dominated central Albu.

Yet, even the trees succumbed when soil once more became sparse and lacked depth. Moorland gorse, heathers, and lichens formed a beautiful, multi-hued crown. The mountains of Penn-inus were not as tall or craggy as those in the north. Indeed, they could be climbed by man and beast with little difficulty. They were, however, vast in length and breadth. Scattered bogland, unpredictable weather, and sudden fogs and mists made the range treacherous.

Urard sat back from the fire, nibbling absent-mindedly on a roasted rabbit thigh, and dug thick, gnarly toes into the soft sand. His axe lay by his side. Surrounded by a circle of smooth rocks, the fire of driftwood and grasses crackled joyfully. The blaze radiated heat not altogether needed at meán lae on a dry, late-summer day.

However, the fire proved useful to air damp clothes. A combination of "Since we're close to the sea, we may as well take a bath" and the need to wash gore from their clothes propelled his band to rush into the cold waters. Urard laughed loudly at the childish cries of the fierce warband when the bitterly cold waters of An Mhuir Ó Thuaidh rose over their crotches.

A rustle several paces away caught Urard's attention. Two tousled redheads appeared from beneath a mound of *diallaití*. He was glad the twins, under the watchful eye of Iasg, had been able to nap. They rubbed the sleep from their eyes and, assured they were not dreaming, threw themselves at Urard. Their grip on his neck almost choked him before he gently levered them downwards. Each sat on a muscled thigh as he held them to his chest, enfolding each with a strong, steady arm.

Danu looked up and asked. "Aodán?"

A tear rolled down the Urard's cheek at the girls' concern for their brother. "Your brother lives. He is safe."

"Are *we* safe, Urard?" Brighid asked.

"We've a long journey ahead." Urard looked to the north and squinted slightly as if in thought. "This is an unfriendly land, but your Da has given me a hundred of his best to guard you. Even in the land of the High People, such a warband is not to be trifled with. The Goddess willing, we'll all meet up again."

Their seal of approval prompted another tear to escape Urard's eye as small arms surrounded his considerable girth and squeezed hard.

CHAPTER 20

406 B.C.—Trócaire

He knew he would be sore later but did not care. He moaned in savage pleasure as he thrust upwards and felt her pit embrace his hard manhood. Her riding was particularly fierce and had an urgency absent from their previous encounter. He gazed up, admiring her body. The raven-black hair piled high on her head was a stark, but beautiful, contrast to her alabaster-white skin. He grasped her firm breasts and squeezed hard. He smiled as she gasped in pain. She was not the only one who could be rough.

Finely muscled arms stretched, strong hands with long musician's fingers removed the pins from her hair. The ribbed, bronze pins tapered quickly from an ornately engraved, solid circle with a ruby at its centre to a thin, sharp point. She shook her head, releasing long tresses that fell forward in a warm, lush caress of his chest and face. She felt the approach of her climax and urged him to thrust harder and deeper.

The orgasm was perfect. Her body flushed, and she quivered with pleasure as his seed spurted inside her. There was a fleeting moment of sadness before the hairpins plunged towards his eyes. As the long, slim blades descended, time seemed to pass unbearably slowly for the bowman. His pupils widened briefly in shock. There was no time for anger. The sharp points continued their trajectory, penetrating his eyeballs and then his brain. Clear liquid flowed from his ruined eyes—then blood.

She raised herself slowly and deliberately and stepped away from the body. As she dressed, she glanced at the young man. In a moment of frivolity, she giggled. The rigour of death had immortalised his erection. She wondered how it compared to those of Nikandros or Torcán. Their manhoods were a constant subject of camp gossip. She shook her head. Such thoughts were inappropriate, even if they did cause an extra flutter of warmth between her legs.

***

"Why me?" Tadhg repeated the phrase with mild exasperation as he was guided along a narrow animal track in the woods behind Trócaire.

It was mid-morning. The chill had gone from the weather. Tadhg had eaten a full, hot breakfast and supped on milk cooled overnight in a nearby spring. He sat on a log with his back against the roundhouse wall chewing on a twig to clean his teeth. He was feeling good right up until the family stood before him.

The children, a boy and a girl he guessed were about seven or eight summers, firmly clasped their parents' hands. The da informed Tadhg that the children were picking berries in the forest when they encountered a strange scene. While curiosity initially drew them, fear drove them to drop their baskets and run screaming back to the settlement. Now the boy and girl took Tadhg's hands and led him into the woods, followed by ma and da.

It was a pleasant, secluded glade. The ground was covered with a thick cushion of amber and green pine needles. Overhead the sylvan canopy gave protection from sun and rain. It was a setting that Gràinne and he could have chosen for its privacy. The corpse at its centre ruined the rustic ambience.

No wonder the children were scared. Tadhg took in the scene before him. He turned to the family. "Go back to Trócaire. Wait for me. Say nothing to anyone." Almost before he finished speaking, his guides scurried back along the trail.

The torso was semi-clothed. Red-green plaid pants were pulled down and lay over ankles and feet. Death had preserved an impressive cock. Tadhg took in the ruined eyes—two pools of dark, coagulated blood. *By the Hag, who wanted you dead and why? Perhaps the passion of a jealous lover?* Still, the precision of the stab wounds pointed to premeditation rather than a moment of lost control.

Tadhg shook his head again. *Why?* He gathered branches to place over the body. They would afford some protection from scavengers wanting a snack. As he knelt beside the body, he detected a distinctive fragrance wafting upwards, released by the warming air—the scent of a woman. That he had eliminated half of the population was of little consolation.

A bow lay abandoned several paces away, was the victim an archer or hunter? Tadhg tramped wearily along another path. This time his destination was Áth and a meeting with Conall. The king would not be pleased.

***

Brion woke with a pounding headache, an empty belly, and in dire need of a piss. The residual smell of urine emanating from a pail on the floor suggested this was where he could find relief from one of the three. Still, in his present condition, he doubted he could be that accurate.

Furthermore, he doubted whether he could get his legs to cooperate and leverage him to a standing position. Under his arse, a damp patch in the straw bedding made it plain that, until now, where to piss had not been subject to choice. He sighed.

Relieved of one burden, thirst drew Brion's attention to the narrow-mouthed jug on the floor to his left. He assumed it contained water. The pitcher remained untouched after several tries, apparently too far away from his shaky reach. He tried again without result.

This time his efforts were noticed. A firm hand gently lifted his head, placing the water jug against his lips. Even the small movement made his senses swim. "Drink slowly," said the druid as he looked toward the entrance. "You have a visitor."

"Áine?" croaked Brion.

"Want another guess?" The reply was forced and overly cheerful.

"Gràinne... my partner in crime." Brion's choice of words could have been better.

Gràinne's face fell, and tears flowed down tattooed cheeks as she walked towards the cot. She sat down on its corner, feeling the combination of straw and meadowsweet crunch beneath the pelts that enclosed them. The scent of crushed flowers was a pleasant distraction and masked the faint smell of piss. "I'm so sorry..."

A raised hand, now more bone than flesh, stopped her. "As I hope many have told you, there is neither guilt nor fault to be assigned. It was an accident. I hold no enmity for you."

Gràinne smiled. "Thank you." Standing up, she dipped a cloth into a nearby basin of water. She wrung it out with undue deliberation as if trying to organise her thoughts. Then she gently wiped Brion's haggard face. The long, white scar on his left cheek had sunk and seemed to have dragged the flesh on either side with it, creating a fleshy chasm. Auburn hair hung dull and lank from a shrunken scalp. His face, unshaven for almost a half-cycle of the moon, had the beginnings of a pretty awful beard.

"How bad is it?" asked Brion.

They were words she did not want to hear. "Has no one told ye? Fionnbharr? The druids?"

Brion shook his head and winced at the stabbing pain piercing his forehead. "They may have, but I was likely in no condition to hear or remember." A druid caught the gist of the conversation and raised an eyebrow as if asking, "Should I explain?" Gràinne shook her head, and he dipped his head and exited the chamber.

"Ye have lost yer left arm."

"That explains why I can't lift the water jug," said Brion trying to make light of the devastating news.

"Yer left side was well smashed up, broken collarbone, several broken ribs, *peilbheas* cracked, and thigh bone." Brion let out a long groan, and his emaciated body slipped deeper into the cot.

Gràinne hastily added. "Ye'r healing well. Fionnbharr and the druids have tended ye well. Mongfhionn, too, now that she's back." An uncomfortable silence hung in the air. In desperation, Gràinne blurted, "Ye can feel my tits if ye want!"

In a cot in a far corner of the room, the wounded Deaglán snorted loudly and muttered, "Some people have all the luck."

"What?" Brion was not sure he had heard Gràinne correctly. Maybe his brain was damaged.

"Ye can feel my tits. That seems to make most men happy."

"Thanks for the offer," replied Brion, feigning a nonchalance at odds with his racing pulse. In truth, the idea was very appealing. So much so that he fought to restrain the stirring in his groin. He was unsuccessful. Gràinne's eyes flicked downward.

"Ahhh, I wondered about that. At least yer manhood's functioning." She offered an impish smile. "I can help relieve that 'itch' too." Brion's dilemma was whether to laugh, cry, or accept Gràinne's offer. Instead, he fell prey to a painful bout of coughing. "Well, maybe ye'r still a wee bit weak for that, but the tits are always on offer."

Eventually, getting Brion brought his breathing under control. "Áine would not approve." The easy craic evaporated. Gràinne rose quickly, not wanting to show her contempt. She said goodbye and walked away. Brion sighed, in part at the lost opportunity, and closed his eyes.

Several sunsets later, Brion heard a loud fracas outside. A red-faced Conall dragged a screaming Cassán into the hall. "He's a cripple and useless. Ma says so," shrieked Cassán.

A dagger stabbed into Brion's heart. His son, now seven summers old, had been spoiled by an over-indulgent mother and a fawning nurse. He was overweight to the point of being fat. Unfortunately, Brion had bowed to Áine's wishes in matters related to his son.

Furthermore, he was often not at home. Brion maintained that this was because of his duties as a ceannairí na míle and member of the Chomhairle. In truth, the residence had become an uncomfortable place to rest.

***

"I'm going back to my forests, Conall," said Drostan after taking a long swig of beer.

"What of your people?" queried Conall.

"People are a pain in the arse. Always complaining about something. Trees are beautiful, strong and don't talk back." Drostan stroked his beard. "But I'll leave Carmag and a thousand men with ye. Most of Kartimandu's warriors have been cleared from the forests, but a few warbands may still exist. My warriors are better than yours in the woods." Conall nodded his thanks.

"I'll visit around Lugnasad. See how things are and what yer plans are. We can settle up on our agreement at that time." Conall nodded again, aware that the king had something else on his mind.

"Spit it out, Drostan."

Drostan took a deep breath. "When ye eventually leave, Carmag will go with ye, along with a thousand warriors and as many followers and their kin as want to accompany them." Drostan's tone indicated there would be no argument. Conall looked at the one-eyed king with an eyebrow raised questioningly.

"Why?"

"Old age."

"What?"

The *rígh* laughed, "Ye'll learn that age has a way of putting bad ideas into the heads of even the most loyal friends. A dream can nurture a seed that burrows deep until its roots are so firm that it can do nothing but grow. Carmag is my oldest and dearest friend. He has a brave heart, is a great general, and is loved by his men and the people of the Aos na Coille."

Drostan sighed. "I'd hate to remove his head from his shoulders, should a 'seed' take root one day. Let him adventure with ye. Send him back to me when he has a head of grey hair and can't hold that oversized hammer. Then we'll enjoy the end-years together... as friends."

"I have no problem with that arrangement as long as Carmag agrees." The king grunted. It was a sign that Carmag would have little choice.

"What are yer plans for Brion?" The change of topic surprised Conall.

"I'm not sure I have any beyond him making a good recovery from his injuries. What are you getting at?" Conall looked a little more sternly at the king. Drostan's question roiled him more than he liked to admit. Brion was his best friend and one of the few remaining from childhood. Conall remained furious and hurt at the disrespect shown by Áine and Cassán.

To complicate matters, it also cast a shadow over his friendship with Áine's brother, Íar. The big warrior was duty-bound to support his sister. However, he was heartbroken at having been put in that position. The tension between brother and sister manifested in the curtness of their conversations and the cooling of their relationship. Íar also felt guilty as he had encouraged Brion to court Áine.

Drostan looked up from contemplating the surface of the table. "He'd make a fine king of the Na Mèadaidh and a trustworthy partner on my southern border." Drostan waited a few moments to let Conall consider the proposal.

With some apprehension, Drostan continued. "Look, I disagree with what that *bidse*, Áine, has been saying, but with the loss of his arm, he'll find it hard to reclaim his place within Clann Ui Flaithimh. He can't stand in the shield wall or fight from a chariot or on horseback. *But* he could still run like a mad eejit into battle with us. Maybe a change and a clean break from the past would be better for all."

Conall felt his jaw tighten. It was a topic that he did not want to discuss. At least, not at this time. Drostan recognised the inner turmoil of Clann Ui Flaithimh's king. "There's no rush on this. Consider it. All I ask is that ye discuss it with Brion."

"I will. You have my word on that."

***

Íar slouched over his horse as it splashed through the waters at the crossing at Áth. His usual ebullience was shackled with profound unhappiness and an increasing sense of foreboding. The maelstrom engulfing his sister and Brion showed no end. Still, he clung to the hope that all would be resolved. *Give them time. They'll sort things out.*

Behind Íar trotted five hundred riders. Red and black foxtails attached to the crest of their helmets bounced in rhythm with the horses' gaits. To the rear of the cavalry, a dozen wagons, brimming with weapons and provisions, trundled over the ground on solid wooden wheels. Cattle, oxen, and strings of spare horses brought up the rear.

The final contingent of two hundred men, led by Brocc and Torcán, marched alongside the wagons. Several hundred paces ahead, accompanied by a pack of wolfhounds, Mórrígan's band rode in a skirmish line. One hundred riders were all that remained of her original group. The Huntress and her men rode with sharp blades and vengeance in their hearts.

Clann Ui Flaithimh's advance force was finally in the field. Tasked by Conall and the Chomhairle, Íar's and Mórrígan's orders were to follow and harass Kartimandu's army.

While their numbers had been drastically culled, the High People could still field fifteen thousand fighters. A direct assault would be sheer stupidity. However, using the speed of his horses meant Íar could give the defeated warriors an ongoing nightmare deep into their territory. Left unsaid but a priority, they were to search for Urard and the twins.

Íar's riders tracked along the river plain of the Abhainn Dubh. As they crossed fields that previously housed the camp of the Forest People, the vista was one of rot and decay. No one had taken care of the dead. The High People were long gone, and Clann Ui Flaithimh did not care.

Horses kicked aside half-rotting and partially eaten corpses, releasing clouds of fat blackflies. What meat remained on the bodies heaved with maggots. Scavengers snarled and grumbled from the forest. They were angry that their feasting had been interrupted.

CHAPTER 21

406 B.C.—Trócaire

A bite woke Urard from his doze. He cursed, slapped his shoulder, and then looked at his hand and upper arm. The remains of a blood-engorged cleg formed a dark splotch on his palm. The skin had already become inflamed on his arm and began to throb. "Tuilí," he grumbled. He spat a glob of saliva on the bite. It was an old remedy and would ease, although not prevent, several days of misery and the persistent compulsion to scratch the bite mark. Hopefully, the wound would not become infected.

Urard knew they needed to move. After the skirmish with the pirates, he let everyone rest up for a few sunsets. The time allowed injuries to heal and the men to bid farewell to fallen comrades. It also gave the girls a brief sojourn to recover from their ordeal.

The camp, on a raised, grassy plateau, proved an excellent choice. It kept them close to the coast and had long sightlines inland. There was no lack of forage for the horses. Food for the band was plentiful if restricted mainly to rabbits, fish, and *duileasc.* After Iasg insisted he tried it, Urard was surprised to find he liked the salty tanginess of the red seaweed.

A steady *thunk thunk thunk* interrupted the usual chatter of the camp. It was followed by peals of childish laughter, adult cheers, and the chink of gold. Iasg discovered several sets of throwing knives among the pirates' belongings and sturdy leather shoulder belts to hold them. A few adjustments tailored the cross-belts to fit Brighid and Danu and provided

Iasg with a more durable harness for herself.

Iasg then set about teaching the girls to throw and hit a target. It was an enjoyable way to keep the girls' minds off too many dark dreams. Yet Urard knew Iasg's goal was also to train the twins with a ranged weapon. Brighid's and Danu's skills with Nikandros' swords were impressive. However, Iasg's instruction would further enhance their chances of survival.

A pleasant diversion, the knife-throwing also proved to be welcome entertainment for Urard's warriors. Whenever the girls started to practice, a crowd quickly gathered around. Wagers were quietly made on who would have the most accurate or total number of killing throws.

Still, the riders did not foresee that the girls were fast learners. With a bit of encouragement from Iasg, they turned the drill to their advantage. After the first few sessions, Urard observed a recognisable pattern of which twin would provide better hits on the wooden targets. He also noted that Iasg and the girls' pouch of gold grew substantially.

Urard stood at the sound of rustling in nearby bushes and multiple voices. Scores of shabbily dressed men, women and children skirted the thorn and stake perimeter of the camp. Most ignored Urard's warband; a few glared with impotent anger. The children waved and shouted greetings at Brighid and Danu, who returned the gestures along with some food. The first time the nomads appeared, Urard had grabbed Breith, preparing to dissuade further contact with a few beheadings.

At that time, a hand on his arm restrained him. Iasg spoke with those who appeared to be their leaders and discovered they were of the High People. However, they had been deemed useless and cast out from the settlements. Any wealth they generated was from begging or from the gods.

The shipwreck was considered a part of this bounty. Thus, they were eager to ensure that Urard had no designs on any treasures washed up on the shore. Urard agreed to this arrangement, but their presence still made him uncomfortable.

Urard walked to the centre of the camp and announced, "We move in two sunsets."

***

Conall's arse was numb. He had spent from sunrise to sunset sitting on the carved wooden throne. The only diversion was the occasional skelf that stabbed and lodged in his arse when he shifted position.

His brain was as dead as his arse, and his eyes glazed over as yet another rose to give his opinion... and support. The thick, fetid air in the Great Hall made his head pound. The glum and bored looks on the faces of his Chomhairle told Conall their patience was approaching its limit.

The *Óenach* passed its sixth sunset of eating, drinking, and talking. It took almost a cycle of the moon just to get the flatha from the furthest settlements beyond the Uisce Èireann to attend. In all, two hundred and fifty crowded into Áth's Great Hall. Understandably, everyone wanted to be heard. Unfortunately, many were fond of the sound of their voices, and the unlimited beer lubricated their loquaciousness.

An orderly people of clann, sept and fine, the Celts were ruled by varying levels of flaith-fine. Everyone knew his or her place in the tribe. Position depended on wealth and property. Hence the presence of the cattle owners. The céile or freemen, many of whom had small farms and who formed most of the army, were represented by the ceannairí céad.

Even the fuidhir, the non-free, were represented and brought an unexpected benefit. When their representatives spoke, most took the opportunity to go for a piss, thus letting in a blast of fresh air.

It was a given that Conall, as the clann's chosen king, would get his way. There was no challenger for his position. No one was stupid enough to contest Conall's or the Chomhairle's authority. And only the foolish would object to the Goddess' chosen Hand.

Eventually, the vote was taken, and it was unanimous, to no one's surprise. Clann Ui Flaithimh's army and followers would march after the feast of Lugnasad and the beginning of Autumn. In the meantime, the people would prepare and build the supplies needed for the journey.

✳✳✳

Áine's ailment was an affliction of the mind. It was a disease, which made her behaviour easy to attribute to that of a beautiful but spoilt princess. Her petulant, self-centred actions were brushed off with a knowing smile of indulgence.

However, Áine had a cunning, manipulative mind, which interpreted everything through her twisted perspective. That brain was now free of the anchors that controlled, even enabled, her activities. There was no father, brother, or sister-in-law and, as she saw it, for all intents and purposes, no Brion to restrain her.

After the Óenach, the army, apart from a standing defensive battalion of one thousand under Cúscraid, disbanded. Most returned to their families and former professions. Their orders were to prepare for an autumn exodus. Most of Áine's archers resumed their role as community hunters.

Hunting was a solitary life in the forests that enfolded the tribe's many settlements. Hence, it was the perfect cover for prosecuting Áine's quest to remove all real or imaginary witnesses to her infidelity.

Her second victim was, in her opinion, hardly worth the effort and had not presented much of a challenge. Over-eager to spread her thighs, he spilt his seed in his pants. After assisting him to recover, his lame attempt at rutting was unimaginative.

Indeed, Aine was tempted to end his life before he brought her to a disappointing climax. In the end, she waited, was rewarded, and, in turn, repaid his exertions with a sightless trip to Mag Mell.

Aine smiled at the memory as she closed on her third and final victim. He was a brute. Broad-shouldered and covered in coarse red hair, he had uncouth manners and a mouth that smelled of rotting flesh and vegetables. Aine tracked him, coming upon him as he was skinning a deer.

The weather was warm. Having a practical nature, his pants were discarded to avoid blood stains. As he stood and stretched, Áine licked her lips at his blood-splattered body and manhood. Without ceremony, she slipped out of her clothes and emerged into his line of sight. His fate was assured.

***

"Shite! Not another one." Tadhg hunkered down, taking in the tableau. Measuring each step carefully, he walked the scene. Surrounded by age-old pines with thick trunks, a skinned deer lay partially eaten by scavengers. It was a perfectly ordinary hunting scene at the centre of a small glade. On the other hand, the naked hunter on his knees with his forehead resting against the clearing's single oak tree beggared the explanation.

While aghast at the horror of the man's death, Tadhg admired the ruthless efficiency of the assassin. A thin trail of coagulated blood from his ears to his neck was the sole clue to the cause of his demise. Tadhg shook his head. It took cold-hearted nerve to stab a victim in his ears while in the heights of ecstasy.

He looked around for any token of the assassin. The tree's rough bark had captured a long, narrow sliver of skin and blood. That, at least, explained the position of the corpse. A pleasant zephyr of wind tripped through the glade, drawing Tadhg's attention back to the tree. He reached out and plucked several hairs from the bark. They were long... and dark. Without the breeze, they would have gone unnoticed. Tadhg thanked the Goddess and returned to Trócaire.

Hidden in the trees, Áine watched Tadhg jog away from the clearing. Tadhg was quickly becoming a concern. She doubted he would be taken in by any attempted seduction. For a moment, she was tempted to let an arrow solve this problem but reconsidered, relaxed her grip on the bow and put the shaft back into the quiver that hung on her belt.

***

Deaglán, Fionnbharr, and Tadhg sat around the fire. Tadhg had brought food and beer for them all, so his companions were instantly suspicious. While good-natured, Tadhg was known to be relatively parsimonious with his gold and rarely splurged out.

Finally, after the idle chat, Deaglán said, "Out with it, Tadhg. What do you want?" Tadhg inhaled deeply. He had taken another look at the most recent body before it was carried to the funeral pyre and had re-thought what he knew about the murderer.

"You know that I'm investigating the murders of the bowmen?" His friends nodded. "Well, it is fairly obvious that the killer is a woman."

Deaglán snorted. "Ignoring children leaves about three thousand viable suspects."

"The murder weapons are thin, sharp blades," said Tadgh. "Two were killed through their eyes. The third had his brains scrambled through his ears. All had stiff cocks, so she seems to have enjoyed them before delivering judgement and sentence."

"The Hag, Tadhg. You'll put me off my food," said Fionnbharr.

"The third is of most interest. Obviously, the bowman preferred to stand and deliver." Tadhg chuckled at his jest. The others looked on grimly. "There were blood and pieces of skin on the bark and a few strands of long, dark hair."

"So now," said Deaglán, showing more interest, "we are looking for a woman with long dark hair and a scabby graze on her back."

"Dark hair, yes. The problem is that most women have long hair. Many also dye their hair. Probably we're down to a thousand women! What about the cut, Fionnbharr?"

"That's of little use. Do you know how many people come to the healers for salves and poultices for cuts and grazes? Look at the number of children. Besides, if this is a woman of status, she would send her maid or slave. The only way I might get involved would be if the wound became infected or needed stitching." Tadhg raised his eyebrows. "No, I haven't seen anyone with what you've described."

"What about the disease?"

Fionnbharr leaned forward. "What disease?"

"The last victim had a rash around his cock and the inside of his thighs. A bit around his mouth, too."

"Describe the rash," said Fionnbharr. Tadhg, observant by nature, provided a vivid picture of the shape and colour of the skin eruptions.

"I'm no healer, but that sounds like the pox to me," said Deaglán.

"I'll not inquire how you know about that," said Fionnbharr, "but you're right." The healer turned to Tadhg. "The victim appears to have been infected with the pox, and likely, so is your killer." Tadgh looked hopeful until Fionnbharr said, "The pox is common among the tribe. The healers see many cases daily." Seeing his friend's disappointment, Fionnbharr said, "I'll watch for anything strange over the next moon cycle. That's when any symptoms will raise their heads."

Tadhg smiled. "Thanks. Now eat and drink up. I don't want this to go to waste."

***

It was a cycle of the moon since she had disposed of the final member of the trio. Her indiscretion and the subsequent remedy were consigned to the past. As she sat on a flat stone, dipping long toes into the cool waters of the Abhainn Dubh, Áine was content that her status in the community was secure. However, she detected a growing ill feeling towards her due to her deteriorating relationship with Brion. This puzzled Áine. In her mind, she was merely realistic.

The Law was very flexible when it came to hand-fasting. Separation was simple and straightforward. Ironically, this was especially so for the female partner. Áine could, as a right, claim all property she brought to the relationship. Her dowry was substantial, given that her father was Deda Mac Sin, Rí of Curraghatoor.

Additionally, she had the right to a significant proportion of Brion's property. The more Áine considered her potential wealth, the more she favoured cutting the cords of hand-fasting. She could consolidate her wealth, make a tearful return home to Curraghatoor, and attract a new partner. She was her Da's favourite. Áine chuckled. *My Da will believe any tale I concoct.*

Áine absent-mindedly parted her legs and rucked up her dress until it rested above her knees. She fingered the dark bush between her thighs and thought to pleasure herself. An annoying prickle ended the impulse. A rash had recently appeared under the coarse, lush hair. So far, Áine had given it little thought. Rashes and crabs were a part of life. When she returned to Trócaire, she would have her maid purchase salves and herbs from the healers.

Of more concern was the persistent morning nausea and vomiting. The same had occurred when Áine was pregnant with Cassán. Áine's heart skipped a beat. *I cannot be with a child.* She feverishly reviewed her options. A visit to the old crones and their pointed sticks was out of the question. Their success rate was abysmal, and she wondered why anyone chose to risk death by bleeding out. Some herbs could be administered, but their efficacy was not guaranteed.

Her only other alternative was one she contemplated with distaste. She could seduce Brion, but it made her nauseous to think she would have to humble herself before him and rut a cripple.

***

Deaglán had not fully recovered. The druids said it would be another cycle of the moon before his collarbone fully healed. However, he had moved back into the roundhouse he shared with Brocc and Torcán. Since his friends had left with Íar and Mórrígan's force, he had the residence to himself.

Brion, under protest but at the insistence of Conall, remained at the royal broch in Trócaire. Áth remained in ruins after the invasion of Kartimandu. A sullen Áine was told to remove her belongings and move to a much smaller roundhouse with Cassán and her staff.

Except for Crum Dubh and a group of druids who specialised in healing, most priests left Na Mèadaidh to re-establish authority over their flocks.

Fionnbharr passed the small wooden shed adjacent to Trócaire's main hall by chance. The building was used primarily to dry and store herbs and other plant-based medicines. However, it was also used as a dispensary for those same treatments.

As usual, a small queue had gathered, patiently waiting as a druid interpreted the colourful descriptions of actual and perceived maladies. The dour priest dispensed a mix of therapies to the sick and stern admonitions to those he considered malingerers.

The woman at the head of the queue was known to Fionnbharr. She was a mature, well-proportioned woman of good repute and not prone to associating with the less inhibited members of the community.

The lady looked highly uncomfortable. Her face and neck flushed the colour of her red cloak. Beads of sweat formed on her forehead and trickled down her cheeks, causing her to pad her face persistently with a small square of cloth. She took the proffered medicines, lowered her head, and rushed away.

Fionnbharr inquired as to what the woman needed. With disapproval, the druid answered, "Herbs to undo a pregnancy and salve for an infection." The druid paused and added caustically, "An infection being between her thighs." Fionnbharr shook his head because he knew the woman was Áine's only maid. He went in search of Tadhg.

***

The rash between Áine's legs spread, albeit slowly, with frequent applications of the salve. It was painful to piss, and her pee smelt stronger, to her disgust. The herbs to rid her of the unborn did not appear to have any effect other than making her shite more frequently.

Thus, Áine's disposition was foul. It was a mood which deepened as she watched Tadhg and his friends. A few nights previously, she overheard snippets of a discussion between Tadhg and Fionnbharr. During the friends' conversation, Tadhg said, "I'm convinced it's her, but the evidence is not watertight." Áine's patience had reached its limit.

***

The arrow penetrated between Tadhg's scapula and ribs, exiting his upper chest. Fortunately, Tadhg remained favoured by the Goddess. Hence, rather than puncturing or tearing, the iron barb nicked his right lung, narrowly missing several major blood vessels. Tadhg pitched forward, and blackness overtook him.

When he awoke, Tadhg tried to sit but failed miserably. With a cry of pain, he fell back into the cot. Around his bed, Conall, Fearghal, Mongfhionn, Crum Dubh, and Brion waited anxiously. Outside, his friends paced up and down, vowing retribution on Tadhg's attacker.

Conall put a reassuring hand on Tadhg's shoulder and said, "Rest. You were lucky to be on a well-trodden path between Áth and Trócaire. Otherwise, you would already be in Mag Mell. Fionnbharr and Deaglán have already spoken of what they know." Conall nodded towards the entrance. "Your brothers and Deaglán will keep you company and dissuade future attempts on your life."

Outside the healing hall, Conall turned to face the group; his face was infused with cold rage. Haggard and still quickly exhausted, Brion slumped down on a tree stump. He could not believe that Áine was responsible, yet every sign pointed in her direction. The question of "why" may have been answered by Crum Dubh when he described Áine's outburst on hearing of Brion's injuries.

"Tadhg and the dead will have justice," said a thin-lipped Conall. "It's bad enough to lose friends and warriors during battle. I'll not have an assassin in my camp." He glanced pointedly at each of them. "At first light, bring Áine to the Hall to be heard *and* judged."

***

The morning sky flushed pink. A beautiful and frequent sight, it was also the portent of poor weather. Casually alert, Cúscraid and Nikandros leaned against either side of the Great Hall's doorframe as Conall strode out from the Hall. Behind him followed Mongfhionn, Fearghal, Crum, Brion, and Nikandros. None held welcoming looks.

"It's máen-lae. Where's Áine? She was to be here at first light," snapped Conall.

Áine's maid stepped forward and bowed. Her voice trembled as she spoke. "My mistress is sick and asked me to attend in her absence. I am to report all that is said in full." Her gaze dropped to mud-spattered feet.

"You are a loyal servant," said Conall, "and I lay no blame on you. *But*, if your mistress expects this excuse to be taken seriously, she is mistaken." Conall made a quarter turn and addressed a brace of guards. "Go to the home of Áine Ni Dedad. Prevail on her to attend. If she resists, drag her to this hall."

The men had not made more than two steps when a plainly angry Áine stepped from behind a nearby building. In the Hall, Áine stood before her judges. Her boldness reflected her reality and belief that in protecting herself, she had done nothing wrong and committed no crime. "Our friend, Tadhg, was almost murdered," said Crum Dubh. "A black arrow with red and white fletching was the weapon." Áine offered no response.

"Three of your archers, all males, met their deaths at the hand of an… assassin." Crum's words were deliberate. He stood and held Áine's gaze. "This cannot and will not be tolerated."

"I fail to see what this has to do with me," said Áine.

"The murderess, for indeed the perpetrator of the foul deeds is without doubt female, has long, black hair. She may yet have traces of a graze on her back." A faint tick flickered at the corner of Áine's eyebrow but was quickly brought under control. "She also has an infection, for her final victim had the pox."

It took every fibre of Áine's body to hold her hands steady when told the source of the interminable itch between her legs. Her breathing grew shallow. A sheen of sweat coated her forehead. Crum continued. "The lady is also with child. Her maid fetched herbs to undo the condition."

The person before them transformed. The creature they knew as Áine slipped away, and in her place was a dispassionate predator. "You have no murder weapons. You have no motive. You cannot place me at the scene of the crimes. I am a Princess of Curraghatoor. You have no right to judge me."

"I have every right to judge you. However, I find it curious you chose the word 'weapons' and are so convinced we do not have them," said

Crum. "As for a motive. Look to your infidelity." Áine's cheeks flushed.

The Druid paused as Brion rose and said, "Let your hair down, Áine."

"Pardon?"

"Let your hair down," repeated Brion. White-faced, Áine tugged the twin hairpins. As her hair cascaded over slim shoulders, Brion pointed. "I believe we have the weapons."

"They are simple hairpins," hissed Áine through thin lips. "No more, no less."

"Bring me milk in a shallow pan." There were questioning looks from all around the table at Crum's request. The Druid smiled. "An old trick. Watch." The pins were laid side-by-side in the milk. Within a short time, thin, red swirls drifted to the surface. "It is hard to wash away all traces of blood."

Crum turned to Conall. "I am satisfied that the body of proof points to Áine Ni Dedad as the murderer of three men and the assailant of Tadhg Ó Cuileannáin." Crum paused. "Are there contrary opinions?" The tight, drawn, and sorrowful expressions on his comrade's faces told him all he needed.

"Áine Ni Mac Dedad will pay the *éiric* demanded by the Law for each of the dead and Tadhg. Until the child's birth, she will be treated according to her status as a Princess of Curraghatoor. She will be permitted to retain one maid and one slave. Furthermore, she will remain in her home guarded to forestall escape."

It appeared to those seated that an immense burden had been lifted from Áine's shoulders. Her bearing changed. Head held high and her back straight, she looked at her judges with haughty disdain. She knew her wealth was without measure. The éiric, while severe, would not be beyond her resources. She smiled. She was victorious. She bowed to Crum Dubh in acceptance of her punishment and turned to walk away.

"I have not finished, Áine Ni Dedad," said Crum. "You have willfully separated the body from the soul. In doing so, you have sacrificed your own body and soul. My judgment is that from this day, you are cast out from Clann Ui Flaithimh. As is my right under the Law, I sentence you to death. The punishment will be carried out when the child is born."

The scream from Áine was long and loud. "No!" She fell to her knees and pounded the wooden floor until her hands bled. It was the most human act from the princess in a long time. The Great Hall fell ominously silent as she gathered herself and rose to face her judges.

"You are mistaken if you can enforce this unjust punishment. My brother, Íar, will defend me upon his return." She smiled in cold hostility. "Remember, too, half of my brother's cavalry remain in Na Mèadaidh. Are you sure of their loyalty?"

"Remove the foul stench of her presence." Conall rose and directed a final command to the guards, "She is not to speak to anyone save her maid and the members of the Chomhairle."

As Áine was escorted from the Hall, Fearghal said, "An unpleasant business. Sadly, the lady is right. This is not over."

Conall rubbed his chin, nodding his agreement. "Transfer Áine's archers to Mòrag. Send a unit of shields with them. Mòrag and Brandubh have pestered me about this since the battle for Áth. Now may be a propitious time to accede to their request."

"The cavalry?"

With a resigned shrug, Conall asked, "What can we do? I can't put guards on five hundred horsemen. It's just not practical. I hope most are loyal to Clann Ui Flaithimh, their king and, in Íar's absence, to Nikandros. Many have taken up with and have children by partners well-distant from their birthplace at Curraghatoor." Conall sucked in a long breath. "Speak to the riders' ceannairí céad. Remind them of where their loyalty lies and who holds their oath."

Fearghal nodded. As he turned to walk away, Conall placed a scarred hand on his arm. "I will show no mercy to any who rebel, whether through avarice or misplaced loyalty. Make sure the riders understand."

CHAPTER 22

406 B.C.—Trócaire—Autumn

Pytheas' black-sailed bireme halted with a crunch on the gravel and sand beach. He looked around the northern bank of the Linne Foirthe, and his gaze fell upon the clutch of beached Votod-Daoine ships. The merchant in him automatically calculated the worth and utility of the vessels. They were of a different design than his flat-bottomed, cedar-wood galleys. Nevertheless, they were sturdy, seaworthy ships.

He already envisaged using the boats to ferry ingots of tin and other metals from the mines in the southwest of Albu across the ill-named *Muir nIocht*—the Merciful Sea—to Gaul and beyond. Leaving a small guard to watch over his vessel and new property, Pytheas set a steady pace and headed north to Trócaire.

***

The Greek patted his expanding belly, mentally chastised himself for not getting enough exercise, and then held up his jug for more beer. The Forest People and Clann Ui Flaithimh brewed strong, bitter-tasting beverages mainly from barley and flavoured with meadowsweet, heather, and honey. Or indeed anything that the brewer might have had close by on the day.

Pytheas, as a rule, steered clear of the innocent-looking but deadly liquid the Celts called "*uisce beatha*"—the water of life. In his experience, every nation and tribe had such a drink. On most occasions, prudence guided him away from all such concoctions. He debated whether to introduce Conall and Drostan to wine on his next visit. If favourably received, it could be a profitable future business. At worst, he would have a supply of alcohol that he could trust.

Midway through the evening feast, Pytheas casually mentioned doing Conall a favour by removing the stranded boats from the beach at Linne Foirthe. There was a loud guffaw from a happily drunk Drostan. The one-eyed king pointed a leg of barely roasted lamb, still dripping juices, at the sailor. "Those are my ships, ye thief!"

Pytheas feigned shock at Drostan's words. "I did not know that the king of the great forests and his people had become sailors and merchants. Am I to see the ships of the Forest People sail the waters of An Mhuir Ó Thuaidh, the Muir nIocht, or even the Great Sea?" The merchant raised his hands in mock horror. "How will I survive the competition?"

"Ye'r a sarcastic, overconfident bastard… and a foreigner." With a raised eyebrow, Drostan asked, "Now that we've settled ownership, what's yer offer?" Conall listened with amusement as the two men haggled over the vessels' worth. Both men were shrewd negotiators with an eye for a deal.

Eventually, they came to a mutual accord. Both recognised it would be more profitable for the boats to haul cargo. Hence, a partnership was born. Witnessed by Conall, they shook on a covenant to split the profits from the sale of whatever load the vessels would carry.

"There is, of course, one problem we need to solve," said Pytheas.

"What?" Drostan was instantly suspicious.

"The ships need crews, and your people are not sailors." Pytheas looked at Conall with a smile. "Conall's men have sailed the northern lochs. Perhaps they could be persuaded."

"The Hag's arse, not a chance," slurred Fearghal. Having drunk too much, his head rested on Mongfhionn's ample cleavage. Shouts of "Bloody well, right!" came from the leaders around the tables. Drostan and Pytheas frowned at the glitch in their plans.

Conall offered a solution. "There are many Votod-Daoine still to be sold. Some should know how to sail their vessels."

Pytheas looked at Conall. "Slaves cannot be trusted, especially on a boat."

Drostan called for another fill of beer and leered approvingly at the generous curves of the young woman who served him. An experienced server, she paused long enough for the king to slap her arse before sashaying away from the table. "Much as I hate to admit it, I agree with Pytheas. What's to stop the bastards from taking over the ships and sailing off? They owe us nae loyalty."

"Give them their freedom in exchange for an agreed period of service. Reward them as you would normal crews. There'll always be bad apples, but having three or four armed guards on each boat will negate that problem."

Pytheas scratched his head, then rubbed his chin, "It might work. One of my men would captain each ship." Drostan grumbled half-heartedly about losing gold by being unable to sell the slaves but recognised an excellent plan.

"When the time comes, will you use the ships to transport us?" Conall asked.

"Are you sure, Conall?" replied Pytheas with a genuine concern for the young king.

"You and you people could have a good life here. From what Drostan tells me, the Votod-Daoine are weak. You could invade, conquer the tribe and take its lands if you needed more space. At a stroke, you would control the Linne Foirthe. Wealth greater than that of many kings would be your reward..." he paused and smiled, "...with the right partner, of course."

"That's not my destiny, Pytheas. One day, I'll stand before the gates of Rome... alone or with my army. I'll take the life of my enemies, or they'll take mine."

The merchant sighed. Conall's words were no surprise. "There are two possible routes across the Muir nIocht. To the southeast, the channel is narrow. It is no wider than the distance between northern-Ériu and Maol Chinn Tíre. However, the waters are rougher, and the currents are more unpredictable. It is a route well-used by slavers, and your people would be too attractive to resist.

"The southwestern routes are about four, maybe five times the distance, but safer. The main port, a fortified headland, is situated midway between and south of the hillforts of *Rinn-Campáil* and *Mai-Dùn*. From the forts to the coast, well-travelled avenues are used by metals, grain, and wool traders. On the far side of the Muir nIocht, rivers and roads are frequented by tin and wine merchants. Many lead into the heart of the lands of Gaul, to the Great Sea… and to Rome."

"Your face betrays you, my friend. What are you not telling me?"

A long swallow of beer was followed by another before Pytheas continued. "The wealth of southern Albu, especially the southwestern lands, is in their tin and copper mines and grain. A score or more hillforts jealously protect the grain grown by those under their protection. It is stored in deep storage pits within each fort.

"The local kings and chieftains will not be happy with a large army and its followers tramping through their lands. At the least, you will probably be challenged by the kings of Rinn-Campáil and Mai-Dùn.

"If you successfully negotiate your passage through these lands, defend against almost certain attacks while your people embark, and survive the sea journey, you will land in Gaul. It is a vast land with hundreds of barbarian clans.

"Each tribe's sole ambition is to dominate their neighbours. Clann Ui Flaithimh will not be welcome, and your presence will be resisted. Also, remember, Conall, your enemy, Marcus Fabius Ambustus, has deep coffers of gold to recruit or bribe the barbarians to do his dirty work."

Conall sighed. "The people have given their assent to my mission. We'll set out a cycle of the moon after Lugnasad Bealtaine. The Goddess willing, we will join with Mórrígan and Íar… and my children." Conall's eyes misted over at the mention of his children. His deep sorrow for his kidnapped daughters was a heavy weight on his heart. "Plan to have our vessels waiting for us when summer returns."

"As you wish." At the mention of Conall's children, a grimace momentarily crossed the merchant's swarthy face. He had heard of a confrontation between the pirate, Orestes, and a band of northern warriors near the Abus estuary. Rumours told of the rescue of two young girls. Yet Pytheas kept his own counsel. In his heart, Pytheas prayed that it was Brighid and Danu, but he had no wish to raise Conall's hopes only to have them crushed later.

That said, beer had not entirely dulled Conall's sharp eyes, and he wondered at the passing moment of sadness in his friend's eyes.

***

Lugnasad marked the beginning of the harvest season. Bonfires flared across the ridge of the Sleá and in the many communities of Clann Uí Flaithimh. The feast of Lugnasad had something for everyone: religious ceremonies, athletic contests, feasting, drinking, and trading. It was a celebration for young and old, rich and poor. This season, it was a way for the tribe to put behind them the recent conflict with the High People and the unpleasantness surrounding Áine.

Those with inflamed passions and too much beer attempted unabated coupling with multiple partners. The more conservative couples followed the traditional and at least initially monogamous route of handfasting. As soon as girls had their first bleeding, they were legally able to be mated.

Well-meaning parents endeavoured to arrange suitable matches for their offspring. The more avaricious sought to trade their daughters for gold or power. It was a custom open to abuse, especially by those who should have held to a higher standard. Conall ground his teeth until his jaw ached when he recalled the depravity of Eochaidh Ruadh and his penchant for young girls.

Not only Conall but many of his Chomhairle expressed reservations about the custom, yet they were helpless to act decisively. It was broadcast widely that no girl fourteen summers or less should be forced into coupling. Sadly, the Law provided little support to their cause.

Crum and his druids' hands were tied by the Law. However, they wielded it whenever possible to protect the youngest girls from abuse—albeit after the fact. Yet the cries and tears of many went unheard and unseen. Compensation was scant comfort for innocence lost.

***

In the blackness of a moonless night, he made an eccentric way back to his home. His stomach was stretched with overeating, and his head was befuddled with beer. Finally, at his entrance, he dismissed the guards with a quick flick of his hand and a slurred, "The hounds will protect me."

With a tired grunt, he unbuckled his weapon belt, pulled off his tunic and pants and tossed them across the room. They narrowly missed the banked fire in the middle of the room. He fell into his cot with a satisfying thud. Barely was the brat pulled over his body when sleep took him.

It seemed a pleasant dream. The covers lifted briefly as a warm body slipped beneath them. Two fingers were placed over his lips. The hand smelled of meadowsweet, violets, and heather. A whispered "Shhhh" was accompanied by the brush of her soft shape against him. Her hand caressed his belly and then was between his legs, cupping, squeezing, and stroking gently. His manhood responded.

The covers fell away as she raised herself up and straddled him. Long hair brushed over his chest, teasing his nipples. She bent over, biting, licking, and sucking his nipples until they stiffened. Her breasts pressed against him, soft yet firm against his muscled chest. Instinctively, he reached out to hold one.

He playfully pulled and twisted a nipple made stiff from her aroused state. She responded with a moan and then lifted up her hips. He felt the soft bush rub on his cock, teasing his hardness. She lifted herself up slightly and then sheathed him in silky wetness.

The first time she rode him hard, revelling in the feel of his fingers as they grasped her arse and pulled her breasts into his demanding mouth. As they climaxed together, she cried out loudly and savagely. She smiled and rejoiced as she felt his seed inside her. He made to open his eyes, but she kissed them closed. He prepared to speak, but she stopped him. This time her full lips pressed down on his. It was a night for actions, not words.

She slipped from his bed before dawn, savouring the musky smells of sweat and their ardent coupling. He looked at peace, snoring gently. Covering herself, she walked unsteadily towards the exit. She winced; their passion had been vigorous. She did not need light to know her body was a mosaic of bites and bruises. The throbbing fullness of her pit brought a huge smile to her face. She patted her belly. She felt full but knew she would have to wait until the expected time of her bleeding to know for sure.

His senses burst into action as a golden shaft of sunlight played over his face. Wet tongues licked the sleep from his eyes. "Get off, you brute!" Smiling, Conall tickled the hounds' ears before pushing the broad heads away. He stood up and stretched. With a smile, he remembered the vividness of his dream. The tenderness of his nipple made him wince, and a look of puzzlement appeared on his lips.

A strange vision indeed.

CHAPTER 23

40 B.C.—Penn-inus

The dead rotted in the fields around Áth and the Abhainn Dubh, food for maggots, ravens, and wolves. Others waited in chains in camps or on jetties. They contemplated a bitter life of slavery, never to see or hold their children or lovers again. Angry voices rose, cursing their captors and Kartimandu equally.

Of the remainder, ten thousand were hale and fit for battle; five thousand were the walking wounded. They tramped sullenly across the rolling, forested hills that traversed northern Albu's lowlands. Soon the mountains would merge with the northern tip of the Penn-inus. Once again, they would look upon a familiar landscape of open heather moors, deep glens, upland rivers, and meadows.

Kartimandu's army was in disarray, and their air of invincibility was shattered. This generation had never tasted defeat. They had always been the hunter, never the prey. The humiliating losses laid on them by Conall trampled their pride into the dirt and left them flailing in the heavy mire of defeat.

Never before did they have cause to look fearfully over their shoulders. Tribes like the *Na Daoine Fiadhaich*—The Wild People—had bowed the knee to them. Today, they and others emerged from their hillforts to taunt, snap and bite.

Ualraig glanced at Kartimandu. Each blamed the other for the catastrophic campaign, yet each needed the other more than ever. Away from attacks by the Sídhe and the druids, Kartimandu's powers recovered. Her hold over the minds of her chieftains increased with each sunset.

With Ualraig's acquiescence, the remainder of his elite became uneasy enforcers of the queen's will. Dissent was put down brutally and visibly. Behind them lay a bloody trail of the staked, the disembowelled, and the headless. All sacrificed to an angry, spectral queen. Even under the new rules, fighting between the hundreds of clans and warbands was commonplace.

In the driving wind and rain and with *Cnoc-Naomh*, the hillfort of the Wild People, behind them, they trudged southwards. Their goal was the hillfort of An Balla-Leac. Located in a broad, level valley that almost carved the Penn-inus in two, An Balla-Leac was very much under construction.

Its location was a massive mound in the valley guarded on three sides by mountains. A single rampart of stone and wood, the height of three men, enclosed the knoll. The hill had the potential to be a massive stronghold capable of housing many thousands of people. Indeed, Kartimandu had envisaged the site as an alternate home to Dùn Caen.

Ualraig looked over his shoulder, hoping for news from his scouts. An Balla-Leac was a half-cycle of the moon distant, and Clann Ui Flaithimh's riders were getting closer. The ball of yarn that was Kartimandu's tribe unravelled more every day.

***

In many ways, the driving rain off the lowland mountains was a relief from the persistent drizzle of northern Albu. It was brutal and relentless, like the landscape. The moisture intensified an orchestra of scents from wildflowers, meadows, and bogs. At first, the land breathed and then choked as if drowning.

Water formed in pools, some deep and deadly. Bogs overflowed, waterfalls gushed, cascading down steep hillsides, and rivers burst banks, submerging fields. Sheep and goats fled to higher ground. Crops rotted unharvested in the ground. The rain's bounty was unrelenting.

Íar and the slower-moving advance troops tramped a weary and wet path. Unencumbered by wagons, cattle, and infantry. Mórrígan's riders were a thousand paces ahead. Mórrígan sat miserable upon a sodden diallait. Her clothes were sopping wet, and her hair was plastered flat against her head and shoulders. She could barely see beyond a hundred paces and continually wiped the rain from her red-rimmed eyes.

She smelled of sweat, piss, and shite. The latter two she blamed on her horse. "Five sunsets," she moaned. "It has rained without stopping for five bloody sunsets." As she swivelled to face her riders, her arse squeezed water from the diallait as if it was a sponge. Her band was as wretched looking and ill-humoured as she.

It was not as if the going was hard. Apparently, a bored god had formed the mountains. The deity dropped an enormous pile of dirt and granite in a rough line from coast to coast and folded it over and over as if kneading bread. Then, as an afterthought, he had patted the peaks into a roughly level plateau. There were natural inclines from the forested foothills to the summit. Once attained, the land rolled on and on in soft folds of browns, greens, and purples with splashes of brightly-coloured wildflowers.

The only blight on the landscape, apart from the weather, was of human origin. Random examples of Kartimandu's justice dotted the trail. Some still gasped in naked agony as they hovered between life and death. Mórrígan's band's response was quixotic.

Sometimes the riders would put the unfortunate out of their misery. At other times they would shrug and canter past. Rarely was a killing blow or arrow administered as an act of mercy. It was a distraction to break up the misery of the weather and the monotony of the hunt.

They knew they were gaining on Kartimandu's army. The number of wounded unable to keep up with the main force became more numerous and frequent. *She's a cold bitseach, driving her main body onward but leaving her injured to the mercy of the hunters.* And yet, in the same circumstances, might not she do the same? Many of the wounded boldly showed signs of defiance, and Mórrígan felt no guilt in sending them to Mag Mell. If no resistance was offered, the injured were left to the mercy of Íar's forces.

***

Mórrígan sat up straight. A snarl rumbled from her lips. The presence of several massive, standing stones engraved with tribal markings confirmed that this was a border between tribes. The hilly land was little different, but the territory of the Wild People was behind them. For the first time, Mórrígan looked upon the Penn-inus and the kingdom of the High People.

This was the land she would wreak terrible revenge upon. Kartimandu and Ualraig had taken her daughters. The people of the High People would pay a heavy price until they were delivered safely into her arms. The Huntress pointed south and shouted, "This is your king's and my command. Kill all who resist. Burn their homes and crops. Drive them from their farms, their communities, and settlements. Destroy what they treasure."

The riders raised weapons and shouted in raucous agreement. Mórrígan realised that the rain had ceased and the howling wind had become a gentle breeze. In the east, a beautiful double-arced rainbow dominated the grey sky. *The Goddess is pleased.*

As she looked down on her Huntress, the Goddess nodded in agreement.

***

It was a late-summer evening when the final ship crunched to a halt on the pebble beach. Cuán Ó Néill tossed a bag of gold to the captain, bowed a final thank-you, and leapt over the side rails into the surf. Ignoring the bone-chilling waters, he waded ashore to be greeted by friends who grasped his arm with painfully enthusiastic strength. Backs were slapped and embraces exchanged. The hugs were deemed manly due to their brevity and spine-crunching force that would have made a fully-grown bear proud.

A scream of "Da!" made him turn swiftly. It was followed by the happy cries of two small boys as they hurtled down the beach and launched themselves into his arms. Behind them walked a tall woman whose presence and noble bearing would grace the ranks of any assembly. Bláithín Ni Néill was a beauty notable for the rare combination of red hair and deep blue eyes.

Cuán bowed, smiled, and disentangled himself from his boys. He welcomed her with a lingering kiss and a hug that would have cracked the ribs of a lesser woman. In return, Bláithín placed a single kiss on the lip-shaped birthmark on Cuán's neck. It was a perfect match for the outline of her lips. Lore had it that the mark appeared after the first kiss they shared. Cheers rang out along the beach and the shore's grassy verge.

It had been six cycles of the moon since Cuán had seen his family. Things had not gone well for many of the Craobhach, Ó *Néill*, and *Ruad* clans since the humiliation of Macha Mong Ruad, the High Queen of Ériu, at the hands of Conall Mac Gabhann and the Sídhe.

After the battle of Ráth na Lairig Éadain, Macha, shamed before her nobles and under the geis pronounced by the Sídhe, withdrew from society, choosing a reclusive life at *Emain Macha*. Yet the queen did not relinquish her throne. In her eyes, she had fought too long and suffered much to achieve her position. At first, she ruled through her partner, Cimbáeth—the former High King—and a hand-picked Chomhairle.

Two things conspired to change Macha's perception and the tone of the final years of her reign. Time dulled her recollection of events. After three summers, the geis became a distant memory. In her interpretation of events, the queen chose to believe her humbling and the geis was a dream rather than something that actually took place. The second was the demise of Cimbáeth, who died by the plague fulfilling the geis laid on him.

Cimbáeth's death should have been a sufficient reinforcement of the Sídhe's warnings, but his demise was a lingering one. Thus, its impact was diminished. Cimbáeth was a prudent king, a brave warrior, and a good influence on Macha… while he lived. With his death, the wheels came off the chariot, and Macha's mind turned to revenge. Her Chomhairle, eager to please, knelt in obeisance. Macha assembled a brood of vipers: corrupt Brehons, greedy nobles, and warriors with little conscience.

Many of the leaders and nobles of the northern Ulaid clans, such as the Ó Néills and the Ruads, were influential, with loyal armies. They were also closely aligned with the famed Cróeb Ruad and thus commanded respect. In diplomacy, however, the desire to influence the seat of power is often accompanied by sacrificing the weak.

The Ulaid nobility maintained open lines of communication and a policy of appeasement. They uttered faux protests as Macha vented her spleen on the minor nobles of the Ó Néill, Ruad, and Craobhach clans.

In truth, the Ulaid nobility hoped an assassin's blade would remove Macha. It was a reasonable expectation. The geis on Macha said she would die childless and be assassinated by the knife with which she tried to murder Conall's children. The nobles reckoned that in a few more summers, Macha would be gone and a more reasonable male High King enthroned.

Meanwhile, Cuán Ó Néill and many of his kin and friends became Macha's victims. They were stripped of cattle, lands, and status by arbitrary judgments from bought Brehons. Many were pronounced outcasts and, along with their families, slain on sight. With few options, many chose to go into hiding in the gleannta of north-eastern Ériu.

The fly in the Macha's strategy was that Cuán Ó Néill and a good number of his friends were also members of the Cróeb Ruad. Blunt signals from the powerful Cróeb Ruad leadership indicated they had reached the limits of their patience. If the nobles did not get off their arses and do something, the Cróeb Ruad would insert themselves brutally into Ulaid politics.

The proclamation sent tremors through the Ulaid elite, so they grudgingly opened their coffers to pay for bribes and ships. Over the spring and summer, Ulaid families were spirited from homes and sanctuaries, reappearing briefly at the port of *Domach Dith* before embarking for northern Albu. Macha was furious, but she could ill afford to confront the Cróeb Ruad. They were her bulwark against the armies of the Connachta.

***

The first Ulaid exiles to land in Albu set up camp a thousand paces inland in the domain of the Wild People. The encampment was several sunsets march south of the tribe's chief hillfort at Cnoc-Naomh. Their presence was an unwelcome surprise for the local tribe, who protested in the usual manner of fighting first and negotiating if unsuccessful.

Warriors were dispatched to throw the Ulaid invaders back into the sea. Cuán, however, had foreseen this possibility. Led by his brother, Lonán Ó Néill, the first two hundred and fifty to make the beach of Albu were his best and most belligerent fighters—a right pack of bastards.

Cowed by Kartimandu, the Wild People had rarely left their *dùin*, and their warriors lacked battle nous. They were beaten back by the invaders from Ériu. Thus, the king of the Wild People faced two choices. Gather up an overwhelming force to defeat this new enemy, which would likely be at a high cost in men and gold. Or come to an accommodation, which he could stomach, and, more importantly, sell to the tribe.

In the end, events came to the rescue of the king. After an extended period of submission and paying tribute, the defeat of Kartimandu opened up favourable opportunities for revenge and plunder. Thus, the king agreed the Ulaid could temporarily remain on his land and then turned his raiders to harass the retreating forces of Kartimandu.

For such a large island, there were surprisingly good communications within and between Albu and Ériu. This was primarily based on the principal trading routes: wagon pathways, rivers, and scattered ports. Not long after Cuán's appearance, a message was relayed to the king of the Wild People, informing him that the leader of the group from Ériu had arrived. An invitation to Cnoc-Naomh, for Cuán, his family and a suitable guard was issued.

At Cnoc-Naomh, Cuán learned of the Battle of the Abhainn Dubh. He discovered that Conall, the scourge of Macha Mong Ruad and, to an extent, the author of Cuán's predicament, was now Rí Ruirech of Clann Ui Flaithimh. A mongrel tribe with a mix of Ériu and Cinn Péinteáilte. He also learned of an advanced warband making a steady path south towards An Bella-Leac. Of more than passing interest was that some of Clann Ui Flaithimh sported tattoos similar to his.

Cuán's visit to Cnoc-Naomh went exceptionally well. This likely had to do with him stating that he intended to march with all speed to An Bella-Leac and link up with Conall's force. Overjoyed to hear that his guests would leave, the king of the Wild People offered food, cattle, supplies for the journey, and a few scouts who knew the region well. Cuán gracefully accepted the offer. After all, it would avert the immediate need for him to raid the king's farms and settlements.

***

Giggles bubbled from Brighid and Danu like water from a mountain spring. Tears in their eyes, they watched as Urard rubbed a sore and numb arse. He intended his actions to be unseen. The sounds from behind him told him he was unsuccessful.

The giant still grumbled about having to ride but found he was becoming more comfortable on horseback. In fact, he was beginning to enjoy the experience. That said, he continued to lament about having to sit with legs splayed across the broad back of his mount. He forever complained he was becoming as bow-legged as the other riders *and* smelled of horse shite and sweat.

Urard's band stuck to the coastal pathways that wended their way between the dunes and forest. In this, they were guided by Iasg's knowledge and her clandestine meetings with elders from the small fishing communities scattered along the eastern shores of middle Albu. The settlements, although in the territory of the High People and under Kartimandu's rule, were fiercely independent. Their loyalty lay with the sea and Manannán Mac Lir, who provided security and sustenance.

Regularly, Urard sent a score of his riders deeper into the forestland. They raided farms, carrying off cattle and other necessary supplies. There was an uneasy acceptance of the forays. Urard's men took no more than they needed. Additionally, their presence discouraged the bands of marauding outlaws and brigands that sprang up in Kartimandu's absence.

Such gangs had no qualms about setting fire to farms after raping and killing the inhabitants. Urard's riders also hunted wild pigs, vicious tusked beasts that snuffled and rooted in the forest debris, and the more placid but skittish red deer. Some were traded with the fishing villages. They always appreciated the fresh meat as it made a welcome change to a diet of fish and shellfish.

As Urard approached the source of the Abus estuary, he was faced with a choice. In the distance, beyond dense forestlands, and to the west was Kartimandu's seat of power, the stronghold of Dùn Caen. The fort sat in a lowland valley in the shadow of the mountains.

Dùn Caen was a hillfort in the purest sense of the description. A tall hill rising out of the land and fortified with ramparts and ditches cut into its banks. Hill-based forts were more common in middle and southern Albu. The dùin in northern Albu favoured rock and wood fortresses built on high crags or coastal headlands.

In the end, the horses determined Urard's plan. He needed a supply of oats and forage for the winter. They would move into the forests and travel south and then west towards the southern farmlands and the grain trade routes. Urard hoped they would find a haven for the winter at the far end of the Penn-inus, well away from Dùn Caen.

Iasg breathed in, filling her nostrils and lungs with memories of the ocean she loved. As she gazed at the broad back of Urard, she had no regrets… and many plans.

CHAPTER 24

406 B.C.—An Balla-Leac

Ravens soared and dipped, sweeping low to investigate as Mórrígan's warband thundered out of the curtain of rain, destroying all that lay before them. Farmhouses and shelters smouldered, sending ghost-white plumes of mist into a pale sky. Small settlements were razed, their walls broken and scattered over the muddy earth.

Unharvested crops were trampled, and stored grain was piled into wagons. Animals snuffled and bawled as their new owners herded them away. Squawking chickens' lives ended with stretched necks. Swiftly plucked and roasted, they provided a quick meal for the raiders.

Swirls of blood mingled with rivulets of rainwater trickling across yards and fields. Mórrígan's intent was not to kill because that did not serve her purpose. The inhabitants of the dwellings and settlements were well outnumbered by her riders and poorly armed. A sensible, pragmatic resident would run.

Indeed, the Dark Huntress preferred if the homeowners did not stand. She wanted them to flee in fear, telling all of the destruction visited on them. However, in the heat of despair and anger, many of the men: fathers, grandfathers, and sons, chose to fight and died. It was a tragic waste of courage and blood.

Strong women, hands calloused from working in the fields or grinding grain on heavy kern stones or burned with yarn as they wove garments on rickety wooden looms, faced the ruination of their lives. Some fought with anger, sorrow, and fear and died alongside their men. Others grabbed whatever they could and shepherded daughters and young children away from the slaughter. Most headed to the heather moorlands of the Penn-inus and An Balla-Leac.

The Huntress' quest for vengeance helped her keep the darkness within her at bay. As her band left another scene of destruction, Mórrígan felt the eyes of the dead on her back, which was unsurprising. Their skulls were staked, a warning for all to read.

*****

Kartimandu surveyed the chaos that churned around An Balla-Leac and railed at Ualraig in frustration. The spate of tears and cries for help from subjects evicted from their lands elicited little empathy from the queen. The rabble was a hindrance. Worse, they occupied the inner fort, leaving her army to mill around the valley floor outside the defences.

Ualraig's scouts reported the fate of the army's injured. Slaughtered and stripped of items of value by tribes that formerly paid homage to Kartimandu. They told of a land scorched by fire and soaked in blood. Of the advancing cavalry of Clann Ui Flaithimh, now only a few sunsets away. Haughtily dismissed by the queen, Conall's blood-oath of no mercy echoed loudly in Ualraig's ears.

"Should we fight?" asked Kartimandu. Despite the recent disasters, the queen endeavoured to create an atmosphere of normality. Apart from the fine scar on her shoulder, her body was sheathed perfectly in green paint. The tent was not as splendid as her self-esteem would have preferred, yet it was the largest pavilion in the camp. Slaves and servants saw to her every need.

"Well?" The queen's impatience surfaced.

No one could ever describe Ualraig as a lap dog… or a diplomat. He looked at the queen and scratched an irregularly shaped nose moulded by combat. It was an act that irritated Kartimandu. She saw it as another step in her commander being too familiar, too much at ease in her presence. Previously, he had respected and feared the queen and her power.

Now, Kartimandu was unsure of Ualraig's motivation. Tired and irritated, he had not slept for several sunsets and sorely missed his family. Thus, he was minded to let the queen wait for a response. Unfortunately, as the army's commander, he knew quick action was required. The bones of his neck creaked at what he was about to propose, for it placed him firmly alongside Kartimandu.

"The army will expel all civilians from An Balla-Leac. By force if necessary.

"Two thousand injured have caught up with our forces. Along with five hundred volunteers, they will garrison and defend An Balla-Leac… to the last man." Ualraig held Kartimandu's dark stare. "Are your powers sufficient to ensure the men will not abandon the fort?" Bristling at the implied insult, the queen nodded. "Good. The remainder of the army will retreat across the moors to Dùn Caen. There we will winter and prepare our defences."

"You expect that barbarian king to pursue us?"

Ualraig snorted and waved his hand contemptuously at An Balla-Leac. "This motley group of injured, enthralled misfits will not stand long against Conall's army. Hopefully, they can delay him enough to allow us to escape to Dùn Caen. You have lit the cold flame of vengeance in Conall, his queen, and commanders. Only the handing over of his daughters might have stayed his wrath, but that is not an option, is it?" Kartimandu's silence was telling.

"You have no idea where the children are. Do you?"

"Your impudence goes too far, Ualraig."

"Bah! If I had any sense, I would leave you with the consequences of your stupidity and remain with the forlorn at An Balla-Leac. At least I would have a hero's death." Kartimandu seethed. She had long decided Ualraig would give her the pleasure of a prolonged and painful death.

For three sunsets, sullen anger swept the hillfort of An Balla-Leac. Once again, the people: families, farmers, labourers, and craftsmen, were forced from their refuge and makeshift homes. Livestock and stores of food and grain were seized and taken to the fort. Those who resisted suffered the same fate meted out by their enemies. Cracked skulls, broken bones, and death.

***

Íar pointed to the low hill in the distance. The green-capped mound rose up from a gently undulating, forested valley. Although not significantly elevated, the hummock was spread over a massive area. The bluff warrior reckoned the rise would comfortably sustain over a thousand cattle. "We've no choice. The ráth has to be taken. Without it, our people will not survive the winter snows and storms." The single snowflake that landed on his beard bore witness to his statement.

An Balla-Leac was a work in progress. Only the inner defences, consisting of a single rampart and ditch, were complete. Several thousand could be comfortably housed within the inner walls. The fortification, cut into the limestone hill, was three spears in height and had a facing ditch eight paces wide and six deep. The trench had its challenges and traps. Adding to Íar's problem, a man-high, wooden stockade topped the earthwork.

The ráth's single entrance faced east. A sturdy gate constructed from broad vertical oak planks braced with cross-pieces and secured with a heavy crossbar protected the gateway. Guard towers set back from and held in place by wooden beams that jutted from the rampart flanked either side of the gate. Similar posts on the western, southern, and northern-facing walls gave the hillfort commanding views of the surrounding land.

Sprouting diagonally away from the gateway were two spurs of rampart and stockade. Their function was to channel an attacking force into a confined open area before the gate. Men placed on these spurs would throw down on an attacking force, almost without reprise.

Staggered rows of white-grey rocks and sharpened stakes were sunk into the dirt. It would appear that a cavalry attack was anticipated. The land surrounding the fort was cleared to form the killing area. Íar cursed. *That bastard Ualraig knows how to set up his defences. He's almost as good as Cúscraid.*

Mayhem ensued within and around An Balla-Leac as people fled and the High People's army retreated. Cries and pleadings for protection were answered with a boot in the arse or the flat side of a spear. The disorderly mass streamed southwards away from the fort to the coast, the forests, and the mountains. While calculating their chances of survival, Kartimandu's army growled, cursed, and fell back towards Dùn Caen.

***

Mórrígan stated the obvious. "Over two thousand defend that ráth, Íar. We've six hundred cavalry and two hundred shields. The only way we win is to draw them out of the fort and hit them with the cavalry and the archers." She paused. "I don't think the commander of An Bella Leac will be that stupid, do you?" The small group, which included Torcán, Brocc, and her brothers, concurred.

Íar scowled. "Agreed."

"So what are we talking about?" Torcán asked with a grin. "A glorious assault, death, and then feasting in Mag Mell?" He thought for a moment. "Do they feast in Mag Mell? If we're dead, we'll not need food or beer. There'd better be women." He sighed. "At least we'll be immortalised in one of Tadhg's sagas."

"Arsehole! I'd hate to think that even you would be stupid enough to consider that a viable plan," said an exasperated Íar. The glint in Torcán's eyes did little to convince Íar that the bull-necked brawler jested.

"Starve them out," said Brocc. "The one thing we can do is keep them penned up in the fort."

"You're a disappointment, Brocc," Torcán mocked his friend. "Too much common-sense and strategic thinking. You must be looking for a promotion." The small group laughed. Íar stroked his bushy, red beard, and for the first time since leaving Áth joined in with a resounding belly laugh that was heard in An Balla-Leac. Mórrígan smiled. It was good to have the old Íar back.

***

Soft leather boots muted Cador's footfall as he tramped along the walkway on An Balla-Leac's stockade. In the still air before dusk, the steady thud of his footsteps echoed around the fort. It was a comfort to his men since they had little else to smile about.

The thickset commander cursed as his cloak slipped from his shoulder. High winds were not the cause, for they had lost their bluster mid-afternoon. Instead, his left arm, or more accurately, the lack of a left arm, was the source of his annoyance. Cador swore again as thick fingers, more used to gripping an axe or sword, fumbled with a gem-encrusted brooch. It was a gift from a long-dead lover.

He knew full well his task was impossible. His commission held only the promise of a good death, which he considered an acceptable reward. At fifty summers, Cador was well past his prime as a fighter. A tattooed, bald head distracted from his grey-white beard.

The veteran considered it an ominous sign that he ranked among the best fighters in An Balla-Leac. The defenders had, at best, one thousand men and women fit to fight. Not enough to adequately man the stockade. As for the rest, numbering around fifteen hundred, they were the sick, the wounded and the crippled.

Inside the fort, the air was rank. Yellow-green pus oozing from scabby wounds and the blackened stumps of limbs and fingers contributed to the odour. Harsh, racking coughs and explosive, wet sneezes sprayed a mist of infection into the air. Vermin gnawed on the bones of the dead and nipped the toes of those too sick to move. Cador shivered. *Could the Otherworld be worse than this?*

As night descended, watch lights flickered into life along the stockade. Smoky, yellow-orange flames spluttered against darkening skies, and the rancid smell of burning fat permeated the evening air. Cador cursed. Each torch on the defences of An Balla-Leac seemed to have its twin as campfires burst into flame on the semicircle of hills surrounding the fort.

They can't have many warriors. Ualraig assured him that the Clann Ui

Flaithimh numbered less than a thousand. Perhaps the enemy had been reinforced. Cador and his defenders had been besieged in An Balla-Leac for seven sunsets. If the enemy had superior numbers, why did they not attack?

Cador continued his walk around the perimeter, encouraging the men and women he passed. He shared jests, made wagers, and drank gut-rotting homebrews. In the flickering light, the defenders' gaunt, drawn features were a reminder that food was scarce. The commander clutched the small wooden effigy that hung on a thong around his neck. It was buffed smooth from rubbing and darkened by age and sweat. He offered up a prayer to Brighid. His prayer was simple. *Bring me bad weather.*

***

A third force watched the siege of An Balla-Leac from a camp on the moors. Cuán Ó Néill pointed to the bonfires on the hillside. "Our friends have lit welcoming fires to guide us."

"Are they friends?" said Bláithín. "Apart from their ability to terrorize a vast tract of land, we know little about them, only wild tales and rumours. Just because they're from Ériu doesn't make them allies."

"I agree, my love. But if we are to thrive, we'll need their strength. In the morning, I will take half our warriors and meet with our fellow exiles."

Bláithín nodded and opened her arms. "The children are asleep. We should take advantage of a rare moment of privacy." Cuán smiled.

***

Seven sunsets had passed since An Balla-Leac had been blockaded. The quintet rode at a moderate trot along the north-facing side of the fort. Torcán, designated as the "one most likely to start a fight", was left behind in temporary command of the camp.

Íar prayed to the Goddess it was a wise decision. *Surely, there were enough wise heads around the young man to prevent a major disaster.* Íar's band guided their mounts in a wide semi-circle to face the ráth's entrance. He hoped the commander of An Balla-Leac was in a more reasonable mood to negotiate.

A shower of stones buried themselves in the dirt before them. A few cracked against boiled leather armour and helmets but were little more than an annoyance. Íar sighed and looked pointedly at Mórrígan. The Huntress nodded to her brothers.

The three dismounted, slipped bows from their backs, nocked arrows, and quickly sent a score of the black-shafted missiles arching towards the ramparts. All were highly skilled bowmen and picked their targets well. A dozen defenders cried out and pitched forward to lie in the dirt before the gate.

Cador appeared in one of the guard posts. "If another stone is thrown, I'll cut off the hand of the person who chucked it." He looked down at Íar. "Well, we've made small talk. What do you want?"

Íar moved a few paces to the front of the group and removed his helmet. He scratched his scalp and felt the morning breeze attack the sweaty, dampness of his long, red hair. With arms outstretched and in a bold voice, he said, "Leave. Take your warriors and depart. There's no honour in this fight."

"Is there honour in any fight?" Cador responded. "Our position is strong. You're outnumbered. We've no reason to retreat."

"You and I know your defenders are ill or disabled. Hunger has shrunk their bellies. You will starve. You cannot thrive on water alone. Winter comes. I need this ráth for shelter for my people. An Balla-Leac *will* fall. Take your men. Fall back and rejoin your army at Dùn Caen. We can fight in the spring."

It was a reasonable offer, and there was despair in Cador's reply. "My orders are to hold. Kartimandu has set the minds of the garrison, and they'll not run."

"To the last man," said Íar sorrowfully and saluted Cador.

"To the last man," replied Cador and bowed.

***

Cuán pursed his lips. "What part of *we want to be friends* did they not understand?" The question was pitched at the burly chieftain, standing to his right. The man, a head taller than Cuán, laughed and pointed to Torcán.

"He's a young pup. Looking to show he's a hard man."

"That may be the case, but he has two hundred shields and six hundred riders to back him up. A pitched battle is not what I want, Lonán."

"He made a bad decision and likely knows it. Give him a way to save face."

Cuán guessed at what his brother was considering. "Just don't kill him. I want allies, not more enemies."

Torcán looked at the warriors massed five hundred paces before him. *Shite! How did I get myself into this one?* The answer had he thought about it, was simple. In his estimation, the earlier envoy had been a bit full of himself. So, he sent him away with a flea in his ear without listening to the message.

As he inspected Cuán's men, even an eejit could see they would not be dismissed lightly. Íar would be furious if Torcán lost half his men in a brawl. The deep-purple mark on his throat burned. It was a painful reminder that Íar was not the only or the most forbidding one who would have a say in his fate. The Sídhe had admonished him previously for foolish behaviour.

It disturbed the young ceannairí céad, still just twenty-four summers old, that the two hundred shield-men behind him had started taking bets on how he would extricate himself from the situation. Gossip circulated among the ranks in anticipation of an entertaining tableau. To a man, Torcán's men were mainly Cróeb Ruad and had instantly recognised the tattoos on the upper arms of the envoys. One coughed to gain Torcán's attention and pointed.

Lonán Ó Néill, Cuán's second-in-command and elder brother, strode forward several paces and stopped. He made a great show as he laid his shield face-down on the heather and followed this with his weapons. Already stripped to the waist, he wore red and black plaid pants and calf-high, laced-up boots. His long dark brown hair was pulled back and tied with a thong. With a broad smile, he took several steps more, coming to a halt midway between the two forces.

"A fight. Man-to-man," shouted Lonán. "No weapons save what the Goddess gave us at birth."

"What's the prize?" asked Torcán.

Lonán tugged his beard. "We talk." Then he added, "If I win, we talk, and we'll drink your beer and eat your food. If you win, you drink our beer and eat our food. I am Lonán Ó Néill of the Ulaid and Captain of the Cróeb Ruad. Name your champion." There was a rumbling of recognition among the Clann Ui Flaithimh contingent at Lonán's name. Torcán groaned. *Bloody northerners!* He imagined a long list of those in the tribe who would happily queue up to kick his arse.

"I accept," Torcán called out, although he had little choice. "I am Torcán Ó Dubhghaill, of the tribe Clann Ui Flaithimh." He paused and added, "Acting commander of this fine body of men." Braced with a cheer from his men, he walked forward.

The opponents circled, taking the measure of each other. Lonán saw his opponent was young but no stranger to battle. The taut, muscular chest and thick arm muscles were well-marked with scars old and new. He smiled. "Looks like you use your head a lot."

Torcán looked puzzled and then laughed at the reference to the long, horizontal scar on his forehead. Torcán assessed his challenger. By his reckoning, this Lonán would stand a healthy comparison with Urard and Íar, two of the biggest warriors he knew.

Torcán charged first, as usual, leading with his head. A resounding "Ooooph!" exploded from Lonán as Torcán connected with his abdomen. The blow was followed by a skull to the chin that rattled Lonán's teeth and snapped his head back. Torcán then kneed Lonán in the balls.

Lonán staggered back a few paces, which was just as well. Torcán felt as if his head had hit a stone wall. *Did the man eat rocks to have a stomach that hard?* He shook his head to clear the annoying buzzing sound and refocus his eyes, blearily aware that Lonán had recovered.

With a bellow of anger tinged with embarrassment at being caught unawares, Lonán charged. Torcán made an understandable, if incorrect, assumption that Lonán would hit him head-on. He crouched slightly and braced his feet. For a man of his size, Lonán was sprightly. Bulging thigh muscles added speed. At the last moment, he sidestepped and thrust out a stiff arm.

Had the limb connected with Torcán's throat, the young man would have made the journey to Mag Mell. Instead, the arm caught Torcán on his upper chest, knocking the wind out of his lungs and tossing him up and backwards. He landed on hard ground. Torcán felt as if he had been hit with a bar of iron. However, Lonán had not finished. While Torcán lay helpless on his back, Lonán kicked him in the head, belly, and balls.

By then, both camps had come together and enclosed the combatants in a large circle. Having taken the measure of the two men, they began the honoured practice of setting odds and making wagers. Loud cheers and shouts of advice rang out for both fighters. As Torcán got to his feet, he could not help but notice that those cheering for him appeared much fewer than for Lonán. He charged. With a slap of bodies and loud grunting, the two fighters clashed in the centre of the ring.

Long arms surrounded Torcán, hands clasped and pulled. Bones in his spine grated against each other. Ribs bent inwards, moving towards that moment when they would crack. Torcán responded with a swift headbutt that broke Lonán's nose and his crushing hold. The taller man sneezed, splattering Torcán's face in bloody snot.

Fists battered Lonán's ears until they pulsated purple and red. The men broke apart and circled each other slowly and much more warily. With rasping breaths, they came together once more. Fists smacked against flesh as they pounded each other's torsos with stabbing punches amid sharp grunts of pain.

One more time, their sweat-covered torsos separated, and the fighters stepped back a pace. In a rare moment of clarity, it dawned on

Torcán that Lonán was pulling his punches. The older man's hazel-amber eyes glinted, recognising what had finally penetrated the younger man's skull. It was a challenge that Torcán was unable to resist. With a roar, he hunched his shoulders and charged. Lonán moved to close the gap.

Torcán's chin met the knuckles of Lonán's right fist. This time it was no feint. Stubbornly, Torcán refused to accept the message from his brain that the fight was over. The follow-on left to the base of his skull put the contest beyond doubt. Torcán stumbled, falling face-first into the heather. His last thoughts before unconsciousness were that the flowers smelled pleasant, and he was glad Lonán had pulled *that* punch.

The fight had been bloody, furious, and fleeting, lasting little longer than a leisurely morning piss after an evening of drinking. Torcán groaned as he drifted back to consciousness. His head and body ached. His jaw felt as if it were shattered, and his knuckles were swollen and skinned.

Lonán's hand on the nape of his neck lifted his head slightly, and he felt cool water trickle over his face and into his mouth. "I'm glad you look as bad as I do," Torcán slurred, his brain not yet synchronous with his mouth.

Lonán laughed and then winced. "A broken nose and a few cracked ribs, you bastard. You fight well, if a bit predictably."

"I'll be supping broth for a while, and we'll both be pissing blood for the next few sunsets," said Torcán. Then he added, "Maybe you could give me a few tips." The older man nodded and lay back on the cool earth. It had been a close fight, too close.

***

The raucous cheering of both groups of warriors subsided abruptly. Those gathered backed away to allow five riders to walk their mounts to where the Torcán and Lonán lay. All watched as Íar and his companions removed their helmets and surveyed the scene. Íar bent over his horse's shoulder and said, "Would you like to tell me what in the Hag's name is going on here?"

Torcán attempted to stand but only reached a sitting position before he puked. "Negotiations," he mumbled through spit, vomit, and swollen lips. Íar raised an eyebrow. Torcán continued with a weak flourish of his hand. "I've negotiated with our Ulaid brothers. They will join us for our assault on An Balla-Leac and, with Conall's consent, will become part of our clann." The short speech exhausted Torcán, his eyes glazed over, and he slumped onto the heather and wildflowers.

At a loss for words, Íar looked to Mórrígan, who quickly shrugged her shoulders in an "It's your problem' gesture." They were rescued when Cuán stepped forward and bowed. "Perhaps some introductions would be appropriate, then lots of discussion over food and beer." Íar nodded in relief and signalled for Cuán to continue.

"I am Cuán Ó Néill, Rí Clochar and Captain of the Cróeb Ruad. My men, numbering one thousand, and our families have been exiled from our homeland by Macha Mong Ruad." Cuán paused and smiled towards Torcán.

"While this young and somewhat impetuous warrior's negotiating strategy is unconventional, his heart is in the right place. Both our peoples need shelter for the coming winter. I propose we join forces to capture An Balla-Leac."

Íar dismounted and walked to grasp Cuán's forearm. "Agreed." With a quizzical look at Torcán and Lonán, he asked, "Who won the *negotiations?*"

Cuán laughed, "According to the gold that changed hands, my brother, Lonán. However, I prefer to think of it as an honourable draw."

***

A sympathetic god answered Cador's prayer. Fierce thunder and lightning storms lashed the exposed uplands. Borne on southwesterly winds, hail the size of mistletoe berries flayed an exposed Clann Ui Flaithimh encampment. A few unfortunates were laid out by chunks of ice the size of a fist.

The heavy rains made bogs overflow, and their dark waters deep and treacherous. The heather and the gorse-covered landscape became sodden. Forced off the moorland, Íar and Cuán's people moved to the forested foothills of Penn-inus. The storms eventually abated after a quarter-cycle of the moon.

Cador's hand rested on the wooden fence. A few snowflakes danced along the walkway, harbingers of a cold winter. He felt the last weak rays of a mid-autumn sun on his back. He would miss simple pleasures such as this. The nights were cold, not just chilly. His bones ached, and his joints were stiff. His head thumped, and his stomach rumbled from lack of sustenance.

The storm had brought relief from attack but not from hunger. Besieged, the garrison still had no path to replenish its stores. After half and then quarter rations, the food was long exhausted. No one had seen a dog, cat, or rat recently. A dozen men had been executed for eating human flesh. Cador shivered, repulsed at the thought.

Wasted bodies defended the fort. Many were barely alive and were little more than skin-draped skeletons. Only the thrall of Kartimandu kept them in place. The cloying smell of burnt flesh filled his nostrils. Many of the injured had succumbed to disease or just did not have the nourishment needed to heal. A section of the fort had been set aside for funeral fires. Ominously, its area had doubled in the past few sunsets.

The sound of shields and weapons made his hand instinctively move to the smooth, ivory pommel of his sword. Like its owner, the sword had few embellishments. The blade's long edges were sharp, rust-free, and oiled. It was a tool to be used, and as he looked around, he saw it would soon be put to work. Strangely, Cador's spirit lifted. Soon he would feast in Mag Mell.

From the northern forest, large groups of warriors jogged into place around the hillfort. They halted on the slopes of An Balla-Leac's mound, just beyond the range of his slings. Even at a distance, their bearing told Cador none were strangers to battle. They had an economy of movement, only taking time to check that weapons could be released quickly from fleece-lined sheaths. Wooden shields were strapped to strong backs.

Cador smiled thinly. The position of the shields and the fact that some carried makeshift scaling ladders told him his walls would soon be under threat. The men were semi-naked. Clothes did not restrict or constrain their sword arms. Thongs of leather tied up long hair—even long beards. None would allow an opponent to pull them onto a blade. A small group of riders accompanied them. Cador watched as they dismounted, slid bows from their backs and nocked arrows. All were strangely quiet.

He turned and strode along the wooden walkway to the hillfort's entrance. The slap and splash of several thousand bony hoofs pounding through a water-logged landscape sent a ripple of anxiety through his forces. Yet, it was not these that Cador feared most. Instead, it was the two hundred veterans who followed at a quick jog and the fifty mounted archers who accompanied them.

He did not have enough fit men and women to defend the perimeter. The five hundred Ualraig gave him, the best of Cador's fighters, were concentrated at the eastern entrance. The Clann Ui Flaithimh riders could not be allowed in the fort.

Cador watched a wagon trundle slowly forward. Its solid wheels dug deep ruts in the rain-softened terrain. It stopped at the end of the chalk-speckled dirt track leading to the fort's gates. On its bed lay two large tree trunks. Each had an end fashioned into a blunt point hardened by fire.

***

Íar nodded to the shields, and two dozen brawny men stepped forward. Thick ropes were laid on the ground adjacent to the wagon, and the cut trees were pulled and levered onto the lines. The men stood back evenly spread between the battering rams and waited. Alongside and behind, the remainder of the two hundred adjusted shields and weapons. A group with axes stood to the fore.

At Íar's dip of his head, Mórrígan dismounted and slipped on her helmet. The black plumes at its crest flared in the morning breeze. The other archers followed her lead. Their orders were to kill anyone who threatened the ramming party. Arrows were nocked, and targets were selected.

Mórrígan's arrow flew straight. Her first victim clutched at a scrawny throat as the iron barb entered and exited in a gush of blood and strings of flesh. As the missile left her bow, another was nocked, and another target was chosen.

The lightly defended spurs that overlooked the killing zone were cleared ruthlessly. When the archers, and a band of shield-wall fighters, scaled the dirt and limestone ramparts, there was little opposition. With the advantage of being at a level height, the bowmen cowed or picked off those in the gate's guard posts and those standing on either side. They were not troubled by the handful of Cador's slingers whose aim was erratic and who caused little more than an annoyance. Their efforts ended when having exposed their position, arrows punched through nearly transparent flesh.

Within the killing triangle was a wagon's breadth path through the large rocks and sharpened stakes to allow supplies to reach the fort. Muscles straining and with loud shouts, the ramming teams lifted the massive logs and marched steadfastly forward. On each side, they were guarded by the shields of their comrades.

Sweat dripped from burly bodies as they built momentum and swung the rams to and fro. The sharpened boles were released with a bellow, bashing against the gates. Splinters scattered; some pierced the ramming team's exposed flesh. The gates gave enough to absorb the impact but remained unbroken. The men groaned and began to lift and swing the logs once more.

The thud of wood on wood was the signal for Cuán. With a shout and a sword flourish, he charged up the slope towards An Balla-Leac's ramparts. Around the perimeter, his men followed. The Goddess favoured them. While the fort's walls were strong and the surrounding ditches deep and wide, they were sparsely populated with stakes and iron thistles.

More aggravation to the attackers was the inevitable profusion of blackthorn bushes. Long, sharp spines pierced any patch of open skin as they trod across the ditch's floor. That the bottom was an ankle-deep sludge of shite, piss, and the decaying debris of daily life multiplied the risk of infection.

The attackers scaled the muddy walls of the perimeter ditches and pitched ladders against the ramparts. Iron hooks were hurled upwards, seeking purchase on the wooden stockade while archers provided cover. Flights of black shafts arching over the fence, keeping heads down. Only skin-draped skeletons rallied to confront him when Cuán hauled himself over the palisade and dropped onto the fence's walkway. Although frightening in aspect, they were no match for Cuán's men.

Behind the eastern gates, Cador waited with his five hundred fighters. He knew it would not be long before the gates finally yielded under the battering. His walls were already lost. Soon they would face an enemy at their back and front. The veteran sighed. There was little he could do except die with dignity. He looked at the resigned looks on the small group whose minds were not in thrall to Kartimandu. They shrugged. They were soldiers and warriors who die and go to Mag Mell. That was their lot.

The gates crashed open with a loud squeal of twisting iron hinges. Bits of wooden debris floated down as Cador registered the disgust on his enemy's face. Íar's men were met first, not with blades, but with the stench of disease and decay. A few emptied their morning meal on the dirt as rank odours flowed over the attackers. For Cador, the smell was of trivial concern compared to the human devastation created by Kartimandu.

"Shields forward!" bellowed Íar.

Torcán and Brocc's men formed a column the width of the entrance, locked shields and marched forward. The column scythed through Cador's malnourished men, and the High People retreated, regrouping at the centre of the fort. This action prolonged their lives. Cador's veterans were surrounded by a barrier of the sick and the injured.

The riders entered the ráth, although the horses resisted going forward amid an atmosphere corrupted with rotting flesh and spirits. Surrounded and outnumbered, Cador's force glared defiantly, shouting weak challenges and curses at their enemy.

Íar's force stood with weapons at their sides, unwilling to attack the feeble enemy before them. Íar looked helplessly at Mórrígan and Cuán. The Dark Huntress spoke quietly, "Kill them. They are diseased, and their minds are not their own. It will be a mercy."

With a shake of his head, Íar moved his horse forward and called out to Cador. "Please go. Take your men and go. We'll not harm you."

Cador bowed. "You mean well and are an honourable man, but the lady is right. Give us a swift death so we may proudly enter Mag Mell." With a final cry, Cador raised his sword. "Attack!" The outcome was settled swiftly. Those who could move charged towards their opponents and were met with a hail of javelins and arrows. Those who avoided the missiles were executed with a sword or axe blow.

However, the Goddess kept the bean sídhe from Cador. He knelt at the centre of his command, shouting and screaming for a quick death. His voice was hoarse with anger realising no one would give him relief. Finally, Íar walked his horse to stand alongside Cador and hit him with the flat end of his axe.

"Tie him to a horse. Give him food and water. The Goddess will decide his fate."

***

It took an entire cycle of the moon before An Balla-Leac was inhabitable. For many sunsets, the smoke from funeral pyres rose to darken the skies. Eventually, the stench of the dead and the diseased faded. Íar was thankful for the handful of druids who had accompanied his force. It was their efforts and prayers that cleansed the fort of its ghosts.

The hillfort's buildings were torn down and burned. The stockade, washed many times, would forever hold battle stains. The rebuilding of the ráth to provide for its current occupants and Conall's expected arrival in the spring took everyone's minds off the past horrors.

Ever aware of a possible attack by Kartimandu, Íar oversaw the building of an outer rampart, which encompassed the entire mound on which the ráth sat. Íar's and Mórrígan's thoughts soon turned to how they could make the winter unpleasant for the Kartimandu and Ualraig.

CHAPTER 25

406 B.C.—Winter

Conall stepped outside the broch, shivered, and drew the wolf pelt that trimmed the neck of his heavy winter cloak closer. Smothered in fleece-lined leather boots, his toes still shrank from the chill. The land around Trócaire was blanketed in thick, pristine snow. *Frigid and beautiful.*

Gusts of bone-chilling winds blew drifts of white powder over dark thatched roofs and against the grey-brown walls until the dwellings slowly disappeared. Crystal fringes hung from ragged eaves and sparkled with the colours of the pastel winter sky.

It was the season when trails of white mist flowed from frozen, snot-plugged noses. Lips bled as dry skin cracked. Even with the protection of wraps and scarves, inhaling produced frozen nose hairs and a lungful of ice crystals. The days were short and dark.

Nature hibernated. Man stayed inside unless there was an emergency. There was no war and few raids. Winter's harsh embrace brought peace. Killing was more problematic in inclement seasons. Driving a sword through multiple layers of wool, fleece-lined cloaks, and pelts was practically impossible. The smallest warrior became a hulking, frost-covered giant.

A misery-inducing fall of freezing rain moved south over the mountains and across the Sleá. Trócaire and its sister communities were scourged for three sunsets. Following the storm, the silence was broken by the crack of trees and branches falling under the weight of the transparent glaze.

Nevertheless, the vista evoked awe in all but the dead. The ice-en-crusted landscape glittered pink and silver-grey as the morning sun rose above the horizon. Conall high-stepped through knee-deep snow and rolled over the deeper drifts that overflowed walls. Without fire pits, the settlement's dwellings would have chilled below survival temperature. Families would have fallen into a permanent slumber.

As it was, Conall was thankful the storm had not lasted longer. The broch's store of kindling and peat was severely depleted. He wondered how the rest of the community fared. There were always those who stored too little. Faced with the horrors of no fire or warmth, they canni-balised their home, even the thatch, to feed the flames. Yet the cold hands of the winter gods still reached in and took them.

With good intentions, some foolishly ventured outside to forage for wood. Most became part of the frozen landscape. Their misery was muf-fled as ice first numbed and then entombed them. Their final sluggish thoughts were of despair for themselves and those left behind.

Spotting the smoky trail which arched above Trócaire, Conall cursed, changed direction, and tramped quickly towards the crossing at Áth.

***

A heavily pregnant Áine was mounted on a large salt-and-pepper grey mare. Behind her, a continually whining Cassán sat astride his pony. He drew no sympathy from his mother. Fifty riders stood in a protective cir-cle around them. All were loyal, although mainly to the promise of gold. Silent on cloth-muffled hoofs, they cantered to the ford. The mounts crashed through a finger-deep layer of ice and into the river.

About to guide their horses up the frozen, snow-covered bank, the band encountered an apparition. The horse was so black the rider ap-peared to float above the bank. As the early morning sun rose above the horizon, shafts of light glanced off the rider's polished armour. A chill breeze made the red plumes on his helmet flare and the edges of his black cloak flap.

"You will return to Trócaire for judgment," bellowed Nikandros.

It was a reasonable plan, and the timing was good. I have been betrayed. "He's only one man," spat Áine, recognising the Spartan. "Kill him."

The helmet turned, and a bronze bracer glinted as a hand was raised. A series of hisses startled horses, already unhappy to be standing in the ice-cold waters of the Abhainn Dubh. On the riverbank, fire baskets were uncovered. A hundred archers stood alongside.

The sound of feet crunching through frost-covered snow drew attention to the double row of shields. Two hundred of Cúscraid's men blocked any unapproved retreat. The chink of harness and tack drew the deserters' attention back to the riverbank. Nikandros was accompanied by the rest of the cavalry. Their loyalty to Conall and Clann Ui Flaithimh was unqualified.

"Throw your weapons into the river and dismount. *Now!* You will be taken to the Great Hall and judged" Nikandros' arm described a full semi-circle. "These men are unhappy at giving up the warmth of their fires and women. Do not try their patience further."

"*Attack!*" shrieked Áine. Cassán wailed.

In response, her "loyal" guard tossed their weapons into the river, dismounted, and led their horses to the river's eastern bank. They had gambled and lost. Their horses were led away, and the rebels frisked and taken away between two rows of heavily armed men. Not-so-subtle murmurs of, "Try to escape, and I'll gut you," dispelled any thoughts of an appeal to comradeship or making a run for it.

Conall arrived at the ford, along with Fearghal, Mongfhionn, Brion, and Crum. They watched Áine, still mounted and standing in the middle of the crossing. "Walk your mount slowly towards us, Áine," said Conall. "You'll be escorted to the Great Hall, given warm clothes, food, and a hot drink." Áine trembled in the cold and hesitated. "You'll not be harmed for the unborn child's sake." Resigned to her humiliation, Áine grasped the reins and steered her horse towards Trócaire.

***

The prisoners were lined up against the Great Hall's walls. They were not shackled, but each was flanked by two guards. At the high table, Conall sat with the Chomhairle. Áine had been fed, provided a change of warm clothing, and knew she would not be harmed. Seated at the far end of the high table, she clasped a warm mug and sipped the spiced milk. Retreating to her version of the world, Áine lost any interest in the proceedings. Cassán, still wailing, was given into the care of his nurse.

Conall stood and faced the prisoners. "You chose badly... very badly." He sighed deeply and said, "You'll be taken outside. Before this building and the people, you'll be executed. Your heads will be staked as a reminder to others who may waver in their loyalty to the tribe and its chosen king." There was no response from the prisoners save a soft intake of breath and a prayer for a sharp blade.

Stripped to their pants, the prisoners shivered, and their teeth chattered. A flint-eyed executioner stood before each man. At each captive's back, another waited. All stood with swords drawn. Their faces betrayed no emotion save for a scornful curl of the lip in disgust. No one would cheat death on this morning.

At a signal from Fearghal, a gasp rose from the crowd. Each of the front-facing warriors took a step forward, put a hand on a prisoner's shoulder and plunged their blade into the traitor's gut. Dark iron blades exited their backs, spraying those behind with blood. The sword was twisted and moved horizontally, from side to side. Guts slithered to form steaming piles on the snow-covered ground. They were marginally ahead of the body to which they were still attached.

It was not a swift death and not meant to be. The Goddess judged how soon the condemned entered Mag Mell. For those she favoured, the sword pierced a vital organ or cut an artery, and death would be quick. Miscreants and unbelievers, whom the Goddess had no affection for, suffered a lingering death in the snow. The few who remained alive at dusk were released with a blade to the throat.

Fearghal watched as Áine returned under escort to her home.

"Nikandros must have received good information to be in the right place at the right time."

Conall frowned. "Áine took away her maid's reputation without a thought. At that moment, she forfeited the lady's faithfulness, which hitherto had been a wall of protection."

CHAPTER 26

405 B.C.—Winter

Raised in south-eastern Ériu, Bréanainn Dhá Lámh was a stocky, fresh-faced brawler of average height and indeterminate intellect. Thrown out by an aristocratic family grown tired of his two talents of getting into trouble and spending their money, Bréanainn took to the by-ways of Ériu and the role of an adventurer.

For several years he was moderately successful at cattle raiding, kidnapping, and robbing anyone who travelled the pathways connecting the island's rátha and larger communities. Rich or poor, he made little distinction in his choice of victim. Although, with a prudence that was at odds with his generally thoughtless character, he steered away from killing nobles, Brehons, and druids.

Those who knew Bréanainn were well aware that he had shite-for-brains. Thus, it was his good luck and others' misfortune that he met Téide Bán. Named for the milky paleness of her skin and later for her dyed-blonde hair, Téide was slender and small. She barely came up to Bréanainn's shoulder.

Téide speech was interspersed with an attractive lisp which proved to be a unique, identifying characteristic. Whereas Bréanainn bludgeoned his way through life, Téide's talents were founded on innate cunning and intelligence.

Her diminutive presence and innocent mien belied the menace that resided in her twisted mind. She could cut a throat or slide a blade between ribs with a proficiency and enthusiasm few could match.

Their plundering across southern Ériu brought the duo considerable wealth and a sizeable following of society's outcasts. Soon, they became a force to be reckoned with and one that the local *ríthe* in their fortresses could ill afford to ignore. Unfortunately for the pair, and as often is the case, wealth's companions were cupidity and betrayal.

Téide's vaunted instinct for sensing threats let her down. An ill-advised attack on a wagon train near the fort of Ráthgeal proved to be a trap. Thus, she and Bréanainn ended up in irons before the Rí of Ráthgeal and a trio of stern-looking Brehons. The remainder of their band achieved a final notoriety. Mounted on spears, their heads provided an honour guard for Bréanainn and Téide as they were dragged along the muddy path that led to the gateway of the ráth.

The outcome of the Brehons' judgment was never in doubt. The Law favoured reparation and compensation rather than execution, even for murderers. Thus, and in accordance with the Law, their wealth was distributed as equitably as possible to the kin of those they murdered and stole from. A hefty percentage also found its way into the coffers of Ráthgeal's king.

In a final twist of the dagger of justice, Bréanainn and Téide were declared outcasts. The sentence meant anyone could kill them on sight and not face punishment. The pair were stripped, shaved, and whipped as entertainment for the locals until their backs were bloody. Saltwater was poured over their wounds, sadistically adding to their pain under the banner of mercy.

***

Following their trial and judgement, Bréanainn and Téide were dumped into a solid-wheeled wagon and driven to the coast. There a boat waited. The vessel's captain had been paid to drop them off on the western coast of middle Albu, a journey from sunrise to dusk.

Having already received payment, the seaman could merely have sailed a few thousand paces beyond the shore and tossed the pair into the sea. No one would have known or cared, and no one would have blamed him. However, the captain was an honest man. After a relatively smooth crossing of the *Ler Ériu* and with a parting smile, he tossed the pair into the bone-chilling waters about five hundred paces from the shore. "Enjoy the swim, arseholes."

"*Tuili!*" roared Bréanainn. He spluttered at the inrush of salt water into his open mouth. Ungainly attempts to stay afloat were made impossible by his shackles. Finally, with lots of thrashing, he disappeared beneath the water. Thus, Bréanainn was surprised to feel his feet touch a sandy bottom.

Embarrassed, he stood up to find the waters lapping around his belly. This section of the coastline had a long sloping beach. "Tuilí," he muttered again, then looked around for his partner in the half-light of dusk. After several shouts, they located one another and quickly waded to the beach.

It was a half-cycle of the moon after Imbolg. The weather was bitterly cold. Snowflakes no longer melted when they touched Téide's skin. Numb with cold, she shook uncontrollably, and her teeth chattered wildly. She could not talk because her brain had almost shut down. Any movement was painful and sluggish.

"Run, bitseach! Run or die," shouted Bréanainn in her frost-tipped ears. A harsh grip on her arm dragged her towards the shore.

The pair stumbled bare-footed, breathless, and cold past a small farm holding. There, they stopped to steal a hammer, iron spikes, coarse sacks, and animal blankets from an outhouse. Bréanainn considered forcing his way inside one of the roundhouses, buried up to their eaves by banks of deep snow, but Téide dissuaded him. Even a small farm would have an extended family of twenty or thirty adults. Neither of the two was in any condition for a fight.

At some stage, the gods took pity. Wandering in a mountainous country with no sense of direction, they eventually staggered into a cave. It appeared deserted, although they were past caring about such niceties and too tired to explore. Téide was impressed that Bréanainn, after many curses, managed to get a small fire going.

In truth, it was very much trial and error, striking flint stones and iron, until a random spark arched tantalisingly into the air before settling on some dry grass. The outcasts were chilled to the bone, but the beginnings of a fire ignited a dim hope that they might survive.

"It will be warmer this way," said Bréanainn. Laying a blanket on the frozen ground, he pulled Téide to him with her back to his chest and covered them with the remaining rags.

"Just keep that thing between your legs in its place," snorted Téide. She felt Bréanainn's muscular arms and legs wrap around her. There was something oddly comforting about the mixed bouquets of the smoky fire, cattle-shite-covered blankets, and the natural body odour of Bréanainn. In the flickering light, Bréanainn could not see her smirk.

"Your imagination is running away with you. My cock and balls fell off in the freezing water," grunted Bréanainn. Exhausted, he fell silent temporarily before he commenced snoring.

Enfolded in Bréanainn's arms, Téide turned around and examined his face in the half-light of the dawn. She wondered if hers looked as bad. The bastards who had shaved them had not been careful and used dull blades. She gently touched her face. It felt puffy, bruised, and tight with scabby cuts. The phantom fingers of a cold draught stroked her head, and she shed a tear for her lost hair. Apart from a few random tufts, her scalp was as bald as a baby's arse.

A few of Bréanainn's slashes had the potential to become scars. Selfishly, Téide hoped that was not the case for her. Like ageing, men wore scars better than women. Téide's appraisal was matter-of-fact. Neither was attracted to the other. He was the brother, the family's black sheep she never had. Both were content for that situation to continue. Besides, she had witnessed Bréanainn's preferred rutting style. It was, at best, angry and violent.

Téide stretched her arms and pushed him. "Wake up, you lazy

bastard. Stoke the fire. We've clothes and food to steal before we freeze or starve to death."

***

The wagon trundled over the rutted, frozen path. Iron springs scraped and squealed. Axles turned in hubs that needed grease. An old man sat on the driver's bench and flicked a whip at the scrawny oxen pulling the wagon. Only a bulbous, red nose and eyes, half shut as he squinted at the glaring, snow-covered terrain, were visible.

His hands, weathered and stiff with age, were covered in rags, a sop to the snow and sleet-laden southwesterly wind that chilled his bones. The last winter had taken two of his fingers and the same number of toes. The blue-black patina and lack of feeling in others told him he would lose more this winter.

A boy of no more than ten summers old sat at his side. The child was well hopped up against the elements. He had been delighted to accompany the old man. It was a break from the suffocating closeness of the family's roundhouse. The thick, stale smells of unwashed bodies, farts, full piss-buckets, and the musky scents that accompanied the grunting of some older ones clogged his nostrils and clung to hair and clothes.

The old man understood the boy's incessant flow of animated chatter and comments about animal and bird tracks. It drew occasional but appreciative grunts from the old man. He loved his grandson. It was a hard life into which the child had been born. Any respite was good. When he stood up and pointed, the old man's attention quickly focused on the slight figure that emerged from the forest. The person was female, naked, and ran towards the wagon.

As the grand-da reached for the hand-axe hidden under the folds of his cloak, he sensed he was too late. He was right. The wagon lurched as someone dropped onto it. A thick branch, wielded as a club, crushed the back of his thin skull. More blows pulped his head as he slumped forward. He was dead after the first strike. The subsequent bashes were amusement for his attacker.

Speechless, the young boy stood in shock as his grand-da died. Yet his grief was short. A cold hand reached up and pulled him to the ground. His last vision was of a bald, pale-faced demon who, with a quick twist, snapped his neck. The dull crack echoed across the valley. Animals and birds fell silent, and for a moment, the wind ceased, mourning the murder of the child.

It was a perfect result from Bréanainn and Téide's perspective. Once scraped clean of brain and gore, the old man's clothes would fit Bréanainn. The boy's clothing was a good size for Téide. Inside the wagon, they found sacks of oats and salt. Although not a wonderful discovery, they could make decent hot meals with the addition of wild berries and pine nuts.

They could sell the wagon and oxen in one of the many settlements. The cart would not be recognised if they chose one far enough away. The old man had a hand-axe and a good knife, so they were armed. Above all, they now had transportation.

CHAPTER 27

405 B.C.—Trócaire—Imbolg

The winter feast of Imbolg was celebrated with giant bonfires that left circles of scorched ground amid the deep snow. The people of Clann Ui Flaithimh, knowing that spring was just over the horizon and that the days would soon lengthen, danced around the fires. Their cheeks were ruddy with the weather and beer. Women carried the future of the tribe in their wombs. The fruit of Bealtaine was ready to be delivered.

Conall watched the festivities, amused at the antics of his people. His reticence to fully embrace the festivities reflected his natural shyness and role as king. Unreserved carousing was not for the Rí Ruirech of Clann Ui Flaithimh. On this occasion, Brion stood somewhat unsteadily beside his friend. The bronze tankard grasped in his right hand was lifted once more, and again its contents almost made it past Brion's lips. Conall laughed.

"It's as well you're not paying for that beer. You've wet the snow more than your throat."

Brion looked ruefully at the cup and its contents. "And I'll likely piss the rest away." The two friends were not the chattiest of people. Still, having started and with the beer consumed giving freedom to his tongue, Brion continued, "I'll be taking Drostan up on his proposition."

In his heart, Conall knew that his friend would choose to accept the offer. Indeed, looking at it objectively, it would be foolish of Brion to decline Drostan. While selfishly disappointed at losing a close friend and advisor, Conall knew it was the best outcome. "Brion Ó Cathasaigh, Rí of Na Mèadaidh has a certain ring to it." Brion chuckled as Conall toasted him with a clash of mugs. "Will you re-build Dùn Na Mèadaidh?"

"Nah, the spirits of the dead can have the cursed place. Cúscraid and I have mulled it over. The rocky crag south of Áth, on the opposite side of the river, is a much better location. Once spring arrives, Drostan has promised labour to build the ráth."

"You can have use of men from Clann Ui Flaithimh until we leave." Brion smiled appreciatively. "A hundred from the shield wall will remain. Fifty cavalry and spare horses too." Brion was about to protest but was halted by a raised hand. "I'll hear no argument on this. You need a connection to your homeland and friends who always have your back." Brion dipped his head in thanks.

"And what of her?"

Conall's eyes watched as Gràinne walked past. The thick, fleece-lined cloak could no longer hide her belly. Gràinne stopped to chat with an older woman. She laughed as the lady pushed back the bundle of furs to reveal the heat-flushed face of a baby. Gràinne pointed to her swollen stomach, and they both chuckled.

Brion chose to misinterpret Conall's question. "Áine's daughter, Sorchae, fares well given the unfortunate start to her life. Born early and to *that* woman." The last words were spewed from Brion's mouth like tepid beer. "I hear the baby is a fighter. The Goddess was merciful, and the child has avoided the pox." Conall looked at Brion with a raised eyebrow. His friend shrugged uncomfortably. "I've nothing to do with Áine. The child is not mine, Conall. Her future is for Íar to decide."

"And the other? There are strong rumours," asked Conall.

"Gràinne has chosen to remain with Clann Ui Flaithimh. I'll acknowledge the child as mine, and they'll always be welcome at my ráth." Brion paused and looked into his friend's face. "Gràinne is like a sister to you. I hope her child will be welcome and safe in your home."

Conall growled, offended that the subject was raised. "As if that is in doubt."

An uncomfortable cough from Brion presaged his next words. "Connections have been made between you and the child Mòrag will soon deliver." It was a change of topic that Brion regretted raising. He later blamed it on too much beer. A grunt, the setting of Conall's jaw, and the view of his back as he tramped away told Brion he would get no answer to his question. That Mórrígan was his sister deepened the future king of the Na Mèadaidh's concern.

***

The Sídhe's mare was sixteen hands tall and pure black, apart from having white socks and a lightning-shaped, white blaze. Its large blue eyes accentuated the horse's striking appearance. A cycle of the moon after Imbolg, Mongfhionn sat on the mount, watching the people and army of Clann Ui Flaithimh march past with enthusiasm and raucous good humour. Banners and flags were hoisted aloft. The bodhráin pounded out a deep rhythm.

On the Sleá, the war horns of the Forest People sounded out Drostan's farewell and were joined by the horns of Clann Ui Flaithimh. All wished Conall's tribe well on the journey. Earlier, led by Conall and his Chomhairle, the tribe offered up sacrifices to the Goddess. The muddy waters of the Athain Dubh hid a king's ransom and enough armour to fit a small army.

The procession was impressive. Two wagons wide, the tribe tailed back over two thousand paces. Like a slow-moving river, it carved a meandering path. The centipede's thousands of feet travelled at the speed of its lowliest members—the teams of oxen that pulled the heaviest of the wagons. The foot soldiers of Clann Ui Flaithimh formed the vanguard, Carmag's Forest People, and Brandubh's Ravens, the rearguard.

Bands of cavalry charged up and down the semi-orderly civilian core. Until the borders of the Votod-Daoine and the Wild People were reached and passed, one of their responsibilities was gently shepherding hundreds of children to safety. Apparently, the young ones' goal was to strip every berry-laden bush of its fruit. Once in unfriendly lands, the children would be kept on a much shorter leash.

Few doubted that the journey would try the tribe's fortitude and stamina. Hostile weather, wolves, and warbands were sure to assail the exodus. Invisible yet deadly, disease and infection would relentlessly seek out the weak. Still, the tribe and its leaders had endured tribulation before. They marched forward with confidence.

Mongfhionn rubbed a hand across the pronounced bump that had usurped her usually flat stomach as she watched. She smiled as she caught a glimpse of Fearghal. Ever since he became aware of the child growing inside her, it seemed that she was never out of his sight. His shock that a Sídhe could bear a child amused Mongfhionn.

If anything, the Aes Sídhe and Túatha Dé Danann had a long history of fertility and promiscuity. She knew Fearghal would be a good father if over-indulgent—a fair man and a good Da. He would need to be. The child, a girl, would be a handful...just like her Ma.

***

It was a pleasant spring morning and a good day to ride. Urard grasped the mane of the dapple-grey and swung his leg over its broad, mottled back. The horse barely moved. Its large brown eyes seemed to ask, "Is that the best you can do?" Urard settled his arse on the thick diallait and hooked his feet into the loops in the broad, girth strap. Taking the reins in his hand, he turned the mare around to face Iasg, the twins, and his riders.

"You're all fat from lazing over the winter," he said, and he was right. For some, their only exercise was rutting impressionable young, and some not so young, women in the local farms and settlements. The group cheered and laughed loudly. With a raised eyebrow and mock disapproval, Urard continued. "I also see our band has expanded to include some additional female companions."

His gaze took in the subjects of his chastisement. They quickly averted their eyes, hoping to make themselves inconspicuous. All knew that without Urard's approval, they would be sent home to a humiliating and likely painful reunion with their kin.

"We're heading southwest, towards *An Cnoc* and from there to the southern grain fields and the coast." Urard paused to let his words sink in. "We're at war. If the Goddess has been pleased, then Clann Ui Flaithimh has triumphed, and I expect to face warbands looking for revenge. If the battle went badly, there'll be even more bastards looking to put our heads on a spear."

With a final look at the abandoned fort, which had been their winter camp, Urard turned his mount. Brighid and Danu brought their horses alongside him. Each leaned over in turn and grasped a rough hand. "You will guide us wisely and safely as always, Urard," said Danu. Her sister nodded in agreement. Behind them, Iasg smiled broadly.

***

Íar scoured the horizon for signs of Kartimandu's army. Bealtaine had been celebrated, and spring would soon make way for summer. The winter and, so far, the spring had been quiet. There had been clashes between warbands, but nothing that caused him concern. Most of the skirmishes ended once the thick snow fell. Now that the land was clear of snow and firm enough to walk on, he fully expected to see much more aggressive action from Kartimandu and Ualraig.

With the completion of the inner and outer ramparts and ditches of An Balla-Leac, his defences were in place. Cuán, Lonán, Brocc, and Torcán combined to organise the internal fortifications. Should Ualraig decide to attack, they would be outnumbered ten-to-one. Nevertheless, with the addition of Cuán's men, he was in a much better position than when he had departed Áth.

Messengers informed Íar that Clann Ui Flaithimh had set out on their trek. So far, there was no estimate of when they would be reunited. Still, shelters were erected in anticipation of the tribe's arrival. Íar hoped that blackened timbers and ashes would not greet Conall.

Each day, he walked the ramparts, straining eyes, and ears, hoping for news of Conall's arrival from the north. Mórrígan and her hundred had been sent deeper south to terrorise settlements and be a thorn in Kartimandu's side. His cavalry patrolled the moors of the Penn-inus closest to the hillfort.

At the same time, Íar prayed that Kartimandu's and Ualraig's army had been destroyed by fire, plague, or anything that would slow them down. He knew that every preparation had been made. *Why are the hairs on my nape standing up like the thorns on a gorse bush?*

CHAPTER 28

405 B.C.—Summer

The hillfort and settlement of An Cnoc lay inside the southern edge of Kartimandu's territory. It sat back less than twenty paces from a ridge of limestone cliffs and overlooked the River Gwy to the west. The Gwy, one of Albu's primary waterways, carved a deep, narrow gorge through the land and marked the southern border of the High People. To the north and east, a landscape of gently rolling, green hills added to the pleasing vista of the settlement.

An Cnoc formed the northern tip of a triangle that linked two key trade centres. Its long history as an intermediary and staging post for slavers was the foundation of the settlement's wealth. No slave boarded ships that smelled of death and despair without a commission paid to the elders of An Cnoc.

Farming's rapid growth in the more clement and open grasslands of the southwest presented An Cnoc's leaders with even more opportunity. Before long, no grain of wheat or oats moved north without An Cnoc benefitting.

An Cnoc's status as a generator of immense wealth was protected by three powerful and disparate interests—the slavers, the grain warlords, and Kartimandu. Incredibly and foolishly, the elders never felt the need to erect high walls or retain a garrison. In their minds, an attack on An Cnoc would bring savage reprisals from its benefactors. Thus, they could not envisage anyone being that stupid.

The tide of their fortune changed when Kartimandu marched to invade northern Albu. An Cnoc's young and able had few prospects. The settlement's wealth resided firmly in the grasp of a few privileged families. Thus, they joined the queen's army in search of plunder and fame.

Reluctantly, the settlement elders hired workers to excavate a deep perimeter ditch to encircle the community. Limestone rock from local quarries was used to build a wall on the inner side of the trench. It was an attempt to transform An Cnoc into a proper hillfort. True to form, the settlement's leaders were miserly, the workers unskilled, and the quality of work mediocre.

Yet An Cnoc quickly settled into a familiar routine. Then came the shocking news of Kartimandu's defeat by Conall. The young men of An Cnoc were dead or remained part of the army that was now camped around the stronghold at Dùn Caen.

Still, Kartimandu's defeat and the loss of their young men would not have interrupted the gathering of wealth at An Cnoc save for one crucial factor. Kartimandu's treasury was empty. The queen needed gold to ensure the continued loyalty of the chieftains and defend against Conall. Thus, it was not long before the elders of An Cnoc were commanded to appear before the queen.

With the settlement's men dead or absent and the elders at Dùn Caen, the hillfort of An Cnoc was left in the hands of fewer than two hundred women and children. Their only protection was the new rampart, which already showed the signs of shoddy construction.

Fate assigned An Cnoc one further turn of the wheel. It was the home of Ualraig's partner by hand-fasting and his two daughters. The scene was set for the gods to play.

***

"You're sure of the information?" Bréanainn asked between loud cracks, sucks, and slurps as he used fingers and tongue to remove marrow from the pile of broad bones before him. He rarely had sufficient leisure time to indulge his love for the nutty-flavoured treat. Téide looked on with disapproval while carving slices of elder and tripe from the platter before her.

"Yes. The settlement is unguarded. Only women and children remain. It is said that the wealth of kings is buried within its walls. Easy pickings for us."

Bréanainn growled. He pointed a greasy finger at Téide and then at his face. "The last time *you* told me that, I ended up with these scars, and my back whipped bloody." Téide glared at him but said nothing. "Also, have you considered we'll be stealing from Kartimandu, the slavers, and the grain lords? There will be no place in Albu to hide and no mercy from anyone if we're caught."

"It's your choice," said Téide with a gleam in her eye. For her, the topic was settled. She knew Bréanainn's avarice would eventually bring him around.

The outcast from Ériu thought hard. In a relatively short time, he and Téide had gathered about two hundred miscreants—outlaws, murderers, rapists, and thieves. They successfully raided trade caravans as they carted grain to and from the storage pits in the southwestern hillforts. A promising slave and kidnap business expanded their business. After each raid, they disappeared into the mountains of the midwest.

Bréanainn scratched his arse and sighed. Their band was happy because he and Téide did the thinking and made them wealthy. Yet An Cnoc was tempting. One big haul and he could take a ship across the Muir nIocht and live the life of a king on the shores of the Great Sea. He looked at Téide. "If this goes wrong, I'll skin you alive."

She smiled. "When?"

"No sense in wasting time. We'll march to the Gwy at sunrise."

***

The outcasts crossed the Gwy several sunsets later, circling An Cnoc to approach the fort from its more accessible eastern side. In the settlement, the senior women of the community watched with increasing alarm as the obviously ill-intentioned mob came closer.

They considered locking the gates but thought that would provoke the bandits to violence. In any case, few in An Cnoc were proficient with arms. Their best hope was to be raped. The miscreants, having satisfied their lusts, would go somewhere else. They prayed to Brighid for mercy, but the goddess was no friend to Kartimandu or those who had supported the queen.

Everything went precipitously wrong when Bréanainn asked, "Where is the gold?" Truthfully, the women did not know. Furthermore, the area was littered with limestone caves, so there were innumerable possibilities. The settlement's elders passed the location of the treasure caves from eldest son to eldest son. It had been so for generations.

Bréanainn's face flushed scarlet, believing they were stalling or willfully refusing to answer. He walked up and down the line of frightened women and children, shouting and screaming at them. His frustration and disbelief at their pleadings of ignorance added fuel to his wrath. Gold fever addled his thinking. Behind him, his band's mounting discontent exacerbated a finely balanced situation.

He grabbed one mother's youngest child, a boy of no more than six or seven summers, and cut his throat. The mother screamed and fell to her knees. Her arms clutched her daughters tightly to her. The young girls were torn from her grasp, their léine ripped, and their bodies violated. Their screams turned to whimpers, and their whimpers to silence.

The mother, as good as dead from losing her children, waited. It was not long before dirt-ingrained hands rent her clothes, leaving her naked before her friends. Rough hands pawed at her breasts and between her legs. Fists pommelled her face and belly. The shock made her dumb, and the savagery took her mind.

The mother's silence infuriated Bréanainn, and before the community, he rutted her brutally and sadistically. When he was finished, she was tossed to his men. It was the siren call for mayhem. Women and children ran to the far shadows of An Cnoc, hoping to escape the slavering, murderous pack.

There was no escape. The gates were shut and barred. The hillfort was small, the walls too high. Small children and babies were torn from sobbing mothers, clubbed, speared, and tossed aside. Young and old, male and female, were brutally and repeatedly despoiled to satisfy unbridled lusts. The feral horde carried on without ceasing and without mercy until, late into the night, the fort's buildings were set alight.

***

Iasg pointed to the west, where a red-orange glow pulsated. The smell of burning wood drifted on the night breeze. "An Cnoc lies there."

"I think you're right," said Urard.

"Should we investigate?"

"In the morning. The girls are asleep, as are half the men. We don't know what we'll face or their numbers." The shadows hid the concern on his face. "What has been done, has been done. We can't change that." Iasg nodded. She moved closer and held the warrior's massive hand. He did not resist.

***

Mórrígan's warband followed the Gwy river until dusk and made camp on its western side. So far, their mission had been accomplished with the usual efficiency. Settlements and farms were destroyed. The people were killed or chased off to add grist to the legend of *An Fiagaí Dorcha*. Curious about the glow in the distance, Mórrígan pointed it out to Bricriu and Beacán.

"I thought we were the only ones burning settlements."

Bricriu shrugged. "It's no business of ours. Probably an internal fight. Let them kill each other."

Usually, Mórrígan would have agreed with her brother, but something tugged at her. She sighed. "The river will take us in that direction. We'll investigate what is going on tomorrow."

***

Téide shook Bréanainn roughly with no result. It was close to meán lae, and the fires had died down. Scattered, smouldering debris sent thin curls of soot into the sky. Few of the gang's members were awake. The dead lay wherever and however they had been discarded. She shook Bréanainn again and was rewarded with a backhanded smack that raised a bruise on her cheek. "Bastard," she shouted and kicked him in the balls.

Bréanainn sat up and fumbled to unsheathe his knife. "I told you I'd cut your throat if you failed me again."

"Don't threaten me, Bréanainn," Téide replied. "You'd be dead before that knife cleared its scabbard." The menace in her tone halted her partner's movement. "If you ever hit me again, your next sleep will be your last."

"You failed. There's no gold," said Bréanainn, rising unsteadily to his feet. He looked around for something to wash the foul taste from his mouth. Téide tossed him a leather pouch. He drank and then spat its contents at her feet. "Water!"

"You'll need a clear head. We have company," snapped Téide. "And I didn't fail. *You* didn't find the gold." Bréanainn scowled as he splashed cold water over his shaved head. His formerly lush, red-brown hair had never quite grown back. Téide also reflected that his boyish good looks had been replaced with a face pulled into ugly puckers and ridges. The scars left by the blades used to shave him. The duo climbed the steps cut into An Cnoc's rampart and looked to the east.

"Shite! Where did they come from? We need to move." A note of panic gave Bréanainn's voice an unattractive whine.

Téide put a hand on his arm. "Not so fast. I've heard rumours of a warband guarding an Ériu warlord's twin daughters. If it's true, the girls will fetch a good ransom or price as slaves."

"They're mounted, fool. They'll run us down and slaughter us," Bréanainn said through gritted teeth. "This is folly. We should escape across the Gwy while there is still time."

"We have twice their numbers. Horses are of little use in the forest. We should cross the Gwy, make for the trees, and lie in wait for them."

"And why will they follow us?"

His partner looked at Bréanainn scornfully. She swept her hand over the fort and said, "After the slaughter here, every warband within a sunset's ride will be looking for us."

Bréanainn spat and then bellowed to his followers. "On your feet. Run or die!"

***

"The rats are abandoning the barn." Iasg pointed to the scramble of figures flowing out of An Cnoc. "Some only partially dressed."

Urard scowled. "When we get closer, keep the girls and the other females with you. Don't enter the fort unless I call."

"Ye'r not expecting a friendly welcome?"

"I always hope to be pleasantly surprised, but rarely am." Urard held his hand above his head and said, "Two lines, twenty paces apart. The first rank will enter the hillfort with me, and the second will stand guard at the entrance. Unsheathe weapons."

Inside An Cnoc, clouds of flies rose. The bodies of babies, young children, and women were strewn in the dirt like garbage. Many had multiple stab wounds from spears and swords. Some had been bludgeoned to death, and others strangled. Pregnant women had been sliced open, and baby and mother speared. Bloody thighs and arses abounded.

Urard dismounted, dropped to his knees, and beat his hands in the dirt. Like a roll of thunder, his great bellow rose into the air. It was a cry that cursed Bréanainn and his followers and promised retribution.

The Goddess heard the outpouring of grief. The wailing of the innocents still rang in her ears. She dipped her head. Urard's axe, Breith, would be both judge and executioner.

Looking around An Cnoc, Urard's despair deepened the lines on his weather-worn face. "These people suffered severely. Horrors were visited on them that no one should endure. I pray they are in *Tir inna n-Óc* or *Tir Tairngire*, where they will suffer no more. Only the shells that were their bodies lie before us.

For a moment, Urard studied the rampart walls. "Place the corpses in the ditch. We'll collapse the walls of the fort on them. An Cnoc will be their tomb." Sombre-faced men dipped their heads in silent accord. They breathed with relief when he said, "Tonight, we'll camp outside the fort. When we have buried the dead, we will hunt the vermin and show no mercy."

***

Across the Gwy, Téide heard Urard's cry, and the colour drained from an already pale face. She turned to Bréanainn. "I can guarantee they'll come for us."

***

Urard's lament reached the ears of Mórrígan, although she did not realise who it was. The smouldering settlement was a hive of activity. She paused on a hill overlooking An Cnoc and the Gwy to consider her next move. In the distance, men and women carried objects of irregular size from An Cnoc and laid them along the perimeter ditch. The task ceased just before dusk.

As dusk fell, Mórrígan led her band across the Gwy. Once on the other side, they wrapped bony horse hoofs in fleeces and rags around the metal tack. The riders continued their advance on An Cnoc in muffled silence.

The Huntress saw the fort's ditch was ringed with torches. Pairs of riders patrolled the perimeter. She thought it odd the warband had camped outside the fort, forgoing the protection of its walls. What were they guarding? A faint odour of carrion wafted on evening breezes. She had smelled worse. At the sound of a horse nickering, Mórrígan turned.

"There's death here," said Bricriu, guiding his skittish mount alongside his sister. Bricriu, now twenty-one summers, had a talent for foresight. It was not well-developed since it disturbed him, and he tried to ignore it.

"Select ten as our guard. Tell your Beacán to stay with the rest. They should follow, but a few hundred paces behind." Bricriu bowed.

***

Urard's scout ghosted past the main body and the small forward group. He smiled. The riders were good, very good, but he was better. It was why he had been selected for Urard's warband. When he was far enough from the band that the night's noises would cover him, he lengthened the stride and pace of his mount.

Mórrígan walked her horse towards the fire at the camp's centre. The flames rose into the night sky and were unnaturally high for a cooking fire casting great light and deep shadows. "The Hag, you could celebrate Bealtaine with that bonfire," said Bricriu.

The Huntress inclined her head towards her brother. "I think we're expected." The flames were an effective barrier to discerning who was beyond as a wall.

The shouted command was anticipated. "Dismount. No funny business. We've eyes on you and your other friends. We've had a very unpleasant day, so a good fight might be the perfect way to end it. What do you want?" Mórrígan recognised the brogue, if not the person. She chuckled, remained on her horse, and took a chance.

"I am Mórrígan Ni Cathasaigh, Queen of Clann Ui Flaithimh, hand-fast partner to Conall Mac Gabhann, King of Clann Ui Flaithimh. I am also known as An Fiagaí Dorcha—The Dark Huntress." Mórrígan paused. "I am also not known for being patient, so perhaps some deference would be appropriate."

A loud guffaw on her right startled the queen, and, for a moment, she thought she was badly mistaken. The high-pitched screams that followed made her reach for her bow until she heard a single word.

"Ma!"

Jumping from her horse, Mórrígan ran in the direction of the screams. She fell to her knees as Brighid and Danu emerged from the shadows. Tears cascaded down her cheeks as she held them in her arms, and worry lines faded. "Thank the Goddess."

The queen glanced around, searching and hoping. When Urard stepped out of the darkness, she said, "I am and will always be in your debt, Urard." In due time, she ordered, "Damp that bloody fire. I can't see beyond my nose, but our enemies will mark the spot well."

There was little sleep that night, for both bands had many tales to share. Mórrígan looked curiously at Iasg and thought she deserved a better name than "Fish". Brighid and Danu were obviously taken with the young woman. Given the glances from Iasg to Urard, it was plain that Iasg held hope for more than friendship. Mórrígan smiled, remembering Urard's selfless devotion to protecting her in the past. *Iasg is a lucky girl.*

***

"Show me." Urard grimaced at Mórrígan's words but rose and led the way. The twins jumped up to accompany their Ma but were halted by a firm "No." The queen had heard enough over the morning's meal to know it would not be a sight for children's eyes. Mórrígan nodded to Iasg. Pleased at the queen's approval, she guided the girls away.

As the pair walked the perimeter ditch, Mórrígan was horrified at what she saw. The Huntress knew more than her share of violence and death, but this savagery gave her hope that her sins were less dark.

"It's not our fight, Urard," said Mórrígan.

Urard remained silent but guided Mórrígan to a place further along the ditch. He pointed. Laid side-by-side, as if in each other's arms were two girls. The queen gasped. Their appearance was such that they could have been Brighid's and Danu's sisters. The cause of their death was awful.

"With respect, my Queen, it *is* our war," said Urard. "This was not a fort that could fight back. These were women and children, not warriors. They were raped, abused, and slaughtered. We would not treat our livestock in this manner." Mórrígan was troubled but unconvinced. Her mouth opened to speak, but she was stalled by Urard's raised palm.

"Your daughters have a price on their heads. Today, pirates, Kartimandu, and the Roman, Marcus Fabius Ambustus, hunt them." Indicating the other side of the gorge through which the Gwy ran, he said, "The vermin who carried out this evil lie in wait for only one purpose. To take Brighid and Danu. Can you allow that possibility?"

"Leadership seems to agree with you, Urard," said Mórrígan. With a long sigh of resignation, she turned back to An Cnoc. "Complete the burial of the dead, Collapse the walls on the ditch so that neither man nor animal will disturb their rest." Urard dipped his head.

"Then we'll set a snare for this nest of rats."

***

The plateau sat like a massive, tilted anvil, surrounded by narrow river plains and deep-sided gorges. The thickly wooded peak broadened to merge with the moorlands of the Penn-inus. Bréanainn and his outlaws camped on the promontory of land nearest the river.

"We should move," said Téide.

It was three sunsets after the slaughter at An Cnoc. Bréanainn looked at Téide and shook his head. "First, you want to stay, then you want to run. The girls are with that warband. They are the only possible profit from this miserable raid. I'll not throw that away."

"I've a bad feeling about this. Trust me. There'll be other targets."

With more than a little irritation, Bréanainn looked at Téide, "You've not been the same since An Cnoc. Perhaps you're losing your taste for our way of life." He pointed to a small string of horses, "Take two and leave. No hard feelings." Téide scratched short, tufted hair and stood up.

***

Mórrígan scowled. "I'm not happy about this, Urard. I've only just been reunited with my daughters, and now you want to use them as bait."

"The forest is thick. It gives the vermin an advantage. A way is needed to force them from its protection. The girls will be safe. Iasg will be at their side," replied Urard. Mórrígan huffed but called to her riders and rode for the nearest ramp to the plateau.

Urard scrutinised the meán lae skies. The weather had been surprisingly temperate recently. On this day, the firmament was populated with fluffy clouds that spun leisurely across its blue-grey expanse. The more imaginative among his band were convinced that their shapes resembled gods. A smoky trail in the distance told him that Mórrígan was in place. He turned to Iasg and the twins. "Be careful."

Screaming, Brighid, Danu, and Iasg urged their mounts down the steep, crumbling limestone slope. Horses and riders plunged into the cold waters. The beasts snorted as their thrashing legs tried to find the river bottom. With more shrieks, the girls and Iasg slipped off water-logged diallaits and into the river. Caught in the current's grasp, they were pulled slowly, inexorably towards the opposite bank.

The lack of plunder made Bréanainn's band of outcasts increasingly irritable and quarrelsome. Now, they could not believe their luck. The gods had delivered their prizes into their hands. Ignoring furious shouts from Bréanainn and Téide for caution, the fractious mob dashed for the river.

Slipping and sliding down grass and dirt banks to the water's edge, many tumbled into the river. They stretched out grasping hands to the girls, but to their confusion, the girls drifted no closer. Indeed, the trio seemed to float back towards the far bank.

The outlaws howled in frustration, and more plunged into the Gwy. At this point, the river was about twenty-five paces wide and slow-moving. It was shallow, coming up to the chests of most of the warriors. With weapons held high, they pushed against the river current to pursue their receding prizes. Angry, they watched as Iasg and the twins scrambled from the river onto the bank.

Brighid and Danu turned, shrugged off the ropes around their waists, laughed, and bared their arses. Suspicions of a trap finally percolated the outcasts' minds. When unseen hands ushered the twins into the woods, fear gripped the brigands tighter than the river mud.

Perfectly camouflaged by the intricate designs that covered her body, Mórrígan moved like a ghost through the leafy forest. Wolfhounds circled and ran back and forth before her. Behind, her warband stretched across the table in a loose skirmish line. Closer to the Gwy, the plateau narrowed, and the row would close in. All had bows ready and arrows laid on the strings.

The canopy was not as dense as in the vast pine forests of Northern Albu. Green scrub and wildflowers abounded where the sun's golden light shone through. Each patch of verdant growth spread until constrained by the deeper shadows of the woods. The forest's trees were well-spaced, providing the perfect cover for archers.

Téide sensed a trap and wished she had ridden off instead of standing with Bréanainn. She shouted over the mounting chaos, "Forget the eejits in the river. They're as good as dead. Look to the trees." A howl from a wolfhound was joined by others, confirming her suspicions.

Men and women stared, wide-eyed and fearful, toward the sound. A soft swish in the air was followed by the *thunk* of iron arrowheads embedding themselves in trees, interspersed with shrieks of pain as others pierced flesh.

Alongside Téide, a woman grasped at the shaft firmly embedded in her breast. Blood and froth bubbled from her mouth, a sure sign that the arrowhead had punctured a lung. *It would be a mercy to kill her.* Téide's thought was cut short as a massive grey shape hurtled towards her.

In the lull between arrow volleys, the hounds breached the camp's pitiful defences. A growl in her ear was followed by a sharp pain as she was shouldered aside. She hit the ground, faintly aware of blood streaming down the left side of her head.

Bréanainn crawled beside his partner. Her ear was gone, and a flap of flesh hung from cheek to jaw. He grimaced at her appearance. The attack on the camp was well-organised and unexpected. *I should have listened to her.* He seized his weapon when an arrow struck his shoulder, spinning him around and dropping him to the forest floor. His head cracked against a fallen tree trunk. In the few moments before he regained his senses, his band had been ravaged by snapping jaws and hundreds of arrows. Worse, the attackers had not shown themselves.

"Cowardly bastards!" shouted Bréanainn.

The river was a muddy red. Bodies drifted with the current. Some sank, leaving a trail of bubbles to mark their final breaths. Fifty of Bréanainn's band died in the first volley of Urard's javelins. Stranded in midstream and well within throwing range, their plight was helpless. Ropes were tossed into the river. Hoping for mercy, some chose to grab on and were pulled to the riverbank.

Others turned and attempted to retreat. Urard led half of his riders into the Gwy. His prey soon found that horses fared much better than they against the river current. The ragged force tried to scramble out of the water. Those who remained in the water suffered split skulls and backs laid open with vicious downward slashes of sword and axe. Others clambered up the gorge slope and loped towards the camp.

Mórrígan halted her advance. At her signal, bows and quivers were set aside. There was the soft swish of swords unsheathed and the tug of axes from belt loops. Some palmed throwing knives from leather baldrics. The Huntress held her long, bone-handled daggers in her hands. Mórrígan listened until she heard the screams and snorts of Urard's mounts.

With a loud shout of *"Ionsaí!"* Mórrígan charged forward. Her wolfhounds quickly bounded ahead, forming a snapping, snarling shield. Close behind, her band shouted tribal cries and curses. On the opposite side of the camp, Urard leapt from his mare and began to swing Breith. Men fell before him like hay before the sickle. Mórrígan and Urard fought their way across the encampment to each other, and the mêlée was over.

Téide looked into Mórrígan's face of cold rage and shivered. There was no trace of mercy in the glittering emerald eyes. And so, in a final act of rebellion, Téide spat at the queen. The fist that punched her almost broke an already dislocated jaw. Her knees buckled, and she fell onto the dirt, hawking up blood-flecked vomit and phlegm. To add insult to injury, Urard kicked her in the belly. Being female garnered no sympathy from her captors.

A short time later, Bréanainn sat on the stump of an oak tree, gazing about and snorting in disgust. Less than half of his band survived. Yet the dead were fortunate, for their trials were over. The captured, injured, and limbless stared with vacant, hopeless eyes. The stupid grinned gormlessly, incapable of envisioning the range of punishments that could be their fate. A shaven-headed giant strode past, dipped his head, and addressed the Huntress.

"What have you decided?"

"Suddenly, I'm queen again," answered Mórrígan.

"You were always a queen," said Urard.

"Conall's the decision-maker. Suggestions are welcome."

"I doubt we can duplicate the pain suffered by their victims."

"We could try, but would that make us any different from them?" Mórrígan gestured at the landscape. "It's so remote here that whatever we do, it's unlikely to be a lesson to dissuade others from doing the same." Mórrígan inhaled deeply; she had made up her mind.

"Are the blades ready?" Urard nodded and gripped Breith.

Mórrígan pointed to Bréanainn and Téide, "Bring those two forward. Strip them and stake them. They can watch their band's punishment as they die."

Téide gazed forward with a stone-faced determination to not give her executioners any satisfaction. Impalement was never a good end. Her captors had two choices. The first was to drive a stake into the ground, leaving the sharp end pointed upwards. She would be lifted up and lowered onto the point. The stake would slowly move through her body until her arse rested on the ground.

Téide would be forced to kneel on all fours with the second option. A rough stake would be hammered into her arse or between her legs. Spitted like a pig, she would then be lifted up, and the end of the stake dropped into an arms' length hole. It was a judgment call as to which was the worst option.

Some say the anticipation of pain is the greater punishment. Téide disagreed as she felt the sharpened end of the stake on her arse. The tuilí seemed to leave it pressing against her flesh for a long time. The knock of iron on wood made her bite down hard on her lip. "I've had worse in my arse!" she shouted defiantly through bloody lips.

Several blows later, satisfied with their efforts, the executioners lifted her up and dropped the end of the stake into the prepared hole. Téide could not prevent the raw scream torn from her chest. She saw the flesh above her breasts distend as the point pressed to break free. Her legs attempted to push up to relieve the pressure. The blunt side of an axe broke her thighs. She slumped, muttering incoherently.

Bréanainn was not quite as phlegmatic. He screamed, shouted, cursed, and fought every step as he was stripped. Four men lifted him across a broad fallen tree. Another placed the stake against his arse and hammered it into yielding flesh. Finally, as for Téide, the stake and body were dropped into a hole. The stake bit through Bréanainn's torso, erupting from his chest. His screams resounded through the forest but soon ebbed to pitiful whimpers and sobs.

Mórrígan watched the remaining outlaws with hard eyes. Some prayed to their gods for mercy. Others hoped that their fate would not be as bad as their leaders. The Huntress stood before a small group of females and shook her head as if trying to understand.

"You never lifted a hand to stop the atrocity at An Cnoc." She sighed and turned to Urard. "They have no need of their hands."

Shrieks of terror echoed through the forest as, one by one, the women's hands were stretched across fallen trees and neatly removed at the wrist. Pale-faced women looked on bloody stumps as their lifeblood seeped away. A few reached the campfires and cauterised the flow; most didn't. The few who did were the stupid ones.

By this time, the men were on their knees, begging for forgiveness and promising to lead a life of piety and servitude. Mórrígan looked at them with disgust. "Count yourselves lucky the Sídhe is not with us, for her vengeance is sacrificial." To her riders, she said, "Strip them. Cut their cocks and balls off and remove their right hands." Howls of protests were soon replaced with shouted curses. Their captors had seen the slaughter of An Cnoc and were in no mood to show compassion.

The riders had long departed, and sunset approached. The bean sídhe had called Bréanainn's spirit. Téide looked at her partner and whispered a hoarse, "Bastard!" Finally, her eyes fluttered, and her heart failed. Téide's eyes opened as she entered the darkness of the Otherworld. "No!"

CHAPTER 29

405 B.C.—An Balla Leac

Kartimandu was a sad and shallow vessel. She could not understand the love Ualraig had for his hand-fast partner and children. Her empathy for other people and their emotions was fickle, focusing exclusively on how her subjects could please her and satisfy her quixotic whims. Therefore, when a distraught Ualraig barged into her chambers, knocking her servants aside like straw, she was furious at the intrusion.

The queen was aware of the deaths of those at An Cnoc and Ualraig's loss. Her thoughts, however, were directed at the Clann Ui Flaithimh raiders. Scouts had informed her incorrectly that the thieves had stolen *her* gold. This threw fuel onto the flames of her ire. Neither Ualraig's family nor the dead of An Cnoc came into her reckoning.

Her emotionally neutral, if not hostile, response to Ualraig's pain poured oil on the fire rising in her general's breast. She refused to countenance an immediate attack on the Clann Ui Flaithimh forces at An Bella-Leac. Yet Kartimandu's instincts were well-founded. It was a foolish plan.

An attack on An Bella-Leac would necessitate dividing the High People's army. A sizeable force would be needed to defend Dùn Caen while most of her warriors engaged Conall. Worse, they would fight a Clann Ui Flaithimh army entrenched behind well-fortified battlements.

What Kartimandu failed to recognise was that Ualraig's anguish had a simple remedy. He needed arms to hold him, an understanding bosom for his head, and a sympathetic ear. A confrontation could have been avoided had the queen been remotely compassionate. She would have persuaded him that his demand for action was reasonable but untimely. Ualraig was a good commander. After mourning and reflection, he would probably have arrived at a similar conclusion.

Instead, the queen saw herself as the victim and was insulted by Ualraig. "Get out of here before I have you arrested, imprisoned and executed." Her response resulted in the soft swish of a blade unsheathed. In the briefest moment, the iron blade was at her throat, bringing a shriek of pain from the queen. She felt a thin trickle of blood course down her neck. The blood did not worry her, but the iron did.

Slaves and servants ran for their lives, and the news quickly spread around Dùn Caen. Outside the queen's roundhouse, two factions faced off: those loyal to the queen and those to Ualraig. Inside her quarters, Kartimandu glared at Ualraig while attempting to control the searing pain that the mere touch of iron on her skin produced. She could not influence her commander. His anger was too great. In his red-rimmed eyes, she recognised the signs of madness.

Kartimandu was sure Ualraig was on the verge of cleaving her head from her neck. To forestall an agonising death, she fell to her knees. Inwardly seething and swearing revenge, she looked up at Ualraig's face and begged him to let her depart Dùn Caen with her elite guard. She took his snarl and the lowering of his sword as consent.

***

The sun was high in the sky when Kartimandu, Queen of the High People, stood proudly in her royal chariot. She led a guard of one thousand warriors out of the gates of Dùn Caen. Ualraig had given her a day to make ready and leave. Crowds watched silently and nervously from the ramparts. While still within earshot of Dùn Caen, Kartimandu halted her chariot.

She stood arms apart and held upwards. In an unnaturally loud voice which echoed across the valley, the queen cursed Ualraig. She condemned him to a lingering death and the Otherworld, where he would never be united with his family. Finally, she lifted her voice against the people of the High People, cursing them with slavery, pestilence, and death for many generations.

Dread gripped the people as they slunk away from the sandstone fortifications until only one remained. With unblinking eyes, the tragic figure king of the High People stared, not at the departing Kartimandu but north towards An Bella Leac. Ualraig was about to fight a war based on a false report, but then, is that not often the case?

As for Kartimandu, she had previous dealings with the king at Rinn-Campáil and considered he could be brought under her influence. Thus, she began a journey to the hillfort and refuge in southwestern Albu.

***

"Any news?" asked Brocc. His teeth ripped bloody pink meat from a rib that had the briefest of caresses with the flame.

Torcán, who preferred his meat well done, if not burnt, wrinkled his nose. "That pig's still alive." Brocc grinned broadly. His uncommonly white teeth were a striking contrast to the yellowed and rotting teeth in the broader population. *Perhaps if I just sliced a slab of meat off passing livestock, my teeth would look that good.* Torcán shuddered at the notion.

The pair were at a meeting of the Council at An Balla Leac. Besides Íar, Cuán, Lonán, and the most senior of the druids, at Cuán's request, the group also included his hand-fast partner, Bláithín.

"The defences are as good as we can make them. Strong inner and outer walls of rock, dirt, and wood. Deep, wide ditches," said Cuán. "We have over a thousand fully fit fighters. Another two hundred are injured or sick. Now that Mórrígan has gone south with her riders, Íar has about five hundred horses. Unfortunately, we have no archers or slingers."

Cuán paused and sipped on cold spring water. "We don't have enough fighters to fully man the ramparts. With apologies to the Lady Bláithín, we're in deep shite if a large force attacks us."

"Maybe we should construct another defensive berm with the shite Íar's horses generate. That should test their stomachs and boots." Íar offered a token look of disapproval but grinned, despite himself, when Torcán continued. "How do you convince any woman to rut when you smell of horse-shite and piss?"

"Young bastard. Curb your mouth, or you'll be permanently assigned to shovelling, said shite." Torcán feigned horror at Íar's suggestion.

"What news from the north?" asked Brocc.

"We know that Conall has left the lowlands. I'm hoping they'll be with us within a cycle of the moon. Certainly, before Kartimandu's attack."

***

The rain lashed down, a silver-grey curtain of misery. Íar screwed his eyes into a narrow squint as he peered south towards the forested slopes. Beyond the foothills, a few scattered copses survived on the moors. The soil and bogland provided nourishment for mainly smaller flowers and bushes.

Íar was thankful for the shelter of the watchtower. Instead of being soaked to the skin, he was merely wet. The sun would not break through the cloud today. He shook his head. It was hard to tell the difference between the fog blanketing the land and the low cloud.

"Did you hear that?" Brocc had the ears of a fox.

"The only thing I hear is the Hag's rain."

Brocc shook his head. "I thought I heard shouts from the hillside."

"I hope you're wrong. With this weather, it's been five sunsets since our last scouts were sent out. An army can move a fair distance in that time." Íar stroked his beard. "Send runners to Cuán and the captain of my riders. Suggest to Cuán that he should double the men on the outer perimeter. Tell my captains to have the cavalry ready to ride." Brocc hurried away.

The rain ceased during the night, and a butter-yellow sun rose above the horizon. A light mist drifted over the fields and trees. Hundreds of puddles, many like small ponds, reflected the sun's weak rays as fragmented rainbows. There was no breeze.

Stomachs rumbled in anticipation of breaking their fast. Bread baked on hot stones and griddles, stews and oatmeal simmered in iron cauldrons, and flesh roasted over slumbering fire pits brought to life with peat and wood. Men and women stood palms out over braziers. They stretched their arms and legs and stamped feet to drive the dampness from their bones.

It was meán lae when a flock of ravens broke from the forest. The dense, black cloud soared upwards, hurling a raucous *kraa kraa* at those who had disturbed their peace. They came to rest on the stockade of An Balla Leac's inner rampart.

Brocc scratched the long scar on his left forearm, a gift from his first skirmish. He had been just fifteen summers old. A finger-wide tress of white hair swept back from his forehead, contrasting with his auburn-red mop of curls. The striking feature appeared shortly after the tragic death of his friend Labhraidh. The wiry ceannairí céad was popular with his warriors. They laughed when he pointed to the ravens.

"What do you think? A good omen or not?"

A soft voice behind him answered, "I think we should take it as a good sign. They feel safe, at least here." Startled by the almost silent appearance of Bláithín, Brocc's hand instinctively went to his sword. A smooth but strong hand touched his lower arm. "Not yet. There'll be plenty of fighting soon."

It took a moment for Brocc to realise that the warrior before him was Cuán's partner, Bláithín. Brocc's eyes were drawn instinctively to the round shield she carried in her left arm and the short-handled, double-bladed axe in her right. *An axe? What woman carries a bloody axe?*

Bláithín had discarded her long *chiton* for a light red tunic and matching pants. The latter was tucked into soft leather boots. A boiled leather breastplate, plainly moulded to her figure, was held firmly in place by broad leather straps, which buckled at her spine. Her hair was pulled back from her face and fell down her back in a single, long, thick plait. Finally able to tear his eyes from the breastplate, Brocc began to stammer, "My

Lady…"

She held up her hand and smiled. It was a gesture which said, "Poor boy, retreat now." Full lips parted. "No doubt what you were about to say was both well-intentioned and chivalrous. For that, you have my thanks. However, the last man to request that I move to a safer location still bears a scar from this blade." She nodded in the direction of Cuán and laughed at a whimsical memory. "Ask him."

Brocc, regaining a measure of composure, observed the tattoo on Bláithín's right shoulder—a sword with a red branch entwined around it. "I was unaware that the Cróeb Ruad included females among their number."

Bláithín's smile widened. "It's an honorary membership. Cuán and Lonán insisted. My sister, Aoibheann, has a similar one." Brocc dipped his head. It seemed the proper response. Privately, he believed it highly unlikely that the Cróeb Ruad proffered invitations to join its ranks without good cause. Further exploration of the topic was cut short by the roar of thousands of voices and blasts of horns braying from the foothills. Ualraig's army stepped from the tree line, slapping weapons against shields.

"Choose your stand, My Lady. May the Goddess be with us." Then Brocc turned and roared, "Any man or woman who can hold a sword. Go to the walls, *now!*"

Cuán watched the High People's army stride from the forest onto the rain-soaked ground. Known as quite a religious man, he said, "I hope everyone made the appropriate sacrifices this morning. We'll need all the help we can get."

Beside him, Lonán and Torcán nodded. Around the outer perimeter rang the sounds of armour being checked and weapons made ready for easy access. They were followed by the clink of gold and silver armbands and heavy torcs being adjusted. Everyone had their quirks and superstitions before the battle. They brought calm to the space between preparation and fighting.

"Let me take two hundred outside the gates," said Torcán. "Kartimandu and Ualraig fear the shield wall."

Cuán raked him with a stern look. "I have heard much of the Clann Ui Flaithimh formation, and, undoubtedly, my warriors will learn that tactic." His hand swept a semi-circle pointing to the enemy's ranks before continuing. "However, you would be outnumbered ten thousand to two hundred. Those are foolish odds, whose only result is a journey to Mag Mell." Torcán began to protest, and Cuán's voice rose.

"When *you* have fought to a glorious death, who will protect the women and children from rape and slavery?" Torcán reddened, and the mark on his throat burned. Cuán rasped, "Our walls are solid. We'll defend the outer perimeter as long as possible. Then we'll retreat to the inner walls." He added with a grim smile, "There'll be more than enough killing to satisfy even you."

***

Ualraig's chieftains were unhappy and looked at their new king with deep unease. Not long after the banishing of Kartimandu, the might of the High People, a not insignificant force, was marched at speed across wet moorland and dank bogs. Little thought was given to their welfare or the state in which they would arrive. They were inadequately supplied and poorly equipped.

They left behind family and loved ones in a home vulnerable to attack. The curses of Kartimandu rang vividly in their minds. With a brutality that Ualraig would not have previously tolerated, the grumblings of the men were smothered. Hundreds of bodies found a final resting place in the black bog waters of the Penn-inus.

Yet stepping from the tree line, the High People were finally presented with a target for their simmering anger. Ualraig stood on the moorland heights. Behind him, the remaining half of the army waited. At his signal, a great *barrr-ewww* wailed from the war horn aide beside him. The horde on the valley floor rushed forward. In truth, it was not much of a charge. The recent weather had spoiled the field, spawning another gripe from the men. The "old" Ualraig would not have attacked on such unfavourable ground.

The High People sloshed and splashed their way forward. Long before they closed on the hillfort, the rear ranks sank into the mire created by the boots of those in front. Many floundered in the deeper ponds. Others broke ankles, falling victim to flooded animal setts and burrows. At less than a brisk walking pace and panting from the exertion, they converged on the outer ditch of An Balla Leac.

Maintaining aggressive defiance is challenging when soaked, covered in mud and slime, and faced with a ditch brimming with rainwater. Only the sleek bodies of rats broke the water's surface. The combatants muttered curses and showered the defenders with little more than sullen faces and glowering looks. The taunts of the defenders did little to improve the besiegers' disposition.

The outer rampart of An Balla Leac, built with limestone, dirt, and wood, was three spears high and two spears wide. From this platform, it took little effort to pitch a javelin beyond the ditch. Five hundred men on the southern curve of the rampart grunted and lofted their missiles into the air. After three volleys, the rats in the trench feasted on fresh meat and blood.

Water splashes followed shrieks of pain as iron punched through frail flesh, and the dead and injured tumbled into the trench. Many were pushed by comrades or used as stepping stones. Bloodied, Ualraig's army howled in anger and frustration. Those with dry slings pitched stones at the defences. It proved little more than an irritation, although Íar wished he had kept a corps of Mórrígan's bowmen.

A band of the High People charged across the dirt causeway. The path to the fort's gate was broad and could comfortably be defended by a score of men standing side-by-side. Unfortunately for the attackers, after the rains, it was a slick of mud bordered on both sides by walls that extended out from the main rampart. A storm of javelins and rocks thundered down from those positioned on the wall. Few survived the gauntlet to the gate.

Ualraig's men retreated. They had little choice. There would be no breaching of the walls of An Balla Leac. To add to their misery, as they turned their back on the ráth, Íar's previously hidden cavalry took to the field. Advancing from behind the hillfort, they rode with hunting horns blaring and screaming battle cries. Horses splashed through the muddy ground throwing up clods of dirt.

The riders soon closed the distance. Yet, even for the mighty beasts, it took great effort to reach the trailing edge of the High People. The riders hefted javelins and threw three salvos into the rump of the fleeing foes. Spearheads entered backs and exited chests in a gush of blood and bone. The tardy and the injured were put down with a slashing blade and left to rot in the mud.

That evening the attackers' fear was not of future battles but of Ualraig, who capriciously selected and punished those he deemed responsible for the withdrawal. Ualraig's camp resonated with cries of pain and loud curses. Those who tasted the lash of the whip were fortunate. Other leaders judged lacking sufficient enthusiasm for battle were disembowelled, and their bodies left where they fell.

***

The ring of axes and the groan of trees falling in the forest greeted the dawn. Cuán looked southward. Íar and his riders had already departed, using the morning mists as a cloak. As usual, their mission was to harass the enemy. Once more, horns reverberated on the hilltop, urging Ualraig's warriors to battle.

This time they were better prepared. Timbers were carried and dragged across the muddy landscape. Roughly hewn branches forming makeshift ladders were hefted on scabby shoulders. "A more serious attempt," muttered Cuán.

Lonán looked at his brother. "My advice. Position Torcán and a hundred men on the causeway. It'll give the attackers a distraction—a target. The bridge is narrow, and with cover from the side walls, he'll hold."

"Agreed." Lonán turned to walk away, but Cuán stopped him with a hand on his arm. "Make it clear to Torcán he is to hold the causeway. He is *not* to go on a romp around the battlefield."

The water in the perimeter ditch had receded. Still, enough remained to cover the thick stakes waiting to impale those doomed by Fate. As the besiegers neared the edge of the trench, bloated corpses called to them with farts and escaping bubbles. Pinkish-white foam trailed from dead lips. The cadavers' skin was a ghastly shade of green and marked by rat bites.

The High People were in a fouler mood this day. Curses and vulgarities were shouted. Those with shields slammed weapons against them until several volleys of javelins muzzled them. The dead collapsed with a final moan into the fetid waters. The injured screamed as life seeped from their broken and torn bodies.

A tremendous bellow rose from the attackers, and the horde parted. Under cover of a shower of slingshots, huge men carried split tree trunks to the rim of the ditch. Cuán watched as the timbers were raised on their ends and dropped across the trench. It was simple and effective. *The bastards used those at the front to soak up our javelins and then kept our heads down with their slingers.*

"Weapons and shields ready," roared Cuán. "Prepare to defend the wall." A hail of High People's curses and screams beat down Cuán's words as they stormed across the makeshift bridges.

Torcán was having a great day. Front and centre of the twenty-man-wide shield-wall, he stabbed and slashed with unrestrained relish. Not a deep thinker, the mound of bodies and body parts that grew before the young fighter was meaningless. Neither the cries of pain nor their demise would disturb his sleep. They were not part of or allied to his tribe and had little value.

When the battle was over, Torcán would prepare his armour and weapons for the next fight. He would sluice his blood-spattered body in the cold waters of a nearby river, eat and drink his fill. Then he would find a young woman willing to spread her legs. Torcán knew his end would be bloody and violent, which did not worry him. He had no fear of death, and because of this, he was a very dangerous opponent.

The blood of the besieged and besieger stained the greenish-white limestone ramparts. Individual duels and minor melees broke out along the length of the defences. Famed for their fighting skills, the reputation of the Cróeb Ruad claimed that each member was worth ten of any other tribe. Yet the numbers of the Ualraig's army took their toll as more scampered across rough logs and clambered up rickety ladders. With too few defenders, too thinly spread, Cuán knew he had no chance of holding the walls.

Cuán's goal was to be a nuisance and cause as much injury as possible. He surveyed his bloodied warriors, exhaled, and called his young aide to his side. There was little sense in throwing lives away. "Sound the retreat." Relieved, the boy nodded vigorously and blew several blasts on his trumpet.

First, the massive gates opened, allowing Torcán's company to fall back. Torcán's lips pulled back in a wolfish grin. As Cuán's men retreated from the outer walls, Torcán was joined by another hundred shields. The glory of a fighting rearguard immortalised by Tadhg beckoned. Torcán's men locked shields and hurled taunts at the approaching High People.

Positioned outside the hillfort, Íar blew a battered bronze horn. At the signal, his riders charged the rear of the High People. The tail of around one thousand men had yet to cross the perimeter trench. Soon they found themselves slashed by long-handled axes and cavalry swords. Many were bowled over by the heavy-muscled mounts onto the stakes in the ditches. Others had skulls and bones cracked by hard hoofs. Several passes shredded the High People's flank to bloody rags.

On the moor, Ualraig watched his force breach An Balla Leac's perimeter. He snarled an order at his chieftains, the war horns rang out, and his elite scrambled down the hillside. He would take An Balla Leac and wait for Conall. The man Ualraig held responsible for the murder of his family would suffer greatly before the bean sídhe took him.

***

"It's a dangerous game ye'r playing," said Carmag.

He poked a twig at an annoying piece of gristle lodged between two molars. Eventually, the offending piece of meat was flicked from its location, only to disappear into Carmag's beard. Carmag stood with Conall's inner group of commanders on the northern moorland overlooking An Balla Leac. The acoustics were excellent in the valley. They heard Cuán's bellowed orders and watched as the defenders made an orderly withdrawal to the inner perimeter.

"The walls look solid. Almost as good as my own work," said Cúscraid. The tall, sandy-haired general looked puzzled. "There seem to be more warriors down there than set out from Trócaire."

Conall nodded. "Indeed, many more." He looked at the sun riding its zenith. "And that's why our plan will work. They've enough to man the inner defences fully. The walls are thick and high, and the stockade is solid. Whoever is in command of the defences appears to be competent. They'll stand firm until sunset."

Casually, he turned to Nikandros. "Take your riders and find Íar. The cavalry should be reunited." The Spartan smiled, inclined his head, and threw a leg across his black horse.

***

As darkness descended, Ualraig's men celebrated their triumph. Bellies were filled as they gorged on stores abandoned when Cuán's forces retreated to the citadel. A few buildings were set alight, but this was frowned upon by Ualraig. When caught, the arsonists were tossed onto the fires they had created.

Ualraig wanted An Balla Leac intact. While the madness of misplaced grief gripped Ualraig's mind, he recognised the benefit of having the hillfort as a stronghold. Yet the strength of the inner defences and the force that resisted him rankled Kartimandu's successor. He foresaw a long siege.

In the pre-dawn, the flames of hundreds of torches flickered along the inner ramparts of An Balla Leac. Cuán paced the walkway behind the stockade with Bláithín and Brocc. The wall was fully manned and not just with professionals. Anyone who could hold a spear, sword or axe joined the fighters. All expected a brutal and bloody day, yet none stood down at the thought. Below, Ualraig and his army were camped comfortably within the outer perimeter.

Daybreak shattered Ualraig's thinking. Hundreds of fire arrows scraped sooty fingers across the pink skies. They were followed by the solid, staccato *thunk* of multiple iron arrowheads sinking into wooden buildings and the shrieking as iron pierced flesh. The damp wood resisted at first before curls of smoke floated upwards. Finally, the timber surrendered and burst into flames. With a cry of rage, Ualraig stormed up the stone steps of the outer walls. He gazed at the landscape and cursed. Conall had arrived before he had taken the inner walls.

A bemused Cuán stared to the south. *Where on earth did they come from?* Then he snorted. *The clever bastard used us as bait to snare Ualraig.* Unable to decide whether he was angry or relieved, the Cróeb Ruad commander roared with laughter and then bellowed, "Prepare to advance on my signal."

"I think your wake-up signal was fairly effective," said Fearghal adjusting his longsword more comfortably on his back. He settled his shield on his left arm and tugged on the reins of his horse. Finding Fearghal on a horse was rare. He mistrusted them, and they returned the favour, but Íar had finally found him an easy-going, blue roan. Fearghal and the horse had reached an understanding. He would not ride the beast too often. In return, the mount would allow him to remain on its back.

Conall looked at Fearghal and laughed. "Shall we go negotiate with Ualraig and Kartimandu?" Conall was unaware of the plight of the High People's queen, although Mongfhionn had indicated some disturbances in the spirit domain. The group had only trotted a few paces when Mongfhionn appeared alongside them. Fearghal was not amused. "I told you to stay at the camp," he snapped, his face darkening. "You've only just given birth to our daughter."

The Sídhe's cheeks flared berry-red, and a feral snarl told all to stay well out of the conversation. "Two things, Fearghal Ruad. First, I was carrying *your* daughter. I was neither ill nor diseased. Second, I am of the Aes Sídhe. Save the Goddess and the Ancient Ones. No one tells me what I should or should not do." Fearghal managed a deep-throated growl, suggesting the subject was far from settled.

That said, Mongfhionn's demeanour was not entirely the fault of Fearghal. The new life her body nourished had clashed with the Ancient ways of her spirit and roundly won the battle. Thus, from conception, until the baby uttered its first cry, Mongfhionn's powers had diminished.

Indeed, the Sídhe became as helpless as the child she bore. Only recently had she regained a measure of her former abilities, and even this was fragmented and unreliable. That she was also cut off from Brighid and Danu and had no knowledge of their current state exacerbated the Sídhe's fragile disposition.

"*Eejit!* Perhaps, now we have aired our squabbles and entertained this noble audience, we should follow Conall. I believe he wants to discuss terms with the High People."

A raised eyebrow, a quick shake of the head and a steely glare from Conall informed the warring couple that they should keep him out of their quarrel. A scowl from the Sídhe signalled to the remaining members of the group that further maintenance of their adolescent smirks and grins would have painful consequences.

Conall glanced back at his army. The strident sound of Clann Ui Flaithimh's roars greeted the Goddess in the skies. At its core, two thousand warriors stood in two ranks. Red shields emblazoned with black ravens jutted forward toward An Balla Leac. Before the shield-wall stood the archers. On the right wing, Brandubh's Ravens ritually stomped the ground with naked feet and slammed spears against wooden shields. On the left, Carmag's thousand howled in concord with the reverberations of the tribe's war horns. At the rear, Íar's cavalry fought to control mounts restless with the scent of promised battle.

With a scowl, Conall pulled on Toirneach's reins. A sharp nod of the big horse's head twisted Conall's wrist. It was Toirneach's way of saying, "Don't take your problems out on me." Conall laughed and slapped the mount's shoulders. A gentle tug and rider and horse trotted harmoniously towards the outer gates of An Balla Leac. The negotiating party followed.

Twenty paces from the causeway, Conall halted and called out, "Send out Kartimandu and Ualraig. Surrender the hillfort or die." The response was a clatter of spears and rocks flung from the walls. It had little impact other than agitating the horses.

"I'm not sure you've grasped the difference between negotiation and an ultimatum," opined a waggish Fearghal. Crum Dubh chuckled.

Conall glowered at his commanders with no effect, sighed, and turned to face the ramparts. "Warriors of the High People, you are trapped. You have been poorly led. You have no food or water to survive a siege. Yield An Balla Leac. Surrender your leaders, leave your weapons, and return to your homes."

Fearghal responded to a quizzical look from Conall. "Better."

The response from Ualraig was a tirade of curses and swearing. This disturbed Conall. He considered Ualraig a brave and excellent commander and a shrewd tactician, not a hothead. *What has changed the man?* Ualraig's rant culminated in him informing Conall that Kartimandu was not at An Balla Leac and that he was the leader of the High People. Perhaps power had gone to his head?

More perplexing were Ualraig's final words. *"Child killer!"* They were spat with a shower of saliva and phlegm. Puzzled, Conall shook his head and turned to his companions.

"Move the army back a thousand paces. This may be a long siege." To Brandubh, he said, "Use your archers and slingers to harass those on the ramparts." The prince of the Ravens dipped his head. After a moment's thought, Conall said, "Íar, send a rider to Sárán. We'll likely need him to organise supplies of food and weapons." Íar inclined his head as Conall added, "Your riders are to ensure no one escapes from the fort."

***

Ualraig's warriors burst from the outer gates of An Balla Leac like the foul-smelling pus expelled from a festering scab. Three sunsets had passed since Conall's demands. The beer stores had been consumed during the opening celebrations. To assuage the inevitable effects of dehydration, any water had been guzzled down the morning after. There was no access to fresh water as the spring for the hillfort was located within the inner defences. Those who risked climbing over the ramparts were hunted down by Íar's cavalry.

Ualraig's options were limited. Send his army out to fight or watch them die of thirst. His army was not trained to defend. They were marauders who knew only how to attack, rape, and to plunder. If he waited much longer, they would be too weak to do that. Ualraig knew he had to get his men out of An Balla Leac quickly. Furthermore, the forces in the inner defences were a sword at his back, making his rear increasingly vulnerable.

With admirable ruthlessness, the High People's king sent the weakest out first. The first wave would assault Conall's divisions while Ualraig readied his veterans and probed for failings in his enemy. As the forlorn stormed forward, Ualraig's elite moved through the gateway and formed up just beyond the perimeter ditch. Ualraig had learned from Torcán's stand at the causeway. He positioned a small rear-guard force to hold the entrance against an attack on his rear by Cuán.

In the shrinking no-man's-land between the adversaries, ravens held the horde of the High People in contempt. They swaggered with a rustle of blue-black feathers immune to the sounds of the tramp of feet, rough-throated cries, and the rap of weapons against shields. At a silent command, the wings of the flock beat in unison. The birds swept upwards, dipping and soaring, a black cloud against the morning sky's yellows, pinks, and purple-grey hues. With a loud *kraa kraa*, they permitted the battle to commence.

In less than a heartbeat, the first salvos of stones and arrows flew. Brandubh roared, encouraging his archers and slingers to keep up their devastating barrage. A wounded animal bloodied by the hunter, Ualraig's army howled with frustrated anger. They slipped on gore, stumbled over the fallen and trampled comrades into the mud, but they did not stop... until Conall's javelins broke the heart of the onslaught.

Two thousand stood in Conall's shield wall. With a loud shout of "*Fág an Bealach!*" a storm cloud of iron was released. Moments later, stunned adversaries gazed at each other and the slaughter. Less than half of Ualraig's first wave remained standing. The sighs of the dead were exhaled as a ghostly whisper. They were followed by the sobbing of those pinned to the earth. Almost two thousand lay injured or dead.

The warband chieftains who survived the storm shouted frenzied orders to those still able to fight. Urgency penetrated shocked minds, uncertain whether to retreat or fight. Carmag's war horns sounded, and, hammer swinging, he led his men through the gore. On the right wing, Brandubh called for spears and shields and charged. The remnant of the Ualraig's first surge was crushed. A single horn blew a long mournful note, and the Cinn Péinteáilte wings returned to link again with the shield-wall.

In An Balla Leac, Cuán's warriors exited the inner defences and scythed through the High People's injured. Abandoned by Ualraig, their fate hung on the mercy of Clann Ui Flaithimh. Ualraig's strategy was cold-hearted, but few challenged its necessity. Clann Ui Flaithimh's warriors were in no mood to take or care for prisoners. Hence, the demise of the abandoned was swift.

A small stubborn force prevented Cuán from joining the main affray. Reckoning that the shield-wall would be better at grinding through, he sent Torcán against them. It was a slow process, as twenty faced off against twenty. Cuán paced the yard with Lonán and cursed the lack of progress. Lonán said, "We could always send the men over the wall and use the timber bridge to cross the ditch." Cuán rounded on him, and Lonán raised his hands. "A jest, brother."

Cuán cursed his stupidity when he realised no one held the ramparts protecting the hillfort's main entrance. It was the flaw in Ualraig's plan. "Thanks, Lonán." Lonán looked puzzled at the change in Cuán's demeanour. "Send men to scavenge spears, javelins, rocks, and cauldrons of hot water and cinders." Cuán pointed to the ramparts. "Place men on the walls that guard the causeway." Lonán grinned.

The plan worked better than Cuán had envisaged. A hail of rocks, spears, and various burning materials dislodged the High People, allowing Torcán's squad to gain control of the dirt bridge. Meanwhile, more of Cuán's men clambered up the stone steps that led to the main ramparts. They hurled javelins at the rear of Ualraig's elite, forcing them to move away from the perimeter ditch and closer to Conall's main force.

***

Ualraig's remaining chieftains were unhappy. The grumbling of their men grew louder as they witnessed the slaughter of friends and comrades for no gain. Their numerical advantage had disappeared, and the Clann Ui Flaithimh army threatened both back and front.

It could not be called a fight when men and women were harvested like ripe corn. The field before them was filled with misshapen bodies, guts, and scattered limbs. Above, ravens waited to feast on the corpses. In the forests, enticed by the taint of blood carried on the gusting winds, predators gathered outside their dens.

"Sue for peace." The tall, dark-haired chieftain looked Ualraig in the eye. Ignored, he repeated his request. "Sue for peace. We can't win here."

In the past, the chieftain had been a good friend and counsellor. On this day, in Ualraig's mind, he was a traitor. In the blink of an eye, Ualraig's dagger punched into the man's belly. The warrior hissed in pain and spat a glob of blood and saliva into Ualraig's face. He fell to his knees before tumbling forward to die face down in the slop.

"Any others?" snarled Ualraig, his eyes challenging those before him. He turned to face the enemy. "We'll attack and slaughter the bastards." Ualraig sensed a lack of accord and turned around. A dozen chieftains had shifted their stance, and a dozen spears were levelled at him. The brother of the man, who lay in the mud at Ualraig's feet, spoke with anger in his voice.

"Sue for peace, Ualraig."

"I am your king. You'll do what *I* command."

"You're not a goddess like Kartimandu. You're just a man, Ualraig, and your mind is sick. Sue for peace or join my brother." Ualraig looked in desperation at his captains and the men and women behind them. There was no hope for him in their faces. He spat at the rebels, turned, and tramped towards the Clann Ui Flaithimh lines.

***

"Ualraig approaches," said Fearghal.

Conall looked up and watched Ualraig halt midway between the two armies. Ankle deep in the bloody slop of battle, Ualraig waited. Conall removed his ornate gold and silver helmet and handed it to Fearghal. He smiled thinly as he adjusted his chainmail and checked his shield and weapons.

"I should go see what he wants."

With a quick shake of braided hair, Conall strode towards Ualraig. They had never been friends, although Conall respected Ualraig as a leader and had some measure of sympathy for him having to serve Kartimandu. As he drew closer, the hackles on the back of Conall's neck stood up. He sensed that all was not right. Ualraig's posture spoke of barely restrained fury. As Conall came to a halt, he was shocked to see Ualraig's countenance was that of a stranger. He had seen that manic look too many times.

"*Child-killer!*" Ualraig shook as he screamed. White flecks of spit flew into the air. "You murdered my family." Taken aback, Conall paused.

This appeared to antagonise Ualraig further. He railed at Conall, uttering curses and repeating *"Tuill. Child-killer!"* repeatedly.

"I know nothing of your family. None in my army are responsible for their deaths." Conall prayed to the Goddess that his declaration was true. He knew Mórrígan and Urard had travelled deep into the High People's territory. With his jaw set, Conall said, "You, Ualraig of the High People, kidnapped my daughters. Where are they? Where is Kartimandu?"

"Kartimandu is gone. Your children are likely slaves or dead. *You* slaughtered my family."

The two men faced one another, each consumed by wrath and each accusing the other of heinous deeds. Both were wrong. "I warned you what would happen if my daughters were not returned to me. Go back to your army. Tell them to make peace with their gods. It's time to die." Conall turned his back on Ualraig.

Snarling, Ualraig brought his sword up and took a pace forward. His ankle turned on a severed limb, and Conall grunted as Ualraig's sword struck his back below his left kidney. Still, Ualraig's gleeful shouts of victory, even if a dishonourable one, were premature. Before it could do more than bruise his side, the blade was turned away by Conall's mail.

Anticipating the follow-up slash to his neck, Conall crouched, raised his shield, and swivelled. Ualraig's sword scraped harmlessly off the shield's curved surface. Conall's axe swept in a semi-circle. Ualraig leapt backwards but was too late to avoid the viciously sharp edge slice across his belly. Blood welled, but Ualraig's wrath was more profound than the cut, and he attacked. The ring of sword and axe against shield sounded again and again as the men traded blows.

They fought in a slurry of gore. Unable to find solid ground, the duellists slipped and circled continuously. Shields battered torsos, bosses broke ribs, and blades slashed flesh. A swish of displaced air and stinging pain reminded Conall he had foregone the use of his helmet. He swore as Ualraig's sword sliced his ear and cheek. Hot blood trickled down Conall's neck.

He lost his footing and stumbled to the ground. Conall dragged his shield across his body in time to prevent Ualraig's sword from cleaving his back to the spine. With a howl, Conall thrust the head of his axe upwards before Ualraig could straighten up. It caught Ualraig a glancing blow on the jaw and travelled upwards, breaking teeth and ripping flesh from his face.

A burst of axe strokes shattered Ualraig's round, wooden shield. The High People's king flung it aside and pulled a dagger from his belt in time to deflect an axe swing that would have opened up his side.

Fearghal watched the duel in a stew of fiery emotions along with the Clann Uí Flaithimh leaders and warriors. He raged at the shameful attack on Conall but was helpless and unable to intercede. All that he could do was prepare the army to attack once the duellists had finished. If Conall died, Fearghal swore that none of the High People would be spared.

Meanwhile, the High People's chieftains and warband leaders watched the combat in dismay. Ualraig's actions had shamed them and increased their peril. They argued furiously over what they could do when the fight ended. All agreed the enemy would attack and that their position—a slice of bloody meat caught between two snapping jaws, was hopeless.

Ualraig's concentration flitted momentarily from madness to sanity, allowing Conall to slam the boss of his shield hard against Ualraig's stomach, pushing ribs into his kidney and spleen. Ualraig exhaled sharply and howled at the intense pain. Immediately, Conall brought the iron rim of the shield down hard on Ualraig's left foot, crushing bones and severing toes.

The High People's king limped back a step to steady his position. His crossed dagger and sword barely slowed the downward swing of Conall's axe. The curved blade tracked a path down Ualraig's face, splitting nose and lips in twain. Blood and snot flowed from the ruined nose. Sensing the battle ebbing, Ualraig marshalled his strength and dove forward for a final flourish. Feinting with his sword, the triumph in his eyes was precipitous as he stabbed the dagger into Conall's side.

In his madness, Ualraig had forgotten about Conall's mail. Ignoring the dagger, Conall swatted Ualraig back with his shield and swung his axe. Ualraig bellowed in pain and anger as his sword fell to the ground. It was still grasped in his hand. The bloody stump spurted bright blood as he looked around for a weapon. A follow-up backward axe slash left Ualraig's head barely attached to his neck. It flopped backwards, allowing him a final vision of the accusing faces of his men.

With Ualraig dead, the remaining High People's chieftains understood their only path from the battlefield was to surrender. They dropped their weapons, fell to their knees with their hands on their heads and waited, hoping their enemy would be merciful.

The terms of surrender were harsh. One in five leaders and one in ten of the rank and file, over five hundred men and women, were executed, and their heads mounted on spears along the ramparts of An Bella Leac. Those remaining were stripped of their possessions, given food and water, and pointed toward Dùn Caen.

Conall turned to Fearghal as they watched the defeated army retreat. "I wouldn't have won against a sane Ualraig." Fearghal protested that this was not so. Yet in his heart, he knew Conall was right.

CHAPTER 30

405 B.C.—An Balla Leac

With the battle for An Balla Leac over, the people of Clann Ui Flaithimh flowed from their hilltop and forest camps to take up residence in the hill-fort. With their usual dry wit and sarcasm, the civilians pointed out that the army had destroyed the buildings which would have housed them. Íar and Cuán agreed with the sentiment. Indeed, Íar complained they would not have erected them in the first place had they known Conall would burn the buildings down.

Ere long, someone proposed a feast to celebrate the victory over the High People and to welcome the new friends from Ériu. Conall and Cuán were formally introduced, and after deliberations lubricated by beer, Cuán and his partner, Bláithín, accepted Conal's invitation to become part of the Chomhairle.

As usual, the irreverent humour of the Ériu was evident. Shouts of "Not more bloody Northerners" were countered with retorts of "*Póg mo thoin!*" and calls for another round of drinks.

With little more than minor scorching, An Balla Leac's Great Hall was one of the few buildings that had survived intact. Aromas of food, fire, and body odour thickened the already heavy atmosphere inside. Peat and wood smoke hovered in thick ribbons between oak beams and thatch.

The Hall thronged with ruddy-faced revellers gorging on roasted meat. Copious volumes of beer were swilled down with a fervour that suggested the world would end before sunrise. As the carousing inside and outside the Hall ebbed and flowed, Conall reclined comfortably on the pelts that covered the rough wooden chair that served as his throne.

Although at the centre of the celebrations, Conall was alone and troubled. He did not know the fate of his daughters or his queen. As soon as the tribe had recovered from their festivities, they would spend a short time at An Balla Leac gathering supplies. Then the tribe's trek south in pursuit of his family and the fulfilment of the Sídhe's geis would resume.

He started as a frothing jug of beer was slammed down on the table before him. Conall grinned at a rosy-cheeked and unsteady Fearghal. "Your melancholy worries the people, Conall. Don't sour their celebrations. Get off your arse and drink with them."

Conall stood, raised the jug, shouted, "*Slántu!*" and drained the vessel. The Hall's occupants cheered loudly, emptied their mugs, and called for refills.

***

Íar paced the wooden floor of the Great Hall. His anger was such that his face was the same colour as his mane of hair. His fists clenched and unclenched repeatedly, signalling his torment. The veins in his neck threatened to burst. Before him sat Conall and the Chomhairle. In a far corner, oblivious to the storm raging around her, was Áine.

"My sister is a Princess of Curraghatoor. You cannot execute her like a common criminal. *I* won't allow it."

Crum Dubh looked at Conall. A quick nod of the head gave the Druid permission to speak. "Your sister murdered three men and put an arrow in Tadhg's back. He narrowly missed a journey to Mag Mell. She fomented rebellion among the cavalry, which led to the death of fifty of *your* men. Áine has been judged according to the Law and found guilty."

The Druid paused and, with compassion, said, "I am truly sorry for your distress, but the fact is that your sister is a murderer. She is an outcast from Clann Ui Flaithimh. *Your* king had every right to put her to death long before this, but he waited until you could meet with her one last time."

"For pity's sake, look at her. She is diseased with the pox. Her mind is gone. Show some mercy."

"She showed no mercy to her victims and has been judged according to the Law. Her execution will take place in two sunsets." Conall spoke resolutely and yet with deep sadness. "The Law is for everyone, Íar. We can't pick and choose to whom it applies."

Íar roared defiantly. "No! I will take my sister and my cavalry and return to Curraghatoor."

Conall exhaled sharply. "I'll forget that you said that, as will all present. Similar foolish words from your sister caused the deaths of many. You're an honourable man. How many lives do you want on your conscience?" Íar slumped to his knees. His shoulders shook with racking sobs. Conall stepped down from the high table, walked to where Íar knelt and laid his hand on his friend's head. "Take your sister home, Íar. Make good use of the time she has left."

***

The party stood on a grassy knoll. Overhead, a butter-gold sun shone brightly in a pale blue sky. A gentle zephyr cooled the summer heat. It should have been a day for pleasant pastimes, lovers' trysts, and childish games. A baby's cries were quietened with a wet nipple and replaced with gentle sucking. Tears rolled down the pale, freckled face of the wet nurse.

She cried for the child in her arms and the mother who stood twenty paces distant. There was no recognition in Áine's eyes, only the glimmer of madness conferred by the pox. The salves and herbs of the healers could do little to stop the ravages of the disease on her body and mind. It was thanks to the Goddess and an early birth that the child was borne without infection.

"Stand aside, Íar," Conall spoke gently, but his manner showed he would brook no argument. "The axe-man has been well paid. It will be quick."

Instead, Íar placed himself between the executioner and his sister. Scarred hands held his axe. "No one will take the head of my sister, daughter of Rí Deda Mac Sin and Princess of Curraghatoor."

Behind him, in a moment of recognition, a white-faced Áine whispered, "Thank you, Brother." They were Áine's last words. With tears streaming down his ruddy face, Íar turned to face his sibling.

"Find peace, my sister."

Two hands gripped the axe's throat as it swung in a short semi-circular arc. Áine's head toppled from her swan-like neck to the lush grass. As her body came to rest, a hand briefly rose as if to wave a final goodbye to Íar. He looked at the axe stained with his sister's blood and hurled the weapon away with a cry of rage. Only the cries of the child halted him from walking away.

"The child, Íar. Think of the child?" said Conall.

"Sorchae Ni Íar is innocent of her mother's wrongdoing. She is my adopted daughter and a Princess of Curraghatoor." Íar took the tiny baby, swaddled in summer clothing, into his outstretched arms. They were enveloped in puffs of wildflower seeds as Íar tramped down the hillside. The occasional cry of the child and the sobs of Íar marked their receding presence.

CHAPTER 31

405 B.C.—Rinn-Campáil

On a chalky hilltop surrounded by rolling hills and fields of corn sat the hillfort of Rinn-Campáil. Three high ramparts, topped by chalk and earthen walls and wooden stockades, protected the hillfort. The ráth housed around five hundred residents, although its population more than doubled during harvest times and festivals.

The hillfort was the sentinel protecting numerous farms in south-western Albu. It also stored the grain harvests. As a major regional commercial, cultural, and religious centre, it was rivalled only by Mai Dùn to its west. Rinn-Campáil's army was feared throughout the region and imposed the ráth's status and sphere of influence with brutality, bribery, and assassination.

Rinn-Campáil was tidy and well laid out, with the king's residence and shrines at its centre. Chalky roads and pathways connected its buildings. Family roundhouses hugged its walls, adding another layer of protection to its defences. The granaries and grain storage pits were located to the southwest. The western gateway allowed the livestock to be driven to pastures and water.

The eastern approach to Rinn-Campáil was broad enough for two chariots. As Mórrígan led her riders along the road, their mounts kicked up clouds of fine, chalky dirt. The summer was warm and dry, a striking and pleasant contrast to the rains that swept the Penn-inus and northern Albu.

Most of her riders covered their mouths with cloth squares to spare them from the choking dust. Many rode with naked torsos save for breastplates and bracers. Unaccustomed to the constant hot sun, they winced as their pale skin reddened and blistered. Fevered itching was accompanied by flurries of flaking skin.

Mórrígan was conscious of being watched. Guards stood on the convoluted maze of ramparts that loomed over Rinn-Campáil's eastern entranceway and funnelled the party towards its wooden gates. As they approached shouting distance, Urard nudged Mórrígan, dipping his head toward one figure standing on the rampart. "That's obviously him."

Caradog, king of Rinn-Campáil, was an imposing man… and he knew it. He rarely passed a still pond or polished bronze plate without, and with some justification, admiring himself. Caradog was almost twenty hands in height and broad-shouldered. Long sun-bleached blonde hair, braided into a single thick plait, fell from the crown of his head to midway down his back. The sides of his head were shaved, save for two thin braids tipped with coloured stones that hung on either side of his skull. Long, drooping whiskers framed his mouth.

A lifetime in southern Albu's sun had burned Caradog's body a pleasing golden brown. His torso gleamed with aromatic oils applied frugally and meticulously by his slaves. Contained in clay amphorae, the oils were a gift from traders in Gaul. Indeed, Caradog treasured the oil almost as much as gold and silver.

The king was vain but no stranger to battle. Scars crisscrossed his ruggedly sculpted body. Large, calloused hands rested on the jewelled pommel of a longsword. With unblinking eyes, he watched Mórrígan's party approach.

"You may enter along with a small guard. The rest of your band will camp outside." It was a reasonable restriction with no significant sacrifice or insult. The weather was fair, and the grass lush. The king's deep voice surprised Mórrígan. She had anticipated and possibly hoped for a lighter tone as evidence of imperfection.

Along with her daughters, Urard, Iasg and a guard of ten, Mórrígan passed through the gates of Rinn-Campáil. An aide guided them to their assigned quarters, located within a stone's throw of Caradog's residence. Before long, they were given food, water, and an invitation to eat with the king after dusk.

***

A few thumps with the flat end of Urard's axe elicited an appropriate response, and the doors of Caradog's banqueting hall were flung open. Wood smoke billowed out, surrounding the group. A stocky guard looked them up and down and said, "No weapons, apart from your daggers." His accent was difficult to understand and had a heavy emphasis on the "r". Mórrígan shrugged; many Ulaid accents were equally impossible.

The guard pointed to several wooden barrels, "Leave them there. They'll be safe." Mórrígan nodded and her band disarmed. As they crossed the lintel, the guard held up his hand, "What about them?" He nodded toward the knives and swords that Brighid and Danu carried.

"Children's toys. They like to think they're grown-up," said Mórrígan. The guard grunted, and they passed into the chamber. The room was not as big or imposing as Áth's Great Hall but seated fifty comfortably. The floor was laid with flat stones. Long, brightly coloured drapes fell from wooden beams, obscuring the walls. Caradog occupied an ornately carved throne. Behind the king hung an array of banners, shields, and weapons. Trophies of past glories, Mórrígan surmised.

Two plump pouches thudded onto the table before Mórrígan as she took her seat. Eyebrow raised, she looked at Caradog, awaiting an explanation. "My information is that you killed Bréanainn and his band. There was a price on the bastard and his whore's heads. The reward is yours by right. That pack of thieves and murderers cost me a lot of gold and trade. A pity about An Cnoc. It will take us time to replace the services the community provided."

Mórrígan inclined her head and smiled. "A pleasant surprise. Thank you. Perhaps some formal introductions are in order." A quick flourish of Caradog's hand consented to her proceeding. "These are my daughters, Brighid and Danu and my brothers, Bricriu and Beacán. The giant is the guardian of my daughters and a faithful friend. His name is Urard. His companion is Iasg."

The queen paused. "As for me, I am Mórrígan Ni Cathasaigh, Queen of Clann Ui Flaithimh, and hand-fast partner of Conall Mac Gabhann, Rí Ruirech of Clann Ui Flaithimh, also known as the Hand of the Goddess." There was a sharp intake of breath as Mórrígan made her final introduction. "Some also know me as An Fiagaí Dorcha."

"We have heard of the Dark Huntress. Most of the stories are not at all flattering. Death and destruction appear to be your constant companions."

"Only for my enemies. At Rinn-Campáil, I am in the company of friends, am I not?"

Caradog twisted and tugged at his moustache. "Perhaps we could be better friends." He raised his hand at Mórrígan's startled and not-too-happy look. "No, I don't refer to *that* type of friendship. Certainly not with your family present." The glint in Caradog's eyes suggested that the king was not altogether truthful. He pointed to the bags of gold. "There is more where that came from. My captains tell me that your riders look very capable. I would pay well for cavalry."

"Mercenaries?" questioned Mórrígan. The king dipped his head. "That will not be possible. Our destination is the coast and a rendezvous with Pytheas the Greek and our tribe. With your permission, we will remain in Rinn-Campáil for a half-cycle of the moon." She smiled and pointed to the gold. "We can pay for accommodation and supplies."

Caradog frowned. The king was unused to having his advances, romantic or otherwise, spurned. He was also aware of the contest at An Balla Leac and that the Clann Ui Flaithimh and their famed king were already marching southwards. He doubted Mórrígan was as well informed. "You're my guests," he said, waving his hand dismissively at the offer of gold. "Stay as long as you wish. Perhaps, I can come up with a better argument for you to stay on a more permanent basis."

"You're very gracious."

Mórrígan chewed on a slice of roast pork, washing it down with a pleasantly flavoured beer. She wiped her mouth with her hand and asked, "What can you tell me about the journey to the coast and the trading ports on this side of the Muir nIocht? Your highways seem very well maintained. An army could travel very quickly along them."

The king scowled. "Mounted, the journey is not long, maybe two or three sunsets. To get to the coast, you'll have to circumvent the fort of *Mai-Dùn*." Caradog's enmity towards Mai-Dùn was evident as he ferociously spiked a large slice of beef with his dagger before transferring it to his open jaws.

"That bastard, Dai, will never let you cross his land without a large bribe or a fight." As he ripped and ground the meat between perfect teeth, bloody juice dribbled down impeccably coifed whiskers. He pointed the dagger at Mórrígan. "If you want to get past Mai-Dùn and to the coast, then you should reconsider my offer. Dai will have to be removed or defeated."

∗∗∗

"You don't believe that arsehole, do you?" asked Urard as they left the feast and ambled towards their accommodation. The moon was full, the sky cloudless, and the night pleasantly warm. Mórrígan breathed in myriad scents of wildflowers in the surrounding pastures. Her nose wrinkled as she sampled her smell—a mix of stale sweat, horse shite, and smoke. *I need a bath.*

Turning to Urard, who exuded a similar body odour, she said, "No. It would appear there are two warlords in this region. Either may be friends or enemies." Then, as an afterthought, she added, "Get acquainted with the gatekeepers at the southwestern entrance."

∗∗∗

Mai-Dùn squatted like a giant toad amid a cluster of low hills. The hillfort was a five-sunset journey southwest from Rinn-Campáil and a half-sunset

321

from the coast and major ports. The fort was prosperous and influential. By all accounts, most considered Mai-Dùn to be the largest ráth in Albu, rivalling An Balla Leac in importance, although that depended on a strict definition of "hillfort".

Surrounded by farms, and copper, iron, and tin mining communities, it was no surprise that it exerted a benevolent stranglehold on the region's economy. Mai-Dùn was a sanctuary to those who bowed the knee to its king, Dai. And a dangerous enemy to those who rebuffed his generosity.

Dai, Rí of Mai-Dùn, was a cantankerous old man. Set in his ways, he cursed his fifty-nine summers. He had lived far too long. Fate and the gods had conspired to deprive him of a hero's death. Dai did not care what his subjects believed, yet he imagined he was a fair ruler. To his way of thinking, he acted for the good of his kingdom.

Any who disagreed could like it or lump it. Most accepted it because, despite the king's curmudgeonly ways, he had built Mai-Dùn into a bulwark against his peoples' enemies and a significant economic force. His nobles and landowners were fat, happy, and wealthy. Labourers were treated as well as any. As for the slaves, well, they were slaves.

It was mid-morning, and Dai took his usual walk around the massive ramparts of Mai-Dùn. He was deep in thought. His spies in Rinn-Campáil constantly informed him of Caradog's ambitions. Caradog had removed his elderly father, murdered his rivals, and exiled his sisters. Now, he had turned his ambitions to uniting the many disparate tribes in southern Albu.

Unsurprisingly, Caradog coveted Mai-Dùn and its wealth. Rinn-Campáil's king followed an aggressive militaristic strategy of enlarging his army with conscripts and mercenaries. Expansion and loyalty were purchased at the point of a sword and the promise of wealth… or death. So far, he had been successful and controlled much of the land north and east of Mai-Dùn.

What disturbed Dai in the most recent reports was the rumour that Caradog had bought the services of a sizeable company of cavalry. A band of mounted warriors could upset the region's finely poised balance of power. Dai looked over the triple ramparts, stockades, and ditches of Mai-Dùn.

The elderly king favoured a defensive strategy. While his retainers were not the same calibre as Caradog's, they stood behind the most substantial walls in Albu. As Dai scratched his neatly trimmed, grey-white beard, he decided that the fort's two entrances needed an immediate upgrade.

**

The land of Albu, while vaster than Ériu, could not be considered a large island. As the raven flies, a mounted rider could trot from its northern tip to its southern coast in about ten sunsets. An army could march the same distance in the cycle of the moon. However, warriors face human and natural barriers.

Distances are complicated by mountains, deep valleys, forests, rivers, and lochs. Added to this are the weather and season. It is also a given that an army moves at the pace of its slowest link, which in the case of Clann Ui Flaithimh, were the wagons pulled by teams of oxen.

In an exodus, people are also a significant challenge. They invariably carry sickness and disease and attract the attention of predators—human and animal. Packs of wolves stalked the travellers. To the yellow-eyed hunters, the people of Clann Ui Flaithimh were a slow-moving and abundant food source. The old and the weak kept the animals' bellies full.

Local warbands and roving bands of outlaws proved incapable of resisting the mirage of promised wealth. Fortunately, most were disorganised, poorly armoured and not battle-ready. Like the clouds of midges that hung around the people and animals, they were an irritant to be swatted. In the dusty wake of the people, ravens pecked the eyes of those whose lives were thrown away fruitlessly.

Conall sat on Toirneach. He gulped tepid water from a hide water pouch and wiped the sweat from his forehead. His helmet was strapped to his mount. The black stallion cropped the lush grass on the small hill as his master surveyed the long snake that was the people of Clann Ui Flaithimh.

The tortuous train of man and beast had left the mountains and moors of the Penn-inus far behind. As far as he could see, the landscape before him comprised low, rolling hills. The roads were undoubtedly better, so travel should be less gruelling for his people and army. The weather was improving, with less rain, frequent, prolonged days of sunshine and blue skies.

"We need to keep them moving," said the Sídhe to Conall. Mongfhionn cradled a baby girl, or more accurately, she provided access to her breast to a demanding infant. "And you, get that stupid grin off your face, old man." The last comment was aimed at Fearghal, who was hopelessly and helplessly entranced by the additional capacity that childbearing had bestowed on Mongfhionn. The Sídhe converted the beginning of a smile, she was not immune to Fearghal's boyish charms, into a snarl. "As I said, we need to keep moving."

"Why?" Conall was curious and a bit perturbed. There was urgency in the Sídhe's voice. "What have you seen? Have your powers recovered?"

"I have been experiencing more dreams recently, and my spirit can travel farther."

"And?"

"Brighid and Danu are safe and with their mother."

"And?"

"The fuath lives. Kartimandu's path may cross with theirs. She blames the twins for her fall from power and seeks revenge."

Conall turned to his commanders. "According to Pytheas, the two major hillforts in the southwest are Rinn-Campáil and Mai-Dùn. The closest is Rinn-Campáil. I will leave five hundred men, a hundred slingers, and two hundred riders under the command of Eirnín. They should be sufficient to guard the people. The rest of the army will march for the nearest fort."

***

Plagued with conflicting dreams and nightmares, Mórrígan did not sleep well. As morning grasped the day, she awoke agitated and was more than a bit sharp with everyone. Ordinarily vigilant, on this sunrise, the queen bordered on paranoia.

Rarely were Brighid and Danu allowed out of her sight and preferably only a few paces away. Even Iasg, the twins' constant companion and Urard loitering nearby were insufficient to mollify Mórrígan. Urard joked the queen would put halters on the girls if they would stand still long enough.

As expected, Caradog's invitation to dine arrived. The aide, typically quite a chatty lad, was withdrawn, and his eyes fixated on his bare feet. In fact, the more Mórrígan thought about it, there was a worrying atmosphere within the hillfort. There did not appear to be the same hustle and bustle of activity. Most of the residents stayed indoors, and all avoided eye contact.

"Send a man to our camp beyond the walls. Tell them to approach the western gateway. If anyone asks, they can plead better grass for the horses."

Urard dipped his head. "You suspect something?"

"Visions and nightmares. My spirit says something is not right."

"Now that you mention it, the folk have been a bit subdued. Even the livestock are quiet. Maybe there's a big storm coming. You know how folk and animals get when the weather changes," said Urard.

"There's a storm coming. Of that, I am sure. It's the nature of it that worries me. At this evening's feast, only you, my brothers, Iasg and the twins will accompany me. The rest of the guard will remain close, outside, and fully armed." As Urard turned, Mórrígan rested a hand on his forearm.

"Make sure Brighid and Danu are fully armed. Keep Breith as near as possible. This evening my armour will be my paint." Urard's eyebrow twitched. Mórrígan chuckled. "The Sídhe will be proud of me."

"Oh, be quiet, Urard. They'll wash off." Iasg gave the huge, complaining man a slap on the arse and walked over to Brighid and Danu. Urard's protest was directed at the swirling, indigo-blue designs Mórrígan insisted on painting on his face and shaven skull. Mórrígan had also applied similar sigils to her brothers, Iasg and the twins. Far from grumbling, Brighid and Danu were delighted with their face paint. The rest of the group was not quite so sure, but the thought of angering Mórrígan overruled any misgivings or protests.

✷✷✷

"Who died?" The booming voice of Urard cut through the brooding silence in the feasting hall like a dagger through soft cheese curds. "We'd better not fart. Everyone will know who did it." The twins giggled. Iasg sighed benignly, and Mórrígan threw him a stern look. As they sauntered forward, Caradog lifted his head to acknowledge their presence and waved them to empty seats at his table. The effort seemed an enormous strain.

"There's something wrong, Urard. Caradog is not seated on his throne," Mórrígan whispered, motioning for the small group to halt midway down the aisle. In the typical boisterous atmosphere of Rinn-Campáil's feasting room, Mórrígan's murmur would have been among many and unheeded.

The voice behind the throne sent a chill down Mórrígan's spine. "There's nothing wrong. I am the new queen of Rinn-Campáil." Kartimandu stepped from behind the throne and sat down. Like bark around a tree, the dark wood seemed to enclose her. She looked at Caradog. "This weak-minded fool and his men now follow me." There was fury in Caradog's eyes as he fought Kartimandu's control. The strain of the fight was evident by the sheen of perspiration on the queen's brow and the throbbing pain in her head.

Angrily, Kartimandu sought to bring her powers to bear on Mórrígan's group. At that instant, Mórrígan's cloak fell to the floor, and she stepped in front of her band. The sigils on her body glowed as the spirit of Dark Huntress clashed with the green-skinned queen. Behind her, the painted swirls on the others shimmered.

"It would appear that my powers have grown while yours have not," said Mórrígan.

"Seize them!" screeched a furious Kartimandu.

In unison, Urard, Iasg, and the twins pulled and threw all eight daggers hidden in Brighid and Danu's baldrics. All save one struck the throne. The eighth sliced along Kartimandu's cheekbone, piercing her earlobe. Blood welled from the wounds, trickling down green-painted cheek and neck. Chaos quickly descended as the queen screamed at the iron that boiled her blood.

Around the room, Caradog's men shook their heads as if released from a trance. Caradog jumped up, roaring, and reached for his sword. The queen's guard emerged from behind the wall hangings. In the confusion, Caradog and his people were shoved aside and received cracked skulls from sword pommels and clubs as the guard moved to protect their queen.

Beacán and Bricriu quickly drew the sheathed swords strapped to the girls' backs. They flanked the group as Mórrígan ushered them out of the wooden doors. Beyond the feasting hall, they grabbed the rest of their weapons and jogged to the corral and their mounts.

Torches flickered over the western gates as they approached. More of Kartimandu's elite emerged from the shadows. Streaks of blood on their torsos and faces told the fate of Caradog's guards.

Urard's axe flashed silver in the moonlight. Black blood gushed from chests slashed to the bone. The steady impact of iron arrowheads finding their targets drew cries from Kartimandu's warriors. Mórrígan's brothers and the twins' blades quickly finished those that remained standing. Breith's razor-sharp edge ended the skirmish as the axe split the locking bar on the gates.

"Mount up," ordered Mórrígan and swung up on her horse. Hoofs thundered along the rain-parched road towards Mai-Dùn.

CHAPTER 32

405 B.C.—Mai-Dùn

A southerly wind caressed the hill where Rinn-Campáil perched. The breeze carried the tang of sea salt but could not mask the taint of decay. Conall's army halted several hundred paces from the hillfort's walls. They waited for a reaction, good or bad, to their presence but were met only with brooding silence. It was not a total stillness if the intermittent sounds of ravens within the fort were counted. Still, their cries made the silence more intense.

Conall shifted on the thick, red diallait and scratched his arse. His backside was numb from the ride, and his ears rang with the rising chorus of complaints of sore arses from the cavalry and blistered feet from those marching. "Setting an example for the men?" Mongfhionn guided her mount alongside.

He snorted, as did his horse, and nodded towards the fort. "It's ominously quiet."

"*She* has been here," said the Sídhe. "I smell her corruption."

"Is she still in the fort?"

Mongfhionn hesitated. "I don't think so, but be careful." Conall smiled. It was unusual to see the Sídhe waver. As far as he could remember, she had always been confident, even arrogant, in her words and pronouncements.

The birth of her daughter, Neamhain, had conferred a gentler, warmer, and less certain nature on Mongfhionn. The temporary interruption of her powers made her seem less Aes Sídhe and more human. Conall felt guilty. At this moment, he yearned for the return of the "old" Mongfhionn in all her awful magnificence. A hand on his forearm interrupted his thoughts. "Have no concerns." Conall heard wistful regret in the Sídhe's voice. "My powers are almost restored."

Deaglán, Tadhg, and Torcán marched past the fortifications lining the path to Rinn-Campáil's entrance. A hundred each of shield-warriors and slingers tramped in their wake. Deaglán and Torcán carried on an animated conversation. The main subject of which was the influx of young women who accompanied Cuán's warriors. Deaglán was at pains to impress on his friend that a confrontation with an angry Cróeb Ruad father, at best, would be bruising. At worst, he could find his renowned manhood cut off.

In contrast to his companions, Tadhg quietly reflected on recent events. The birth of Gràinne's baby girl was a shock. The scars on his back and chest, caused by Áine's arrow, tightened, and throbbed. *How should I feel?* He had been recovering from his wounds for much of Gràinne's pregnancy. Hence, Tadhg had not entirely taken in the implications of her swelling belly. He knew the wee'un was not his and had a fair idea of the father's identity.

Tadhg's musings came to an abrupt end. His two friends had stopped and were staring at him with raised eyebrows. "The Hag, being a father must make you deaf, Tadhg," remarked Torcán. "Another reason for me to avoid parenthood." Deaglán laughed. Tadhg scowled.

"What?"

Deaglán pointed to the fort's entrance. "We were looking for our celebrated solver of mysteries to give an opinion on how we should proceed." Tadhg looked up and peered at the tall, wooden gates. He sighed. *Eeejits!*

"Why don't we just walk through the entrance? The gates are open." Deaglán and Torcán squinted at the gates. This time they saw that the gates were indeed a hand's breadth open.

"Bloody eyes like a hawk," muttered Torcán, falling in as Tadhg marched on.

Tadhg turned to look at his friends. "I'm not the father."

"Shite!" exclaimed Torcán softly; Deaglán wondered if saying "Sorry" was appropriate.

***

The forward group navigated the maze of newly constructed ramparts guarding the entrance of Mai-Dùn. The impressive, curved walls were three spears high and augmented by guard towers and firing platforms. They would undoubtedly slow down an attacking force, leaving them vulnerable to spears, slings, and bows. Indeed, to anything that could be thrown or tipped over the walls.

Mórrígan stood in the oblong killing zone before two sets of solid oak gates between high dirt and rock banks. A guard tower was anchored to the segment of the rampart connecting the twin gates.

The captain of the guard peered at the riders before him. "Go away."

"I would like to speak with Dai, Rí of Mai-Dùn. I have information he needs to hear."

"He's sleeping and can't be disturbed." The rejoinder carried a note of irritation.

The Huntress looked to the sky. She reckoned it was around meán lae. "The sun is high in the sky. Surely the king cannot be in his cot?"

"He's an old man. He needs his rest. Go away." At the captain's signal, a score of defenders appeared on the ramparts readying slings and spears.

Mórrígan sighed. "Our intentions are friendly. Why do you threaten us with slings and spears? Remove your men from the walls. Or perhaps you would like a demonstration of my archers' skills?"

At a nod from the queen, her bowmen dismounted, retrieved bow staffs from their backs, and nocked arrows. Mórrígan pointed to Urard. "I should also point out that this large man with his equally oversized axe is not known for his patience. Open the gate, or I will have him carve it into a thousand splinters."

The captain shifted his stance uneasily, for he had not intended the conversation to go downhill quite as rapidly. Usually, visitors were not as dogged. It did not help that a young warrior, eager to prove his worth, raised his spear at that moment. "No!" shouted the captain, holding his hands high.

The young man was about to hurl the spear when several arrows slammed into the weapon's shaft, diverting it. The remaining missiles made a bloody mess of the young man's throwing hand and arm, spinning him around. He fell from the running platform, landing in the yard. Quivers of arrows thudded into the wooden stockade, startling those behind. A few others joined their wounded comrade.

The captain of the guard peered over the stockade at Mórrígan. Her face now featured a ferocious scowl. "Your king!" she called out through clenched teeth. The captain nodded and scurried off.

A massive oak locking bar scraped against rock and dirt as it was withdrawn into deep slots in the walls. Yet not so quickly, to give the impression of surrender and not so tardy as to further anger those waiting, The high gates swung inward with the shrill sound of iron hinges. Dai strode forward, supported by a hundred of his best men. Although below average height, the king had a commanding demeanour.

"I am Mórrígan, Queen of..."

"I know who you are. I'm old, not senile. I do have scouts beyond these walls," said Dai. He looked over his shoulder and frowned at the wounded guard. "This eejit has left me with little choice other than to let you enter, if only to compensate for his lack of common sense. Enter. My aide will show you where your band can rest. Your men can eat with mine in the barracks.

"I expect you and a small group to dine with me." The king spoke to one of his men. "Have boys follow the horses with shovels. We'll be ankle-deep in horse shite before we know it."

***

While not unsociable, Dai preferred to keep mass celebrations to an absolute minimum. Small gatherings were his preference. The hall to which Mórrígan and her party were escorted was big enough to seat fifty comfortably while allowing the servants sufficient space to do their job without mishap.

Four solid oak tables formed a square around the open log fire at the centre of the room. Three tables had bench seating; the fourth had individual carved seats. Dai's throne stood at the centre. The room had a thatched roof. Like Rinn-Campáil, brightly coloured hangings covered the rough wooden walls. A mix of hardwoods laid down in an attractive pattern and colouring formed the floor. Imported cedarwood beams added a touch of colour and a fragrant bouquet to the room.

Dai greeted his guests with reserved warmth. To everyone's surprise, the king insisted Brighid and Danu sit on either side of him. He loudly proclaimed that they were likely better company than the adults. He admired the twins' baldrics and promised they would have an opportunity to demonstrate their knife-throwing skills later.

Brighid and Danu instantly loved Dai and conferred the status of grand-da on him. Seated to his right were Brighid, Mórrígan, Beacán, and Urard; on his left, Danu, Bricriu, Iasg and the commander of Mai-Dùn's army. Around the other tables sat Dai's sons and daughters with their families and a selection of his nobles.

No one could accuse Dai of stinting on hospitality. The variety of roasted and boiled meats, bread, cheeses, fruit, and vegetables was impressive, and the drink flowed without end. The king even provided entertainment in the form of musicians and storytellers. It was a pleasant evening, but Kartimandu's malevolent advance hovered like a dark cloud over those assembled.

"Our walls are strong. Our army experienced," said Dai. "My people will find sanctuary and protection within Mai-Dùn. It has always been this way and always will be."

"With respect, you have not fought an enemy like her. Kartimandu has enthralled Caradog and his people. Rinn-Campáil's gold and the promise of plunder, slaves, and rape have drawn an army of mercenaries, outlaws, and bandits to her. An army the size of which you have never faced marches on Mai-Dùn. Your warriors are brave, and your people stalwart…"

Mórrígan paused to look into Dai's blue eyes and shook her head. She saw a stubborn man but a king who cared for his people. "Your walls are not high enough to prevent the bitseach from capturing the minds of your men, women, and children. Her victory will be complete and bloodless until she enters your gates. Then the slaughter, the culling of your tribe, will begin."

Dai slumped back on his throne. He knew Mórrígan's assessment was honest. Indeed, his spies gave him similar reports, but he feared little could be done to stop Kartimandu. After all these years, perhaps, the gods had finally heard his complaints and prepared a death in battle for him.

He stood and held up his mug of beer. "We will fight!" he shouted. The cry was taken up by all present. "And Mórrígan, The Dark Huntress and Queen of Clann Ui Flaithimh, will stand with us." Dai smiled at Mórrígan and then turned to face the room. "Eat and drink well. War is upon us. Tomorrow, we inspect our defences."

***

"The spawn of the Hag!" Deaglán cursed as the party trudged reluctantly towards the centre of Rinn-Campáil. Weapons were redundant. Instead, warriors gripped amulets, praying for protection against the malevolence that assaulted their senses. The druids' monophonic incantations implored the Goddess to bind the evil surrounding them. Too late, many tried to avert their eyes, but the horror was inescapable. Stomachs heaved as men fought to keep their gorge.

Women, children, and the elderly hung from the stockade that crowned Rinn-Campáil's walls. Most were unrecognisable, surrounded by clouds of fat, blue-black flies. Flesh heaved as thousands of maggots feasted on dead meat. Long tails of guts hung from bellies slashed open to the spine. Still attached with umbilical cords to their mothers, the unborn dangled, swinging slowly in the zephyrs that danced around the fort. The ground beneath the corpses was soaked in blood.

Mongfhionn stood above the fort's entrance. One hand reached for the skies, and the other held her oak staff. In the breeze, the Sídhe's long blonde hair rose in gentle waves. Her white léine, trimmed in black and red, formed a diaphanous cloud about her.

The Sídhe's long, haunting cry ascended to the skies. Rinn-Campáil's horror kindled a fire that fully restored the Sídhe's powers. Previously clear and blue, the sky darkened to threatening indigo. Forks of lightning danced on the horizon. Long rolls of thunder reverberated as the Goddess welcomed the return of her servant.

Fearghal stood beneath Rinn-Campáil's entrance and cursed Kartimandu with all his heart and soul. Although mindful of the dead, Fearghal's was a selfish anger. He mourned the loss of a gentler Mongfhionn whose spirit had found peace. With a cry of unbounded wrath, Fearghal swore that his blade would separate Kartimandu's head from her neck.

***

In Mai-Dùn, Mórrígan looked to the darkening skies from the safety of one of the fort's watchtowers. Steel-grey rods of rain beat the wooden frame. On the wind, she heard Mongfhionn's great cry of anger. Mórrígan turned to Dai. "The Lady Sídhe has returned." Dai shivered and once more wished he had travelled beyond the veil long ago.

The rain did not bother Kartimandu, for she came from the water. The enormous underground reservoirs of southern Albu were her sources of power and fed her. Yet Katimandu's face reflected her rage at Mongfhionn, the scar that would always be seen, and the ear that would never be whole. She drove her army towards Mai-Dùn. She would capture Conall's daughters and make him and his accursed partner kneel and watch as she sacrificed them.

CHAPTER 33

405 B.C.—Mai-Dùn

Mai-Dùn thronged with men and women. They huddled in small groups, watchful and fearful. Innocent of the storm around them, children screamed, laughed and played, ignorant and unaware. Anyone, farmers, labourers, and artisans, who could wield a weapon were assigned a place on the walls.

The civilians looked nervously at the warriors in their midst. Not skilled in battle, they knew they were another layer of armour for the fighters. Their job was to deflect, guard, and, if needed, die. Everyone on the ramparts wore painted sigils. Swirling black, white, and blue designs intensified grim faces into sombre masks.

Dai stood beside Mórrígan and stared at Kartimandu's mongrel army arrayed in the grain fields to the northwest. Low morning mists swirled around the horde. Unaccustomed to his painted sigils, Dai screwed up his face. He reluctantly allowed his face to be painted as an example to his people.

"This makes a pretty mask," said Dai, scratching his forehead. "Perhaps, if we survive, we'll do it again at Lugnasad." The king's well-known sarcasm was oddly comforting to those around him. "Will these symbols protect my people?" he asked.

Mórrígan smiled. It was but a few days, yet she had grown to like the king. Beneath the irascibility, his judgment was well-founded. He had a genuine affection for his people and they for him. "If your men think it will work, it has fulfilled its purpose." She pointed to the livestock pens. "If it prevents filling those, then it is a victory."

The cattle that formerly occupied the holdings now grazed on meadow grass far from the fort, guarded by young boys and girls. In their place, confused citizens began to trickle into the pens. They were the first; the most vulnerable, whose minds had already succumbed to Kartimandu.

Dai spat on the wooden walkway. For such a fastidious man, the act summed up his anger at Kartimandu's assault.

***

Kartimandu looked at the faces before her with ill-concealed contempt. It was not her nature to feel remorse, yet the queen fleetingly regretted her quarrel with Ualraig. The news of his death at An Balla Leac had surprised her. Still, Ualraig was a warrior, and warriors kill or die. Few saw the white hairs of old age. Fewer wanted to see them.

The newly crowned queen of Rinn-Campáil peevishly stamped a foot on the dirt floor of her pavilion. No. Ualraig had deserted her and left her without an experienced general. There would be no forgiveness for him. She toyed with the idea of returning to Dùn Caen to assume the throne of the High People. They were a broken tribe; many would bow their knees, hoping she would return their former glories. *Perhaps, after I deal with Conall.*

Kartimandu swore and brushed a fly from her cheek. A plague of the creatures had followed her from Rinn-Campáil. Her finger touched the long scar that marred a previously flawless face. Rage welled up in Kartimandu's breast. She would see the Dark Huntress dead and bring Conall to his knees. The witch, Mongfhionn, she would banish to the mounds of dirt which gave birth to her.

With a curl of her lip, the queen turned to face her captains. The leaders of the upcoming assault on Mai-Dùn varied from the dumb and brutal to the capable but mentally hamstrung Caradog.

The former ruler of Rinn-Campáil glared at Kartimandu. His eyes were a mosaic of broken blood vessels. Bloody sweat-stained sallow cheeks reflected Caradog's inner turmoil as he struggled to regain control of his senses. His mind fought her, and his hands twitched, yearning to feel the smooth pommel of his sword and daggers.

She had misjudged the king's mental fortitude. Of more concern, pacifying Caradog required a constant drain on her resources. Left with no alternates, the queen was forced to rely on the loyalty of the many bands of mercenaries she attracted. She did not need to use her powers to ensure their compliance.

The treasury of Rinn-Campáil and the grain pits and towers of Mai-Dùn were more than sufficient to reward the vermin. They would remain trustworthy and their minds unfettered for as long as avarice and lust ruled their actions.

The ties of the tent flap whipped sharply against the pavilion's hide walls. Kartimandu regarded Cunobelinus as he entered. Insolent and too confident in his limited abilities, the *de facto* leader of the mercenaries was a battering ram with a brain.

Not surprisingly, he carried a club. Circles of iron ringed its shaft, and its head was studded with short, iron spikes. Calloused, massive hands covered in thick, white scars and with stone-hard knuckles spoke of a lifetime of brawling. The mercenary preferred his fighting close and very personal. The queen's pert nose crinkled as the first wave of the mercenary's earthy smell reached her.

"Well?" said Kartimandu. "What is your plan for taking Mai-Dùn?"

Cunobelinus' squinting, brown eyes swept the tent. Most chose not to meet his gaze, and others feigned disinterest. He looked into and held Kartimandu's eyes. Beyond the rage and thirst for vengeance, he saw that, more than anything, her desire was to be worshipped.

For now, he needed to avoid becoming a puppet like Caradog. So, Cunobelinus dropped to his knee and paid obeisance to the queen. Kartimandu was pleased but not deceived and waved her commander to stand. "I asked you a question, mercenary."

"I walked Mai-Dùn's perimeter this morning. The fortifications: walls, ramparts, and ditches, are strong. A child with a few rocks could hold the fort. The pathways to both entrances are a maze with, I suspect, many traps. As soon as we attack, the walls guarding the northwest entrance will be filled with warriors armed with anything that can be thrown at or poured down on us."

"Are you making excuses already?" Kartimandu's tone was menacing. Her patience, a fragile thread at the best of times, was about to break.

The mercenary smiled and stabbed a dirt-ingrained finger at Caradog. "*He* will order his people to attack the western gate. Their bodies will spring the traps and bear the brunt of missiles. They will attempt to breach the defences if they reach the gates." Cunobelinus inhaled and hacked up a glob of spit. "They will die, but their corpses will be a ramp for my mercenaries and your elite."

The scrape of soft leather boots on the dirt floor drew eyes to Caradog. Blood-tinted sweat stung inflamed eyes as the king dragged his feet a pace towards Kartimandu, but his strength ebbed, and he collapsed on the dirt. Cunobelinus laughed and spat on the prostrate king.

"Useless bastard."

***

Teams of spirited horses pawed the earth and chomped on metal bits. Heavily armoured vehicles, brightly painted creta garlanded with flags and banners, rocked on spoked wheels. Chariots were not a tactic if stealth was required. They were, however, highly effective in putting the fear of the Hag into the enemy. Gràinne whooped and yelled with unrestrained enthusiasm as she drove her command forward, cutting a broad swathe across the grain fields.

Naked as the day she was born and longsword grasped firmly in both hands, Gràinne slashed down on the hapless warrior who avoided the spinning scythes. Her tortured leg muscles lacked the strength to put her beyond sword range. With a dull thud and muted crack, the well-honed edge of the longsword met the shaggy-haired skull of the enemy.

It was no contest. The woman's skull clove in two. Gore and brains splattered the cret's fern-green walls. The corpse continued its final steps on earth until both heart and mind agreed that she was dead. It flopped over and rested in a field of yellow gold.

The hopes of the fifty unwashed outcasts and bandits marching to Mai-Dùn to claim their share of the fort's gold and violate and despoil the residents were dashed. They had caught the attention of Gràinne's band. No match for Gràinne's carbaid, they quailed as the vehicles bore down on them. That most of their wounds were on their backs gave proof of the futility of running. The skirmish was swift, bloody, and final.

Gràinne's chariots scouted ahead of Clann Ui Flaithimh's army. Tasked with keeping pace with Kartimandu's force, they were to harass but not to get captured or killed. They were to send a message and sow doubt in Kartimandu's and her commanders' minds. Looking around the blood-soaked field, Gràinne pondered the practicality of her orders. Dead mercenaries made poor messengers.

New, silvery-pink lines on her belly wove a delicate design, curling around and between the indigo-blue designs that made her one of the Cinn Péinteáilte. The lines tingled. Gràinne scratched at the pattern and smiled. It was a permanent reminder of her daughter, Brianag, who travelled in the vanguard of Clann Ui Flaithimh.

A frown passed briefly over Gràinne's painted face. Her relationship with Tadhg was doomed. Adopted by Fearghal and Mongfhionn, she had taken Fearghal's name and returned to the comfort of Conall's tent. She hoped Tadhg had moved on, which given his recent carousing with Deaglán and Torcán, appeared to be the case.

Gràinne sighed deeply; pleasure and pain were close companions. Grabbing the chariot rail, she swung onto the cret's platform, raised her sword, and pointed towards Mai-Dùn. "Let's put the fear of the Hag into the *págánaigh*!" she shouted. A roar of approval met her command.

***

"How long before we face Kartimandu?" asked Conall, looking at those gathered around the campfire. Mongfhionn, Bláithín, and Mòrag were dispersed between Brandubh, Carmag, Cúscraid, Crum, Cuán, Deaglán, Fearghal, Íar, and Nikandros. Fearghal opined that the seating was strategic since it did not allow the women to gang up on the men. Deaglán pondered if the fact that he was at the discussion was a sign he was getting old. Within earshot of the group, Tadhg and Sárán waited. Their input would be decided by the range of the conversation.

"The bitseach is two sunsets from us," answered Fearghal. "We'll not arrive at Mai-Dùn before the siege commences." Conall shifted uneasily on the log. The closer he got to Mórrígan and his daughters, the more anxious and impatient he became. The duties of being Rí Ruirech of the tribe chafed against those of being a father.

"Do we know if our people are guests or prisoners?"

"I sense that Mórrígan is not in any harm from the king of Mai-Dùn," said Mongfhionn. "Still, Kartimandu is throwing up a strong net of power around her army. It makes spying with any degree of certainty difficult… even with the help of Crum's druids." Crum smiled thinly. He knew how much any acknowledgement of other powers pained the Sídhe.

"What do we know about Kartimandu's army?"

Conall turned to Íar, who responded with a grunt and angry look. Exasperated, Conall snapped, "Do I need a new commander of my cavalry?" Those around the fire supported Conall. Sympathy for Íar's feelings over Áine's execution had reached its limit, and all were weary of his moody demeanour. The air was heavy with silence as Íar rose, snapped a bow at Conall, turned his back, and strode off. Furious, Conall looked at Nikandros.

"Well?"

"Best guess is about ten thousand warriors. Over half are mercenaries, and about one thousand are Kartimandu's elite. The rest are Caradog's men. The main problem is the mercenaries because Mai-Dùn holds the promise of massive wealth. Parasites from across the south of Albu, some even from north of Dùn Caen, flock to Mai-Dùn. If we don't finish this quickly, we could face double the numbers."

"What's the state of Mai-Dùn's fortifications, Cúscraid?" Conall's master of defence scratched his arse and moaned loudly to emphasise his pain. The taciturn commander was another who hated riding. His arse and thighs felt like they were on fire and missing several layers of skin. The various witches' brews and salves recommended by his so-called friends did little to relieve his misery while seeming to cause them great merriment. Still, he had no choice if he wanted to survey Mai-Dùn.

"I hope Mórrígan and her party are guests. I'd hate to have to breech Mai-Dùn's ramparts. In the absence of other less worldly influences, a handful of defenders could hold that hillfort until the end of the world."

Conall said, "Mongfhionn and Crum, I look to you to restrain the 'other influences.'" All present slipped into their own thoughts. The silence was disturbed only by the cracking of wood burning on the fire.

***

Side-by-side, Dai and Mórrígan walked the forward ramparts of Mai-Dùn. The intimidating hulk of Urard walked a few paces behind. The lie of the land directed Kartimandu's horde as they tramped towards the western gates.

"They outnumber us by ten to one. Not good odds," commented Dai.

Mórrígan chuckled. "The Cróeb Ruad warriors in my army would claim this is perfect odds. They say that there's little glory in an even fight."

Dai grunted something obscene and turned to survey the interior of the fort. The cattle pens brimmed with those whose minds had been touched by Kartimandu's madness. Most gazed sullenly around. A small, more agitated group became more violent, hurling curses, shite, and rocks at the guards who patrolled the corral's perimeter fence. The few who attempted to breach the compound were encouraged back with clubs and spears.

"I never thought I'd have to treat my people like animals," said Dai. His face was flushed red with sorrow as much as anger, making his white beard stand out like snow on sandstone.

"Perhaps you should have paused to consider the wisdom of driving the druids from Mai-Dùn and its environs. Those 'bloody fanatics in black cloaks' would be useful now."

"Bah! Hindsight never makes a mistake," Dai answered. "I did the priests a good turn. From what I hear, they're happy as pigs in shite at *Choir-Gaur*." As Dai turned to face his enemies, Mórrígan looked closely at the older man. She hoped his health was robust and he would last the battle. Dai's presence was needed to embolden his men to fight for their homes and families.

***

Kartimandu stood on a large limestone outcrop overlooking the battle-field on its northern side. From her position, she could smell the salt tang of the sea on the wind and feel its power as it hurled waves against the white cliffs.

She was less impressed with her ragged army as it half-marched, half-staggered towards the fort. Cunobelinus and Caradog watched alongside the queen as Caradog's men shuffled towards the twin gateways of Mai-Dùn. The mercenary pointed to Caradog's forces and laughed. "Sheep to the slaughter."

The queen ignored him. She was concerned about Caradog. It consumed too much of her power to keep the king of Rinn-Campáil compliant. The tall king's usually impeccable appearance, along with his hygiene, was a quickly fading memory. He looked and smelled more like a vagrant than a king.

She wanted him broken like a stallion. Broken and compliant, he would make an excellent puppet for her to rule the south of Albu and allow her to regain her former tribe. Instead, she saw livid hate in his eyes and helplessness at his inability to change the situation.

***

Wings stretched wide to catch the warm updrafts from the earth below. The pair of eagles glided gracefully above Mai-Dùn. In the grey-blue summer sky, they soared high, calling to each other, taunting and teasing each other. The Goddess and Fate held their positions above the field.

It was not long before their play was interrupted by a smaller, although deadly, predator that swooped across their line of vision. While the eagles' flight held elegance, the hawk's movement spoke of speed and violence. Banded by white eyebrows, her red eyes showed no fear as she glared at the eagles. The shrill *kree-ah* of the hawk rose higher and higher.

"Free Caradog. He has suffered enough."

"Cease your pleadings. It is not fit for a hunter or a deity," screeched the Goddess. "Your acolyte was a narcissistic cur who thought only of himself. He deserves his lot."

Fate flapped his great wings and wheeled around the hawk in a long smooth glide as effortless as it was graceful. The cry came. "His destiny is mine. It has been decided." The long black talons that opened before the hawk's eyes were a sign Fate would brook no dissent.

***

Kartimandu and Cunobelinus ignored Caradog, turning their attention to the upcoming encounter. Nonetheless, Kartimandu sensed something awry. There was the merest hint of a boot slowly dragged on the dirt, and a weary breath exhaled. Cunobelinus would have ignored the tug on his belt had it not been followed by a sharp pain in his lower back.

Surprised, Cunobelinus swung around, lifting his club as he prepared to strike. A thin line of drool trickled from the corner of Caradog's lips, making Cunobelinus hesitate. The creeping slackness on the right side of the face of Rinn-Campáil's king looked like melting wax. His arms hung limp and useless at his side. With a twisted smile, Caradog pitched forward to lie at Kartimandu's feet. An ephemeral breath whispered, "*Striapach.*" In death, Caradog had earned his freedom.

"Shite! The bastard stabbed me!" shouted Cunobelinus holding up a hand wet with blood. The dagger remained lodged, hilt-deep, in his lower back. "Send for a healer." Irritated, he kicked Caradog's corpse several times.

"Does that make you feel better? Kicking a dead man's corpse?" The queen looked at Cunobelinus, one derisory eyebrow raised.

"If you can find a better use for the body, feel free. In the meantime, I need a healer. Then you'll know if you've also got a dead general." Cunobelinus sat down, clutched his back, and breathed heavily as the wound throbbed. "Remember, without me, you'll never take Mai-Dùn."

***

"Just like old times, Urard," Mórrígan spoke as she watched the enemy move closer to the wooden stakes that marked the distances for her archers and Dai's slingers.

"No, you are queen," responded the giant warrior. He pointedly dipped his head toward Brighid and Danu. "I have new charges to protect and will, with my life if needed." Mórrígan sighed. Urard was right. She had left the awkward, naïve young girl on the ramparts of Ráth Na Conall. She nodded her agreement to Urard and raised her bow.

"Archers, choose your targets. Slingers ready," she shouted. The Dark Huntress' arrow was first in the air and was quickly followed by a storm of wood, stone, and iron.

Battles dim the senses. Screams of pain and cries of victory plug ears as efficiently as wax. A bed of meadowsweet cannot cloak the cloying stink of blood, shite, and decay. The taste of dust, gore and bitten flesh remains long after many horns of beer. Torn and broken bodies overload the eyes of the living. The steadying grasp of a hand can help a friend or push a blade into the flesh of an opponent.

Funnelled by Mai-Dùn's maze of walls and ramparts, the first wave of attackers stumbled into concealed traps of stakes and iron thistles. Smaller holes caused them to trip and break ankles. Those behind trampled the first wave. Snares and iron-teethed traps grabbed, snapped, and maimed. Soon the rush slowed to a hesitant jog. It was then that the cauldrons of boiling water, oil, and glowing red-orange embers were upended.

Shrieks echoed off Mai-Dùn's ramparts, for there was no escape. The walls were three times the height of the tallest man. The press behind gave those at the front no path of retreat. Small wooden shields and leather armour offered little protection. Skin blistered and sloughed off. The stench of boiled and broiled flesh ascended on the ensuing warm mist. On the defences, the Mai-Dùn's garrison tied scraps of cloth around mouths and noses to stem the smell.

Like water escaping a torn pouch, the attackers burst from the narrow paths where many of their comrades had been killed and mutilated to reach open ground. They stood before the twin gates of the fort. Their exhilaration at the freedom of space and fresh, untainted air was short-lived.

Rocks, arrows, and slingshot loads launched from the stockade of Mai-Dùn flayed their flesh. A thrusting spear was a mercy to those who surmounted the ramparts with ladders and hooks. For others, their last sight was of smoke-stained cauldrons disgorged. Swollen tongues blocked screams from tortured throats.

As Cunobelinus predicted, the dead formed a fleshy ramp against Mai-Dùn's walls. "Do you intend to let Caradog's entire force die on the walls of Mai-Dùn?" asked Kartimandu. "It seems a waste. There *is* another entrance."

Cunobelinus flicked a black *creabhar* from his cheek, but not before it bit him. He scratched at the inflamed wound and cursed. The pain, however, provided a momentary distraction from the injury in his back. The healers had removed the dagger, cleaned the gash, stuffed it with bog moss, and bound it tightly. They assured him that while the stab was deep, it had not pierced any vital organs. When he looked into their eyes, he knew they lied.

He considered Kartimandu's observations. Mai-Dùn's southeastern entrance was not as well guarded but presented a similar challenge to the western gate. Torturous paths to a protected gateway. If he divided the army, they would face slings and bows as they tracked along the perimeter ditch.

His scouts, those that survived, told him of chariots that hunted like a pack of wolves, picking off the isolated and the weak. He would not… could not risk more of his mercenaries to the spinning scythes. The main Clann Ui Flaithimh army was steadily advancing. He needed to be inside Mai-Dùn within another sunset or face being the meat between two sets of jaws.

The mercenary leader grunted and called his messenger. "Set up two battalions of slingers, one on either side of the western path, to the fort. Maintain a steady barrage on the ramparts. That should keep the heads of Mai-Dùn's defenders down. I want the ramparts cleared." Cunobelinus turned to the queen. "We'll breach the walls and gates by dusk. I expect your spears to watch our backs."

Kartimandu nodded as if in agreement. She was not accustomed to taking orders, especially not from an outcast. She would take her vengeance on Cunobelinus, but for now, she needed him and his men.

CHAPTER 34

Horns blared as showers of stones rained down on Mai-Dùn's ramparts. Men and women ducked and weaved as they fell back from the walls abutting the primary defences. Some, felled by the missiles, were dragged away by friends who grasped clothes, limbs, and hair.

Within Mai-Dùn, Mórrígan and Dai sought shelter from the storm in the guard tower. Mórrígan swore at the insistent staccato of stones striking wood. Along the ramparts, others hugged the wooden stockade. Shields were raised to deflect the sharp rocks.

Even without the presence of their king, Caradog's warriors continued to attack the defences, although in a mindless, disorganised fashion. They charged forward recklessly with numbed senses and no fear in their eyes. Many were struck down by the slings of their mercenary allies.

A young woman grabbed the sharpened ends of the stockade and began to haul herself into the guard tower. She glanced at the occupants. Anguish and anger disfigured a face that was pretty beneath the blood and dirt—blue-eyed, blonde hair with thick tresses and golden skin.

Her life abruptly ended when Iasg's thrown knife punched a hole in her forehead, and Mórrígan's arrow entered her open mouth. At that range, the shaft tore out the back of her head. A hand's length of feathers remained and fluttered briefly in the wind before the body fell backwards. The rage on her lips was silenced as blood filled her throat. Another corpse joined the heap of anonymous dead.

347

"Such a waste," said Dai. Deep sadness filled his mien as he gestured to the mounds of the broken and dead who lay before the defences of Mai-Dùn.

"It looks worse than it is," said Mórrígan, somewhat unsympathetically. "Mai-Dùn's maze restricts how many they can throw at us. Likely there are only a few hundred dead and the same injured. We're still massively outnumbered." The Huntress looked directly at Dai. "These are not their best. They were sacrificed. We should prepare for what is to come."

***

Cunobelinus observed the proceedings, called his captains to him, and issued orders. Horns sounded out, and messengers ran with the new instructions. The attackers withdrew, leaving only corpses and the maimed scattered over the paths that led to the gates.

He turned to Kartimandu, "Should the Clann Ui Flaithimh army arrive before I've taken the fort, use Caradog's mindless rabble to disrupt their advance." The queen nodded but obviously had her mind on other issues. Cunobelinus growled, "Do not let me down. My iron club can smash your pretty head to a pulp."

Kartimandu's reaction was swift. Cunobelinus fell to his knees in searing pain. His head felt as if his brain had been opened up. "Do not presume that you can better me, servant. You are a well-paid mercenary and nothing more. Challenge me, and I will destroy you. I very much doubt you can match Caradog's resilience."

***

Mórrígan grudgingly conceded the tactic was working. Many small groups, each containing about a score of well-armed mercenaries, zigzagged towards the walls. Bows and slings quickly became redundant.

Battering rams thudded against the gates. Ladders slapped against the ramparts. Grappling hooks found purchase in the wooden stockade. The fence held, but minor skirmishes broke out along its length, where mercenaries scaled and scrambled over its jagged points.

Many were summarily dealt with as Mórrígan's long knives slashed throats and punched holes in lightly armoured chests. In Urard's hands, Breith swatted and dismembered with contemptuous ease. Iasg's throwing knives were long gone, and she fought alongside Urard with a pair of throwing axes.

Dai, through ragged breaths, complained of burning arm muscles and a lack of fitness. The king was modest. Age had slowed him down, but experience more than adequately compensated. Flourishes with his longsword cut down opponents like a scythe in a harvest corn field.

A lull in the battle turned Mórrígan's attention to Brighid and Danu. Backs to the stockade and wedged into adjacent corners of the guard post, the twins were wide-eyed with fear. They were also childishly excited by the events surrounding them. Faced with the prospect of the gates being overrun, Mórrígan turned to Urard.

"Take my daughters, Iasg, and a hundred men and fall back to the Great Hall. It's a solid, defensible building." Urard opened his mouth to protest, but the queen held up her hand. "Also, take the riders you came with. Fifty will guard my daughters with their lives if needed. The remainder's task will be to counter incursions. My band will fight alongside Dai's men on the ramparts until that becomes untenable."

"As you wish." Urard was unhappy at leaving the fight for the ramparts, but his orders from Conall were to find Brighid and Danu and keep them safe. He was not about to defy both the king and queen.

"We'll miss his axe," remarked Dai as Urard and Iasg departed with their charges.

"Better that than my daughters' blood painting the walls of this post," snapped Mórrígan.

Dai raised his hands, "I have no quarrel with your judgment. I have grown fond of Brighid and Danu. Perhaps, I could persuade you and your handfast partner to stay at Mai-Dùn when this is over?"

Mórrígan smiled, but there was sadness in her eyes. "Perhaps." Their wishful musings were interrupted by a roar and fresh waves of the unwashed. Both turned to face their attackers.

***

Cunobelinus was frustrated... and in considerable pain. The mercenaries' general stood on the far end of the ramparts that abutted the main walls of Mai-Dùn. He clutched his side while roaring commands and directing his fighters to weak points on the walls. Still, Cunobelinus could not press his advantage home despite his numerical advantage.

The bastard defenders were a solid line along the short span of the western ramparts. Both sides were bloodied, but his men had taken more damage and left more bodies on the blood-engorged dirt. Cunobelinus watched uneasily as dusk's red and grey hues crept closer. He knew time was short.

With one dark eye, the mercenary watched his warriors. His "army" was a jigsaw puzzle with a myriad ill-fitting pieces. Each bit was unique, led by men and women with conflicting talents. They had widely ranging capacities to think beyond satisfying their immediate needs. They were specialists in smash, rape, and run, not war or campaigns. It was by force of will and brute strength that Cunobelinus held their loyalty, but that lessened with each failed assault.

Still, Kartimandu and her elite force were of more concern. He had little doubt that the queen would betray him. It was her nature, and she could not resist the compulsion. The question was, when? Their forces were roughly matched. The queen had her elite guard and control of what remained of Caradog's army. Cunobelinus held the mercenaries.

Even with the attacks on Mai-Dùn, he had lost a relatively minor portion of his original force. He just had not been able to overcome the fort's defences. Cunobelinus exhorted and cajoled his army into a final assault for the day. Perhaps, this time, they could push the defenders from their redoubt.

***

The mercenary leader never knew how close he came to victory. As his primary force attacked the gates and western walls of Mai-Dùn, several enterprising warbands overwhelmed the widely dispersed defenders on the northern and southern-facing ramparts. One band was summarily executed by Urard's riders, who quickly cantered into their midst. Knocked aside by broad-shouldered horses, the mercenaries fell victim to swinging axes and slashing swords.

Nevertheless, several bands dropped into the pens holding those intoxicated with Kartimandu's insidious powers. They carved a bloody furrow through the mentally disturbed but unarmed civilians, finally bursting through the fencing that constrained them.

The pen's guards, surprised by the mercenaries and rush of men, women, and children escaping the corrals, hesitated and fell to enemy blades. Minds controlled by Kartimandu proved merciless. With teeth and bare hands, they strangled, bit, scratched and ripped the throats and eyes of the guards, many of whom were kin.

Urard watched as the tide of the demented and the avaricious swarmed towards the Great Hall. He ushered Iasg and the twins inside. "Lock the doors. You don't open for anyone but me or the queen." Ten were selected to guard the doors. "You will die before you let anyone enter the Hall," Urard instructed. None protested.

He turned to his riders. "Kill the mercenaries. Try not to kill the residents, but don't take chances." Finally, Urard issued his orders to the remaining members of his squad—about two score men and women. "Two rows. Form a semi-circle at the front of the Great Hall. Kill all who attempt to pass."

Urard's orders had an immediate if unexpected, impact on the mercenaries. Seeing Clann Ui Flaithimh warriors move to protect the Great Hall, their leaders reasonably if incorrectly, assumed the building was the repository of Mai-Dùn's wealth. Therefore, with a flurry of shouted commands, they gathered and rushed towards it. "Eejits!" growled Urard. "*Fág an Bealach!*" With a roar of curses and battle cries, Urard's shield-wall strode to meet the mercenaries.

Unaccustomed to fighting as a team, the outlaws focused on single opponents only to find arms chopped off, thighs slashed open, and sides pierced by their target's immediate neighbours. The attackers' leaders met their end with ruthless efficiency as Urard's axe swung. Sharper than any other blade and powered by Urard's strong arm muscles, Breith cut through neck flesh, sinew, and bone with contemptuous ease. Two heads flew backwards, eyes blinking in surprise, while the corpses fell forward.

Panic took hold of the outcasts. They turned, scattered, and hoped to escape. Caught between Urard's shields, fully intent on making certain no one survived, and the cavalry approaching their rear, some chose to fight, and others ran. A small group dropped their weapons and fell to their knees, hoping for mercy. Compassion was not in Urard's mind. In the eyes of the Law, the mercenaries were little more than rabid dogs. To a man and woman, they were put down.

Dai appraised the destruction as the skirmish at the Great Hall drew to a bloody end. He cursed Kartimandu and groaned in sorrow at the bodies of his people scattered around the fort. A clack and thud against the stockade drew his attention to the onslaught. In the dimming light of dusk, a shadow hurled itself over the fence, swinging a club wildly. More by Serendipity, the weapon caught Dai a glancing blow to the base of his skull.

The king slumped to the floor. A trickle of blood seeped from his ears and nose. "No!" screamed Mórrígan. Pivoting, she slashed the assailant's throat to the bone. The attacker gurgled, and his hands frantically tried to stem gouts of blood. In a fit of anger, Mórrígan slashed again. The warrior's head flopped against his back, held only by a few strings of muscle. She seized his legs and tipped him over the wooden fence.

A single horn blown ended the battle. The mercenaries withdrew, spitting bloody saliva and curses at Mai-Dùn's defenders. In the guard post, Mórrígan knelt beside the pale king and sobbed.

***

Anger and wariness charged the atmosphere in Kartimandu's pavilion. The queen, seething at what she perceived as Cunobelinus' inadequate leadership, threatened to replace him with one of his captains. Yet, none wanted the position or intended to accede to her wishes. They were veterans who did not trust nobles of any shade or colour and had been hand-picked by Cunobelinus.

Sensing their rebellion, Kartimandu fought to bring her wrath under control. The livid scar on her cheek glowed starkly white against the green sigils, accurately indicating her demeanour. She addressed Cunobelinus. "Having failed to take Mai-Dùn, what is your plan?" Truthfully, Cunobelinus' concern was not Mai-Dùn but the armies of Clann Ui Flaithimh. His last scouts had not returned. Hence, he played for time.

"What's *your* knowledge of the army of Conall? How close are they?"

Kartimandu flinched. The throbbing, dull ache in her head was a clear sign that the Sídhe neared. She had seen the passing of Samhain, Imbolg, and Bealtaine without interference from the Sídhe. Now her hope rested on a demi-goddess such as Mongfhionn growing bored and seeking entertainment elsewhere. Her wish was in vain.

In recent days Kartimandu experienced fierce spikes of unbearable pain as the Sídhe rent asunder the curtains of shade protecting her mind. Kartimandu's nights, and sometimes days, were filled with terrible visions of a painful demise. It did not help that Mórrígan's powers had strengthened.

Still, Kartimandu's will remained exceptionally strong. She gathered her thoughts, and once more under control, she rounded on Cunobelinus. Holding his stare with unflinching green eyes, she said, "Clann Ui Flaithimh's army draws closer. That is what I know. What I do *not* know is your plan of attack."

Cunobelinus spat on the dirt floor. The saliva was speckled with blood. "My plan? I plan to survive. You'll place Caradog's remaining warriors under my command. You can retain your guard, but I'll decide where they fight." Allowing no time for a rejoinder, the mercenary leader spun on his heels and marched from the tent. He had little confidence that the queen would comply.

***

The camp was unnaturally quiet. Weapons, armour, chariots, and horses were muffled. No fires gave away their presence. Men stifled coughs and sneezes and spoke in hushed tones. In the half-light and mists of pre-dawn, the army moved purposefully, silently, into position and waited.

The sky accommodated Conall's strategy. The sun glided up through the thick band of clouds that hugged the horizon, bathing the land in pastel shades of pink, orange and yellow. Then, having reached the boundary of the cloud, it seemed to pause for dramatic effect before bursting onto the stage. Rays of copper and gold flooded the land around Mai-Dùn. The beauty was glorious and beguiling.

***

During the night, some mercenary bands decided there was no profit to be made in the venture and slipped away. It irritated Cunobelinus, and should he survive, he would take revenge on the cowards. Still, his combined forces at least matched the numbers of the foe he faced. If he were victorious, the gold and grain of Mai-Dùn would be worth the blood about to be spilt.

Now the mercenary leader stood beside Kartimandu. From their vantage point, they surveyed the enemy's entire army. "Shite! The Hag ram a stake up my arse and get it over with!" declared Cunobelinus.

Clann Ui Flaithimh's army stood no more than five hundred paces distant. Bright gold, black and red banners were held aloft. The riot of colour was accentuated by the brightly dyed pants many of the fighters wore. The two Cinn Péinteáilte divisions wore nothing save the dark designs painted and tattooed on their pale skins.

Conall sat on his black horse. The gold and silver helmet glittered, and the black plumes falling from its raven crest flared in a slight morning breeze. On either side of Conall were arrayed his commanders.

Behind him, the shield-wall of two thousand stood in two rows; each spaced an arm's length apart. Behind the shields, Cuán's thousand

Cróeb Ruad jostled good-naturedly yet very much alert for the command to attack. To their rear, the horses and chariots waited.

On Conall's right, Brandubh and Mòrag's Ravens stood in two ranks of five hundred. Slings and bows were taken from pouches and sheaths; stones were placed, and arrows nocked. On Conall's left, Carmag's Forest People howled and raised axes, clubs, and spears. Soon the remainder of Clann Ui Flaithimh took up the refrain.

Weapons clashed against shields, and feet stomped on the grass and dirt. The sound was ferocious. In Mai-Dùn's entrance guard post, Mórrígan smiled bitterly and issued orders to be ready for battle.

A long, primal howl rent the silence of the early morning. It was quickly echoed by an ululating yowl from the walls of Mai-Dùn. Both calls hung in the sky so all could experience the dread they embodied. A flock of ravens rose from the cover of the grassy slopes to add their hoarse *kraa kraa*. Warriors on both sides trembled.

A commotion in Clann Ui Flaithimh's ranks drew Cunobelinus' attention to a grey-cloaked figure sitting astride a black horse. The horse cantered alongside Conall and halted. The king inclined his head, and a hundred men and women were dragged forward. Naked, with hands bound behind their backs, they were kicked, pushed, and pulled until they stood in clear view of Kartimandu's patchwork army.

Mongfhionn dismounted, and her cloak fell to the ground. She stood before the unhappy group, sheathed in golden sunlight. Curling sigils shimmered over the Sídhe's body. In her hands, two cruelly curved bronze knives reflected the sun. It had been a long time since Mongfhionn's blades tasted blood.

The first group to be sacrificed were unfortunate. Their agony was heightened with Mongfhionn's unpractised and hesitant slashes. However, by the time the Sídhe reached the last of the hundred, she eviscerated bellies and slashed throats with merciless efficiency. The host of Clann Ui Flaithimh shuddered, thankful she was on their side.

Mongfhionn turned to face the enemy, her milk-white body

splattered with gore and blood. With arms held high, she howled and made two final slashes in the air. Standing on the limestone outcrop before Mai-Dùn, Kartimandu cried out. Her hands went to her throat and came away stained with blood from two thin, shallow cuts.

Alongside the queen, Cunobelinus cursed. The message was unmistakable. No quarter would be given.

***

Behind the ranks of Conall's army, the sound of horns and the thumping rhythm of bodhráns set hearts racing. As one, the army marched forward. Stunned by the show of strength and a nightmarish fear of ancient prophecies, Kartimandu found no solace in the might of her army.

Thus, the queen acted no differently than any self-respecting tyrant. She leapt into her chariot and fled south towards the coast, accompanied by her thousand-strong guard. Unsurprised, Cunobelinus cursed the receding back of Kartimandu. He turned to his captains.

"We need an escape route from this trap. Concentrate your attack on the southern wing of the Clann Uí Flaithimh." The warband leaders grunted their sullen acceptance. "The assholes from Rinn-Campáil will be our diversion. They will assault the centre of Conall's formation.

"They'll be slaughtered, but they're disposable. The diversion and our numbers should allow us to break through. Once through, we'll head for the coast. I doubt the king of Clann Uí Flaithimh will be interested in chasing down a thousand scattered warbands."

Cunobelinus' plan was reasonable. Many would die, but more would survive to kill and plunder another day. However, even sensible strategies change once spoken, rarely for the better. Cunobelinus committed a fatal error. He overlooked that the men and women of Rinn-Campáil remained in the Kartimandu's thrall. Mid-flight and with a contemptuous laugh, the queen severed the gossamers binding the minds of Rinn-Campáil's men and women to her.

Chaos immediately descended. Dazed Rinn-Campáil fighters recovered their sensibilities and realised they were caught between two armies.

A few prescient leaders quickly grasped the situation. They judged that the more significant threat was the army of Clann Uí Flaithimh. Thus, with a pragmatism based on aiding the likely winner, the Rinn-Campáil warriors turned on their former "allies".

Conall shook his head at the turn of events and signalled for the advance to halt. Beside him, a bemused Fearghal said, "So, do we pick a side or just let them kill each other and fight who's left?" Conall rubbed the stubble on his chin. He had two problems. First, Kartimandu had fled the field and was heading south. Second, he needed to know if Mórrígan, Brighid, and Danu were safe inside Mai-Dùn.

As if reading his thoughts, Fearghal said, "I'll pursue Kartimandu. I'll take the cavalry, Gràinne's chariots, and half of Cuán's men. That fuath has a reckoning to face. You do what's best here." Conall nodded in assent.

At the thump and lurch of her chariot, Gràinne reached for her longsword, stopping only when Fearghal growled, "Can you drive this thing?" She was momentarily speechless, distracted by the veteran's hard-muscled and agreeably hairy chest.

"Well?" Fearghal's gruff voice brought her back to reality. She nodded briskly. Fearghal stared at the chariot's driver, and he got the message. Somewhat relieved, he handed the reins to Gràinne and leapt from the cret.

"What are you waiting for?" Fearghal pointed south, where Kartimandu was little more than a smudge on the horizon. "We've a queen to kill." Gràinne smiled, screamed orders to the rest of her chariots, and they hurtled across grain fields.

To their left, Mongfhionn and Nikandros commanded Clann Uí Flaithimh's cavalry. The Spartan was in a foul mood, his bronze armour glinting and red plumes flaring. Despite lengthy pleadings and entreaties, his friend, Íar, had refused to take charge of the cavalry. Nikandros felt betrayed, and he knew Conall was furious. To the rear, Lonán Ó Néill led the Cróeb Ruad contingent at a fast jog.

Conall called Brandubh and Mòrag to his side. The prince of the Ravens was usually comfortable in Conall's presence. However, today and recently, he had felt uneasy, especially when his sister accompanied him. Mòrag had done little to discourage the rumours and gossip that strongly suggested that Conall was the father of her newborn son. For his part, Conall seemed embarrassed by the overt expression of affection that Mòrag thrust upon him.

"Take your Ravens and archers to within striking range of the mercenaries. That would be a good location." Conall pointed to a grassy mound to the north of the fight. "Use your slings and bows to weaken the bastards." Brandubh smiled in agreement as Conall added, "I'll send the remainder of Cuán's group to protect your flanks."

Mòrag stepped a pace closer and said, "Thanks." With obvious deliberation, she adjusted the leather cross-straps that restrained her breasts before turning around to accompany her brother. Conall rubbed his forehead, frowning. Perhaps Brandubh and he could encourage Mòrag to return to her tribe in northern Albu. *Some hope.*

***

Kartimandu was not a tactician. That she could see the coastline to her right *and* left should have signalled the trap into which she guided her warriors. Yet all she wanted was to put distance between her and those following.

Thus, the queen was focused on the well-kept and faster road she travelled. It was a route frequently used by tin traders. At low tide, they would transport ingots on pack animals to the island that sat offshore and thence onto the ships anchored in the deeper waters. Waves breaking on a pristine, white-sand shore finally alerted Kartimandu to the danger.

The queen screamed in rage. She also suffered an attack of well-founded panic. On two sides, the coastlines gradually narrowed until they met to form the blunt apex of the promontory. Fearghal's forces were quickly blocking any potential retreat to the north. As she frantically looked for an escape route, Kartimandu hissed orders to her guard. They were to defend and protect their queen to the death.

To Fearghal's puzzlement, Gràinne pulled up their chariot well short of the line of spears that faced them. Mongfhionn, Nikandros, and Lonán came alongside. "Why have we stopped?"

"I've fought Kartimandu's elite before," answered Gràinne, "They'll nae give in. They'll fight to the last man." She pointed to the hedge of spears. "The horses will not break through the spears. They will turn around. It's their nature."

"Javelins," said Nikandros.

"Doesn't seem quite fair," responded Lonán. "No glory in killing from a distance."

"They know of our javelins," said Gràinne, "They'll use their shields better this time. At best, we'll kill or injure one or two hundred."

Fearghal scratched his damp head. The gentle summer breeze that circled his head was a pleasant relief from his sweat-soaked helmet. "Javelins," he said to Nikandros. "If we only kill a hundred, it's still less to fight." The Spartan nodded, mounted his horse, and trotted to the cavalry. With a roar, the riders galloped, red foxtails swinging from helmets towards Kartimandu's defensive lines.

"I think it's time we stretched our legs," said Fearghal, grinning.

Lonán laughed. "Torcán is going to be pissed he missed this fight." Shouted orders to the waiting Cróeb Ruad were followed by a cry of "*Cróeb Ruad, go Brách!*" The shields, with Fearghal, Gràinne, Lonán, and the Sídhe at their head, jogged and then charged the enemy.

As Gràinne predicted, Nikandros' riders caused relatively minor damage to Kartimandu's elite. The horses swerved away from the spiky row of spears, coming to a halt a score paces from the line. Fearghal's command was in full voice fifty paces short of their enemy's lines. Weapons were raised above a mix of burnt and bronzed shoulders.

As they swept past the cavalry, Nikandros dismounted and grabbed his doru. *I'm not going to miss this.* The black-shafted spear felt good in his calloused hands as he ran to join the attack. Not a people to forego a good fight, the rest of the cavalry alighted and entered the fray with their long-bladed swords and long-handled axes.

Spears, swords, and axes carved bloody gashes in unarmoured flesh. Sandy ground quickly became a morass of gore, shite, and guts. Shields battered torsos and broke ribs. Adversaries clashed against each other with unfettered ferocity. The roars of frenzied fighters became grunts as men and women fought face-to-face.

Kartimandu's elite was stubbornly unyielding. Blindly loyal to the queen, they fought a senseless and futile battle. Only those without the ability to hold a sword or spear ceased fighting. Pride would not let these warriors beg. With anguish in their eyes, the mortally injured and crippled waited for a mercy blade.

***

Kartimandu scrambled down the steep dunes bordering the coast-line. Her feet plunged calf-deep into the soft sand, slowing her flight. Breathless, she finally reached the edge of the shifting sands. Momentum drove her onto the stone and pebble ribbon between the dune and beach. The queen cursed loudly as she stubbed toes and cracked nails.

Close behind, jogged Fearghal, Gràinne, and Mongfhionn. Kartimandu swore. Exhausted in the dash for her life, she sensed that her pursuers were not extending themselves. They breathed hard, but un-like her, not painfully so. She felt their steady pulse rate as blood pumped through demanding muscle. Kartimandu ran, but to where and for what purpose?

The hopelessness of her predicament ended with a sharp pain in her back, and she fell to the sand. From the waist down, her body was numb, unresponsive to her demands to rise and flee. A javelin thrown by Fearghal lodged in her lower back, severing the queen's spine. Ironically, the paralysis negated the usual impact of iron on her body. She spat sand from her mouth and waited. It was not long before three shadows stood over her.

"Do it," snarled Kartimandu. "I'll not beg."

"And I'll show no mercy," spat Fearghal.

A tattooed arm raised a longsword. The searing pain lasted a brief moment. When the sword lifted, blood dripped from its point onto the sand. Kartimandu's severed head lay beside her body. "Burn the body and head… separately," commanded Mongfhionn. "There can be no pity. We can leave her no opportunity for rebirth."

***

Ambition had led Cunobelinus into a cul-de-sac of diminishing returns. He had few options which would not result in his death. The bitseach queen of Clann Ui Flaithimh and her band of killers had retaken the ramparts that jutted from the main walls of Mai-Dùn.

Systematically and with appalling accuracy, they picked off the remaining mercenary leaders. To his north, the slingers and archers of Clann Ui Flaithimh were sending a hail of rock and iron into his midst. That they were also killing or injuring the Rinn-Campáil fighters caught at the interface of the two combatants did not appear to deter them.

The mercenary leader swung his club two-handed, crushing another head. Pink-grey brain matter oozed from the cracked skull. He breathed slowly and painfully because he had taken several blows to his side, causing his wound to bleed. Wrapped around his lower back, the bandage had a growing crimson stain. Ironically, he vanquished the Rinn-Campáil traitors. Any who survived scattered, hoping to avoid both mercenaries and Clann Ui Flaithimh.

Two-thirds of Cunobelinus' mercenaries were in good fighting order. Still, he was in a battle that his head and heart told him he could not win. Furthermore, there was no sign from Clann Ui Flaithimh that they would countenance his surrender. As he looked west, he noted grimly that Conall, having let Caradog's men cause as much damage as possible, had resumed his march towards him. These were men and women with fresh arms and bodies. *What hope do I have?*

Brandubh commanded the Ravens to cease slings and take up spears and shields. With a shout, he and Mòrag led the charge against the mercenaries' northern flank. Simultaneously, Carmag lifted his hammer in the air. Horns blasted out as the Forest People and Ravens flowed towards Cunobelinus' southern flank. In the centre, Conall's shield-wall, supported by Cuán's Cróeb Ruad, picked up the pace and jogged towards Cunobelinus.

Worn out by days of constant fighting and assailed on all flanks, the mercenaries were no match for the approaching enemy. They could put up little resistance to Conall's revenge-seeking attackers. The skirmish was quick and brutal. The stench of gore, piss and shite filled the air.

Heads and limbs cleaved from warm bodies lay in small heaps across the battlefield—the last stand of comrades. Shouts and war cries were replaced by the injured's whimpering and the grunts of men and women as they laboured to finish the fight.

With a roar of defiance, Cunobelinus rallied his warbands in one final attempt to break free of the snare. His boldness was short-lived. The mercenary leader's face met the blunt end of Carmag's hammer. At that moment, Cunobelinus' head became a bloody pulp. His arms flailed around before his body slumped to join the sludge of battle debris.

The strife over Mai-Dùn and its riches were finished. It was time to strip the enemies' bodies of anything of value, mete out justice, and burn the dead. For Conall, the challenge was separating punishment from vengeance.

CHAPTER 35

405 B.C.—Mai-Dùn—Autumn

To the people's relief, the siege of Mai-Dùn was lifted. Rousing cheers and prayers of the victors flowed to a Goddess basking in her Hand's and Huntress' victory. Yet, the fervent joy clashed with cries for retribution and vengeance.

After several days of discussion between Conall, Crum, Fearghal, Mórrígan and the Sídhe, one in ten mercenaries was selected by ballot. Along the ramparts, hundreds of heads were mounted on spears. Their vacant eyes gazed across golden corn fields to others staked beyond the fort and left to the wolves and ravens.

The fortunate not to be selected for execution were given a choice, slavery or death. About half chose death. For several sunsets, the axes of Clann Ui Flaithimh fell on naked necks and rose, dripping blood. Again, the earth drank its fill of blood.

Yet Conall's victory was tinged with sadness. Surrounded by family, close friends, and even several druids, Mai-Dùn's king lay on his bed, hovering between life and death. No doubt the king would pass away; the question was when. Brighid and Danu were inconsolable as they sobbed beside Dai's cot. They had found a Grand-da, only for him to leave them.

Mórrígan blinked away tears for a man she had known less than the cycle of the moon. Yet she had grown to respect and love him as a king... and a father. A cough drew everyone's attention to Dai. A weak hand signalled Mórrígan to come closer. She bent her head to hear the king's softly spoken words.

"Tell them to stop mourning. I got what I yearned for, a hero's death. The Goddess is good." Mórrígan bit her lip and dipped her head. Dai's hand gripped her wrist. "Would you have stayed?"

The queen of Clann Ui Flaithimh smiled wistfully. "Yes. Yes, I would." She looked up. Conall watched his queen with sadness and regret. The bloody path to vengeance again opened as the road to redemption receded. Mórrígan heard the mournful wailing of the bean sídhe and glanced down. Dai of Mai-Dùn journeyed to Mag Mell.

***

Conall sat on the cliff top overlooking the Muir nIocht. It was a pleasant day. He enjoyed the soothing repetition of waves crashing on the beach and the tang of salt and sea in the air. Beside him, Toirneach munched on spiky grass and swatted flies with his long black tail. A pair of wolfhounds chased rabbits through the maze of dunes that bordered the bluff.

A second horse nickered, and a soft thud on the packed sand and grass signalled its rider had dismounted.

"You came," said Conall.

"You asked," responded Íar.

"You do little that I ask." Unlike the quiet that previously the two friends had shared with comfort, the silence was strained,

"I'm unsure."

"I'm your friend, but firstly, your king. Your oath is to me... to the clann."

Conall pointed to the headland and the ships and queues of people and beasts waiting to embark. "It will be Bealtaine before all depart. If you're unsure of your loyalties and duties by then, you will be a danger to me... the people... and your friends. You will *not* be welcome."

The second horse squealed with displeasure at being interrupted in its conversation with Toirneach but did Íar's bidding. It nuzzled the tall warrior as if to say, "All will be well." Íar swung a leg over the horse's back and settled his arse on the thick diallait. *I hope so.*

Conall turned to watch Íar ride away. "I hope so too, friend."

***

In the harbour, beyond the camp, ships bobbed on a green-grey sea, awaiting their cargo. The sun was intense, and the sky a soft, powder blue. The crowds parted as Mórrígan and Conall strolled through the massive coastal encampment. Mórrígan paused and put a steadying hand on Conall's arm.

"Wait for me. This will not take long."

Caught off balance, Conall nodded and watched as Mórrígan walked away. Her gait and bearing had changed to that of a predatory cat. She was naked apart from the curling designs that almost entirely covered her lithe, but by no means skinny body. A cold finger traced Conall's spine. *Shite!* Mórrígan's path was disconcerting.

The Dark Huntress' prey stood several hundred paces away, chatting animatedly with friends and kin. As was the custom of the Cinn Péinteáilte, all were naked save for a loincloth. Some had foregone even that small token of modesty in the warm sun. Skin glistened with a fine coating of sweat, and previously reddish tones were changing to pleasing golden or dark tans. Brandubh and his sister were a striking couple, well-loved by the Ravens and admired by the greater Clann Ui Flaithimh.

Acknowledging Mórrígan's presence, Brandubh turned to greet her with his usual broad smile and welcoming embrace. Mòrag bit her lip and held her baby closer to milk-laden breasts as if for protection. The child did not appear to object to being near to both warmth and food.

Mórrígan slipped from Brandubh's hug and took several steps towards Mòrag. The crowd shrank back. Mòrag stood a head taller than Mórrígan and was voluptuous without being fat. Layers of firm muscle were the foundation for soft curves. She was every inch a warrior.

Yet, of the two, it was Mòrag who felt intimidated on this day. She watched as Mórrígan smiled and held out her arms. The request was apparent and could not be refused. With a brief cry of annoyance, the child was passed over. "A beautiful and healthy baby, Mòrag," said Mórrígan.

"What is his name?"

Someone exclaimed, "*The Hag!*" The crowd edged back further.

With a nervous lick of her lips, Mòrag answered. "Barra… Barra Mac Conall."

Mórrígan lips lifted at the edges. It was an unnerving smile; her tattoos seemed to flow around and shroud the baby. "A strong name. No doubt he will be a great leader… like his father." She turned to Brandubh, who, along with Conall, stood nearby and handed the child into his arms.

The movement was swift. In the briefest of moments, Mórrígan closed the gap between her and Mòrag. Few witnessed, but all heard the loud slaps on Mòrag's face—one on each cheek. The princess was stunned and unprepared for the punch to her belly that followed. She fell to her knees, gasping for breath, only to find her long hair grasped tightly and her head snapped back to expose her throat. Mòrag heard the swish of a blade drawn from a sheath and the cold touch of steel on her neck.

"The Hag, Mórrígan. No!" Conall moved towards his queen. A glare from emerald eyes so deep as to appear black stopped him.

Mórrígan bent down, and her lips touched Mòrag's ear. "Open your legs for others if you wish, *striapach*. Open them for *my* partner again; this blade will remove your head from your shoulders. Have I made myself clear?"

"Yes, my Queen." Mòrag's voice was faint but distinct. Beads of sweat trickled down her skin.

"Stand." As Mòrag raised herself up, the queen turned to face Brandubh. "The child should be with his mother. Return him to your sister." The relief on Conall and Brandubh's faces was palpable. Turning to the hushed crowd, Mórrígan called out, "Barra Mac Conall is as my son. He, *and* his mother, are welcome in my home and will be treated respectfully among Clann Ui Flaithimh."

She added in a more ominous tone, "From this day, there will be no more talk of this."

At the edge of the crowd, Fearghal turned to Mongfhionn.

Neamhain suckled happily at the Sídhe's breast. "Sounds very like something you would have said."

The Sídhe smiled. "Yes, it does, doesn't it?"

***

Marcus Fabius Ambustus, Pontifex of Rome, was purple with rage. Now fifty-eight summers old, he had been informed Conall Mac Gabhann and Clann Ui Flaithimh had started the sea journey to the shores of Gaul.

Worse, it had transpired that Quintus, his eldest son, had contracted with the pirate Orestes to kidnap the daughters of the barbarian king. With some justification, Marcus screamed at a shocked Quintus.

"Fool! You have given the barbarian more credibility than he deserves. Worse, word has reached Rome of how this 'brave' barbarian rescued his daughters and slaughtered the pirates. Many in Rome judge him a hero for ridding the Great Sea of its worst menace. Our house is tainted with your incompetence."

In the antechamber to Marcus' private suite, Gaius Aurelius Atella waited. A smirk played on his tanned face. Typically, Gaius took little pleasure in the sufferings of others. Still, he was willing to make an exception for Marcus and his sons.

The raised voices within Marcus' chambers left little doubt about his anger and the subject of that passion. Finally, there came the shout that Gaius had been expecting. "Send that bastard, Gaius, in."

Iron-nailed soles clacked crisply and confidently as Gaius traversed the smooth stone floors of the outer chamber and entered Marcus' room. He ignored the scowls of the Ambustus brothers and Quintus' simmering rage. Coming to a halt several paces before Marcus, Gaius slapped a hand across his breastplate and bowed. Though not as obsequiously as Marcus would have preferred. Gaius knew it would irritate the older Roman. Although his actions may have been justified, hubris was, to some, a failing of the young man.

"What news have you of the barbarian?"

Gaius knew that Marcus was well-informed. Thus, there was little point in being evasive. "Conall's forces and followers have begun to land in northern Gaul. By late spring of next year, they will be fully transported. His army is about five thousand. Conall also lists several thousand Picti among his troops and at least one thousand of Ériu's famed Cróeb Ruad.

"His cavalry numbers over one thousand. He has archers. A group of twenty druids, as equally comfortable with a sword as their chanting, accompany him. Also, one, Mongfhionn, the Sídhe, who I believe you and your sons have met before, accompanies him.

"Mórrígan, his partner, also known as the Dark Huntress, is by his side. They have at least ten thousand followers. Many are artisans and craftsmen. From a small band of farmers, Conall has welded an army and birthed a tribe... Clann Ui Flaithimh."

Gaius halted at the explosive grunt from Marcus. "Anything else?" Marcus asked, unable to resist sarcasm and irritated by Gaius's obvious admiration for the barbarian king. The Pontifex would have liked to dismiss Gaius' report as wild speculation. Unfortunately, his informants confirmed Gaius' words.

He glanced from Gaius to his sons. Bile rose up, burning his gullet. His sons were no match in battle or politics for the soldier who stood before them. For that alone, he hated Gaius. Marcus would have embraced Gaius as a son at one time, but that galley had long sailed.

"Take your bastard troops and travel to meet this barbarian. You will take gold and letters of promise with you. Get to know him. Assess his forces. Bribe him and his leaders where possible. Corrupt him. Assassinate him. Send envoys to the barbarian tribes to alert them to this invasion of their lands and the rewards for bringing me his head." Marcus leaned forward. "Stop him before he reaches Rome."

Gaius looked with piercing blue eyes into Marcus' bloodshot, red-rimmed eyes. He considered using the dagger that hung from his belt for a moment. There was no doubt in his mind that he could kill Marcus and his sons. Instead, he nodded his assent, took several steps backwards, turned and strode to the door.

THE END

BACKGROUND

In Conall's time of 400 B.C., the distance from Rome (and Greece) was approximately correlated with an increasing oral tradition and few written records. This is especially the case for the Celts generally, and the Gaels (Irish, Scottish, and Manx) and Brythonic Celts (Welsh, Cornish, and Bretons) in particular. Hence, there is a high reliance on archaeology.

Yet, the archaeological record, although fascinating, is open to disagreement in interpretation. Thus, authors can slip through the chinks in history and pose "maybe" or "what if?" questions and flesh out the bones of the actors.

The Conall series is based on an era where the boundaries of myth, legend, and reality are blurred. Were the Aes Sídhe truly demi-goddesses, or were they people who just had an excellent grasp of nature and how the mind works?

Conall III: The Sisters sees the entry of Kartimandu, Queen of the Aos na h-Àirde (The People of the Heights). The character is based loosely on Cartimandua, queen of the Brigantes, who appeared later in history and was famous for her dealings with the Romans. Cartimandua's principal forts were at Almondbury (*Dùn Caen*) and Stanwick (*An Balla Leac*). Since names are often recycled over and within generations, I have little guilt in proposing a similarly named queen at an earlier age.

Giving Kartimandu's nature a mystical twist was irresistible as a counterbalance to the Sídhe. Also, to some extent Mórrígan, whose powers are developing. Hence, Kartimandu became a *"fuath"*. Traditionally, the fuath is a malevolent, highland water spirit inhabiting the sea, rivers, freshwater, or sea lochs.

***

A word on the society of the Gaels. "A place for everyone and everyone in their place" aptly sums up Ancient Gaelic culture. The foundation was the Brehon Laws or *'Fénechas'*, a system of law and jurisprudence that predated all similar European legal systems and was written in the people's language. In contrast, Anglo-Saxon laws were written in Latin or Norman-French.

The Fénechas emanated from the wisest heads of the nation, the Brehons. They were obeyed and venerated without prescription or coercion. This was primarily due to the Laws being widely seen as designed to promote and secure the nation's well-being.

The Gaelic tribal system had three divisions: *clann*, *sept*, and *fine*. The clann was composed of a number of septs, and each sept was formed of multiple of fines. Society was divided into six classes: kings of various levels from Rí of a single tuath or district to Ard-Righ or High King. The office of the Rí at any level was always elective; professionals; flatha or nobility; freemen possessing property; freemen possessing no or little property; and the fuidhir—the non-free (slaves). The complex political, social, and military system was based on the possession of wealth. Land, cattle, and crops were highly valued.

Punishments for criminal and civil crimes were primarily based on a system of fines and reparations. The *"éiric"* was defined as the fine for separating the body from the soul, whether murder or manslaughter. In the case of particularly heinous crimes, a criminal could be expelled from the tribe or clann and its territory.

The person became an outlaw or outcast without rights or protection under the Law. If he (or she) remained within the tribe's lands, anyone might kill him (or her) as a wild beast or a mad dog. The Brehons retained the right to execute a wilful murderer who was considered to have lost his soul and body. Slavery was deemed a reasonable punishment for criminals guilty of capital offences but whose lives were to be spared.

***

The story of Fin Cop (*An Cnoc*), where I reunited Mórrígan with her daughters, is a tragedy and mystery based on a recorded event.

The massacre threw a spanner into the works of those who believed that Iron Age Britain was a peaceful, agrarian society. The interpretation that the numerous hillforts of Britain were farming settlements or status symbols also took a hit.

According to archaeological records, around 400 B.C., the high-status hillfort of Fin Cop, a relatively new construction in the southern Pennines, witnessed the slaughter of women, teenagers, children, and babies, some unborn.

Hundreds were stabbed, strangled, stripped, and tossed into the fort's perimeter ditch. The attackers then collapsed the fort's 13-ft high limestone wall on top of the bodies. There are many theories about the disappearance of Fin Cop's men, but no definitive explanation.

***

Stone circles or henges are a fascinating topic. *Dr Aubrey Burl's gazetteer* lists 1,303 stone circles in Britain, Ireland, and Brittany. The majority of these are found in Scotland (508 sites), England (316), Ireland (187), Northern Ireland (156), Wales (81), Brittany (49), and the Channel Isles (6).

The stone circle where Drostan and Votod fought is based on an area site in *Balfarg, Scotland*. It is one of a complex of related sites associated with ritual and burial from 4000 B.C. to 1500 B.C. Two concentric stone circles existed on the site, and the henge was built within a 200-ft. circular ditch, the soil of which was used to create a large bank surrounding the henge. A large, two-ton slab of stone covering the body of a young male was discovered in the centre of the henge. A flint knife and a finely made, handled beaker were buried with the body.

The reference to *Choir-Gaur* in the battle for Mai-Dùn is, of course, better known as Stonehenge. Much has already been written about Stonehenge. It is a prehistoric monument in Wiltshire, England. The ring of standing stones was constructed from 3000 B.C. to 2000 B.C., with the surrounding circular earth bank and ditch dated to about 3100 B.C.

***

Boats, travel, and trade. The Gaels and their counterparts in Europe used the seas and waterways extensively. Gaelic ships had a flat bottom of four large planks attached to a frame of slender skeleton timbers. These flat bottoms allowed the vessels to sail in shallow coastal waters.

At its broadest point, the ship was probably about eight or nine feet wide with a depth of just under four feet. It would have had an average speed of three to five knots and almost certainly had a square flax or leather sail. Some had a more sophisticated "fore" and "aft" sail configuration. Built of oak, the vessel could carry up to three tons of cargo. These vessels had a long life. Compressed plant fibres were often used to plug leaks.

There were Channel-sailing Celtic ships. Julius Caesar recorded direct experiences of heavy-planked boats when conducting naval operations against the Veneti. Their high bows and sterns protected them from heavy seas and violent storms, as did strong hulls made from oak. The cross-timbers, beams a foot wide, were secured with iron nails as thick as a man's thumb. Anchors were secured with chains, not ropes. Sails were made of rawhide or thin leather to withstand the violent Atlantic winds.

The tin-rich areas of the southwestern peninsula of Britain proved very attractive to continental traders: Greeks, Phoenicians, and Romans. In the time of Conall, Hengistbury Head on the Dorset Coast was developing into an important port. This was due to the shortness of the sea crossing and being strategically close to the region's tin, iron and copper mines and the fertile lands.

Hengistbury Head was a fortified settlement where the headland was cut off from the mainland by constructing two banks and ditches, similar in structure to those at Maiden Castle. The Atlantic seaways linked south-western Britain to *Amorica*, the part of Gaul between the Seine and Loire Rivers, including the Brittany peninsula, western France and, via the Gironde-Garonne, the Mediterranean.

The main trade from Britain centred on tin, copper, and iron. Later, this expanded to wool, grain, cattle and hides, gold, silver, hunting dogs and slaves. The countertrade was Italian wine, ivory chains and necklaces, amber gems, glass vessels and other 'pretty wares.'

***

A few notes on the hillforts mentioned in the story. The proliferation of hillforts in southwestern Britain points to a heavily contested region. Two forts, however, stand out: Maiden Castle (*Mai-Dùn*) and Danebury (*Rinn-Campáil*).

Maiden Castle was first built around 600 B.C. and updated several times. The north-western gateway of Maiden Castle is one of the most complex of any Iron Age hillfort, with no fewer than four lines of defence outlying the inner rampart and gate. It provided multiple opportunities to pour fire into an attacker's flank before he was able to reach the entrance. Today the site still looks impressive, even on Google Earth.

Danebury was occupied from the mid-6th century B.C. until around 100 B.C. The defences were remodelled numerous times. The hillfort's complex gateways support the view that the site was militaristic. The long, curving east entrance maximised the time it would have taken for attackers to enter the fort and allowed defenders on the ramparts more time to hurl missiles. The southwest entrance narrowed, forcing attackers together and causing disarray. The fort was supplied with grain from the surrounding farmsteads. It could hold 20 times more food than the average farmstead, indicating Danebury had a higher status than local farmsteads.

Almondbury (Castle Hill—*Dùn Caen*) and Stanwick (*An Balla Leac*) were the significant hillforts of the *Brigantes*, under Kartimandu in the story and under Cartimandua and Venutius in Roman times. Castle Hill is a striking natural landmark nearly 1,000 feet high, covering some eight acres and surrounded by very steep slopes. In 430 B.C., the summit of Castle Hill raged with fire. Bright red flames and clouds of black smoke climbed high into the sky from the Iron Age hill fort.

Archaeological digs indicated the fort was constructed and

abandoned centuries before the Roman occupation. Stanwick was a vast hillfort comprising over 5.6 miles of ditches and ramparts enclosing approximately 300 hectares of land. The original enclosure dates from around 400 B.C., which was why it was "under construction" in Conall's tale.

Clatchard Craig (*Creag na Clachard*—Craig of the High Stone) was a Pictish hillfort near Newburgh in Fife, Scotland. The fort of Clatchard Craig was situated on a hill 390 feet high overlooking the coastal plain of the Tay. At its centre was a detached pillar of rock, which stood 90 feet tall and 25 feet wide.

The fort's walls were vitrified at some point, suggesting that the site had once been destroyed by fire. Sadly, in the late twentieth century, A.D. Clatchard Craig was destroyed by quarrying for aggregate authorised by the British Ministry of Transport. The "High Stone" was demolished by a single charge of dynamite to make way for the railway. Progress!

SUGGESTED READING

Dr Aubrey Burl, *The Stone Circles of the British Isles* (Yale University Press)

Robert Gardiner, *The Earliest Ships – The Evolution of Boats into Ships* (Conway Maritime Press)

Laurence Ginnell, *The Brehon Laws — A Legal Handbook* (Forgotten Books 2012; originally published 1894)

Angus Konstam, *The Forts of Celtic Britain* (Osprey Publishing Ltd.)

Sarah Macready and F.H. Thompson (Editors), *Cross-Channel Trade Between Gaul and Britain in the Pre-Roman Iron Age*, (Society of Antiquaries of London and Pitman Press, Bath)

GLOSSARY

IRISH GAELIC

An Fiagaí Dorcha (The Dark Huntress)

Ard-Bord (High Table)

Ar shlí na fírinne

Bean sídhe/ mná sídhe (Harbinger of Death)

Bitseach (Bitch)

Bodhráin (Celtic drum)

Brat/brait (cloak)

Breith (Judgement, Urard's axe)

Bróga (Boots/shoes)

Caomhnóirí (Personal Guard)

Carbad/carbaid (Chariot)

Ceannairí céad (Leader of one hundred)

Ceannairí na míle (Leader of one thousand)

Céile (free person)

Céili (Dance)

Chomhairle (Council)

Clann (Tribe)

Craic (Good fun/conversation)

Creabhar

Cret/Creta (Chariot basket)

Cróeb Ruad (Red Branch, Ulaid elite warriors)

Cróeb Ruad, go Brách

Diallait/diallaití (Thick horse blanket)

Dobhran (Otter)

Droimnín (Small lines of hills)

Duileasc (Dulse)

Dùn do bheal! (Shut your mouth)

Eibhear

Eiric (A fine or compensation)

Fág an Bealach

Fénechas (Brehon Laws, The Law)

Fine/ finte (Sub-division of a Sept)

Flaith-fine (Leader of A Fine)

Flaith/flatha (Leader)

Francach

Fuidhir (non-free)

Halla Mór (Great Hall)

Imeacht gan teacht ort (May you leave without returning.)

Ionsaí (Forward/Charge)

Léinte (Tunic/dress)

Lincse (Lynx)

Meán-lae (Midday)

Ní ghéillfear, nó cúlú (No retreat, no surrender.)

Óenach (Tribal gathering)

Págánaigh (Pagans/barbarians)

Peilbheas (Pelvis)

Pit (Vagina)

Póg ma thoin. (Kiss my arse)

Ráth/Rátha (Fort)

Rí/Ríthe (King)

Rí Ruirech (King over Kings)

Seanchaí/Seanchaithe (Storyteller)

Sept (Sub-division of a Clann)

Sídhe (Demi-Goddess)

Striapach (Whore)

Triubhas (Pants)

Tuagh
Tuilí/Tuilithe (Bastard)
Uisce beatha

SCOTTISH GAELIC
Comhairle-Chatha (High Council)
Bidse (Bitch)
Blaeberry
Dùn/dùin (Fort)
Fuath (Malevolent, highland water spirit)
Lince (Lynx)
Meadhan-latha (Midday)
Righ (King)
Strìopach (Whore)

TRIBES/RACES/CLANNS
Aes Sídhe (Race of Demi-Goddesses/ Túatha Dé Danann)
Aos na Coille (the Forest People)
Aos an Eich (the Horse People)
Aos an Fhithich (the Ravens)
Aos na h-Àirde (High People)
Aos nan Con-Seilge (People of the Hounds)
Cinn Péinteáilte (the Painted Ones)
Clann Ui Flaithimh (the People of the Hand)
Connachta (Connaught)
Craobhach (Ulaid clann)
Na Daoine Tùrsach (the People Who Chant)
Na Daoine Fiadhaich (Wild People)
Na Mèadaidh
Ó Néill (Ulaid Clann)
Ruad (Ulaid Clann)
Ulaid (Ulster)

Votod-Daoine (People of Votod)

FESTIVALS

Imbolg (Spring)

Bealtaine (Summer)

Lugnasad (Autumn)

Samhain (Winter)

DRAMATIS PERSONÆ

IRISH GAELS
Ailill Mac Mata
Áine Ni Dedad
Aodán Mac Conall
Aoibheann
Barra Mac Conall
Beacán Ó Cathasaigh
Bláithín Ni Néill
Bréanainn Dhá Lámh
Brianag Ni Brion
Bricriu Ó Cathasaigh
Brighid Ni Conall
Brion Ó Cathasaigh
Brocc Ó Cathasaigh
Cassán Mac Brion
Cimbáeth
Conall Mac Gabhann
Craiftine Ó Cuileannáin
Cuán Ó Néill
Cúscraid Mac Conchobar
Danu Ni Conall
Deaglán Ó Néill
Deda Mac Sin
Eochaidh Ruad
Fearghal Ruad

Fionnbharr Ó Cuileannáin
Íar Mac Dedad
Lonán Ó Néill
Macha Mong Ruad
Manannán Mac Lir
Medb
Mongfhionn
Mórrígan Ni Cathasaigh
Neamhain Ni Fearghal
Seanán
Tadhg Ó Cuileannáin
Téide Bán
Toirneach
Torcán Ó Dubhghaill
Tuathal Mac Conall
Urard

SCOTTISH GAELS

Brandubh Mac Artair (Brother of Mòrag)
Camran Mac Madadh (King of Clachard Craig)
Carmag Mac an t-Sionnaich (Former governor of Cùil Daothail)
Ceana Nic Sèitheach (Sister of Finnean)
Coireall (Seaman)
Crum Dubh (Brother of Drostan)
Diadhaidh (Grandmother of Gràinne)
Drostan Ruadh (Brother of Crum)
Failbhe (Father of Crum & Drostan)
Finnean Mac Sèitheach (Brother of Ceana)
Friseal (Camran's Captain)
Gormal Mac Eachdonn (Son of Eachdonn)
Gràinne Ni Fearghal (Adopted by Fearghal Ruad)
Iasg (Urard's Guide)

Eachdonn Breac (Husband of Ceana)
Mòrag Nic Artair (Sister of Brandubh)
Ròidh Mac Eachdonn (Son of Eachdonn)
Votod (King of Votod-Daoine)

THE ROMANS

Marcus Fabius Ambustus (Pontifex Maximus of Rome)
Quintus Fabius Ambustus (son of Marcus)
Numerius Fabius Ambustus (son of Marcus)
Caeso Fabius Ambustus (son of Marcus)
Gaius Aurelius Atella (Centurion in Marcus' army)

OTHER

Caradog
Dai
Kartimandu
Nikandros
Orestes
Ualraig

LOCATIONS

COUNTRIES
Albu (Great Britain)
Ériu (Ireland)
Gaul (France)

SCOTLAND
Abhainn Dubh (River Forth)
An Mhuir Ó Thuaidh (North Sea)
Áth (Ford, settlement)
A' Chrìon Làraich (Crianlarich)
Clachard Craig (nr. Newburgh in Fife)
Cnoc-Naomh (Hillfort, The Wild People)
Cùil Daothail (Culduthel, nr. Inverness)
Dumha (Mound, settlement)
Dùn Athad (Dunadd hillfort)
Dùn Na Mèadaidh (Fort of the Na Mèadaidh)
Linne Foirthe (Firth of Forth estuary)
Maol Chinn Tìre (Mull of Kintyre)
Sleá (The Spear, Mountain range, lowlands)
Trócaire (Mercy, settlement)
Uisce Èireann (River, north of the Sleá)

ENGLAND
Abus (Humber Estuary)
An Balla Leac (Stanwick)

An Cnoc (Fin Cop)
Choir-Gaur (Stonehenge)
Dùn Caen (Castle Hill, Almondbury)
Muir nIocht (English Channel)
Penn-inus (The Pennines)
Rinn-Campáil (Danebury hillfort, S. England)
River Gwy (River Wye)
Mai-Dùn (Maiden Castle, S. England)

IRELAND
Curraghatoor (Hillfort, S. Ireland)
Domach Dith (Donaghadee, N. Ireland)
Emain Macha (Navan Fort, N. Ireland)
Ler Ériu (Irish Sea)
Ráthgeal (Rathgall Hillfort, S. Ireland)
Ráth Na Conall (Conall's hillfort, S. Ireland)

AFTERLIFE
Mag Mell (Celtic warrior heaven)
Otherworld (Celtic hell)
Tír inna n-Óc (Land of the Young)
Tír Tairngire (Land of Promise)

OTHER
Chios (Greek Island)

ABOUT THE AUTHOR

Born in Belfast, Northern Ireland, internationally published and award-winning author David H. Millar is the founder, owner, and author-in-residence of *A Wee Publishing Company*, a business that seeks to promote Celtic literature, authors, and art.

Millar moved from beautiful but wet Northern Ireland to Nova Scotia, Canada, in the late 1990s. After ten years of shovelling snow, he relocated to warmer climates and settled in Houston, Texas. Quite a contrast!

An avid reader, armchair sportsman, and Liverpool Football Club fan, Millar lives with his family and Bailey, a Manx cat of questionable disposition known to his friends as "the small angry one"!

Millar writes historical fantasy with a Celtic twist. He is the author of the five-volume, ancient Celtic-based *Conall Series* and spin-offs: *The Dog Roses* and *The Blood* Queen.

Excerpt:

CONALL IV:
A Brace of Eagles:
Snaidhm Iolar

CHAPTER 1

405 B.C.—Lugnasad—Southern Albu

Butter-gold and cruelly hooked, the beak ripped a ragged gash across the newborn's throat. Bright, arterial blood splashed the grey stone slab. Denied a final voice, the innocent's lips trembled. A second mortal slash delivered by a pitiless talon laid open the sacrifice's belly. Released from the bonds of skin and muscle, entrails burst forth to lie steaming on the rock's cool, pitted surface.

"Did you receive a message you approve of?" Fate attempted to maintain a haughty distance from the violence, but in this guise, the smell of blood and warm flesh challenged his fortitude.

With a nod of her heavy, golden-brown head, the Goddess replied, "The Ancients have given their consent. I will cross the Muir nIocht and enter the land of the Gauls."

"Gods and goddesses do not usually cross territories."

"Extenuating circumstances. Rome must be stopped. My servants, the druids, must be protected. My Hand must fulfil his destiny. The people need to worship."

"Surely, it is you who needs the people's worship?"

"Bah! Semantics."

Fate changed the topic. "The Roman gods did not protest?"

Such was her distaste for her fellow gods, if the Goddess could have spat, she would have. "The Romans got their gods from the Greeks. Likely the Greeks got theirs from the Egyptians. All the Roman gods desire is to pose for yet more marble statues. Affecting an air of ennui, they abstained."

The scent of the warm flesh and blood tormented Fate. Conversation and debate faded. He screeched at the Goddess, and she returned his cry. Soon there was little left of the carcass but cracked bones and skin. Satisfied, the eagles bent powerful legs and swept upwards. The stones of Choir-Gaur quickly became a grey mirage in the distance.

**

Stripped to the waist, Conall Mac Gabhann, *Rí Ruirech*, king over kings, of *Clann Uí Flaithimh*, sat on the cliff's edge. His perch overlooked the harbour, located at the apex of a roughly equal-sided triangle. The other points were the great hillforts of southern *Albu*—*Mai Dún* and *Rinn-Campáil*. He enjoyed the warmth of the summer sun as he surveyed the array of ships in the harbour. The sound of waves breaking on the shore and the rhythmic clunking of wooden hulls against jetties soothed away his morning headache.

To Conall, it seemed that the longer he sojourned in the pleasant kingdom of Mai Dún, the more frequent were his headaches. Nightmares, in graphic detail, recalled his mother pinned to the solid wooden table with iron spikes through her hands, her dress torn, and her arse bloodied from multiple penetrations. His blacksmith father shackled to the stanchions of the forge, his back charred and eyes sightless, burst by hot irons. Tearless, his last moments were filled with the dying screams of his hand-fast partner.

Conall's little sisters, too young to rape, were tossed aside. Deep gashes across their throats smiled ghoulishly at Conall. Bathed in sweat, he awoke, screaming at the Goddess. "Your Hand needs no visions to remind him of his duty. I will avenge my family and destroy the Romans who paid for the murders." Only the soothing embrace and tears of Mórrígan that splattered his chest restored his sanity.

With an effort of will, Conall pushed the memory aside. Enjoying the juices released, he chewed and sucked on a stalk of coastal grass. He mused that it had probably been pissed on by multiple sheep and goats. A smile ghosted his lips before he stretched his well-toned arms and rolled his muscled neck and shoulders.

Sighing, he pulled soft, calf-high boots over what he considered ugly toes. Slowly, deliberately, as if wanting to delay his return to the myriad daily responsibilities, he criss-crossed and then tied off the boots' long thongs. With an emphatic grunt, the king of Clann Ui Flaithimh stood and slapped dirt, grass, and sand from his *triubhas*—trousers. He bent over, took his axe and shield, and turned about.

Situated in a grassy hollow, a thousand paces back from the cliffs, a random patchwork of tents formed a good-sized village. They gave shelter to the ships' crews. "So many mouths to feed… and gold to pay," muttered Conall. His comment was aimed at no one in particular but was overheard by the small, mahogany-skinned sailor who came into view.

Palm forward, Pytheas held his hand aloft. It signalled that the portly Greek had not quite recovered from the walk up the fairly steep hillside. Conall grinned. "You need more exercise, my friend. Perhaps a stint on the oars of your galley, or I could have Fearghal set you a training regime?"

Partially recovered, Pytheas laughed and stroked a black beard that glistened with jasmine-scented castor oil. "I prefer decadence over austerity." Conall knew the merchant undersold himself. The beard was one of vanity and choice. Unlike many, it did not hide a fragile chin or signal a weak character. Moreover, while in recent years, the Greek's flesh may have gained more fat than muscle, he had proven loyal and resourceful in harsh circumstances.

"Are they all necessary?" asked Conall, his gaze once more focused on the village of sticks and skins.

"The crews and rowers of the galleys make up most of the population. We have ten biremes, one hundred and twenty rowers for each vessel. Then there are the ships' crews: captain, helmsman, piper, shipwright, bow lookout, and five or six sailors per boat. It all adds up." Pytheas looked along the jetties as if searching for something. Then he pointed to the rugged, locally built ships with their rough timbers and high curved bows and sterns. "On the other hand, *they* only need a small crew—far fewer rowers. They are built for carrying cargo, the biremes for war. You need both."

"How long will it take?"

"The ships are contracted for a year. It will likely take that long—maybe more."

Conall snorted, "So, I'm financing your new partnership with Drostan." He spoke of his onetime enemy and now friend, Drostan Ruadh, the one-eyed king of the *Aos na Coille*—the Forest People. Drostan had returned to his beloved forests of ancient pine that stretched from coast to coast in his native northern Albu.

"A happy quirk of fate. It was quite propitious that the ships from the *Votod-Daoine* fell into our hands." Pytheas looked at Conall's face to gauge whether the king of Clann Ui Flaithimh was truly unhappy. The glimmer of a smile that played at the corners of Conall's mouth was reassuring. "You did get the 'preferred' customer rate," said Pytheas with a huge smirk.

"Ha! Spoken like a true merchant. Perhaps I should have become a partner in your venture. At the least, some of my gold would be returned to me."

Pytheas again scrutinised Conall's expression. Was the young king serious? He had become an accomplished fidchell player. Few could read a face that seldom gave clues as to his thoughts. "Drostan would have no objection, and neither would I."

Conall inclined his head, "Perhaps." His attention was drawn to the vessels once more. "How many warriors can the biremes transport?"

"The shipwrights are adding another deck to the galleys. With that, and reducing the number of rowers per ship, they will each carry fifty warriors."

"Not a lot."

"The galleys are flat-bottomed, fast, and highly manoeuvrable. Much better for beach landings and assaults. An almost full complement of rowers and sailors is needed to cope with the worsening weather that is inevitable between now and the festival of Samhain. We also need to be able to outrun any potential attacks. The coastal *Veneti* in *Aremorio* have fast ships and will take to the seas if they see an opportunity for plunder. Plus, there are always Phoenician and Greek slavers looking for easy prey." Pytheas hesitated.

"Well?"

With a cough to hide his embarrassment, Pytheas added, "Then there are the… witches on the island of *Andion*." Conall raised an eyebrow in disbelief. Pytheas coughed. "Sailors are superstitious. The island is ancient, with lots of burial grounds and tall stones. Rumour has it that there is a colony of nine unmarried witches living on the island. They guard a sacred cauldron." Pytheas shrugged and smiled weakly at Conall. "Anyway, the crews will not go anywhere near Andion, especially in the dark."

"Anything else? Huge sea creatures, perhaps?" said Conall with a boyish chuckle.

Pytheas glanced nervously out to sea, "It's not good to mock the sea gods. Neither Poseidon nor your own Manannán Mac Lir is known for having placid natures. Who knows what creatures inhabit the deeps?" With a quick change of topic, Pytheas said, "There is one more thing. At least two-thirds of your men will have to train as rowers. It's the only way to make space for them on the crossing."

"That'll please them," said Conall.

"Sarcasm?" chuckled Pytheas.

"Never!"

***

Conall knew the importance of securing a defensible beachhead in Aremorio. It would determine the mission's success and set the tone and foundation for the wider campaign in Gaul. A strategic blend of captains and warriors was required. Succinctly, Conall explained his thinking to Fearghal Ruad, his battle commander. "They're all sullen, foul-mouthed, foul-smelling eejits… but they're hard bastards who'll get the job done."

Command of the landing rested on the broad shoulders of Lonán Ò Neill. Lonán, the second-in-command of Conall's newest recruits from Ériu's famed Cróeb Ruad—the Red Branch—faced a singular challenge. When he asked for two hundred volunteers, one thousand hopefuls stepped forward. According to Fearghal, himself, a former commander of the Ulaid warriors, Lonán's final selection was a bunch of ugly, toothless killers whose skin had so much scar tissue it was as tough as a boar's hide.

Few were surprised when Conall also nominated Torcán Ò Dubhghaill to be part of the Aremorio landing. Even fewer were surprised at Torcán's jig of glee on hearing the news. Torcán's hundred, as bull-headed as their leader, provided a platoon of the vaunted Clann Ui Flaithimh's shield-wall. It was, however, a possible sign of maturity that the bluff warrior was not overly convinced by the profuse assurances of a safe sea crossing from either the tall and beautiful sídhe, Mongfhionn, or Pytheas.

Memories of stormy sailings on the seas and lochs of northern Albu were all too easy and painfully recalled. So, Torcán flung extra offerings of armour and gold into the sea for Manannán Mac Lir and into a nearby river for the Goddess—better safe than sorry.

The remaining members of the landing party hailed from the mountains and forests of northern Albu. Armed with clubs and spears, Carmag Mac an t-Sionnaich's cohort, totalled one hundred veteran forest fighters. All sported shaggy red hair and bodies covered in elaborate tattoos. It was a sight sure to put the fear of the Hag into the enemy. The women, well, most of them, were distinguished from the menfolk by the lack of bushy, ginger-red beards and whiskers.

The female warriors of Clann Ui Flaithimh were as aggressive as, some said, fiercer than the men. Hence, the raiding party included

Mòrag, the voluptuous princess of the Ravens, and her warband of one hundred spearmen, archers, and slingers. Like many of her tribe and indeed Carmag's Forest People, Mòrag preferred to fight unrestricted by clothing.

Given her undoubted beauty, few grumbled at her lack of attire. Even fewer queried her inclusion in the assault. If any were foolish to suggest that her addition was frippery, the least they could expect was a fist in the face. Underlying Mòrag's welcoming curves was a core of iron. The Raven's leader could trounce any man in the raiding party.

www.ingramcontent.com/pod-product-compliance
Lightning Source LLC
Chambersburg PA
CBHW030648120726
47905CB00001B/116